Edward Payson Roe

A Knight of the Nineteenth Century

Volume Three

Edward Payson Roe

A Knight of the Nineteenth Century
Volume Three

ISBN/EAN: 9783337279387

Printed in Europe, USA, Canada, Australia, Japan

Cover: Foto ©Andreas Hilbeck / pixelio.de

More available books at **www.hansebooks.com**

"Would he never Look Up?"

The Works of E. P. Roe

VOLUME THREE

A KNIGHT OF THE NINETEENTH CENTURY

ILLUSTRATED

NEW YORK
P. F. COLLIER & SON

THIS BOOK

IS REVERENTLY DEDICATED TO THE MEMORY OF

MY HONORED FATHER

PREFACE

HE best deserves a knightly crest,
Who slays the evils that infest
His soul within. If victor here,
He soon will find a wider sphere.
The world is cold to him who pleads;
The world bows low to knightly deeds.

CORNWALL ON THE HUDSON, N. Y.

CONTENTS

CHAPTER XII

CHAPTER XIII

CHAPTER XIV

CHAPTER XV

CHAPTER XVI

CHAPTER XVII

CHAPTER XVIII

CHAPTER XIX

CHAPTER XX

CHAPTER XXI

CHAPTER XXII

CHAPTER XXIII

CHAPTER XXIV

CHAPTER XXV

CHAPTER XXVI

A KNIGHT OF THE NINETEENTH
CENTURY

A KNIGHT OF THE NINETEENTH CENTURY

CHAPTER I

BAD TRAINING FOR A KNIGHT

EGBERT HALDANE had an enemy who loved him very dearly, and he sincerely returned her affection, as he was in duty bound, since she was his mother. If, inspired by hate and malice, Mrs. Haldane had brooded over but one question at the cradle of her child, How can I most surely destroy this boy? she could scarcely have set about the task more skilfully and successfully.

But so far from having any such malign and unnatural intention, Mrs. Haldane idolized her son. To make the paradox more striking, she was actually seeking to give him a Christian training and character. As he leaned against her knee Bible tales were told him, not merely for the sake of the marvellous interest which they ever have for children, but in the hope, also, that the moral they carry with them might remain as germinating seed. At an early age the mother had commenced taking him to church, and often gave him an admonitory nudge as his restless eyes wandered from the venerable face in the pulpit. In brief, the apparent influences of his early life were similar to those existing in multitudes of Christian homes. On general principles, it might be hoped that the boy's future would be all that his friends could desire; nor did he himself in early youth promise so badly to superficial observers; and the son of the wealthy Mrs. Haldane was, on

(15)

the part of the world, more the object of envy than of censure. But a close observer, who judged of characteristic tendencies and their results by the light of experience, might justly fear that the mother had unwittingly done her child irreparable wrong.

She had made him a tyrant and a relentless task-master even in his infancy. As his baby-will developed he found it supreme. His nurse was obliged to be a slave who must patiently humor every whim. He was petted and coaxed out of his frequent fits of passion, and beguiled from his obstinate and sulky moods by bribes. He was the eldest child and only son, and his little sisters were taught to yield to him, right or wrong, he lording it over them with the capricious lawlessness of an Eastern despot. Chivalric deference to woman, and a disposition to protect and honor her, is a necessary element of a manly character in our Western civilization; but young Haldane was as truly an Oriental as if he had been permitted to bluster around a Turkish harem; and those whom he should have learned to wait upon with delicacy and tact became subservient to his varying moods, developing that essential brutality which mars the nature of every man who looks upon woman as an inferior and a servant. He loved his mother, but he did not reverence and honor her. The thought ever uppermost in his mind was, "What ought she to do for me?" not, "What ought I to do for her?" and any effort to curb or guide on her part was met and thwarted by passionate or obstinate opposition from him. He loved his sisters after a fashion, because they were his sisters; but so far from learning to think of them as those whom it would be his natural task to cherish and protect, they were, in his estimation, "nothing but girls," and of no account whatever where his interests were concerned.

In the most receptive period of life the poison of selfishness and self-love was steadily instilled into his nature. Before he had left the nursery he had formed the habit of disregarding the wills and wishes of others, even when his childish conscience told him that he was decidedly in the wrong. When he snatched his sisters' playthings they cried in vain, and found no redress. The mother made peace by smoothing over matters, and promising the little girls something else.

Of course, the boy sought to carry into his school life the same tendencies and habits which he had learned at home, and he ever found a faithful ally in his blind, fond mother. She took his side against his teachers; she could not believe in his oppressions of his younger playmates; she was absurdly indignant and resentful when some sturdy boy stood up for his own rights, or championed another's, and sent the incipient bully back to her, crying, and with a bloody nose. When the pampered youth was a little indisposed, or imagined himself so, he was coddled at home, and had bonbons and fairy tales in the place of lessons.

Judicious friends shook their heads ominously, and some even ventured to counsel the mother to a wiser course; but she ever resented such advice. The son was the image of his lost father, and her one impulse was to lavish upon him everything that his heart craved.

As if all this were not enough, she placed in the boy's way another snare, which seldom fails of proving fatal. He had only to ask for money to obtain it, no knowledge of its value being imparted to him. Even when he took it from his mother's drawer without asking, her chidings were feeble and irresolute. He would silence and half satisfy her by saying:

"You can take anything of mine that you want. It's all in the family; what difference does it make?"

Thus every avenue of temptation in the city which could be entered by money was open to him, and he was not slow in choosing those naturally attractive to a boy.

But while his mother was blind to the evil traits and tendencies which she was fostering with such ominous success, there were certain overt acts naturally growing out of her indulgences which would shock her inexpressibly, and evoke even from her the strongest expressions of indignation and rebuke. She was pre-eminently respectable, and fond of respect. She was a member "in good and regular standing" not only of her church, but also of the best society in the small inland city where she resided, and few greater misfortunes in her estimation could occur than to lose this status. She never hesitated to humor any of her son's whims and wishes which did not threaten their respectability, but the quick-witted boy was not long in discovering that she would not tolerate any of those vices and associations which society condemns.

There could scarcely have been any other result save that which followed. She had never taught him self-restraint; his own inclinations furnished the laws of his action, and the wish to curb his desires because they were wrong scarcely ever crossed his mind. To avoid trouble with his mother, therefore, he began slyly and secretly to taste the forbidden fruits which her lavish supplies of money always kept within his reach. In this manner that most hopeless and vitiating of elements, deceitfulness, entered into his character. He denied to his mother, and sought to conceal from her, the truth that while still in his teens he was learning the gambler's infatuation and forming the inebriate's appetite. He tried to prevent her from knowing that many of his most intimate associates were such as he would not introduce to her or to his sisters.

He had received, however, a few counter-balancing advantages in his early life. With all her weaknesses, his mother was a lady, and order, refinement, and elegance characterized his home. Though not a gentleman at heart, on approaching manhood he habitually maintained the outward bearing that society demands. The report that he was a little fast was more than neutralized by the fact of his wealth. Indeed, society concluded that it had much more occasion to smile than to frown upon him, and his increasing fondness for society and its approval in some degree curbed his tendencies to dissipation.

It might also prove to his advantage that so much Christian and ethical truth had been lodged in his memory during early years. His mother had really taken pains to acquaint him with the Divine Man who "pleased not himself," even while she was practically teaching him to reverse this trait in his own character. . Thus, while the youth's heart was sadly erratic, his head was tolerably orthodox, and he knew theoretically the chief principles of right action. Though his conscience had never been truly awakened, it often told him that his action was unmanly, to say the least; and that was as far as any self-censure could reach at this time. But it might prove a fortunate thing that although thorns and thistles had been planted chiefly, some good seed had been scattered also, and that he had received some idea of a life the reverse of that which he was leading.

But thus far it might be said with almost literal truth, that young Haldane's acquaintance with Christian ethics had had no more practical effect upon his habitual action and thought than his knowledge of algebra. When his mother permitted him to snatch his sisters' playthings and keep them, when she took him from the school where he had received well-merited punishment, when she enslaved herself and her household to him instead of teaching considerate and loyal devotion to her, she nullified all the Christian instruction that she or any one else had given.

The boy had one very marked trait, which might promise well for the future, or otherwise, according to circumstances, and that was a certain wilful persistence, which often degenerated into downright obstinacy. Frequently, when his mother thought that she had coaxed or wheedled him into giving up something of which she did not approve, he would quietly approach his object in some other way, and gain his point, or sulk till he did. When he set his heart upon anything he was not as "unstable as water." While but an indifferent and superficial student, who had habitually escaped lessons and skipped difficulties, he occasionally became nettled by a perplexing problem or task, and would work at it with a sort of vindictive, unrelenting earnestness, as if he were subduing an enemy. Having put his foot on the obstacle, and mastered the difficulty that piqued him, he would cast the book aside, indifferent to the study or science of which it formed but a small fraction.

After all, perhaps the best that could be said of him was that he possessed fair abilities, and was still subject to the good and generous impulses of youth. His traits and tendencies were, in the main, all wrong; but he had not as yet become confirmed and hardened in them. Contact with the world, which sooner or later tells a man the truth about himself, however unwelcome, might dissipate the illusion, gained from his mother's idolatry, that in some indefinite way he was remarkable in himself, and that he was destined to great things from a vague and innate superiority, which it had never occurred to him to analyze.

But as the young man approached his majority his growing habits of dissipation became so pronounced that even his willingly blind mother was compelled to recognize them. Rumor of his fast and foolish behavior took such definite shape as to penetrate the widow's aristocratic retirement, and to pass the barriers created by the reserve which she ever maintained in regard to personal and family matters. More than once her son came home in a condition so nearly resembling intoxication that she was compelled to recognize the cause, and she was greatly shocked and alarmed. Again and again she said to herself:

"I cannot understand how a boy brought up in the careful Christian manner that he has been can show such unnatural depravity. It is a dark, mysterious providence, to which I feel I cannot submit."

Though young Haldane was aware of his mother's intolerance of disreputable vices and follies, he was not prepared for her strong and even bitter condemnation of his action. Having never been taught to endure from her nor from any one the language of rebuke, he retorted as a son never should do in any circumstances, and stormy scenes followed.

Thus the mother was at last rudely awakened to the fact that her son was not a model youth, and that something must be done speedily, or else he might go to destruction, and in the meantime disgrace both himself and her—an event almost equally to be dreaded.

In her distress and perplexity she summoned her pastor, and took counsel with him. At her request the venerable man readily agreed to "talk to" the wayward subject, and thought that his folly and its consequences could be placed before the young man in such a strong and logical state-ment that it would convince him at once that he must "re-pent and walk in the ways of righteousness." If Haldane's errors had been those of doctrine, Dr. Marks would have been an admirable guide; but the trouble was that, while the good doctor was familiar with all the readings of ob-scure Greek and Hebrew texts, and all the shades of opin-ions resulting, he was unacquainted with even the alphabet of human nature. In approaching "a sinner," he had one formal and unvarying method, and he chose his course not from the bearing of the subject himself, but from certain general theological truths which he believed applied to the "unrenewed heart of man as a fallen race." He rather prided himself upon calling a sinner a sinner, and all things else by their right names; and thus it is evident that he often had but little of the Pauline guile, which enabled the great apostle to entangle the wayward feet of Jew, Greek and Roman, bond and free, in heavenly snares.

The youth whom he was to convince and convert by a single broadside of truth, as it were, moved in such an ec-centric orbit, that the doctor could never bring his heavy artillery to bear upon him. Neither coaxing nor scolding on the part of the mother could bring about the formal in-terview. At last, however, it was secured by an accident,

and his mother felt thereafter, with a certain sense of consolation, that "all had been done that could be done."

Entering the parlor unexpectedly one afternoon, Haldane stumbled directly upon Dr. Marks, who opened fire
at once, by saying:

"My young friend, this is quite providential, as I have
long been wishing for an interview. Please be seated, for
I have certain things to say which relate to your spiritual
and temporal well-being, although the latter is a very sec-
ondary matter."

Haldane was too well bred to break rudely and abruptly
away, and yet it must be admitted that he complied with
very much the feeling and grace with which he would take
a dentist's chair.

"My young friend, if you ever wish to be a saint you
must first have a profound conviction that you are a sinner.
I hope that you realize that you are a sinner."

"I am quite content to be a gentleman," was the brusque
reply.

"But as long as you remain an impenitent sinner you
can never be even a true gentleman," responded the clergyman somewhat warmly.

Haldane had caught a shocked and warning look from
his mother, and so did not reply. He saw that he was "in
for it," as he would express himself, and surmised that the
less he said the sooner the ordeal would be over. He therefore took refuge in a silence that was both sullen and resentful. He was too young and uncurbed to maintain a cold
and impassive face, and his dark eyes occasionally shot vindictive gleams at both his mother and her ally, who had so
unexpectedly caged him against his will. Fortunately the
doctor was content, after he had got under way, to talk at,
instead of to, his listener, and thus was saved the mortification of asking questions of one who would not have
answered.

After the last sonorous period had been rounded, the
youth arose, bowed stiffly, and withdrew, but with a heart

overflowing with a malicious desire to retaliate. At the angle of the house stood the clergyman's steady-going mare, and his low, old-fashioned buggy. It was but the work of a moment to slip part of the shuck of a horse-chestnut, with its sharp spines, under the collar, so that when the traces drew upon it the spines would be driven into the poor beast's neck. Then, going down to the main street of the town, through which he knew the doctor must pass on his way home, he took his post of observation.

CHAPTER II

BOTH APOLOGIZE

HALDANE'S hopes were realized beyond his anticipations, for the doctor's old mare—at first surprised and restless from the wounds made by the sharp spines—speedily became indignant and fractious, and at last, half frantic with pain, started on a gallop down the street, setting all the town agog with excitement and alarm.

With grim satisfaction Haldane saw the doctor's immaculate silk hat fly into the mud, his wig, blown comically awry, fall over his eyes, and his spectacles joggle down until they sat astride the tip of a rather prominent nose.

Having had his revenge he at once relented, and rushing out in advance of some others who were coming to the rescue, he caught the poor beast, and stopped her so suddenly that the doctor was nearly precipitated over the dashboard. Then, pretending to examine the harness to see that nothing was broken, he quietly removed the cause of irritation, and the naturally sedate beast at once became far more composed than her master, for, as a bystander remarked, the venerable doctor was "dreadfully shuck up." It was quite in keeping with Haldane's disingenuous nature to accept the old gentleman's profuse thanks for the rescue. The impulse to carry his mischief still further was at once acted upon, and he offered to see the doctor safely home.

His services were eagerly accepted, for the poor man was much too unnerved to take the reins again, though, had he known it, the mare would now have gone to the parsonage quietly, and of her own accord.

The doctor was gradually righted up and composed.

His wig, which had covered his left eye, was arranged decorously in its proper place, and the gold-rimmed spectacles pressed back so that the good man could beam mildly and gratefully upon his supposed preserver. The clerical hat, however, had lost its character beyond recovery, and though its owner was obliged to wear it home, it must be confessed that it did not at all comport with the doctor's dignity and calling.

Young Haldane took the reins with a great show of solicitude and vigilance, appearing to dread another display of viciousness from the mare, that was now most sheeplike in her docility; and thus, with his confiding victim, he jogged along through the crowded street, the object of general approval and outspoken commendation.

"My dear young friend," began the doctor fervently, "I feel that you have already repaid me amply for my labors in your behalf."

"Thank you," said Haldane demurely; "I think we are getting even."

"This has been a very mysterious affair," continued the doctor musingly; "surely 'a horse is a vain thing for safety.' One is almost tempted to believe that demoniacal possession is not wholly a thing of the past. Indeed, I could not think of anything else while Dolly was acting so viciously and unaccountably."

"I agree with you," responded Haldane gravely, "she certainly did come down the street like the devil."

The doctor was a little shocked at this putting of his thoughts into plain English, for it sounded somewhat profanely. But he was in no mood to find fault with his companion, and they got on very well together to the end of their brief journey. The young scapegrace was glad, indeed, that it was brief, for his self-control was fast leaving him, and having bowed a rather abrupt farewell to the doctor, he was not long in reaching one of his haunts, from which during the evening, and quite late into the night, came repeated peals of laughter, that grew more boisterous and discordant as that synonyme of mental and moral anarchy, the "spirit of wine," gained the mastery.

The tidings of her son's exploit in rescuing the doctor were not long in reaching Mrs. Haldane, and she felt that the good seed sown that day had borne immediate fruit. She longed to fold him in her arms and commend his courage, while she poured out thanksgiving that he himself had escaped uninjured, which immunity, she believed, must have resulted from the goodness and piety of the deed. But when he at last appeared with step so unsteady and utterance so thick that even she could not mistake the cause, she was bewildered and bitterly disappointed by the apparent contradictoriness of his action; and when he, too far gone for dissimulation, described and acted out in pantomime the doctor's plight and appearance, she became half hysterical from her desire to laugh, to cry, and to give vent to her kindling indignation.

This anger was raised almost to the point of white heat on the morrow. The cause of the old mare's behavior, and the interview which had led to the practical joke, soon became an open secret, and while it convulsed the town with laughter, it also gave the impression that young Haldane was in a "bad way."

It was not long before Mrs. Haldane received a note from an indignant fellow church-member, in which, with some disagreeable comment, her son's conduct was plainly stated. She was also informed that the doctor had become aware of the rude jest of which he had been the subject. Mrs. Haldane was almost furious; but her son grew sullen and obstinate as the storm which he had raised increased. The only thing he would say as an apology or excuse amounted to this:

"What else could he expect from one who he so emphatically asserted was a sinner?"

The mother wrote at once to the doctor, and was profuse in her apologies and regrets, but was obliged to admit to him that her son was beyond her control.

When the doctor first learned the truth his equanimity was almost as greatly disturbed as it had been on the previous day, and his first emotions were obviously those of wrath. But a little thought brought him to a better mood.

He was naturally deficient in tact, and his long habit of dwelling upon abstract and systematic truth had diminished his power of observantly and intuitively gauging the character of the one with whom he was dealing. He therefore often failed wofully in adaptation, and his sermons occasionally went off into rarefied realms of moral space, where nothing human existed. But his heart was true and warm, and his Master's cause of far more consequence to him than his own dignity.

As he considered the matter maturely he came to the conclusion that there must have been something wrong on both sides. If he had presented the truth properly the young man could not have acted so improperly. After recalling the whole affair, he became satisfied that he had relied far too much on his own strong logic, and it had seemed to him that it must convince. He had forgotten for the moment that those who would do good should be very humble, and that, in a certain sense, they must take the hand of God, and place it upon the one whom they would save.

Thus the honest old clergyman tried to search out the error and weakness which had led to such a lamentable failure in his efforts; and when at last Mrs. Haldane's note of sorrowful apology and motherly distress reached him, his anger was not only gone, but his heart was full of commiseration for both herself and her son. He at once sat down, and wrote her a kind and consolatory letter, in which he charged her hereafter to trust less to the "arm of flesh" and more to the "power of God." He also inclosed a note to the young man, which his mother handed to him with a darkly reproachful glance. He opened it with a contemptuous frown, expecting to find within only indignant upbraidings; but his face changed rapidly as he read the following words:

My dear young Friend—I hardly know which of us should apologize. I now perceive and frankly admit that there was wrong on my side. I could not have approached you and spoken to you in the right spirit, for if I had, what followed could not have occurred. I fear there was a self-sufficiency in my words and manner yesterday, which made you conscious of Dr. Marks only, and you had no scruples in dealing with Dr. Marks as you did. If my words and bearing had brought you face to face with my august yet merciful Master, you would have respected Him, and also me, His servant. I confess that I was very angry this morning, for I am human. But now I am more concerned lest I have prejudiced you against Him by whom alone we all are saved.   Yours faithfully,

ZEBULON MARKS.

The moment Haldane finished reading the note he left the room, and his mother heard him at the hat-rack in the hall, preparing to go out. She, supposing that he was again about to seek some of his evil haunts, remonstrated sharply; but, without paying the slightest attention to her words, he departed, and within less than half an hour rang the bell at the parsonage.

Dr. Marks could scarcely believe his eyes as the young man was shown into his study, but he welcomed him as cordially as though nothing unpleasant had occurred between them.

After a moment's hesitation and embarrassment Haldane began:

"When I read your note this evening I had not the slightest doubt that I was the one to apologize, and I sincerely ask your pardon."

The old gentleman's eyes grew moist, and he blew his nose in a rather unusual manner. But he said promptly:

"Thank you, my young friend, thank you. I appreciate this. But no matter about me. How about my Master? won't you become reconciled to Him?"

"I suppose by that you mean, won't you be a Christian?"

"That is just what I mean and most desire. I should be willing to risk broken bones any day to accomplish that."

Haldane smiled, shook his head, and after a moment said:

"I must confess that I have not the slightest wish to become a Christian."

The old gentleman's eager and interested expression changed instantly to one of the deepest sorrow and commiseration. At the same time he appeared bewildered and perplexed, but murmured, more in soliloquy than as an address to the young man:

"O Ephraim! how shall I give thee up?"

Haldane was touched by the venerable man's tone and manner, more than he would have thought possible, and, feeling that he could not trust himself any longer, determined to make his escape as soon as practicable. But as he rose to take his leave he said, a little impulsively:

"I feel sure, sir, that if you had spoken and looked yesterday as you do this evening I would not have—I would not have—"

"I understand, my young friend; I now feel sure that I was more to blame than yourself, and your part is already forgiven and forgotten. I am now only solicitous about *you.*"

"You are very kind to feel so after what has happened, and I will say this much—If I ever do wish to become a Christian, there is no one living to whom I will come for counsel more quickly than yourself. Good-night, sir."

"Give me your hand before you go."

It was a strong, warm, lingering grasp that the old man gave, and in the dark days of temptation that followed, Haldane often felt that it had a helping and sustaining influence.

"I wish I could hold on to you," said the doctor huskily; "I wish I could lead you by loving force into the paths of pleasantness and peace. But what I can't do, God can. Good-by, and God bless you."

Haldane fled rather precipitously, for he felt that he was becoming constrained by a loving violence that was as mysterious as it was powerful. Before he had passed through the main street of the town, however, a reckless companion placed an arm in his, and led him to one of their haunts, where he drank deeper than usual, that he might get rid of the compunctions which the recent interview had occasioned.

His mother was almost in despair when he returned. He had, indeed, become to her a terrible and perplexing problem. As she considered the legitimate results of her own weak indulgence she would sigh again and again:

"Never was there a darker and more mysterious providence. I feel that I can neither understand it nor submit."

A sense of helplessness in dealing with this stubborn and perverse will overwhelmed her, and, while feeling that something must be done, she was at a loss what to do. Her spiritual adviser having failed to meet the case, she next summoned her legal counsellor, who managed her property.

He was a man of few words, and an adept in worldly wisdom.

"Your son should have employment," he said;

> " 'Satan finds some mischief still
> For idle hands,'

etc., is a sound maxim, if not first-class poetry. If Mr. Arnot, the husband of your old friend, is willing to take him, you cannot do better than place your son in his charge, for he is one of the most methodical and successful business men of my acquaintance."

Mrs. Arnot, in response to her friend's letter, induced her husband to make a position in his counting-house for young Haldane, who, from a natural desire to see more of the world, entered into the arrangement very willingly.

CHAPTER III

CHAINED TO AN ICEBERG

HILLATON, the suburban city in which the Arnots resided, was not very distant from New York, and drew much of its prosperity from its relations with the metropolis. It prided itself much on being a university town, but more because many old families of extremely blue blood and large wealth gave tone and color to its society. It is true that this highest social circle was very exclusive, and formed but a small fraction of the population; but the people in general had come to speak of "our society," as being "unusually good," just as they commended to strangers the architecture of "our college buildings," though they had little to do with either.

Mrs. Arnot's blood, however, was as blue as that of the most ancient and aristocratic of her neighbors, while in character and culture she had few equals. But with the majority of those most cerulean in their vital fluid the fact that she possessed large wealth in her own name, and was the wife of a man engaged in a colossal business, weighed more than all her graces and ancestral honors.

Young Haldane's employer, Mr. Arnot, was, indeed, a man of business and method, for the one absorbed his very soul, and the other divided his life into cubes and right angles of manner and habit. It could scarcely be said that he had settled down into ruts, for this would presuppose the passiveness of a nature controlled largely by circumstances. People who travel in ruts drop more often into those made by others than such as are worn by themselves.

Mr. Arnot moved rather in his own well-defined grooves, which he had deliberately furrowed out with his own steely will. In these he went through the day with the same strong, relentless precision which characterized the machinery in his several manufacturing establishments.

He was a man, too, who had always had his own way, and, as is usually true in such instances, the forces of his life had become wholly centripetal.

The cosmos of the selfish man or woman is practically this—Myself the centre of the universe, and all things else are near or remote, of value or otherwise, in accordance with their value and interest to me.

Measuring by this scale of distances (which was the only correct one in the case of Mr. Arnot) the wife of his bosom was quite a remote object. She formed no part of his business, and he, in his hard, narrow worldliness, could not even understand the principles and motives of her action. She was a true and dutiful wife, and presided over his household with elegance and refinement; but he regarded all this as a matter of course. He could not conceive of anything else in *his* wife. All his "subordinates" in their several spheres, "must" perform their duties with becoming propriety. Everything "must be regular and systematic" in his house, as truly as in his factories and counting-room.

Mrs. Arnot endeavored to conform to his peculiarities in this respect, and kept open the domestic grooves in which it was necessary to his peace that he should move regularly and methodically. He had his meals at the hour he chose, to the moment, and when he retired to his library —or, rather, the business office at his house—not the throne-room of King Ahasuerus was more sacred from intrusion; and seldom to his wife, even, was the sceptre of favor and welcome held out, should she venture to enter.

For a long time she had tried to be an affectionate as well as a faithful wife, for she had married this man from love. She had mistaken his cool self-poise for the calmness and steadiness of strength; and women are captivated by strength, and sometimes by its semblance. He was strong; but so also are the driving-wheels of an engine.

There is an undefined, half-recognized force in nature which leads many to seek to balance themselves by marrying their opposites in temperament. While the general working of this tendency is, no doubt, beneficent, it not unfrequently brings together those who are so radically different, that they cannot supplement each other, but must ever remain two distinct, unblended lives, that are in duty bound to obey the letter of the law of marriage, but who cannot fulfil its spirit.

For years Mrs. Arnot had sought with all a woman's tact to consummate their marriage, so that the mystical words of God, "And they twain shall be one flesh," should describe their union; but as time passed she had seen her task grow more and more hopeless. The controlling principles of each life were utterly different. He was hardening into stone, while the dross and materiality of her nature were being daily refined away. A strong but wholly selfish character cannot blend by giving and taking, and thus becoming modified into something different and better. It can only absorb, and thus drag down to its own condition. Before there can be unity the weaker one must give up and yield personal will and independence to such a degree that it is almost equivalent to being devoured and assimilated.

But Mr. Arnot seemed to grow too narrow and self-sufficient in his nature for such spiritual cannibalism, even had his wife been a weak, neutral character, with no decided and persistent individuality of her own. He was not slow in exacting outward and mechanical service, but he had no time to "bother" with her thoughts, feelings, and opinions; nor did he think it worth while, to any extent, to lead her to reflect only his feelings and opinions. Neither she nor any one else was very essential to him. His business *was* necessary, and he valued it even more than the wealth which resulted from it. He grew somewhat like his machinery, which needed attention, but which cherished no sentiments toward those who waited on it during its hours of motion.

Thus, though not deliberately intending it, his manner toward his wife had come to be more and more the equivalent of a steady black frost, and she at last feared that the man had congealed or petrified to his very heart's core.

While the only love in Mr. Arnot's heart was self-love, even in this there existed no trace of weak indulgence and tenderness. His life consisted in making his vast and complicated business go forward steadily, systematically, and successfully; and he would not permit that entity known as Thomas Arnot to thwart him any more than he would brook opposition or neglect in his office-boy. All things, even himself, must bend to the furtherance of his cherished objects.

But, whatever else was lacking, Mr. Arnot had a profound respect for his wife. First and chiefly, she was wealthy, and he, having control of her property, made it subservient to his business. He had chafed at first against what he termed her "sentimental ways of doing good" and her "ridiculous theories," but in these matters he had ever found her as gentle as a woman, but as unyielding as granite. She told him plainly that her religious life and its expression were matters between herself and God—that it was a province into which his cast-iron system and material philosophy could not enter. He grumbled at her large charities, and declared that she "turned their dwelling into a club-house for young men"; but she followed her conscience with such a quiet, unswerving dignity that he found no pretext for interference. The money she gave away was her own, and fortunately, the house to which it was her delight to draw young men from questionable and disreputable places of resort had been left to her by her father. Though she did not continually remind her husband of these facts, as an under-bred woman might have done, her manner was so assured and unhesitating that he was compelled to recognize her rights, and to see that she was fully aware of them also. Since she yielded so gracefully and considerately all and more than he could justly claim, he finally concluded to ignore what he regarded as her "peculiarities." As for himself, he had no peculiarities. He was a "practical, sensible man, with no nonsense about him."

Mrs. Haldane had been in such sore straits and perplexity about her son that she overcame her habitual reserve upon family and personal matters, and wrote to her friend a long and confidential letter, in which she fully described the "mysterious providence" which was clouding her life.

Mrs. Arnot had long been aware of her friend's infirmity, and more than once had sought with delicacy and yet with faithfulness to open her eyes to the consequences of her indulgence. But Mrs. Haldane, unfortunately, was incapable of taking a broad, and therefore correct, view of anything. She was governed far more by her prejudices and feelings than by reason or experience, and the emotion or prejudice uppermost absorbed her mind so completely as to exclude all other considerations. Her friendship for Mrs. Arnot had commenced at school, but the two ladies had developed so differently that the relation had become more a cherished memory of the happy past than a congenial intimacy of their maturer life.

The "mysterious providence" of which Mrs. Haldane wrote was to Mrs. Arnot a legitimate and almost inevitable result. But, now that the mischief had been accomplished, she was the last one in the world to say to her friend, "I told you so." To her mind the providential feature in the matter was the chance that had come to her of counteracting the evil which the mother had unconsciously developed. This opportunity was in the line of her most cherished plan and hope of usefulness, as will be hereafter seen, and she had lost no time in persuading her husband to give Haldane employment in his counting-room. She also secured his consent that the youth should become a member of the family, for a time at least. Mr. Arnot yielded these points reluctantly, for it was a part of his policy to have no more personal relations with his *employés* than with his machinery. He wished them to feel that they were merely a part of his system, and that the moment any one did not work regularly and accurately he must be cast aside as certainly as a broken or defective wheel. But as his wife's health made her practically a silent partner in his vast business, he yielded—though with rather ill grace, and with a prediction that it "would not work well."

Haldane was aware that his mother had written a long letter to Mrs. Arnot, and he supposed that his employer and his wife had thus become acquainted with all his misdeeds. He, therefore, rather dreaded to meet those who must, from the first, regard him as a graceless and difficult subject, that could not be managed at home. But, with the characteristic recklessness of young men who have wealth to fall back upon, he had fortified himself by thoughts like the following:

"If they do not treat me well, or try to put me into a straight-jacket, or if I find the counting-house too dull, I can bid them good-morning whenever I choose."

But Mrs. Arnot's frank and cordial reception was an agreeable surprise. He arrived quite late in the evening, and she had a delightful little lunch brought to him in her private parlor. By the time it was eaten her graceful tact had banished all stiffness and sense of strangeness, and he found himself warming into friendliness toward one whom he had especially dreaded as a "remarkably pious lady"— for thus his mother had always spoken of her.

It was scarcely strange that he should be rapidly disarmed by this lady, who cannot be described in a paragraph. Though her face was rather plain, it was so expressive of herself that it seldom failed to fascinate. Nature can do much to render a countenance attractive, but character accomplishes far more. The beauty which is of feature merely catches the careless, wandering eye.

The beauty which is the reflex of character *holds* the eye, and eventually wins the heart. Those who knew Mrs. Arnot best declared that, instead of growing old and homely, she was growing more lovely every year. Her dark hair had turned gray early, and was fast becoming snowy white. For some years after her marriage she had grown old very fast. She had dwelt, as it were, on the northern side of an iceberg, and in her vain attempt to melt and humanize it, had almost perished herself. As the earthly streams and rills that fed her life congealed, she was led to accept of the love of God, and the long arctic winter of her despair passed gradually away. She was now growing young again. A faint bloom was dawning in her cheeks, and her form was gaining that fulness which is associated with the maturity of middle age. Her bright black eyes were the most attractive and expressive feature which she possessed, and they often seemed gifted with peculiar powers.

As they beamed upon the young man they had much the same effect as the anthracite coals which glowed in the grate, and he began to be conscious of some disposition to give her his confidence.

Having dismissed the servant with the lunch tray, she caused him to draw his chair sociably up to the fire, and said, without any circumlocution:

"Mr. Haldane, perhaps this is the best time for us to have a frank talk in regard to the future."

The young man thought that this was the preface for some decided criticism of the past, and his face became a little hard and defiant. But in this he was mistaken, for the lady made no reference to his faults, of which she had been informed by his mother. She spoke in a kindly but almost in a business-like way of his duties in the counting-room, and of the domestic rules of the household, to which he would be expected to conform. She also spoke plainly of her husband's inexorable requirement of system, regularity, and order, and dwelt upon the fact that all in his employ conformed to this demand, and that it was the business-like and manly thing to do.

"This is your first venture out into the world, I understand," she said, rising to intimate that their interview was over, "and I greatly wish that it may lead toward a useful and successful career. I have spoken plainly because I wished you to realize just what you have undertaken, and thus meet with no unpleasant surprises or unexpected experiences. When one enters upon a course with his eyes open, he in a certain sense pledges himself to do the best he can in that line of duty, and our acquaintance, though so brief, has convinced me that you *can* do very well indeed."

"I was under the impression," said the young man, coloring deeply, "that my mother's letter had led you to suppose—to expect just the contrary."

"Mr. Haldane," said Mrs. Arnot, giving him her hand with graceful tact, "I shall form my opinion of you solely on the ground of your own action, and I wish you to think of me as a friend who takes a genuine interest in your success. Good-night."

He went to his room in quite a heroic and virtuous mood.

"She does not treat me a bit like a 'bad boy,' as I supposed she would," he thought; "but appears to take it for granted that I shall be a gentleman in this her house, and a sensible fellow in her husband's office. Blow me if I disappoint her!"

Nor did he for several weeks. Even Mr. Arnot was compelled to admit that it did "work rather better than he expected," and that he "supposed the young fellow did as well as he could."

As the novelty of Haldane's new relations wore off, however, and as his duties became so familiar as to be chiefly a matter of routine, the grave defects of his character and training began to show themselves. The restraint of the counting-room grew irksome. Associations were formed in the city which tended toward his old evil habits. As a piece of Mr. Arnot's machinery he did not move with the increasing precision that his employer required and expected on his becoming better acquainted with his duties.

Mrs. Arnot had expected this, and knew that her husband would tolerate carelessness and friction only up to a certain point. She had gained more influence over the young man than any one else had ever possessed, and by means of it kept him within bounds for some time; but she saw from her husband's manner that things were fast approaching a crisis.

One evening she kindly, but frankly, told him of the danger in which he stood of an abrupt, stern dismissal.

He was more angry than alarmed, and during the following day about concluded that he would save himself any such mortification by leaving of his own accord. He quite persuaded himself that he had a soul above plodding business, and that, after enjoying himself at home for a time, he could enter upon some other career, that promised more congeniality and renown.

In order that his employer might not anticipate him, he performed his duties very accurately that day, but left the office with the expectation of never returning.

He had very decided compunctions in thus requiting Mrs. Arnot's kindness, but muttered recklessly:

"I'm tired of this humdrum, treadmill life, and believe I'm destined to better things. If I could only get a good position in the army or navy, the world would hear from me. They say money opens every door, and mother must open some good wide door for me."

Regardless now of his employer's good or bad opinion, he came down late to supper; but, instead of observing with careless defiance the frown which he knew lowered toward him, his eyes were drawn to a fair young face on the opposite side of the table.

Mrs. Arnot, in her pleasant, cordial voice, which made

the simplest thing she said seem real and hearty, rather than conventional, introduced him:

"Mr. Haldane, my niece, Miss Laura Romeyn. Laura, no doubt, can do far more than an old lady to make your evenings pass brightly."

After a second glance of scrutiny, Haldane was so ungratefully forgetful of all Mrs. Arnot's kindness as to be inclined to agree with her remark.

CHAPTER IV

IMMATURE

"IS she a young lady, or merely a school-girl?" was Haldane's query concerning the stranger sitting opposite to him; and he addressed to her a few commonplace but exploring remarks. Regarding himself as well acquainted with society in general, and young ladies in particular, he expected to solve the question at once, and was perplexed that he could not. He had flirted with several misses as immature as himself, and so thought that he was profoundly versed in the mysteries of the sex. "They naturally lean toward and look up to men, and one is a fool, or else lacking in personal appearance, who does not have his own way with them," was his opinion, substantially.

Modesty is a grace which fine-looking young men of large wealth are often taught by some severe experiences, if it is ever learned. Haldane, as yet, had not received such wholesome depletion. His self-approval and assurance, moreover, were quite natural, since his mother and sisters had seldom lost an opportunity of developing and confirming these traits. The yielding of women to his will and wishes had been one of the most uniform experiences of his life, and he had come to regard it as the natural order of things. Without formulating the thought in plain words, he nevertheless regarded Mrs. Arnot's kindness, by which she sought to gain a helpful influence over him, as largely due to some peculiar fascination of his own, which made him a favorite wherever he chose to be. Of course, the young stranger on the opposite side of the table would prove no exception to the rule, and all he had to do was to satisfy himself that she was sufficiently pretty and interesting to make it worth while to pay her a little attention.

But for some reason she did not seem greatly impressed by his commonplace and rather patronizing remarks. Was it pride or dignity on her part, or was it mere girlish shyness? It must be the latter, for there was no occasion for pride and dignity in her manner toward him.

Then came the thought that possibly Mrs. Arnot had not told her who he was, and that she looked upon him as a mere clerk of low degree. To remove from her mind any such error, his tones and manner became still more self-asserting and patronizing.

"If she has any sense at all," he thought, "she shall see that I have peculiar claims to her respect."

As he proceeded in these tactics, there was a growing expression of surprise and a trace of indignation upon the young girl's face. Mrs. Arnot watched the by-play with an amused expression. There was not much cynicism in her nature. She believed that experience would soon prick the bubble of his vanity, and it was her disposition to smile rather than to sneer at absurdity in others. Besides, she was just. She never applied to a young man of twenty the standard by which she would measure those of her own age, and she remembered Haldane's antecedents. But Mr. Arnot went to his library muttering:

"The ridiculous fool!"

When Miss Romeyn rose from the table, Haldane saw that she was certainly tall enough to be a young lady, for she was slightly above medium height. He still believed that she was very young, however, for her figure was slight and girlish, and while her bearing was graceful it had not that assured and pronounced character to which he had been accustomed.

"She evidently has not seen much of society. Well, since she is not gawky, I like her better than if she were blasé. Anything but your blasé girls," he observed to himself, with a consciousness that he was an experienced man of the world.

The piano stood open in the drawing-room, and this suggested music. Haldane had at his tongue's end the names of half a dozen musicians whose professional titles had been prominent in the newspapers for a few months previous, and whose merits had formed a part of the current chit-chat of the day. Some he had heard, and others he had not, but he could talk volubly of all, and he asked Miss Romeyn for her opinion of one and another in a manner which implied that of course she knew about them, and that ignorance in regard to such persons was not to be expected.

Her face colored with annoyance, but she said quietly and a trifle coldly that she had not heard them.

Mrs. Arnot again smiled as she watched the young people, but she now came to her niece's rescue, thinking also it would be well to disturb Haldane's sense of superiority somewhat. So she said:

"Laura, since we cannot hear this evening the celebrated artists that Mr. Haldane has mentioned, we must content ourselves with simple home music. Won't you play for us that last selection of which you wrote to me?"

"I hardly dare, auntie, since Mr. Haldane is such a critical judge, and has heard so much music from those who make it a business to be perfect. He must have listened to the selection you name a hundred times, for it is familiar to most lovers of good music."

Haldane had sudden misgivings. Suppose he had not heard it? This would be awkward, after his assumed acquaintance with such matters.

"Even if Mr. Haldane is familiar with it," Mrs. Arnot replied, "Steibelt's Storm Rondo will bear repetition. Besides, his criticism may be helpful, since he can tell you wherein you come short of the skilled professionals."

Laura caught the twinkle in her aunt's eye, and went to the piano.

The young man saw at once that he had been caught in

his own trap, for the music was utterly unfamiliar. The rondo was no wonderful piece of intricacy, such as a professional might choose. On the contrary, it was simple, and quite within the capabilities of a young and well-taught girl. But it was full of rich melody which even he, in his ignorance, could understand and appreciate, and yet, for aught that he knew it was difficult in the extreme.

At first he had a decided sense of humiliation, and a consciousness that it was deserved. He had been talking largely and confidently of an art concerning which he knew little, and in which he began to think that his listener was quite well versed.

But as the thought of the composer grew in power and beauty he forgot himself and his dilemma in his enjoyment. Two senses were finding abundant gratification at the same time, for it was a delight to listen, and it was even a greater pleasure to look at the performer.

She gave him a quick, shy glance of observation, fearing somewhat that she might see severe judgment or else cool indifference in the expression of his face, and she was naturally pleased and encouraged when she saw, instead, undisguised admiration. His previous manner had annoyed her, and she determined to show him that his superior airs were quite uncalled for. Thus the diffident girl was led to surpass herself, and infuse so much spirit and grace into her playing as to surprise even her aunt.

Haldane was soon satisfied that she was more than pretty —that she was beautiful. Her features, that had seemed too thin and colorless, flushed with excitement, and her blue eyes, which he had thought cold and expressionless, kindled until they became lustrous. He felt, in a way that he could not define to himself, that her face was full of power and mind, and that she was different from the pretty girls who had hitherto been his favorites.

As she rose from the piano he was mastered by one of those impulses which often served him in the place of something better, and he said impetuously:

"Miss Romeyn, I beg your pardon. You know a hundred-fold more about music than I do, and I have been talking as if the reverse were true. I never heard anything so fine in my life, and I also confess that I never heard that piece before."

The young girl blushed with pleasure on having thus speedily vanquished this superior being, whom she had been learning both to dread and dislike. At the same time his frank, impulsive words of compliment did much to remove the prejudice which she was naturally forming against him. Mrs. Arnot said, with her mellow laugh, that often accomplished more than long homilies:

"That is a manly speech, Egbert, and much to your credit. 'Honest confession is good for the soul.'"

Haldane did not get on his stilts again that evening, and before it was over he concluded that Miss Romeyn was the most charming young lady he had ever met, though, for some reason, she still permitted him to do nearly all the talking. She bade him good-night, however, with a smile that was not unkindly, and which was interpreted by him as being singularly gracious.

By this time he had concluded that Miss Romeyn was a "young lady *par excellence*"; but it has already been shown that his judgment in most matters was not to be trusted. Whether she was a school-girl or a fully fledged young lady, a child or a woman, might have kept a closer observer than himself much longer in doubt. In truth, she was scarcely the one or the other, and had many of the characteristics of both. His opinion of her was as incorrect as that of himself. He was not a man, though he considered himself a superior one, and had attained to manly proportions.

But there were wide differences in their immaturity. She was forming under the guidance of a mother who blended firmness and judgment equally with love. Gentle blood was in her veins, and she had inherited many of her mother's traits with her beauty. Her parents, however,

believed that, even as the garden of Eden needed to be
"dressed and kept," so the nature of their child required
careful pruning, with repression here and development
there. While the young girl was far from being faultless, fine traits and tendencies dominated, and, though as
yet undeveloped, they were unfolding with the naturalness
and beauty of a budding flower.

In Haldane's case evil traits were in the ascendant, and
the best hope for him was that they as yet had not become
confirmed.

"Who is this Mr. Haldane, auntie?" Laura asked on
reaching her room. There was a slight trace of vexation
in her tone.

"He is the son of an old friend of mine. I have induced
my husband to try to give him a business education. You
do not like him."

"I did not like him at all at first, but he improves a little
on acquaintance. Is he a fair sample of your young men
protégés?"

"He is the least promising of any of them," replied Mrs.
Arnot, sitting down before the fire. Laura saw that her face
had become shadowed with sadness and anxiety.

"You look troubled, auntie. Is he the cause?"

"Yes."

"Are you very much interested in him?"

"I am, Laura; very much, indeed. I cannot bear to give
him up, and yet I fear I must."

"Is he a very interesting 'case'?" asked the young girl
in some surprise. "Mother often laughingly calls the young
men you are trying to coax to be good by your winning
ways, 'cases.' I don't know much about young men, but
should suppose that you had many under treatment much
more interesting than he is."

"Sister Fanny is always laughing at my hobby, and saying that, since I have no children of my own, I try to adopt
every young man who will give me a chance. Perhaps if
I try to carry out your mother's figure, you will understand

why I am so interested in this 'case.' If I were a physician and had charge of a good many patients, ought I not to be chiefly interested in those who were in the most critical and dangerous condition?"

"It would be just like you to be so, auntie, and I would not mind being quite ill myself if I could have you to take care of me. I hope the young men whom you 'adopt' appreciate their privileges."

"The trouble with most of us, Laura, is that we become wise too late in life. Young people are often their own worst enemies, and if you wish to do them good, you must do it, as it were, on the sly. If one tries openly to reform and guide them—if I should say plainly, Such and such are your faults; such and such places and associations are full of danger—they would be angry or disgusted, or they would say I was blue and strait-laced, and had an old woman's notions of what a man should be. I must coax them, as you say; I must disguise my medicines, and apply my remedies almost without their knowing it. I also find it true in my practice that tonics and good wholesome diet are better than all moral drugs. It seems to me that if I can bring around these giddy young fellows refining, steadying, purifying influences, I can do them more good than if I lectured them. The latter is the easier way, and many take it. It would require but a few minutes to tell this young Haldane what his wise safe course must be if he would avoid shipwreck; but I can see his face flush and lip curl at my homily. And yet for weeks I have been angling for him, and I fear to no purpose. Your uncle may discharge him any day. It makes me very sad to say it, but if he goes home I think he will also go to ruin. Thank God for your good, wise mother, Laura. It is a great thing to be started right in life."

"Then this young man has been started wrong?

"Yes, wrong indeed."

Is he so very bad, auntie?" Laura asked with a face full of serious concern.

Mrs. Arnot smiled as she said, "If you were a young society chit, you might think him 'very nice,' as their slang goes. He is good-looking and rich, and his inclination to be fast would be a piquant fact in his favor. He has done things which would seem to you very wrong indeed. But he is foolish and ill-trained rather than bad. He is a spoiled boy, and spoiled boys are apt to become spoiled men. I have told you all this partly because, having been your mother's companion all your life, you are so old-fashioned that I can talk to you almost as I would to sister Fanny, and partly because I like to talk about my hobby."

A young girl naturally has quick sympathies, and all the influences of Laura's life had been gentle and humane. Her aunt's words speedily led her to regard Haldane as an "interesting case," a sort of fever patient who was approaching the crisis of his disease. Curling down on the floor, and leaning her arms on her aunt's lap, she looked up with a face full of solicitude as she asked:

"And don't you think you can save him? Please don't give up trying."

"I like the expression of your face now," said Mrs. Arnot, stroking the abundant tresses, that were falling loosely from the girl's head, "for in it I catch a glimpse of the divine image. Many think of God as looking down angrily and frowningly upon the foolish and wayward; but I see in the solicitude of your face a faint reflection of the 'Not willing that any should perish' which it ever seems to me is the expression of His."

"Laura," said she abruptly, after a moment, "did any one ever tell you that you were growing up very pretty?"

"No, auntie," said the girl, blushing and laughing.

"Mr. Haldane told you so this evening."

"O auntie, you are mistaken; he could not have been so rude."

"He did not make a set speech to that effect, my dear, but he told you so by his eyes and manner, only you are such an innocent home child that you did not notice. But when you go into society you will be told this fact so often that you will be compelled to heed it, and will soon learn the whole language of flattery, spoken and unspoken. Perhaps I had better forewarn you a little, and so forearm you. What are you going to do with your beauty?"

"Why, auntie, how funny you talk! What should I do with it, granting that it has any existence save in your fond eyes?"

"Suppose you use it to make men better, instead of to make them merely admire you. One can't be a belle very long at best, and of all the querulous, discontented, and disagreeable people that I have met, superannuated belles, who could no longer obtain their revenue of flattery, were the worst. They were impoverished, indeed. If you do as I suggest, you will have much that is pleasant to think about when you come to be as old as I am. Perhaps you can do more for young Haldane than I can."

"Now, auntie, what can I do?"

"That which nearly all women can do: be kind and winning; make our safe, cosey parlor so attractive that he will not go out evenings to places which tend to destroy him. You feel an interest in him; show it. Ask him about his business, and get him to explain it to you. Suggest that if you were a man you would like to master your work, and become eminent in it. Show by your manner and by words, if occasion offers, that you love and revere all that is sacred, pure, and Christian. Laura, innocent dove as you are, you know that many women beguile men to ruin with smiles. Men can be beguiled *from* ruin with smiles. Indeed, I think multitudes are permitted to go to destruction because women are so unattractive, so absorbed in themselves and their nerves. If mothers and wives, maidens and old maids, would all commence playing the agreeable to the men of their household and circle, not for the sake of a few compliments, but for the purpose of luring them from evil and making them better, the world would improve at once."

"I see, auntie," said Laura, laughing; "you wish to administer me as a sugar-coated pill to your 'difficult case.' "

A deep sigh was the only answer, and, looking up, Laura saw that her words had not been heeded. Tears were in her aunt's eyes, and after a moment she said brokenly:

"My theories seem true enough, and yet how signally I have failed in carrying them out! Perhaps it is my fault; perhaps it is my fault; but I've tried—oh! how I have tried! Laura, dear, you know that I am a lonely woman; but do not let this prejudice you against what I have said. Good-night, dear; I have kept you up too long after your journey."

Her niece understood her allusion to the cold, unloving man who sat alone every evening in his dim library, thinking rarely of his wife, but often of her wealth, and how it might increase his leverage in his herculean labors. The young girl had the tact to reply only by a warm, lingering embrace. It was an old sorrow, of which she had long been aware; but it seemed without remedy, and was rarely touched upon.

CHAPTER V

PASSION'S CLAMOR

LAURA had a strong affection for her aunt, and would naturally be inclined to gratify any wishes that she might express, even had they involved tasks uncongenial and unattractive. But the proposal that she should become an ally in the effort to lure young Haldane from his evil associations, and awaken within him pure and refined tastes, was decidedly attractive. She was peculiarly romantic in her disposition, and no rude contact with the commonplace, common-sense world had chastened her innocent fancies by harsh and disagreeable experience. Her Christian training and girlish simplicity lifted her above the ordinary romanticism of imagining herself the heroine in every instance, and the object and end of all masculine aspirations. On this occasion she simply desired to act the part of a humble assistant of Mrs. Arnot, whom she regarded as Haldane's good angel; and she was quite as disinterested in her hope for the young man's moral improvement as her aunt herself.

The task, moreover, was doubly pleasing since she could perform it in a way that was so womanly and agreeable. She could scarcely have given Haldane a plain talk on the evils of fast living to save her life, but if she could keep young men from going to destruction by smiling upon them, by games of backgammon and by music, she felt in the mood to be a missionary all her life, especially if she could have so safe and attractive a field of labor as her aunt's back parlor.

But the poor child would soon learn that perverse human nature is much the same in a drawing-room and a tenement-house, and that all who seek to improve it are doomed to meet much that is excessively annoying and discouraging.

The simple-hearted girl no more foresaw what might result from her smiles than an ignorant child would anticipate the consequences of fire falling on grains of harmless-looking black sand. She had never seen passion kindling and flaming till it seemed like a scorching fire, and had not learned by experience that in some circumstances her smiles might be like incendiary sparks to powder.

In seeking to manage her "difficult case," Mrs. Arnot should have foreseen the danger of employing such a fascinating young creature as her assistant; but in these matters the wisest often err, and only comprehend the evil after it has occurred. Laura was but a child in years, having passed her fifteenth birthday only a few months previous, and Haldane seemed to the lady scarcely more than a boy. She did not intend that her niece should manifest anything more than a little winning kindness and interest, barely enough to keep the young fellow from spending his evenings out she knew not where. He was at just the age when the glitter and tinsel of public amusements are most attractive. She believed that if she could familiarize his mind with the real gold and clear diamond flash of pure home pleasures, and those which are enjoyed in good society, he would eventually become disgusted with gilt, varnish, and paste. If Laura had been a very plain girl, she might have seconded Mrs. Arnot's efforts to the utmost without any unpleasant results, even if no good ones had followed; and it may well be doubted whether any of the latter would have ensued. Haldane's disease was too deeply rooted, and his tastes vitiated to such a degree that he had lost the power to relish long the simple enjoyments of Mrs. Arnot's parlor. He already craved the pleasures which first kindle and excite and then consume.

Laura, however, was not plain and ordinary, and the smiles which were intended as innocent lures from snares, instead of into them, might make trouble for all concerned. Haldane was naturally combustible, to begin with, and was now at the most inflammable period of his life.

The profoundest master of human nature portrayed to the world a Romeo and a Juliet, both mastered by a passion which but a few words and glances had kindled. There are many Romeos who do not find their Juliets so sympathetic and responsive, and they usually develop at about the age of Haldane. Indeed, nearly all young men of sanguine temperaments go through the Romeo stage, and they are fortunate if they pass it without doing anything especially ridiculous or disastrous. These sudden attacks are exceedingly absurd to older and cooler friends, but to the victims themselves they are tremendously real and tragic for the time being. More hearts are broken into indefinite fragments before twenty than ever after; but, like the broken bones of the young, they usually knit readily together again, and are just as good for all practical purposes.

There was nothing unusual in the fact, therefore, that Haldane was soon deeply enamored with his new acquaintance. It was true that Laura had given him the mildest and most innocent kind of encouragement—and the result would probably have been the same if she had given him none at all—but his vanity, and what he chose to regard as his "undying love," interpreted all her actions, and gave volumes of meaning to a kindly glance or a pleasant word. Indeed, before there had been time to carry out, to any extent, the tactics her aunt had proposed, symptoms of his malady appeared. While she was regarding him merely as one of her aunt's "cases," and a very hard one at best, and thought of herself as trying to help a little, as a child might hold a bandage or a medicine phial for experienced hands, he, on the contrary, had begun to mutter to himself that she was "the divinest woman God ever fashioned."

There was now no trouble about his spending evenings

elsewhere, and the maiden was perplexed and annoyed at finding her winning ways far too successful, and that the one she barely hoped to keep from the vague—and to her mind, horrible—places of temptation, was becoming as adhesive as sticking-plaster. If she smiled, he smiled and ogled far too much in return. If she chatted with one and another of the young men who found Mrs. Arnot's parlor the most attractive place open to them in the town, he would assume a manner designed to be darkly tragical, but which to the young girl had more the appearance of sulking.

She was not so much of a child as to be unable to comprehend Haldane's symptoms, and she was sufficiently a woman not to be excessively angry. And yet she was greatly annoyed and perplexed. At times his action seemed so absurd that she was glad to escape to her room, that she might give way to her merriment; and again he would appear so much in earnest that she was quite as inclined to cry and to think seriously of bringing her visit to an abrupt termination.

While under Mrs. Arnot's eye Haldane was distant and circumspect, but the moment he was alone with Laura his manner became unmistakably demonstrative.

At first she was disposed to tell her aunt all about the young man's sentimental manner, but the fact that it seemed so ridiculous deterred her. She still regarded herself as a child, and that any one should be seriously in love with her after but a few days' acquaintance seemed absurdity itself. Her aunt might think her very vain for even imagining such a thing, and, perhaps, after all it was only her own imagination.

"Mr. Haldane has acted queerly from the first," she concluded, "and the best thing I can do is to think no more about him, and let auntie manage her 'difficult case' without me. If I am to help in these matters, I had better commence with a 'case' that is not so 'difficult.'"

She therefore sought to avoid the young man, and prove

by her manner that she was utterly indifferent to him, hoping that this course would speedily cure him of his folly. She would venture into the parlor only when her aunt or guests were there, and would then try to make herself generally agreeable, without an apparent thought for him.

While she assured herself that she did not like him, and that he was in no respect a person to be admired and liked, she still found herself thinking about him quite often. He was her first recognized lover. Indeed, few had found opportunity to give more than admiring glances to the little nun, who thus far had been secluded almost continuously in the safest of all cloisters—a country home. It was a decided novelty that a young man, almost six feet in height, should be looking unutterable things in her direction whenever she was present. She wished he wouldn't, but since he would, she could not help thinking about him, and how she could manage to make him "behave sensibly."

She did not maintain her air of indifference very perfectly, however, for she had never been schooled by experience, and was acting solely on the intuitions of her sex. She could not forbear giving a quick glance occasionally to see how he was taking his lesson. At times he was scowling and angry, and then she could maintain her part without difficulty; again he would look so miserable that, out of pity, she would relent into a half smile, but immediately reproach herself for being "so foolish."

Haldane's manner soon attracted Mrs. Arnot's attention, notwithstanding his effort to disguise from her his feeling; and a little observation on the part of the experienced matron enabled her to guess how matters stood. While Mrs. Arnot was perplexed and provoked by this new complication in Haldane's case, she was too kindly in her nature not to feel sorry for him. She was also so well versed in human nature as to be aware that she could not sit down and coolly talk him out of his folly.

Besides it was not necessarily folly. The youth was but following a law of nature, and following it, too, in much the same manner as had his fathers before him since the beginning of time. There would not be any thing essentially wrong in an attachment between these young people, if it sprang up naturally; only it would be necessary to impress upon them the fact that they were *young*, and that for years to come their minds should be largely occupied with other matters. Haldane certainly would not have been her choice for Laura, but if a strong attachment became the means of steadying him and of inciting to the formation of a fine character, all might be well in the end. She was morbidly anxious, however, that her niece should not meet with any such disappointment in life as had fallen to her lot, and should the current of the young girl's affection tend steadily in his direction she would deeply regret the fact.

' She would regret exceedingly, also, to have the young girl's mind occupied by thoughts of such a nature for years to come. Her education was unfinished; she was very immature, and should not make so important a choice until she had seen much more of society, and time had been given for the formation of her tastes and character.

Mrs. Arnot soon concluded that it would be wiser to prevent trouble than to remedy it, and that Laura had better return speedily to the safe asylum of her own home. She could then suggest to Haldane that if he hoped to win the maiden in after years he must form a character worthy of her.

Had she carried out her plan that day all might have turned out differently, but the advanced in life are prone to forget the impetuosity of youth. Haldane was already ripe for a declaration, or, more properly, an explosion of his pent-up feelings, and was only awaiting an opportunity to insist upon his own acceptance. He was so possessed and absorbed by his emotions that he felt sure they would sweep away all obstacles. He imagined himself pleading his cause in a way that would melt a marble heart; and both vanity and hope had whispered that Laura was a shy maiden, secretly responsive to his passion, and only awaiting his frank avowal before showing her own heart. Else why had she been so kind at first? Having won his love, was she not seeking now to goad him on to its utterance by a sudden change of manner?

Thus he reasoned, as have many others equally blind.

On becoming aware of Haldane's passion, Mrs. Arnot resolved to sedulously guard her niece, and prevent any premature and disagreeable scenes. She was not long in discovering that the feeling, as yet, was all on the young man's side, and believed that by a little adroitness she could manage the affair so that no harm would result to either party.

But on the day following the one during which she had arrived at the above conclusions she felt quite indisposed, and while at dinner was obliged to succumb to one of her nervous headaches. Before retiring to her private room she directed the waitress to say to such of her young friends as might call that she was too ill to see them.

Haldane's expressions of sympathy were hollow, indeed, for he hoped that, as a result of her indisposition, he would have Laura all to himself that evening. With an insinuating smile he said to the young girl, after her aunt had left the table:

"I shall expect you to be very agreeable this evening, to compensate me for Mrs. Arnot's absence."

Laura blushed vividly, and was provoked with herself that she did so, but she replied quietly:

"You must excuse me this evening, Mr. Haldane; I am sure my aunt will need me."

His smile was succeeded by a sudden frown; but, as Mr. Arnot was at the table, he said, with assumed carelessness:

"Then I will go out and try to find amusement elsewhere."

"It might be well, young man," said Mr. Arnot austerely, "to seek for something else than amusement. When I was at your age I so invested my evenings that they now tell in my business."

"I am willing to invest this evening in a way to make it tell upon my future," replied Haldane, with a meaning glance at Laura.

Mr. Arnot observed this glance and the blushing face of his niece, and drew his own conclusions; but he only said dryly:

"That remark is about as inexplicable as some of your performances at the office of late."

Laura soon after excused herself and sought a refuge in her aunt's room, which, being darkened, prevented the lady from seeing her burning cheeks and general air of vexation and disquiet. Were it not for Mrs. Arnot's suffering condition and need of rest, Laura would then have told her of her trouble and asked permission to return home, and she determined to do this at the first opportunity. Now, however, she unselfishly forgot herself in her effort to alleviate her aunt's distress. With a strong sense of relief she heard Haldane go out, slamming the front door after him.

"Was there ever such an absurd fellow!" thought she; "he has made himself disagreeable ever since I came, with his superior airs, as if he knew everything, when, in fact, he doesn't know anything well, not even good manners. He acts as if I belonged to him and had no right to any will or wishes of my own. If he can't take the hints that I have given he must be as stupid and blind as an owl. In spite of all that I can, do or say he seems to think that I only want an opportunity to show the same ridiculous feeling that makes him appear like a simpleton. If I were a young lady in society I should detest a man who took it for granted that I would fall in love with him."

With like indignant musings she beguiled the time, wondering occasionally why her aunt did not ask her to go down and entertain the object of her dread, but secretly thankful that she did not.

At last Mrs. Arnot said:

"Mr. Haldane went out, did he not?"

"Yes, auntie, some time ago."

"I left my other bottle of smelling-salts in the parlor. I think it is stronger than this. Would you mind getting it for me? It's on the mantel."

Laura had no difficulty in finding it in the somewhat dimly-lighted drawing-room, but as she turned to leave the apartment she saw Haldane between her and the door.

Before he had reached any of his garish haunts he had felt such an utter distaste for them in his present mood that he returned. He was conscious of the impulse merely to be near the object of his thoughts, and also hoped that by some fortunate chance he might still be able to find her alone. That his return might be unnoted, he had quietly entered a side door, and was waiting and watching for just such an opportunity as Mrs. Arnot had unwittingly occasioned.

Laura tried to brush past, but he intercepted her, and said:

"No, Miss Laura, not till you hear me. You have my destiny in your hands."

"I haven't anything of the kind," she answered, in tones of strong vexation. Guided by instinct, she resolved to be as prosaic and matter-of-fact as possible; so she added: "I have only aunt's smelling-salts in my hands, and she needs them."

"I need *you* far more than Mrs. Arnot needs her smelling-salts," he said tragically.

"Mr. Haldane, such talk is very absurd," she replied, half ready to cry from nervousness and annoyance.

"It is not absurd. How can you trifle with the deepest and holiest feelings that a man—of which a man—feels?" he retorted passionately, and growing a little incoherent.

"I don't know anything about such feelings, and therefore cannot trifle with them."

"What did your blushes mean this evening? You cannot deceive me; I have seen the world and know it."

"I am not the world. I am only a school-girl, and if you had good sense you would not talk so to me. You appear to think that I must feel and do as you wish.   What right have you to act so?"

"The truest and strongest right.   You know well that I love you with my whole soul.   I have given you my heart —all there is of me.   Have I not a right to ask your love in return?"

Laura was conscious of a strange thrill as she heard these passionate words, for they appeared to echo in a depth of her nature of which she had not been conscious before.

The strong and undoubting assurance which possessed him carried for a moment a strange mastery over her mind. As he so vehemently asserted the only claim which a man can urge, her woman's soul trembled, and for a moment she felt almost powerless to resist.   His unreserved giving appeared to require that he should receive also.   She would have soon realized, however, that Haldane's attitude was essentially that of an Oriental lover, who, in his strongest attachments, is ever prone to maintain the imperative mood, and to consult his own heart rather than that of the woman he loves.   While in Laura's nature there was unusual gentleness and a tendency to respect and admire virile force, she was too highly bred in our Western civilization not to resent as an insult any such manifestation of this force as would make the quest of her love a demand rather than a suit, after once recognizing such a spirit.   She was now confused, however, and after an awkward moment said:

"I have not asked or wished you to give me so much. I don't think you realize what you are saying.   If you would only remember that I am scarcely more than a child you would not talk so foolishly.   Please let me go to my aunt."

"No, not till you give me some hope.   Your blushes prove that you are a woman."

"They prove that I am excessively annoyed and vexed."

"Oh, Laura, after raising so many hopes you cannot— you cannot—"

"I haven't meant to raise any hopes."

"Why were you so kind to me at first?"

"Well, if you must know, my aunt wished me to be. If I had dreamed you would act so I would not have spoken to you."

"What motive could Mrs. Arnot have had for such a request?"

"I will tell you, and when you know the whole truth you will see how mistaken you are, and how greatly you wrong me. Aunt wanted me to help her keep you home evenings, and away from all sorts of horrid places to which you were fond of going."

These words gave Haldane a cue which he at once followed, and he said eagerly:

"If you will be my wife, I will do anything you wish. I will make myself good, great, and renowned for your sake. Your smiles will keep me from every temptation. But I warn you that if you cast me off—if you trifle with me—I shall become a reckless man. I shall be ruined. My only impulse will be self-destruction."

Laura was now thoroughly incensed, and she said indignantly:

"Mr. Haldane, I should think you would be ashamed to talk in that manner. It's the same as if a spoiled boy should say: If you don't give me what I wish, right or wrong, I will do something dreadful. If I ever do love a man, it will be one that I can look up to and respect, and not one who must be coaxed and bribed to give up disgusting vices. If you do not open that door I will call uncle."

The door opened, and **Mr. Arnot entered with a heavy** frown upon his brow.

CHAPTER VI

"GLOOMY GRANDEUR"

MR. ARNOT'S library was on the side of the hall opposite to the drawing-room. Though he had been deeply intent upon his writing, he at last became conscious that there were some persons in the parlor who were talking in an unusual manner, and he soon distinguished the voice of his niece. Haldane's words, manner, and glances at the dinner-table at once recurred to him, and stepping silently to the drawing-room door, he heard the latter part of the colloquy narrated in the previous chapter. He was both amused and angry, and while relieved to find that his niece was indulging in no "sentimental nonsense," he had not a particle of sympathy or charity for Haldane, and he determined to give the young man a "lesson that would not soon be forgotten."

"What is the meaning of this ridiculous scene?" he demanded sternly. "What have you been saying to this child?"

Haldane at first had been much abashed by the entrance of his employer; but his tone and manner stung the young fellow into instant anger, and he replied haughtily:

"She is not a child, and what I have said concerns Miss Romeyn only."

"Ah, indeed! I have no right to protect my niece in my own house!"

"My intentions toward Miss Romeyn are entirely honorable, and there is no occasion for protection."

Reassured by her uncle's presence, Laura's nervous apprehension began to give place to something like pity for the youth, who had assumed an attitude befitting high tragedy, and toward whom she felt that she had been a little harsh. Now that he was confronted by one who was disposed to be still more harsh, womanlike, she was inclined to take his part. She would be sorry to have him come to an open rupture with his employer on her account, so she said eagerly:

"Please, uncle, do me the favor of letting the whole matter drop. Mr. Haldane has seen his mistake by this time. I am going home to-morrow, and the affair is too absurd to make any one any more trouble."

Before he could answer, Mrs. Arnot, hearing their voices, and surmising the trouble which she had hoped to prevent, now appeared also, and by her good sense and tact brought the disagreeable scene to a speedy close.

"Laura, my dear," she said quietly, "go up to my room, and I will join you there soon." The young girl gladly obeyed.

There were times when Mrs. Arnot controlled her strong-willed husband in a manner that seemed scarcely to be reconciled with his dictatorial habits. This fact might be explained in part by her wealth, of which he had the use, but which she still controlled, but more truly by her innate superiority, which ever gives supremacy to the nobler and stronger mind when aroused.

Mr. Arnot had become suddenly and vindictively angry with his clerk, who, instead of being overwhelmed with awe and shame at his unexpected appearance, was haughty and even defiant. One of the strongest impulses of this man was to crush out of those in his employ a spirit of independence and individual self-assertion. The idea of a part of his business machinery making such a jarring tumult in his own house! He proposed to instantly cast away the cause of friction, and insert a more stolid human cog-wheel in Haldane's place.

But when his wife said, in a tone which she rarely used:

"Mr. Arnot, before anything further is said upon this matter, I would like to see you in your library"—he followed her without a word.

Before the library door closed, however, he could not forbear snarling.

"I told you that your having this big spoiled boy as an inmate of the house would not work well."

"He has been offering himself to Laura, has he not?" she said quietly.

"I suppose that is the way in which you would explain his absurd, maudlin words. A pitiful offer it was, which she, like a sensible girl, declined without thanks."

"What course do you propose to take toward Haldane?"

"I was on the point of sending him home to his mother, and of suggesting that he remain with her till he becomes something more than a fast, foolish boy. As yet I see no reason for acting differently."

"On just what grounds do you propose to discharge him?"

"Has he not given sufficient cause this evening in his persecution of Laura and his impudence to me?"

"Thomas, you forget that while young Haldane is your clerk, he enjoys a social position quite equal to that which a son of ours would possess, did we have one. Though his course toward Laura has been crude and boyish, I have yet to learn that there has been anything dishonorable. Laura is to us a child; to him she seems a very pretty and attractive girl, and his sudden passion for her is, perhaps, one of the most natural things in the world. Besides, an affair of this kind should be managed quietly and wisely, and not with answering passion. You are angry now; you will see that I am right in the morning. At all events, the name of this innocent girl, my sister's child, must not be bandied about in the gossip of the town. Among young men Haldane passes for a young man. Do you wish to have it the town talk that he has been discharged because he ventured to compliment your niece with the offer of his hand? That he has been premature and rash is chiefly the fault of his years and temperament; but no serious trouble need follow unless we make it ourselves. Laura will return home in a day or two, and if the young fellow is dealt with wisely and kindly, this episode may do much toward making a sensible man of him. If you abruptly discharge him, people will imagine tenfold more than has occurred, and they may surmise positive evil.''

''Well, well, have it your own way,'' said her husband impatiently. ''Of course, I do not wish that Laura should become the theme of scandal. But as for this young firebrand of a Haldane, there must be a decided change in him. I cannot bother with him much longer.''

''I think I can manage him. At any rate, please make no change that can seem connected with this affair. If you would also exercise a little kindness and forbearance, I do not think you would ever have cause to regret it.''

''My office is not an asylum for incapables, lovesick swains, and fast boys. It's a place of business, and if young Haldane can't realize this, there are plenty who can.''

''As a favor to me, I will ask you to bear with him as long as possible. Can you not send him to your factory near New York on some errand? New scenes will divert his thoughts, and sudden and acute attacks, like his, usually do not last very long.''

''Well, well, I'll see.''

Mrs. Arnot returned to the parlor, but Haldane was no longer there. She went to his room, but, though he was within, she could obtain no response to her knocking, or to the kind tone in which she spoke his name. She sighed, but thought that perhaps he would be calmer and more open to reason on the morrow, and, therefore, returned to her own apartment. Indeed, she was glad to do so, for in her ill and suffering condition the strain had already been too great.

She found Laura tearful and troubled, and could not do less than listen to her story.

"Do you think I have done anything wrong, auntie?" asked the girl in deep anxiety.

"No, dear, I think you have acted very sensibly. I wish I could have foreseen the trouble sooner, and saved you both from a disagreeable experience."

"But uncle won't discharge Mr. Haldane on my account, will he?" she continued with almost equal solicitude.

"Certainly not. Egbert has not done anything that should cause his dismissal. I think that the only result will be to teach you both that these are matters which should be left to future years."

"I'm glad they are distant, for I had no idea that love affairs were so intensely disagreeable."

Her aunt smiled, and after a little time the young girl departed to her rest quite comforted and reassured.

The next morning Mrs. Arnot was too ill to appear at breakfast, and her niece would not venture down alone. Haldane and his employer sat down together in grim silence, and, after a cup of coffee only, the former abruptly excused himself and went to the office.

As might have been expected, the young man had passed a restless night, during which all sorts of rash, wild purposes surged through his mind. At first he meditated hiding his grief and humiliation in some "far distant clime"; but the thought occurred to him after a little time that this would be spiting himself more than any one else. His next impulse was to leave the house of his "insulting employer" forever; but as he was about to depart, he remembered that he happened to have scarcely a dollar in his pocket, and therefore concluded to wait till he had drawn his pay, or could write to his mother for funds. Then, as his anger subsided, a sense of loss and disappointment overwhelmed him, and for a long time he sobbed like a broken-hearted child. After this natural expression of grief he felt better, and became able to think connectedly. He finally resolved that he would become "famous," and rise in "gloomy grandeur" till he towered far above his fellow men. He would pierce this obdurate maiden's heart with poignant but unavailing regret that she had missed the one great opportunity of her life. He gave but slight and vague consideration to the methods by which he would achieve the renown which would overshadow Laura's life; but, having resolutely adopted the purpose with a few tragic gestures and some obscure fragmentary utterances, he felt consoled and was able to obtain a little sleep.

The routine duties at the office on the following day did not promise very much, but he went through them in a kind of grim, vindictive manner, as if resolving to set his foot on all obstacles. He would "suffer in silence and give no sign" till the hour came when he could flash out upon the world. But as the day declined, he found the *rôle* of "gloomy grandeur" rather heavy, and he became conscious of the fact that he had scarcely eaten anything for nearly twenty-four hours. Another impulse began to make itself felt—that of fulfilling his threat and torturing Miss Romeyn by going to ruin. With alluring seductiveness the thought insinuated itself into his mind that one of the first steps in the tragedy might be a game and wine supper, and his growing hunger made this mode of revenge more attractive than cold and austere ambition.

But Laura's words concerning "disgusting vices" recurred to him with all and more than their first stinging plainness, and he put the impulse away with a gesture and tragic expression of face that struck a sere and withered bookkeeper, who happened at that moment to look up, as so queer that he feared the young man was becoming demented.

Haldane concluded—and with some reason in view of Laura's romantic nature—that only a career of gloomy grandeur and high renown would impress the maiden whom yesterday he proposed to make happy forever, but to-day to blight with regret like a "worm i' the bud." He already had a vague presentiment that such a *rôle* would often mortify his tastes and inclinations most dismally; and yet, what had he henceforth to do with pleasure? But if, after he had practiced the austerity of an anchorite, she should forget him, marry another, and be happy! the thought was excruciating. O, that awful "another"! He is the fiend that drags disappointed lovers down to the lowest depth of their tortures. If Laura had had a previous favorite, Haldane would have been most happy to have her meet "another" in himself; but now this vague but surely coming rival of the future sent alternately cold chills and molten fire through his veins.

He was awakened from such painful reveries by a summons to his employer's private office.

CHAPTER VII

BIRDS OF PREY

MR. ARNOT in his widely extended business owned several factories, and in the vicinity of one, located at a suburb of New York, there were no banking facilities. It was, therefore, his custom at stated times to draw from his bank at Hillaton such amounts in currency as were needed to pay those in his employ at the place indicated, and send the money thither by one of his clerks. Upon the present occasion, in compliance with his wife's request, he decided to send Haldane. He had no hesitation in doing this, as the errand was one that required nothing more than honesty and a little prudence.

"Mr. Haldane," said his employer, in tones somewhat less cold and formal than those habitual with him, "we will let bygones be bygones. I am inclined to think that hereafter you will be disposed to give your thoughts more fully to business, as a man should who proposes to amount to anything in the world. In these envelopes are one thousand dollars in currency. I wish you to place them securely in your breast-pockets, and take the five-thirty train to New York, and from thence early to-morrow go out on the Long Island road to a little station called Arnotville, and give these packages to Mr. Black, the agent in charge of my factory there. Take his receipt, and report to me to-morrow evening. With that amount of money upon your person you will perceive the necessity of prudence and care. Here is a check paying your salary for the past month. The cashier will give you currency for it. Report

your expenses on your return, and they will be paid.   As
the time is limited, perhaps you can get some lunch at or
near the depot."

"I prefer to do so," said Haldane, promptly, "and will
try to perform the business to your satisfaction."

Mr. Arnot nodded a cool dismissal, and Haldane started
for a hotel-restaurant near the depot with a step entirely too
quick and elastic for one who must walk henceforth in the
shadow of "bitter memories and dark disappointment."
The exercise brought color to his cheek, and there certainly
was a sparkle in his dark eyes.   It could not be hope, for
he had assured himself again and again that "hope was
dead in his heart."   It might have been caused after his
long fast by the anticipation of a lunch at the depot and
a *petit souper* in the city, and the thought of washing both
down with a glass of wine, or possibly with several.   The
relish and complacency with which his mind dwelt on this
prospect struck Haldane as rather incongruous in a being
as blighted as he supposed himself to be.   With his youth,
health, and unusually good digestion he would find no
little difficulty in carrying out the "gloomy grandeur"
scheme, and he began to grow conscious of the fact.

Indeed, in response to a law of nature, he was already
inclined to react from his unwonted depression into reckless hilarity.   Impulse and inclination were his controlling
forces, and he was accustomed to give himself up to them
without much effort at self-restraint.   And yet he sought
to imagine himself consistent, so that he could maintain his
self-approval.

"I will hide my despair with laughter," he muttered;
"the world cannot know that it is hollow, and but a mask
against its vulgar curiosity."

A good cold lunch and a cup of coffee—which he could
have obtained at once at the hotel near the depot—would
not answer for this victim of despair.   Some extra delicacies, which required time for preparation, were ordered.
In the meantime he went to the bar for an "appetizer,"

as he termed it. Here he met an acquaintance among the
loungers present, and, of course, asked him to take a social
glass also. This personage complied in a manner peculiarly
felicitous, and in such a way as to give the impression that
his acceptance of the courtesy was a compliment to Haldane. Much practice had made him perfect in this art, and
the number of drinks that he was able to secure gratis in
the course of a year by being always on hand and by maintaining an air of slight superiority, combined with an appearance of *bonhomie* and readiness to be social, would have
made a remarkable sum total.

Before their glasses clinked together he said, with the
off-handed courtesy indigenous to bar-rooms, where acquaintances are made with so little trouble and ceremony:

"Mr. Haldane, my friends from New York, Mr. Van
Wink and Mr. Ketchem."

Haldane turned and saw two young men standing con-
veniently near, who were dressed faultlessly in the style
of the day. There was nothing in their appearance to indicate that they did not reside on Fifth Avenue, and, indeed,
they may have had rooms on that fashionable street.

Messrs. Van Wink and Ketchem had also a certain air
of superiority, and they shook hands with Haldane in a way
that implied:

"While we are metropolitan men, we recognize in you
an extraordinarily fine specimen of the provincial." And
the young man was not indifferent to their unspoken flattery. He at once invited them also to state to the smirking
bartender their preferences among the liquid compounds
before them, and soon four glasses clinked together.

With fine and thoughtful courtesy they had chosen the
same mixture that he had ordered for himself, and surely
some of the milk of human kindness must have been infused in the punches which they imbibed, for Messrs. Van
Wink and Ketchem seemed to grow very friendly toward
Haldane. Perhaps taking a drink with a man inspired
these worthies with a regard for him similar to that which

the social eating of bread creates within the breasts of
Bedouins, who, as travellers assert, will protect with their
lives a stranger that has sat at their board; but rob and
murder, as a matter of course, all who have not enjoyed
that distinction.   Whatever may have been the cause, the
stylish men from the city were evidently pleased with Haldane, and they delicately suggested that he was such an
unusually clever fellow that they were willing to know
him better.

"I assure you, Mr. Haldane," protested Mr. Van Wink,
"our meeting is an unexpected pleasure.   Having completed our business in town, time was hanging heavily on
our hands, and it is still a full half-hour before the train
leaves."

"Let us drink again to further acquaintance," said Mr.
Ketchem cordially, evincing a decided disposition to be
friendly; "Mr. Haldane is in New York occasionally, and
we would be glad to meet him and help him pass a pleasant
hour there, as he is enlivening the present hour for us."

Haldane was not cautious by nature, and had been pre-
disposed by training to regard all flattering attention and
interest as due to the favorable impression which he supposed himself to make invariably upon those whose judgment was worth anything.   It is true there had been one
marked and humiliating exception.   But the consoling
thought now flashed into his mind that, perhaps, Miss
Romeyn was, as she asserted, but a mere "child," and incapable of appreciating him.   The influence of the punch
he had drank and the immediate and friendly interest manifested by these gentlemen who knew the world, gave a
plausible coloring to this explanation of her conduct.   After
all, was he not judging her too harshly?   She had not realized whom she had refused, and when she grew up in mind
as well as in form she might be glad to act very differently.
"But I may choose to act differently also," was his haughty
mental conclusion.

This self-communion took place while the still smirking

bartender was mixing the decoctions ordered by the cordial and generous Mr. Ketchem. A moment later four glasses clinked together, and Haldane's first acquaintance—the young man with the air of slight but urbane superiority—felicitated himself that he had "made two free drinks" within a brief space of time.

The effect of the liquor upon Haldane after his long fast was far greater than if it had been taken after a hearty meal, and he began to reciprocate the friendliness of the strangers with increasing interest.

"Gentlemen," said he, "our meeting is one of those fortunate incidents which promise much more pleasure to come. I have ordered a little lunch in the dining-room. It will take but a moment for the waiters to add enough for three more, and then we will ride into the city together, for my business takes me there this evening also."

"I declare," exclaimed Mr. Van Wink in a tone of self-gratulation, "were I piously inclined I should be tempted to call our meeting quite providential. But if we lunch with you it must be on condition that you take a little supper with us at the Brunswick after we arrive in town."

"No one could object to such agreeable terms," cried Haldane; "come, let us adjourn to the dining-room. By the way, Mr. Bartender, send us a bottle of your best claret."

The young man who an hour before had regarded himself as cruelly blighted for life, was quite successful in "hiding his despair with laughter." Indeed, from its loudness and frequency, undue exhilaration was suggested rather than a "secret sorrow." It gave him a fine sense of power and of his manly estate to see the waiters bustling around at his bidding, and to remember that he was the host of three gentlemen, who, while very superior in style, and evidently possessed of wealth, still recognized in him an equal with whom they were glad to spend a social hour.

Scarcely ever before had he met any one who appreciated him as fully as did Messrs. Van Wink and Ketchem, and their courteous deference confirmed a view which he had long held, that only in the large sphere of the metropolis could he find his true level and most congenial companionships. These young men had a style about them which provincials could not imitate. Even the superior gentleman who introduced them to him had a slightly dimmed and tarnished appearance as he sat beside his friends. There was an immaculate finish and newness about all their appointments—not a speck upon their linen, nor a grain of dust upon their broadcloth and polished boots. If the theory be true that character is shown in dress, these men, outwardly so spotless, must be worthy of the confidence with which they had inspired their new acquaintance. They suggested two bright coins just struck from the mint, and "They have the ring of true metal," thought Haldane.

It seemed to the young men that they had just fairly commenced to enjoy their lunch, when a prolonged shriek of a locomotive, dying away in the distance, awakened them to a sense of the flight of time. Hastily pulling out his watch, Haldane exclaimed with an oath:

"There goes our train."

Messrs. Van Wink and Ketchem were apparently much concerned.

"Haldane," they exclaimed, "you are much too entertaining a fellow for one to meet when there's a train to be caught."

"This is a serious matter for me," said Haldane, somewhat sobered by the thought of Mr. Arnot's wrath; "I had important business in town."

"Can it not be arranged by telegraph?" asked Mr. Van Wink in a tone of kindly solicitude.

"One can't send money by telegraph. No; I must go myself."

The eyes of Haldane's three guests met for a second in a way that indicated the confirmation of something in their minds, and yet so evanescent was this glance of intelligence that a cool, close observer would scarcely have detected it, much less their flushed and excited host.

"Don't worry, Haldane," said his first acquaintance; "there is an owl-train along at eleven to-night, and you can mail your check or draft on that if you do not care to travel at such an unearthly hour."

"Oh, there is a late train!" cried the young man, much relieved. "Then I'm all right. I am obliged to go myself, as the funds I carry are in such a shape that I cannot mail them."

Again the eyes of his guests met with a furtive gleam of satisfaction.

Now that Haldane felt himself safely out of his dilemma, he began to be solicitous about his companions.

"I fear," he said, "that my poor courtesy can make but small amends for the loss of your train."

"Well, Haldane," said Mr. Ketchem, with great apparent candor, "I speak for myself when I say that I would regret losing this train under most circumstances, but with the prospect of a social evening together I can scarcely say that I do."

"I, too," cried Mr. Van Wink, "am inclined to regard our loss of the train as a happy freak of fortune. Let us take the owl-train, also, Ketchem, and make a jovial night of it with Mr. Haldane."

"Fill up your glasses, and we'll drink to a jolly night," cried Haldane, and all complied with wonderful zest and unanimity. The host, however, was too excited and preoccupied to note that while Mr. Van Wink and Mr. Ketchem were always ready to have their glasses filled, they never drained them very low; and thus it happened that he and the slightly superior gentleman who made free drinks one of the chief objects of existence shared most of the bottle of wine between them.

As the young men rose from the lunch table Haldane called this individual aside, and said:

"Harker, I want you to help a fellow out of a scrape. You must know that I was expected to leave town on the five-thirty train. I do not care to be seen in the public rooms, for old cast-iron Arnot might make a row about my delay, even though it will make no difference in his business. Please engage a private room, where we can have a bottle of wine and a quiet game of cards, and no one be the wiser."

"Certainly—nothing easier in the world—I know just the room—cosey—off one side—wait a moment, gentlemen."

It seemed but a moment before he returned and led them, preceded by a bell-boy, to just such an apartment as he had described. Though the evening was mild, a fire was lighted in the grate, and as it kindled it combined with the other appointments to give the apartment an air of luxurious comfort.

"Bring us a bottle of sherry," said Haldane to the bell-boy.

"Also a pack of cards, some fine old brandy and cigars, and charge to me," said Mr. Ketchem; "I wish to have my part in this entertainment. Come, Harker, take a seat."

"Desperately sorry I can't spend the evening with you," said this sagacious personage, who realized with extreme regret that not even for the prospect of unlimited free potations could he afford to risk the loss of his eminent respectability, which he regarded as a capitalist does his principal, something that must be drawn upon charily. Mr. Harker knew that his mission was ended, and, in spite of the order for the sherry and brandy, he had sufficient strength of mind to retire. In delicate business transactions like the one under consideration he made it a point to have another engagement when matters got about as far along as they now were in Haldane's case. If anything unpleasant occurred between parties whom he introduced to each other, and he was summoned as a witness, he grew so exceedingly dignified and superior in his bearing that every one felt like asking his pardon for their suspicions. He always proved an *alibi*, and left the court-room with the air of an injured man. As people, however, became familiar with his haunts and habits, there was an increasing number who regarded his virtuous assumptions and professions of ignorance in respect to certain cases of swindling with incredulous smiles.

Mr. Harker, however, could not tear himself away till the brandy and sherry appeared, and, after paying his respects to both, went to keep his engagement, which consisted in lounging about another hotel on the other side of the depot.

Messrs. Van Wink and Ketchem, of course, both knew how to deal the cards, and with apologetic laughter the young men put up small stakes at first, just to give zest to the amusement. Haldane lost the first game, won the second and third, lost again, had streaks of good and bad luck so skilfully intermingled that the thought often occurred to him:

"These fellows play as fair a game as I ever saw and know how to win and lose money like gentlemen."

But these high-toned "gentlemen" always managed to keep the bottle of sherry near him, and when they lost they would good-naturedly and hilariously propose that they take a drink. Haldane always complied, but while he drank they only sipped.

As the evening waned the excitement of the infatuated youth deepened. The heat of the room and the fumes of tobacco combined with the liquor to unman him and intensify the natural recklessness of his character.

There is, probably, no abnormal passion that so completely masters its victims as that for gambling; and as Haldane won, lost, and won again, he became so absorbed as to be unconscious of the flight of time and all things else. But as he lost self-control, as he half-unconsciously put his glass to his lips with increasing frequency, his companions grew cooler and more wary. Their eyes no longer beamed good-naturedly upon their victim, but began to emit the eager, cruel gleams of some bird of prey.

But they still managed the affair with consummate skill. Their aim was to excite Haldane to the last degree of recklessness, and yet keep him sufficiently sober for further play-

ing.   From Harker they had learned that Mr. Arnot had
probably sent him in the place of the clerk usually employed; and, if so, it was quite certain that he had a large
sum of money upon his person.   Haldane's words on becoming aware that he had missed his train confirmed their
surmises, and it was now their object to beguile him into a
condition which would make him capable of risking his employer's funds.   They also wished that he should remain
sufficiently sober to be responsible for this act, and to remember, as he recalled the circumstances, that it was his
own act.   Therefore they kept the brandy beyond his
reach; that was not yet needed.

By the time the evening was half over, Haldane found
that, although he had apparently won considerable money,
he had lost more, and that not a penny of his own funds
remained.   With an angry oath he stated the fact to his
companions.

"That's unfortunate," said Mr. Ketchem, sympathetically.   "There are nearly two hours yet before the train
leaves, and with your disposition toward good luck to-
night you could clean us out by that time, and would
have to lend us enough to pay our fares to New York."

"It's a pity to give up our sport now that we have just
got warmed up to it," added Mr. Van Wink, suggestively.
"Haven't you some funds about you that you can borrow
for the evening—just enough to keep the game going, you
know?"

Haldane hesitated.   He was not so far gone but that
conscience entered an emphatic protest.   The trouble was,
however, that he had never formed the habit of obeying
conscience, even when perfectly sober.   Another influence
of the past also proved most disastrous.   His mother's
weakness now made him weak.   In permitting him to take
her money without asking, she had undermined the instinct
of integrity which in this giddy moment of temptation
might have saved him.   If he from childhood had been
taught that the property of others was sacred, the very

gravity of the crime to which he now was urged would have sobered and awakened him to his danger. But his sense of wrong in this had been blunted, and there was no very strong repugnance toward the suggestion.

Moreover, his brain was confused and excited to the last degree possible in one who still continued sane and responsible. Indeed, it would be difficult to say how far he was responsible at this supreme moment of danger. He certainly had drank so much as to be unable to realize the consequences of his action.

After a moment's hesitation, like one who feebly tries to brace himself in a swift torrent, the gambler's passion surged up against and over his feeble will—then swept him down.

CHAPTER VIII

THEIR VICTIM

HALDANE drew an envelope from his breast-pocket, and laid it on the table, saying with a reckless laugh:

"Well, well, as you say, there is no great harm in borrowing a little of this money, and returning it again before the evening is over. The only question is how to open this package, for if torn it may require explanations that I do not care to make."

"We can easily manage that," laughed Ketchem; "put the package in your pocket a few moments," and he rang the bell.

To the boy who appeared he said, "Bring us three hot whiskey punches—hot, remember; steaming hot."

He soon reappeared with the punch, and the door was locked again.

"Hold your package over the steam of your punch, and the gum will dissolve so that you can open and close it in a way that will defy detection."

The suggestion was speedily carried out.

"Now," continued Mr. Ketchem, "the punch having already served so excellent a turn, we will finish it by drinking to your good luck."

Haldane won the first two games. This success, together with the liquor, which was strong, almost wholly dethroned his reason, and in his mad, drunken excitement he began to stake large sums. The eyes of his companions grew more wolfish than ever, and, after a significant flash toward each other, the gamblers turned fortune against their victim finally. The brandy was now placed within his reach, and under its influence Haldane threw down money at random. The first package was soon emptied. He snatched the other from his pocket and tore it open, but before its contents had likewise disappeared his head drooped upon his breast, and he became insensible.

They watched him a moment, smiled grimly at each other, drew a long breath of relief, and, rising, stretched themselves like men who had been under a strain that had taxed them severely.

"Half an hour yet," said Mr. Van Wink; "wish the time was up."

"This is a heavy swag if we get off safely with it. I say, Haldane, wake up."

But Haldane was sunk in the deepest stupor.

"I guess it's safe enough," said Van Wink, answering Ketchem's questioning eyes.

The latter thereupon completely emptied the remaining package of money, and replaced the two empty envelopes in Haldane's breast-pocket, and buttoned up his coat.

With mutual glances of exultation at the largeness of the sum, they swiftly divided the spoil between them. It was agreed that after leaving the hotel they should separate, that one should go to Boston, the other to Baltimore, and that they should return to their old haunts in New York after the interest caused by the affair had died out. Then, lighting cigars, they coolly sat down to wait for the train, having first opened a window and placed Haldane where the fresh air would blow upon him.

When the time of departure approached, Mr. Van Wink went to the bar and paid both their own and Haldane's bill, saying that they would now vacate the room. On his return Ketchem had so far aroused Haldane that he was able to leave the house with their assistance, and yet so intoxicated as to be incapable of thinking and acting for himself. They took him down a side street, now utterly deserted, and left him on the steps of a low groggery, from whence still issued the voices of some late revellers. Five minutes later the "owl train" bore from the town Messrs. Van Wink and Ketchem, who might be called with a certain aptness birds of the night and of prey.

Haldane remained upon the saloon steps, where he had been left, blinking stupidly at a distant street lamp. He had a vague impression that something was wrong—that a misfortune of some kind had befallen him, but all was confused and blurred. He would have soon gone to sleep again had not the door opened, and a man emerged, who exclaimed:

"Faix, an who have we here, noddin' to himself as if he knew more'n other folk? Are ye waitin' for some un to ax ye within for a comfortin' dhrop?"

"Take me 'ome," mumbled Haldane.

"Where's yer home?"

"Mrs. Haldane's," answered the youth, thinking himself in his native town.

"By me sowl, if it isn't Boss Arnot's new clerk. Sure's me name is Pat M'Cabe 'tis Misther Haldane. I say, are ye sick?"

"Take me 'ome."

"Faix, I see," winking at two or three of his cronies who had gathered at the open door; "it's a disase I'm taken wid meself at odd spells, though I takes moighty good care to kape out o' the way of ould man Arnot when I'm so afflicted. He has a quare way o' thinkin' that ivery man about him can go as rigaler as if made in a mash-shine shop, bad luck till 'im."

Perhaps all in Mr. Arnot's employ would have echoed this sentiment, could the ill luck have blighted him without reaching them. In working his employés as he did his machinery, Mr. Arnot forgot that the latter was often oiled, but that he entirely neglected to lubricate the wills of the former with occasional expressions of kindness and interest in their welfare. Thus it came to pass that even down to

poor Pat M'Cabe, man of all work around the office building, all felt that their employer was a hard, driving task-
master, who ever looked beyond them and their interests to
what they accomplished for him.   The spirit of the master
infused itself among the men, and the tendency of each one
to look out for himself without regard to others was increased.   If Pat had served a kinder and more considerate
man, he might have been inclined to show greater consideration for the intoxicated youth; but Pat's favorite phrase,
"Divil take the hindmost," was but a fair expression of the
spirit which animated his master, and the majority in his
employ.   When, therefore, Haldane, in his thick, imperfect utterance, again said, "Take me 'ome," Pat concluded
that it would be the best and safest course for himself.
Helping the young man to his feet he said:

"Can ye walk? Mighty onstiddy on yer pins; but I'm
athinkin' I can get ye to the big house afore mornin'.
Should I kape ye out o' the way till ye get sober, and
ould man Arnot find it out, I'd be in the street meself
widout a job 'fore he ate his dinner.   Stiddy now; lean
aginst me, and don't wabble yer legs so."

With like exhortations the elder and more wary disciple
of Bacchus disappeared with his charge in the gloom of the
night.

It chanced that the light burned late, on this evening,
in Mrs. Arnot's parlor.   The lady's indisposition had confined her to her room and couch during the greater part of
the day; but as the sun declined, the distress in her head
had gradually ceased, and she had found her airy drawing-
room a welcome change from the apartment heavy with the
odor of anæsthetics.   Two students from the university had
aided in beguiling the early part of the evening, and then
Laura had commenced reading aloud an interesting tale,
which had suspended the consciousness of time.   But as
the marble clock on the mantel chimed out the hour of
twelve, Mrs. Arnot rose hastily from the sofa, exclaiming:

"What am I thinking of, to keep you up so late!   If

your mother knew that you were out of your bed she
would hesitate to trust you with me again."

"One more chapter, dear auntie, please?"

"Yes, dear, several more—to-morrow; but to bed now,
instanter. Come, kiss your remorseful aunt good-night.
I'll remain here a while longer, for either your foolish
story or the after effects of my wretched headache make
me a trifle morbid and wakeful to-night. Oh, how that
bell startles me! what can it mean so late?"

. The loud ring at the door remained unanswered a few
moments, for the servants had all retired. But the appli-
cant without did not wait long before repeating the summons still more emphatically.

Then they heard the library door open, and Mr. Arnot's
heavy step in the hall, as he went himself to learn the
nature of the untimely call. His wife's nervous timidity
vanished at once, and she stepped forward to join her husband, while Laura stood looking out from the parlor entrance with a pale and frightened face. "Can it be bad
news from home?" she thought.

"Who is there?" demanded Mr. Arnot, sternly.

"Me and Misther Haldane," answered a voice without in
broadest brogue.

"Mr. Haldane!" exclaimed Mr. Arnot excitedly; "what
can this mean? Who is *me?*" he next asked loudly.

"Me is Pat M'Cabe, sure; the same as tidies up the office
and does yer irrinds. Mr. Haldane's had a bad turn, and
I've brought him home."

As Mr. Arnot swung open the door, a man, who seemingly had been leaning against it, fell prone within the
hall. Laura gave a slight scream, and Mrs. Arnot was
much alarmed, thinking that Haldane was suffering from
some sudden and alarming attack. Thoughts of at once
telegraphing to his mother were entering her mind, when
the object of her solicitude tried to rise, and mumbled in
the thick utterance of intoxication:

"This isn't home. Take me to mother's."

Mrs. Arnot's eyes turned questioningly to her husband, and she saw that his face was dark with anger and disgust.

"He is drunk," he said, turning to Pat, who stood in the door, cap in hand.

"Faix, sur, it looks moighty loike it. But it's not for a dacent sober man loike meself to spake sartainly o' sich matters."

"Few words and to the point, sir," said Mr. Arnot harshly; "your breath tells where you have been. But where did you find this—and how came you to find him?"

Either Mr. Arnot was at a loss for a term which would express his estimation of the young man, who had slowly and unsteadily risen, and was supporting himself by holding fast the hatrack, or he was restrained in his utterance by the presence of his wife.

"Well, sur," said Pat, with as ingenuous and candid an air as if he were telling the truth, "the wife o' a neighbor o' mine was taken on a suddint, and I went for the docther, and as I was a comin' home, who shud I see sittin' on a doorsthep but Misther Haldane, and I thought it me duty to bring him home to yees."

"You have done right. Was it on the doorstep of a drinking-place you found him?"

"I'm athinkin' it was, sur; it had that sort o' look."

Mr. Arnot turned to his wife and said coldly, "You now see how it works. But this is not a fit object for you and Laura to look upon; so please retire. I will see that he gets safely to his room. I suppose he must go there, though the station-house is the more proper place for him."

"He certainly must go to his own room," said Mrs. Arnot, firmly but quietly.

"Well, then, steady him along up the stairs, Pat. I will show you where to put the—" and Mr. Arnot again seemed to hesitate for a term, but the blank was more expressive of his contempt than any epithet could be, since his tone and manner suggested the worst.

Returning to the parlor, Mrs. Arnot found Laura's face expressive of the deepest alarm and distress.

"O auntie, what does all this mean? Am I in any way to blame? He said he would go to ruin if I didn't—but how could I?"

"No, my dear, you are not in the slightest degree to blame. Mr. Haldane seems both bad and foolish. I feel to-night that he is not worthy to speak to you; much less is he fit to be intrusted with that which you will eventually give, I hope, only to one who is pre-eminently noble and good. Come with me to your room, my child. I am very sorry I permitted you to stay up to-night."

But Laura was sleepless and deeply troubled; she had never seen a laborer—much less one of her own acquaintances—in Haldane's condition before; and to her young, innocent mind the event had almost the character of a tragedy. Although conscious of entire blamelessness, she supposed that she was more directly the cause of Haldane's behavior than was true, and that he was carrying out his threat to destroy himself by reckless dissipation. She did not know that he had been beguiled into his miserable condition through bad habits of long standing, and that he had fallen into the clutches of those who always infest public haunts, and live by preying upon the fast, foolish, and unwary. Haldane, from his character and associations, was liable to such an experience whenever circumstances combined to make it possible. Young men with no more principle than he possessed are never safe from disaster, and they who trust them trust rather to the chances of their not meeting the peculiar temptations and tests to which they would prove unequal. Laura could not then know how little she had to do with the tremendous downfall of her premature lover. The same conditions given, he would probably have met with the same experience upon any occasion. After his first glass of punch the small degree of discretion that he had learned thus far in life began to desert him; and every man as he becomes intoxicated is first a fool, and then the victim of every one who chooses to take advantage of his voluntary helplessness and degradation.

But innocent Laura saw a romantic and tragic element in the painful event, and she fell asleep with some vague womanly thoughts about saving a fellow-creature by the sacrifice of herself. However, the morning light, the truth concerning Haldane, and her own good sense, would banish such morbid fancies. Indeed the worst possible way in which a young woman can set about reforming a bad man is to marry him. The usual result is greatly increased guilt on the part of the husband, and lifelong, hopeless wretchedness for the wife.

CHAPTER IX

PAT AND THE PRESS

PAT having steadied and half carried Haldane to his room, Mr. Arnot demanded of his clerk what had become of the money intrusted to his care; but his only answer was a stupid, uncomprehending stare.

"Hold his hands," said Mr. Arnot impatiently.

M'Cabe having obeyed, the man of business, whose solicitude in the affair had no concern with the young man's immeasurable loss, but related only to his own money, immediately felt in Haldane's pockets for the envelopes which had contained the thousand dollars in currency. The envelopes were safe enough—one evidently opened with the utmost care, and the other torn recklessly—but the money was gone.

When Haldane saw the envelopes, there was a momentary expression of trouble and perplexity upon his face, and he tried to speak; but his thick utterance was unintelligible. This gleam of intelligence passed quickly, however, and the stupor of intoxication reasserted itself. His heavy eyelids drooped, and Pat with difficulty could keep him on his feet.

"Toss him there on the lounge; take off his muddy boots. Nothing further can be done while he is in this beastly condition," said Mr. Arnot, in a voice that was as harsh as the expression of his face.

The empty envelopes and Mr. Arnot's dark looks suggested a great deal to Pat, and he saw that one of his "sprees" was an innocent matter compared with this affair.

"Now, go down to my study and wait there for me."

Pat obeyed in a very steady and decorous manner, for the matter was assuming such gravity as to sober him completely.

Mr. Arnot satisfied himself that there was no chance of escape from the windows, and then, after another look of disgust and anger at Haldane, who was now sleeping heavily, he took the key from the door, and locked it on the outside.

Descending to his study, the irate gentleman next wrote a note, and gave it to his porter, saying:

"Take that to the police-headquarters, and ask that it be sent to the superintendent at once. No mistake, now, as you value your place; and mind, not a word of all this to any one."

"Faix, sir, I'll be as dumb as an oyster, and do yer biddin' in a jiffy," said Pat, backing out of the room, and glad to escape from one whose threatening aspect seemed to forebode evil to any one within his reach.

"He looks black enough to murther the poor young spalpeen," muttered the Irishman, as he hastened to do his errand, remembering now with trepidation that, though he had escaped from his master, the big, red-faced, stout-armed wife of his bosom was still to be propitiated after his late prowlings.

When he entered the main street, a light that glimmered from the top of a tall building suggested how he might obtain that kind of oil which, cast upon the domestic billows that so often raged in his fourth-floor back room, was most effective in producing a little temporary smoothness.

Since the weather was always fouler within his domestic haven than without, and on this occasion threatened to be at its worst, Pat at one time half decided not to run into port at all; but the glimmer of the light already mentioned suggested another course.

Although the night was far spent, Pat still longed for a "wink o' slape" before going to his work, and, in order to enjoy it, knew that he must obtain the means of allaying the storm, which was not merely brewing, but which, from the lateness of the hour, had long been brewed. In his own opinion, the greenness of his native isle had long ago faded from his mental and moral complexion, and he did not propose that any stray dollars, which by any shrewdness or artifice could be diverted into his pocket, should get by him.

Since his wife had developed into a huge, female divinity, at whose shrine it seemed probable that he would eventually become a human sacrifice, and whose wrath, in the meantime, it was his daily task to appease, Pat had gradually formed the habit of making a sort of companion of himself. In accordance with his custom, therefore, he stopped under the high window from whence gleamed the light, for the sake of a little personal counsel.

"Now, Pat," he muttered, "if yees had gone home at nine o'clock, yees wudn't be afeared to go home now; and if yees go home now widout a dollar more or less, the ould 'ooman will make yer wish yees had set on the curbstone the rest o' the night. They sez some men has no bowels o' marcies; and after what I've seen the night, and afore the night, too, I kin belave that Boss Arnot's in'ards were cast at the same foundry where he gets his mash-shines. He told me that I must spake nary a word about what I've seen and heard, and if I should thry to turn an honest penny by givin' a knowin' wink or two where they wud pay for the same, that 'ud be the ind of Pat M'Cabe at the big office. And yet they sez that them as buys news is loike them that takes stolen goods—moighty willin' to kape dark about where they got it, so that they kin get more next time. That's the iditor of the 'Currier' in yon high room, and p'raps he'll pay me as much for a wink and a hint the night as I'll get for me day's work termorrow. Bust me if I don't thry him, if he'll fust promise me to say if any one axes him that he niver saw Pat M'Cabe in his loife," and the suddenly improvised reporter climbed the long stairways to where the night editor sat at his desk.

Pat gave a hearty rap for manners, but as the night was waning he walked in without waiting for an answer, and addressed the startled newspaper man with a business-like directness, which might often be advantageously imitated:

"Is this the shop where yer pays a dacent price for news?"

"It depends on the importance of the news, and its truthfulness," answered the editor, after eying the intruder suspiciously for a moment.

"Thin I've got ye on both counts, though I didn't think ye'd bear down so heavy on its being thrue," said Pat, advancing confidently.

As the door of the press-room, in which men were at work, stood open, the editor felt no alarm from the sudden appearance of the burly figure before him, but, supposing the man had been drinking, he said impatiently:

"Please state your business briefly, as my time is valuable."

"If yer time is worth mor'n news, I'll go to another shop," said Pat stiffly, making a feint of departure.

"That's a good fellow, go along," chimed in the editor, bending down to his writing again.

Such disastrous acquiescence puzzled Pat for a moment, and he growled, "No wonder yer prints a paper that's loike a lump o' lead, when 'stead o' lookin' for news yer turns it away from yer doors."

"Now, look here, my man," said the editor rising, "if you have anything to say, say it. If you have been drinking, you will not be permitted to make a row in this office."

"It's not me, but another man that's been dhrinkin'."

"Well," snarled the editor, "if the other man had the drink, you have the 'drunk,' and if you don't take yourself off, I'll call some men from the press-room who may put you downstairs uncomfortably fast."

"Hould on a bit," remonstrated Pat, "before yer ruffle yer feathers clane over yer head and blinds yer eyes. Wud a man loike Boss Arnot send me, if I was dhrunk, wid a

letther at this toime o' night? and wud he send a letther
to the superintindent o' the perlice at this toime o' the night
to ax him the toime o' day! Afore yer calls yer spalpeens
out o' the press-room squint at that."

The moment the editor caught sight of the business
stamp on Mr. Arnot's letter and the formal handwriting,
his manner changed, and he said suavely:

"I beg your pardon—we have misunderstood one another
—take a chair."

"There's been no misunderstandin' on my part," retorted
Pat, with an injured air; "I've got as dainty a bit o' scandal
jist under me tongue as iver ye spiced yer paper wid, and
yees thrates me as if I was the inimy o' yer sowl."

"Well, you see," said the editor apologetically, "your
not being in our regular employ, Mr.—I beg your pardon
—and your coming in this unusual way and hour—"

"But, begorry, somethin' unusual's happened."

"So I understand; it was very good of you to come to
us first; just give me the points, and I will jot them down."

"But what are yees goin' to give me for the pints?"

"That depends upon what they are worth. News cannot
be paid for till we learn its value."

"Ooh! here I'm rinnin' a grate risk in tellin' ye at all,
and whin I've spilt it all out, and can't pick it up agin,
ye may show me the door, and tell me to go 'long wid me
rubbish."

"If you find what you have to report in the paper, you
may know it is worth something. So if you will look at
the paper to-morrow you can see whether it will be worth
your while to call again," said the editor, becoming impatient at Pat's hesitancy to open his budget.

"But I'm in sore need of a dollar or two to-night. Dade,
it's as much as my loife's worth to go home widout
'em."

"See here, my good friend," said the editor, rising again
and speaking very energetically, "my time is very valuable, and you have taken considerable of it. Whatever may

be the nature of your news, it will not be worth anything
to me if you do not tell it at once."

"Well, you see the biggest part o' the news is goin' to
happen to-morrow."

"Well, well, what has happened to-night?"

"Will ye promise not to mention me name?"

"How can I mention it when I don't know it?"

"That's thrue, that's thrue. Now me mind's aisy on
that pint, for ye must know that Boss Arnot's in'ards are
made o' cast-iron, and he'd have no marcy on a feller.
You'll surely give me a dollar, at laste."

"Yes, if your story is worth printing, and I give you
just three minutes in which to tell it."

Thus pinned down, Pat related all he knew and surmised concerning Haldane's woful predicament, saying in
conclusion:

"Ye must know that this Haldane is not a poor spalpeen
uv a clerk, but a gintleman's son. They sez that his folks
is as stylish and rich as the Arnots themselves. If ye'll
have a reporther up at the office in the mornin', ye'll git
the balance o' the tale."

Having received his dollar, Pat went chuckling on his
way to deliver his employer's letter to the superintendent
of the city police.

"Faix! I was as wise as a sarpent in not tellin' me name,
for ye niver can thrust these iditors. It's no green Irishman
that can make a dollar after twelve o' the night."

A sleepy reporter was aroused and despatched after Part,
in order to learn, if possible, the contents of Mr. Arnot's
note.

In the meantime heavily leaded lines—vague and mysterious—concerning "Crime in High Life," were set up,
accompanied on the editorial page by a paragraph to the
following effect:

With our usual enterprise and keen scent for news, we discovered at a late
hour last night that an intelligent Irishman in the employ of Mr. Arnot had
been intrusted by that gentleman with a letter written after the hour of mid-

night to the superintendent of the police. The guilty party appears to be a Mr. Haldane—a young man of aristocratic and wealthy connections—who is at present in Mr. Arnot's employ, and a member of his family. We think we are aware of the nature of his grave offence, but in justice to all concerned we refer our readers to our next issue, wherein they will find full particulars of the painful affair, since we have obtained peculiar facilities for learning them. No arrests have yet been made.

"That will pique all the gossips in town, and nearly double our next issue," complacently muttered the local editor, as he carried the scrawl at the last moment into the composing-room.

In the meantime the hero of our story—if such a term by any latitude of meaning can be applied to one whose folly had brought him into such a prosaic and miserable plight—still lay in a heavy stupor on the lounge where Pat had thrown his form, that had been as limp and helpless as if it had become a mere body without a soul. But the consequences of his action did not cease with his paralysis, any more than do the influences of evil deeds perish with a dying man.

CHAPTER X

RETURNING CONSCIOUSNESS

MR. ARNOT did not leave his library that night. His wife came to the door and found it locked. To her appeal he replied coldly, but decisively, that he was engaged.

She sighed deeply, feeling that the sojourn of young Haldane under her roof was destined to end in a manner most painful to herself and to her friend, his mother. She feared that the latter would blame her somewhat for his miserable fiasco, and she fully believed that if her husband permitted the young man to suffer open disgrace, she would never be forgiven by the proud and aristocratic lady.

And yet she felt that it was almost useless to speak to her husband in his present mood, or to hope that he could be induced to show much consideration for so grave an offense.

Of the worst feature in Haldane's conduct, however, she had no knowledge. Mr. Arnot rarely spoke to his wife concerning his business, and she had merely learned, the previous evening, that Haldane had been sent to New York upon some errand. Acting upon the supposition that her husband had remembered and complied with her request, she graciously thanked him for giving the young man a little change and diverting novelty of scene.

Mr. Arnot, who happened to verge somewhat toward a complacent mood upon this occasion, smiled grimly at his wife's commendation, and even unbent so far as to indulge in some ponderous attempts at wit with Laura concerning her "magnificent offer," and asserted that if she had been "like his wife, she would have jumped at the chance of get-ting hold of such a crude, unreformed specimen of human-ity. Indeed," concluded he, "I did not know but that Mrs. Arnot was bringing about the match, so that she might have a little of the raw material for reformatory purposes continually on hand."

Mrs. Arnot smiled, as she ever did, at her husband's attempted witticisms; but what he regarded as light, deli-cate shafts, winged sportively and carelessly, had rather the character of any heavy object that came to hand thrown at her with heedless, inconsiderate force. It is due Mr. Arnot to say that he gave so little thought and attention to the wounds and bruises he caused, as to be unaware that any had been made. He had no hair-springs and jewel-tipped machinery in his massive, angular organization, and he acted practically as if the rest of humanity had been cast in the same mold with himself.

But Haldane's act touched him at his most vulnerable point. Not only had a large sum of his money been made away with, but, what was far worse, there had been a most serious irregularity in the business routine. While, there-fore, he resolved that Haldane should receive full punish-ment, the ulterior thought of giving the rest of his employés a warning and intimidating lesson chiefly occupied his mind.

Aware of his wife's "unbusinesslike weakness and senti-mental notions," as he characterized her traits, he deter-mined not to see her until he had carried out his plan of se-curing repayment of the money, and of striking a salutary sentiment of fear into the hearts of all who were engaged in carrying out his methodical will.

Therefore, with the key of Haldane's room in his pocket, he kept watch and guard during the remainder of the night, taking only such rest as could be obtained on the lounge in his library.

At about sunrise two men appeared, and rapped lightly on the library window. Mr. Arnot immediately went out to them, and placed one within a summer-house in the spacious garden at the rear of the house, and the other in front, where he would be partially concealed by evergreens. By this arrangement the windows of Haldane's apartment and every entrance of the house were under the surveillance of police officers in citizen's dress. Mr. Arnot's own personal pride, as well as some regard for his wife's feelings, led him to arrange that the arrest should not be made at their residence, for he wished that all the events occurring at the house should be excluded as far as possible from the inevitable talk which the affair would occasion. At the same time he proposed to guard against the possibility of Haldane's escape, should fear or shame prompt his flight.

Having now two assistant watchers, he threw himself on the sofa, and took an hour or more of unbroken sleep. On awaking, he went with silent tread to the door of Haldane's room, and, afer listening a moment, was satisfied from the heavy breathing within that its occupant was still under the influence of stupor. He now returned the key to the door, and unlocked it so that Haldane could pass out as soon as he was able. Then, after taking a little refreshment in the dining-room, he went directly to the residence of a police justice of his acquaintance, who, on hearing the facts as far as then known concerning Haldane, made out a warrant for his arrest, and promised that the officer to whom it would be given should be sent forthwith to Mr. Arnot's office—for thither the young man would first come, or be brought, on recovering from his heavy sleep.

Believing that he had now made all the arrangements necessary to secure himself from loss, and to impress the small army in his service that honesty was the "best policy" in their relations with him, Mr. Arnot walked leisurely to one of his factories in the suburbs, partly to see that all was right, and partly to remind his agents there that they were in the employ of one whose untiring vigilance would not permit any neglect of duty to escape undetected.

Having noted that the routine of work was going forward

as regularly as the monotonous clank of the machinery, he
finally wended his way to his city office, and was the first
arrival thither save Pat M'Cabe, who had just finished putting the place in order for the business of the day. His fac-
totum was in mortal trepidation, for in coming across town
he had eagerly bought the morning "Courier," and his complacent sense of security at having withheld his name from
the "oncivil iditer" vanished utterly as he read the words,
"an intelligent Irishman in Mr. Arnot's employ."

"Och! bloody blazes! that manes me," he had exclaimed; "and ould Boss Arnot will know it jist as well
as if they had printed me name all over the paper. Bad
luck to the spalpeen, and worse luck to meself! 'Intilligent
Irishman,' am I? Then what kind o' a crather would one
be as had no sinse a' tall? Here I've bin throwin' away
fotry dollars the month for the sake o' one! Whin I gets
me discharge I'd better go round to the tother side o' the
airth than go home to me woife."

Nor were his apprehensions allayed as he saw Mr. Arnot
reading the paper with a darkening scowl; but for the present Pat was left in suspense as to his fate.

Clerks and book-keepers soon appeared, and among
them a policeman, who was summoned to the inner office,
and given a seat somewhat out of sight behind the door.

Upon every face there was an expression of suppressed
excitement and expectation, for the attention of those who
had not seen the morning paper was speedily called to the
ominous paragraph. But the routine and discipline of the
office prevailed, and in a few minutes all heads were bending over bulky journals and ledgers, but with many a furtive
glance at the door.

As for Pat, he had the impression that the policeman within would collar him before the morning was over, and march
him off, with Haldane, to jail; and he was in such a state
of nervous apprehension that almost any event short of an
earthquake would be a relief if it could only happen at once.

The April sun shone brightly and genially into the

apartment in which Haldane had been left to sleep off his drunken stupor. In all its appointments it appeared as fresh, inviting, and cleanly as the wholesome light without. The spirit of the housekeeper pervaded every part of the mansion, and in both furniture and decoration it would seem that she had studiously excluded everything which would suggest morbid or gloomy thoughts. It was Mrs. Arnot's philosophy that outward surroundings impart their coloring to the mind, and are a help or a hindrance. She was a disciple of the light, and was well aware that she must resolutely dwell in its full effulgence in order to escape from the blighting shadow of a life-long disappointment. Thus she sought to make her home, not gay or gaudy—not a brilliant mockery of her sorrow, which she had learned to calmly recognize as one might a village cemetery in a sunny landscape—but cheerful and lightsome like this April morning, which looked in through the curtained windows of Haldane's apartment, and found everything in harmony with itself save the occupant.

And yet he was young and in his spring-time. Why should he make discord with the bright fresh morning? Because the shadow of evil—which is darker than the shadow of night, age, or sorrow—rested upon him. His hair hung in disorder over a brow which was contracted into a frown. His naturally fine features had a heavy, bloated, sensual aspect; and yet, even while he slept, you caught a glimpse in this face—as through a veil—of the anguish of a spirit that was suffering brutal wrong and violence.

His insensibility was passing away. His mind appeared to be struggling to cast off the weight of a stupefied body, but for a time its throes—which were manifested by starts, strong shudderings, and muttered words—were ineffectual. At last, in desperation, as it were, the tortured soul, poisoned even in its imaginings by the impurity of the lower nature, conjured up such a horrid vision that in its anguish it broke its chains, threw off the crushing weight, and the young man started up.

This returning consciousness had not been, like the dawn stealing in at his window, followed by a burst of sunlight. As the morning enters the stained, foul, dingy places of dissipation, which early in the evening had been the gas-lighted, garish scenes of riot and senseless laughter, and later the fighting ground of all the vile vermin of the night with their uncanny noises—as when, the doors and windows having been at last opened, the light struggles in through stale tobacco-smoke, revealing dimly a discolored, reeking place, whose sights and odors are more in harmony with the sewer than the sweet April sunshine and the violets opening on southern slopes—so when reason and memory, the janitors of the mind, first admitted the light of consciousness, only the obscure outline of miserable feelings and repulsive events were manifest to Haldane's introspection.

There was a momentary relief at finding that the horrible dream which had awakened him was only a dream, but while his waking banished the uncouth shapes of the imagination, his sane, will-guided vision saw revealed that from which he shrank with far greater dread.

For a few moments, as he shared vacantly around the room, he could realize nothing save a dull, leaden weight of pain. In this dreary obscurity of suffering, distinct causes of trouble and fear began to shape themselves. There was a mingled sense of misfortune and guilt. He had a confused memory of a great disappointment, and he knew from his condition that he had been drinking.

He looked at himself—he was dressed. There stood his muddy boots—two foul blots on the beauty and cleanliness of the room. So then he had come, or had been brought, at some hour during the night, to the house of his stern and exacting employer. Haldane dismissed the thought of him with a reckless oath; but his face darkened with anguish as he remembered that this was also the home of Mrs. Arnot, who had been so kind, and, at the present time, the home of Laura Romeyn also.

They may have seen, or, at least, must know of, his degradation.

He staggered to the ewer, and, with a trembling hand, poured out a little water. Having bathed his hot, feverish face, he again sat down, and tried to recall what had happened.

In bitterness of heart he remembered his last interview with Laura, and her repugnance toward both himself and what she regarded as "his disgusting vices," and so disgusting did his evil courses now seem that, for the first time in his life, he thought of himself with loathing.

Then, as memory rapidly duplicated subsequent events, he gave a contemptuous smile to his "gloomy grandeur" schemes in passing, and saw himself on the way to New York, with one thousand dollars of his employer's funds intrusted to his care. He remembered that he was introduced to two fascinating strangers, that they drank and lunched together, that they missed the train, that they were gambling, that, having lost all his own money, he was tempted to open a package belonging to Mr. Arnot; did he not open the other also? At this point all became confused and blurred.

What had become of that money?

With nervous, trembling haste he searched his pockets. Both the money and the envelopes were gone.

His face blanched; his heart sank with a certain foreboding of evil. He found himself on the brink of an abyss, and felt the ground crumbling beneath him. First came a mad impulse to fly, to escape and hide himself; and he had almost carried it out. His hand was on the door, but he hesitated, turned back, and walked the floor in agony.

Then came the better impulse of one as yet unhardened in the ways of evil, to go at once to his employer, tell the whole truth, and make such reparation as was within his power. He knew that his mother was abundantly able to pay back the money, and he believed she would do so.

This he conceded was his best, and, indeed, only safe

course, and he hoped that the wretched affair might be so arranged as to be kept hidden from the world. As for Mrs. Arnot and Laura, he felt that he could never look them in the face again.

Suppose he should meet them going out. The very thought was dreadful, and it seemed to him that he would sink to the floor from shame under their reproachful eyes. Would they be up yet? He looked at his watch; it had run down, and its motionless hands pointed at the vile, helpless condition in which he must have been at the time when he usually wound it up.

He glanced from the window, with the hope of escaping the two human beings whom he dreaded more than the whole mocking world; but it was too lofty to admit of a leap to the ground.

"Who is yonder strange man that seems to be watching the house?" he queried.

Was it his shaken nerves and sense of guilt which led him to suspect danger and trouble on every side?

"There is no help for it," he exclaimed, grinding his teeth; and, opening the door, he hastened from the house, looking neither to the right hand nor to the left.

CHAPTER XI

HALDANE IS ARRESTED

AS Haldane strode rapidly along the winding, gravelled path that led from Mrs. Arnot's beautiful suburban villa to the street, he started violently as he encountered a stranger, who appeared to be coming toward the mansion; and he was greatly relieved when he was permitted to pass unmolested. And yet the cool glance of scrutiny which he received left a very unpleasant impression. Nor was this uneasiness diminished when, on reaching the street, he found that the stranger had apparently accomplished his errand to the house so speedily that he was already returning, and accompanied by another man.

Were not their eyes fixed on him, or was he misled by his fears? After a little time he looked around again. One of the men had disappeared, and he breathed more fully. No; there he was on the opposite side of the street, and walking steadily abreast with him, while his companion continued following about the same distance away.

Was he "shadowed"? He was, indeed, literally and figuratively. Although the sun was shining bright and warm, never before had he been conscious of such a horror of great darkness. The light which can banish the oppressive, disheartening shadow of guilt must come from beyond the sun.

As he entered the busier streets in the vicinity of the office, he saw a few persons whom he knew. Was he again misled by his overwrought and nervous condition? or did these persons try to shun him by turning corners, entering shops, or by crossing the street, and looking resolutely the other way.

Could that awful entity, the world, already know the events of the past night?

A newsboy was vociferating down a side street. The word "Crime" only caught Haldane's ear, but the effect was as cold and as chilling as the drip of an icicle.

As he hastened up the office steps, Pat M'Cabe scowled upon him, and muttered audibly:

"Bad luck till yees! I wish I'd lift ye ablinkin' like an owl where I found ye."

"An' back luck till yees, too," added Pat in his surly growl, as a reporter, note-book in hand, stepped nimbly in after Haldane; "it's meself that wishes iviry iditer o' the land was burned up wid his own lyin' papers."

Even the most machine-like of the sere and withered book-keepers held their pens in suspense as Haldane passed hastily toward Mr. Arnot's private office, followed by the reporter, whose alert manner and observant, questioning eye suggested an animated symbol of interrogation.

The manner of his fellow clerks did not escape Haldane's notice even in that confused and hurried moment, and it increased his sense of an impending blow; but when, on entering the private office, Mr. Arnot turned toward him his grim, rigid face, and when a man in the uniform of an officer of the law rose and stepped forward as if the one expected had now arrived, his heart misgave him utterly, and for a moment he found no words, but stood before his employer, pallid and trembling, his very attitude and appearance making as full a confession of guilt as could the statement he proposed to give.

If Pat's opinion concerning Mr. Arnot's "in'ards" had not been substantially correct, that inexorable man would have seen that this was not an old offender who stood before him. The fact that Haldane was overwhelmed with shame and fear, should have tempered his course with healing and saving kindness. But Mr. Arnot had already decided upon his plan, and no other thought would occur to him save that of carrying it out with machine-like precision. His frown deepened as he saw the reporter, but after a second's thought he made no objection to his presence, as the increasing publicity that would result would add to the punishment which was designed to be a signal warning to all in his employ.

After a moment's lowering scrutiny of the trembling youth, during which his confidential clerk, by previous arrangement, appeared, that he might be a witness of all that occurred, Mr. Arnot said coldly:

"Well, sir, perhaps you can now tell me what has become of the funds which I intrusted to your care last evening."

"That is my purpose—object," stammered Haldane; "if you will only give me a chance I will tell you everything."

"I am ready to hear, sir. Be brief; business has suffered too great an interruption already."

"Please have a little consideration for me," said Haldane, eagerly, great beaded drops of perspiration starting from his brow; "I do not wish to speak before all these witnesses. Give me a private interview, and I will explain everything, and can promise that the money shall be refunded."

"I shall make certain of that, rest assured," replied Mr. Arnot, in the same cold, relentless tone. "The money was intrusted to your care last evening, in the presence of witnesses. Here are the empty envelopes. If you have any explanations to make concerning what you did with the money, speak here and now."

"I must warn the young man," said the policeman, interposing, "not to say anything which will tend to criminate himself. He must remember that whatever he says will appear against him in evidence."

"But there is no need that this affair should have any such publicity," Haldane urged in great agitation. "If Mr. Arnot will only show a little humanity toward me

I will arrange the matter so that he will not lose a penny. Indeed, my mother will pay twice the sum rather than have the affair get abroad."

The reporter just behind him grinned and lifted his eyebrows as he took down these words *verbatim*.

"For your mother's sake I deeply regret that 'the affair,' as you mildly term it, must and has become known. As far as you are concerned, I have no compunctions. When a seeming man can commit a grave crime in the hope that a widowed mother—whose stay and pride he ought to be—will come to his rescue, and buy immunity from deserved punishment, he neither deserves, nor shall he receive, mercy at my hands. But were I capable of a maudlin sentiment of pity in the circumstances, the duty I owe my business would prevent any such expression as you desire. When any one in my employ takes advantage of my confidence, he must also, and with absolute certainty, take the consequences."

"Bad luck ter yez!" mentally ejaculated Pat, whom curiosity and the fascination of his own impending fate had drawn within earshot.

"What do you intend to do with me?" asked Haldane, his brow contracting, and his face growing sullen under Mr. Arnot's harsh, bitter words.

"Do! What is done with clerks who steal their employers' money?"

"I did not steal your money," said Haldane impetuously.

"Where is it, then?" asked Mr. Arnot, with a cold sneer.

"Be careful, now," said the policeman; "you are getting excited, and you may say what you'll wish you hadn't."

"Mr. Arnot, do you mean to have it go abroad to all the world that I have deliberately stolen that thousand dollars?" asked the young man desperately.

"Here are the empty envelopes. Where is the money?" said his employer, in the same cool, inexorable tone.

"I met two sharpers from New York, who made a fool of me—"

"Made a fool of you! that was impossible," interrupted Mr. Arnot with a harsh laugh.

"Dastard that you are, to strike a man when he is down," thundered Haldane wrathfully. "Since everything must go abroad, the truth shall go, and not foul slander. I got to drinking with these men from New York, and missed the train—"

"Be careful, now; think what you are saying," interrupted the policeman.

"He charges me with what amounts to a bald theft, and in a way that all will hear of the charge, and shall I not defend myself?"

"O, certainly, if you can prove that you did not take the money—only remember, what you say will appear in the evidence."

"What evidence?" cried the bewildered and excited youth with an oath. "If you will only give me a chance, you shall have all the evidence there is in a sentence. These blacklegs from New York appeared like gentlemen. A friend in town introduced them to me, and, after losing the train, we agreed to spend the evening together. They called for cards, and they won the money."

Mr. Arnot's dark cheek had grown more swarthy at the epithet of "dastard," but he coolly waited until Haldane had finished, and then asked in his former tone:

"Did they take the money from your person and open the envelopes, one carefully, the other recklessly, before they won it?"

Guided by this keen questioning, memory flashed back its light on the events of the past night, and Haldane saw himself opening the first package, certainly, and he remembered how it was done. He trembled, and his face, that had been so flushed, grew very pale. For a moment he was so overwhelmed by a realization of his act, and its threatening consequences, that his tongue refused to plead in his behalf. At last he stammered:

"I did not mean to take the money—only to borrow a

little of it, and return it that same night. They got me drunk—I was not myself. But I assure you it will all be returned. I can—"

"Officer, do your duty," interrupted Mr. Arnot sternly. "Too much time has been wasted over the affair already, but out of regard for his mother I wished to give this young man an opportunity to make an exculpating explanation or excuse, if it were in his power. Since, according to his own statement, he is guilty, the law must take its course."

"You don't mean to send me to prison?" asked Haldane excitedly.

"I could never send you to prison," replied Mr. Arnot coldly; "your own act may bring you there. But I do mean to send you before the justice who issued the warrant for your arrest, held by this officer. Unless you can find some one who will give bail in your behalf, I do not see why he should treat you differently from other offenders."

"Mr. Arnot," cried Haldane passionately, "this is my first and only offence. You surely cannot be so cold-blooded as to inflict upon me this irreparable disgrace? It will kill my mother."

"You should have thought of all this last evening," said Mr. Arnot. "If you persist in ignoring the fact, that it is your own deed that wounds your mother and inflicts disgrace upon yourself, the world will not. Come, Mr. Officer, serve your warrant, and remove your prisoner."

"Is it your purpose that I shall be dragged through these streets in the broad light of day to a police court, and thence to jail?" demanded Haldane, a dark menace coming into his eyes, and finding expression in his livid face.

"Yes, sir," said the man of business, rising and speaking in loud, stern tones, so that all in the office could hear; "I mean that you or any one else in my employ who abuses my trust and breaks the laws shall suffer their full penalty."

"You are a hard-hearted wretch!" thundered Haldane; "you are a pagan idolater, and gold is your god. You crush your wife and servants at home; you crush the spirit and manhood of your clerks here by your cast-iron system and rules. If you had shown a little consideration for me you would have lost nothing, and I might have had a chance for a better life. But you tread me down into the mire of the streets; you make it impossible for me to appear among decent men again; you strike my mother and sisters as with a dagger. Curse you! if I go to jail, it will require you and all your clerks to take me there!" and he whirled on his heel, and struck out recklessly toward the door.

The busy reporter was capsized by the first blow, and his nose long bore evidence that it is a serious matter to put that member into other people's affairs, even in a professional way.

Before Haldane could pass from the inner office two strangers, who had been standing quietly at the door, each dexterously seized one of his hands with such an iron grasp that, after a momentary struggle, he gave up, conscious of the hopelessness of resistance.

"If you will go quietly with us we will employ no force," said the man in uniform; "otherwise we must use these;" and Haldane shuddered as light steel manacles were produced. "These men are officers like myself, and you see that you stand no chance with three of us."

"Well, lead on, then," was the sullen answer. "I will go quietly if you don't use those, but if you do, I will not yield while there is a breath of life in me."

"A most desperate and hardened wretch!" ejaculated the reporter, sopping his streaming nose.

With a dark look and deep malediction upon his employer, Haldane was led away.

Mr. Arnot was in no gentle mood, for, while he had carried out his programme, the machinery of the legal process had not worked smoothly. Very disagreeable things had been said to him in the hearing of his clerks and others. "Of course, they are not true," thought the gentleman; "but his insolent words will go out in the accounts of the affair as surely as my own."

If Haldane had been utterly overwhelmed and broken down, and had shown only the cringing spirit of a detected and whipped cur, Mr. Arnot's complacency would have been perfect. But as it was, the affair had gone forward in a jarring, uncomfortable manner, which annoyed and irritated him as would a defective, creaking piece of mechanism in one of his factories. Opposition, friction of any kind, only made his imperious will more intolerant of disobedience or neglect; therefore he summoned Pat in a tone whose very accent foretold the doom of the "intelligent Irishman."

"Did I not order you to give no information to any one concerning what occurred last night?" he demanded in his sternest tone.

Pat hitched and wriggled, for giving up his forty dollars a month was like a surgical operation. He saw that his master was incensed, and in no mood for extenuation; so he pleaded—

"Misther Arnot, won't ye plaze slape on it afore ye gives me me discharge. If ye'll only think a bit about them newspaper men, ye'll know it could not be helped a' tall. If they suspicion that a man has anything in him that they're wantin' to know, they the same as put a corkscrew intil him, and pull till somethin' comes, and thin they make up the rest. Faix, sur, I niver could o' got by 'em aloive wid me letther onless a little o' the news had gone intil their rav'nous maws."

"Then I'll find a man who can get by them, and who is able to obey my orders to the letter. The cashier will pay you up to date; then leave the premises."

"Och, Misther Arnot, me woife 'll be the death o' me, and thin ye'll have me bluid on yer sowl Give me one more—"

"Begone!" said his employer harshly; "too much time has been wasted already."

Pat found that his case was so desperate that he became reckless, and, instead of slinking off, he, too showed the same insubordination and disregard for Mr. Arnot's power and dignity that had been so irritating in Haldane. Clapping his hat on one side of his head, and with such an insolent cant forward that it quite obscured his left eye, Pat rested his hands on his hips, and with one foot thrust out sidewise, he fixed his right eye on his employer with the expression of sardonic contemplation, and then delivered himself as follows:

"The takin' up a few minits o' yer toime is a moighty tirrible waste, but the sindin' of a human bain to the divil is no waste a' tall a' tall: that's the way ye rason, is it? I allers heerd that yer in'ards were made o' cast-iron, and I can belave—"

"Leave this office," thundered Mr. Arnot.

"Begorry, ye can't put a man in jail for spakin' his moind, nor for spakin' the truth. If ye had given me a chance I'd been civil and obadient the rist o' me days. But whin ye act to'ard a man as if he was a lump o' dirt that ye can kick out o' the way, and go on, ye'll foind that the lump o' dirt will lave some marks on yer nice clothes. I tell ye till yer flinty ould face that ye'r a hard-hearted riprobate that 'ud grind a poor divil to paces as soon as any mash-shine in all yer big factories. Ye'll see the day whin ye'll be under somebody's heel yerself, bad luck to yez!"

Pat's irate volubility flowed in such a torrent that even Mr. Arnot could not check it until he saw fit to drop the sluice-gates himself, which, with a contemptuous sniff, and an expression of concentrated wormwood and gall, he now did. Lifting his battered hat a little more toward the perpendicular, he went to the cashier's desk, obtained his money, and then jogged slowly and aimlessly down the street, leaving a wake of strange oaths behind him.

Thus Mr. Arnot's system again ground out the expected result; but the plague of humanity was that it would not endure the grinding process with the same stolid, inert helplessness of other raw material. Though he had had his way in each instance, he grew more and more dissatisfied and out of sorts. This vituperation of himself would not tend to impress his emyloyés with awe, and strike a wholesome fear in their hearts. The culprits, instead of slinking away overwhelmed with guilt and the weight of his displeasure, had acted and spoken as if he were a grim old tyrant; and he had a vague, uncomfortable feeling that his clerks in their hearts sided with them and against him. It even occurred to him that he was creating a relation between himself and those in his service similar to that existing between master and slaves; and that, instead of forming a community with identical interests, he was on one side and they on the other. But, with the infatuation of a selfish nature and imperious will, he muttered:

"Curse them! I'll make them move in my grooves, or toss them out of the way!" Then, summoning his confidential clerk, he said:

"You know all about the affair. You will oblige me by going to the office of the justice, and stating the case, with the prisoner's admissions. I do not care to appear further in the matter, except by proxy, unless it is necessary."

CHAPTER XII

A MEMORABLE MEETING

MRS. ARNOT had looked upon Haldane's degradation with feelings akin to disgust and anger, but as long, sleepless hours passed, her thoughts grew more gentle and compassionate. She was by nature an advocate rather than a judge. Not the spirit of the disciples, that would call down fire from heaven, but the spirit of the Master, who sought to lay his healing, rescuing hand on every lost creature, always controlled her eventually. Human desert did not count as much with her as human need, and her own sorrows had made her heart tender toward the sufferings of others, even though well merited.

The prospect that the handsome youth, the son of her old friend, would cast himself down to perish in the slough of dissipation, was a tragedy that wrung her heart with grief; and when at last she fell asleep it was with tears upon her face.

Forebodings had followed Laura also, even into her dreams, and at last, in a frightful vision, she saw her uncle placing a giant on guard over the house. Her uncle had scarcely disappeared before Haldane tried to escape, but the giant raised his mighty club, as large and heavy as the mast of a ship, and was about to strike when she awoke with a violent start.

In strange unison with her dream she still heard her uncle's voice in the garden below. She sprang to the window, half expecting to see the giant also, nor was she greatly reassured on observing an unknown man posted in the summer-house and left there.   Mr. Arnot's mysterious action, and the fact that he was out at that early hour, added to the disquiet of mind which the events of the preceding night had created.

Her simple home-life had hitherto flowed like a placid stream in sunny meadows, but now it seemed as if the stream were entering a forest where dark and ominous shadows were thrown across its surface.   She was too womanly to be indifferent to the fate of any human being.   At the same time she was still so much of a child, and so ignorant of the world, that Haldane's action, even as she understood it, loomed up before her imagination as something awful and portentous of unknown evils.   She was oppressed with a feeling that a crushing blow impended over him.   Now, almost as vividly as in her dream, she still saw the giant's club raised high to strike.   If it were only in a fairy tale, her sensitive spirit would tremble at such a stroke, but inasmuch as it was falling on one who had avowed passionate love for her, she felt almost as if she must share in its weight.   The idea of reciprocating any feeling that resembled his passion had at first been absurd, and now, in view of what he had shown himself capable, seemed impossible; and yet his strongly expressed regard for her created a sort of bond between them in spite of herself.   She had realized the night before that he would be immediately dismissed and sent home in disgrace; but her dream, and the glimpse she had caught of her uncle and the observant stranger, who, as she saw, still maintained his position, suggested worse consequences, whose very vagueness made them all the more dreadful.

As it was still a long time before the breakfast hour, she again sought her couch, and after a while fell into a troubled sleep, from which she was awakened by her aunt. Hastily dressing, she joined Mrs. Arnot at a late breakfast, and soon discovered that she was worried and anxious as well as herself.

"Has Mr. Haldane gone out?" she asked.

"Yes; and what perplexes me is that two strangers followed him to the street so rapidly that they almost seemed in pursuit."

Then Laura related what she had seen, and her aunt's face grew pale and somewhat rigid as she recognized the fact that her husband was carrying out some plan, unknown to her, which might involve a cruel blow to her friend, Mrs. Haldane, and an overwhelming disgrace to Egbert Haldane. At the same time the thought flashed upon her that the young man's offence might be graver than she had supposed. But she only remarked quietly: "I will go down to the office and see your uncle after breakfast."

"Oh, auntie, please let me go with you," said Laura nervously.

"I may wish to see my husband alone," replied Mrs. Arnot doubtfully, foreseeing a possible interview which she would prefer her niece should not witness.

"I will wait for you in the outer office, auntie, if you will only let me go. I am so unstrung that I cannot bear to be left in the house alone."

"Very well, then; we'll go together, and a walk in the open air will do us both good."

As Mrs. Arnot was finishing her breakfast she listlessly took up the morning "Courier," and with a sudden start read the heavy head-lines and paragraph which Pat's unlucky venture as a reporter had occasioned.

"Come, Laura, let us go at once," said she, rising hastily; and as soon as they could prepare themselves for the street they started toward the central part of the city, each too busy with her own thoughts to speak often, and yet each having a grateful consciousness of unspoken sympathy and companionship.

As they passed down the main street they saw a noisy crowd coming up the sidewalk toward them, and they crossed over to avoid it. But the approaching throng

grew so large and boisterous that they deemed it prudent
to enter the open door of a shop until it passed. Their
somewhat elevated position gave them a commanding view,
and a policeman's uniform at once indicated that it was an
arrest that had drawn together the loose human atoms that
are always drifting about the streets. The prisoner was followed by a retinue that might have bowed the head of an
old and hardened offender with shame—rude, idle, half-
grown boys, with their morbid interest in every thing tending to excitement and crime, seedy loungers drawn away
from saloon doors where they are as surely to be found as
certain coarse weeds in foul, neglected corners—a ragged,
unkempt, repulsive jumble of humanity, that filled the
street with gibes, slang, and profanity. Laura was about
to retreat into the shop in utter disgust, when her aunt exclaimed in a tone of sharp distress:

"Merciful Heaven! there is Egbert Haldane!"

With something like a shock of terror she recognized her
quondam lover, the youth who had stood at her side and
turned her music. But as she saw him now there appeared
an immeasurable gulf between them; while her pity for him
was profound, it seemed as helpless and hopeless in his
behalf as if he were a guilty spirit that was being dragged
away to final doom.

Her aunt's startled exclamation caught the young man's
attention, for it was a voice that he would detect among a
thousand, and he turned his livid face, with its agonized,
hunted look, directly toward them.

As their eyes met—as he saw the one of all the world
that he then most dreaded to meet, Laura Romeyn, regarding him with a pale, frightened face, as if he were a monster, a wild beast, nay, worse, a common thief on his way
to jail—he stopped abruptly, and for a second seemed to
meditate some desperate act. But when he saw the rabble
closing on him, and heard the officers growl in surly tones,
"Move on," a sense of helplessness as well as of shame
overwhelmed him. He shivered visibly, dashed his hat

down over his eyes, and strode on, feeling at last that the obscurity of a prison cell would prove a welcome refuge.

But Mrs. Arnot had recognized the intolerable suffering and humiliation stamped on the young man's features; she had seen the fearful, shrinking gaze at herself and Laura, the lurid gleam of desperation, and read correctly the despairing gesture by which he sought to hide from them, the rabble, and all the world, a countenance from which he already felt that shame had blotted all trace of manhood.

Her face again wore a gray, rigid aspect, as if she had received a wound that touched her heart; and, scarcely waiting for the miscellaneous horde to pass, she took Laura's arm, and said briefly and almost sternly:

"Come."

Mr. Arnot's equanimity was again destined to be disturbed. Until he had commenced to carry out his scheme of striking fear into the hearts of his employés, he had derived much grim satisfaction from its contemplation. But never had a severe and unrelenting policy failed more signally, and a partial consciousness of the fact annoyed him like a constant stinging of nettles which he could not brush aside. When, therefore, his wife entered, he greeted her with his heaviest frown, and a certain twitching of his hands as he fumbled among his papers, which showed that the man who at times seemed composed of equal parts of iron and lead had at last reached a condition of nervous irritability which might result in an explosion of wrath; and yet he made a desperate effort at self-control, for he saw that his wife was in one of those moods which he had learned to regard with a wholesome respect.

"You have sent Haldane to prison," she said calmly. Though her tone was so quiet, there was in it a certain depth and tremble which her husband well understood, but he only answered briefly:

"Yes; he must go there if he finds no bail."

"May I ask why?"

"He robbed me of a thousand dollars."

"Were there no extenuating circumstances?" Mrs. Arnot asked, after a slight start.

"No, but many aggravating ones."

"Did he not come here of his own accord?"

"He could not have done otherwise. I had detectives watching him."

"He could have tried to do otherwise. Did he not offer some explanation?"

"What he said amounted to a confession of the crime."

"What did he say?"

"I have not charged my mind with all the rash, foolish words of the young scapegrace. It is sufficient for me that he and all in my employ received a lesson which they will not soon forget. I wish you would excuse me from further consideration of the subject at present. It has cost me too much time already."

"You are correct," said Mrs. Arnot very quietly. "It is likely to prove a very costly affair. I tremble to think what your lesson may cost this young man, whom you have rendered reckless and desperate by this public disgrace; I tremble to think what this event may cost my friend, his mother. Of the pain it has cost me I will not speak—"

"Madam," interrupted Mr. Arnot harshly, "permit me to say that this is an affair concerning which a sentimental woman can have no correct understanding. I propose to carry on my business in the way which experience has taught me is wise, and, with all respect to yourself, I would suggest that in these matters of business I am in my own province."

The ashen hue deepened upon Mrs. Arnot's face, but she answered quietly:

"I do not wish to overstep the bounds which should justly limit my action and my interest in this matter. You will also do me the justice to remember that I have never interfered in your business, and have rarely asked you about it, though in the world's estimation I would have some right to do so. But if such harshness, if such disastrous cruelty, is necessary to your business, I must withdraw my means from it, for I could not receive money stained, as it were, with blood. But of this hereafter. I will now telegraph Mrs. Haldane to come directly to our house—"

"To our house!" cried Mr. Arnot, perfectly aghast.

"Certainly. Can you suppose that, burdened with this intolerable disgrace, she could endure the publicity of a hotel? I shall next visit Haldane, for as I saw him in the street, with the rabble following, he looked desperate enough to destroy himself."

"Now, I protest against all this weak sentimentality," said Mr. Arnot, rising. "You take sides with a robber against your husband."

"I do not make light of Haldane's offence to you, and certainly shall not to him. But it is his first offence, as far as we know, and, though you have not seen fit to inform me of the circumstances, I cannot believe that he committed a cool, deliberate theft. He could have been made to feel his guilt without being crushed. The very gravity of his wrong action might have awakened him to his danger, and have been the turning-point of his life. He should have had at least one chance—God gives us many."

"Well, well," said Mr. Arnot impatiently, "let his mother return the money, and I will not prosecute. But why need Mrs. Haldane come to Hillaton? All can be arranged by her lawyer."

"You know little of a mother's feelings if you can suppose she will not come instantly."

"Well, then, when the money is paid she can take him home, that is, after the forms of law are complied with."

"But he must remain in prison till the money is paid?"

"Certainly."

"You intimated that if any one went bail for him he need not go to prison. I will become his security."

"O nonsense! I might as well give bail myself."

"Has he reached the prison yet?"

"I suppose he has," replied Mr. Arnot, taking care to give no hint of the preliminary examination, for it would have annoyed him excessively to have his wife appear at a police court almost in the light of an antagonist to himself. And yet his stubborn pride would not permit him to yield, and carry out with considerate delicacy the merciful policy upon which he saw she was bent.

"Good-morning," said his wife very quietly, and she at once left her husband's private room. Laura rose from her chair in the outer office and welcomed her gladly, for, in her nervous trepidation, the minutes had seemed like hours. Mrs. Arnot went to a telegraph office, and sent the following despatch to Mrs. Haldane:

"Come to my house at once. Your son is well, but has met with misfortune."

She then, with Laura, returned immediately home and ordered her carriage for a visit to the prison. She also remembered with provident care that the young man could not have tasted food that morning.

CHAPTER XIII

OUR KNIGHT IN JAIL

AS Haldane emerged from the office into the open glare of the street, he was oppressed with such an intolerable sense of shame that he became sick and faint, and tottered against the policeman, who took no other notice of his condition than the utterance of a jocular remark:

"You haven't got over your drunk yet, I'm athinking."

Haldane made no reply, and the physical weakness gradually passed away. As his stunned and bewildered mind regained the power to act, he became conscious of a morbid curiosity to see how he was regarded by those whom he met. He knew that their manner would pierce like sword-thrusts, and yet every scornful or averted face had a cruel fascination.

With a bitterness of which his young heart had never before had even a faint conception, he remembered that this cold and contemptuous, this scoffing and jeering world was the same in which only yesterday he proposed to tower in such lofty grandeur that the maiden who had slighted him should be consumed with vain regret in memory of her lost opportunity. He had, indeed, gained eminence speedily. All the town was hearing of him; but the pedestal which lifted him so high was composed equally of crime and folly, and he felt as if he might stand as a monument of shame.

But his grim and legal guardians tramped along in the most stolid and indifferent manner. The gathering rabble at their heels had no terror for them. Indeed, they rather enjoyed parading before respectable citizens this dangerous substratum of society. It was a delicate way of saying, "Behold in these your peril, and in us your defence. We are necessary to your peace and security. Respect us and pay us well."

They represented the majesty of the law, which could lay its strong hand on high and low alike, and the publicity which was like a scorching fire to Haldane brought honor to them.

Although the journey seemed interminable to the culprit, they were not long in reaching the police court, where the magistrate presiding had already entered on his duties. All night long, and throughout the entire city, the scavengers of the law had been at work, and now, as a result, every miserable atom of humanity that had made itself a pestilential offence to society was gathered here to be disposed of according to sanatory moral rules.

Hillaton was a comparatively well-behaved and decorous city; but in every large community there is always a certain amount of human sediment, and Haldane felt that he had fallen low indeed, when he found himself classed and huddled with miserable objects whose existence he had never before realized. Near him stood men who apparently had barely enough humanity left to make their dominating animal natures more dangerous and difficult to control. To the instincts of a beast was added something of a man's intelligence, but so developed that it was often little more than cunning. If, when throwing away his manhood, man becomes a creature more to be dreaded than a beast or venomous reptile, whichever he happens most to resemble, woman, parting with her womanhood, scarcely finds her counterpart even in the most noxious forms of earthly existence. She becomes, in her perversion, something that is unnatural and monstrous; something, so opposite to the Creator's design, as to suggest it only in caricature, or, more often, in fiendish mockery. The Gorgons, Sirens, and Harpies of the ancients are scarcely myths, for their fabled forms only too accurately portray, not the superficial and transient outward appearance, but the enduring character within.

Side by side with Haldane stood a creature whose dishevelled, rusty hair, blotched and bloated features, wanton, cunning, restless eyes, combined perfectly to form the head of the mythological Harpy. It required little effort of the imagination to believe that her foul, bedraggled dress concealed the "wings and talons of the vulture." Being still unsteady from her night's debauch, she leaned against the young man, and when he shrank in loathing away, she, to annoy him, clasped him in her arms, to the uproarious merriment of the miscellaneous crowd that is ever present at a police court. Haldane broke away from her grasp with such force as to make quite a commotion, and at the same time said loudly and fiercely to the officer who had arrested him:

"You may have power to take me to jail, but you have not, and shall not have, the right nor the power to subject me to such indignities."

"Silence there! Keep order in the court!" commanded the judge.

The officer removed his prisoner a little further apart from the others, growling as he did so:

"If you don't like your company, you should have kept out of it."

Even in his overwhelming anxiety and distress Haldane could not forbear giving a few curious glances at his companions. He had dropped out of his old world into a new one, and these were its inhabitants. In their degradation and misery he seemed to see himself and his future reflected. What had the policeman said?—"Your company," and with a keener pang than he had yet experienced he realized that this was his company, that he now belonged to the criminal classes. He who yesterday had the right to speak to Laura Romeyn, was now herded with drunkards, thieves, and prostitutes; he who yesterday could enter Mrs. Arnot's parlor, might now as easily enter heaven. As the truth of his situation gradually dawned upon him, he felt as if an icy hand were closing upon his heart.

But little time, however, was given him for observation

or bitter revery. With the rapid and routine-like manner of one made both callous and expert by long experience, the magistrate was sorting and disposing of the miserable waifs. Now he has before him the inmates of a "disorderly house," upon which a "raid" had been made the previous night. What is that fair young girl with blue eyes doing among those coarse-featured human dregs, her companions? She looks like a white lily that has been dropped into a puddle. Perhaps that delicate and attractive form is but a disguise for the Harpy's wings and claws. Perhaps a gross, bestial spirit is masked by her oval Madonna-like face. Perhaps she is the victim of one upon whom God will wreak his vengeance forever, though society has for him scarcely a frown.

The puddle is suddenly drained off into some law-ordained receptacle, and the white lily is swept away with it. She will not long suggest a flower that has been dropped into the gutter. The stains upon her soul will creep up into her face, and make her hideous like the rest.

The case of Egbert Haldane was next called. As the policeman had said, his own admissions were now used against him, for the confidential clerk, and, if there was need, the broken-nosed reporter, were on hand to testify to all that had been said. The young man made no attempt to conceal, but tried to explain more fully the circumstances which led to the act, hoping that in them the justice would find such extenuating elements as would prevent a committal to prison.

The judge recognized and openly acknowledged the fact that it was not a case of deliberate wrongdoing, and he ordered the arrest of the superior young gentleman who had introduced the New York gamblers to their victim; and yet in the eye of the law it was a clear case of embezzlement; and, as Mr. Arnot's friend, the magistrate felt little disposition to prevent things from taking their usual course. The prisoner must either furnish bail at once, or be committed until he could do so, or until the case could be properly tried. As Haldane was a comparative stranger in Hillaton there was no one to whom he felt he could apply, and he supposed it would require some little time for his mother to arrange the matter. Upon his signifying that he could not furnish bail immediately, the judge promptly ordered his committal to the common jail of the city, which happened to be at some distance from the building then employed for the preliminary examinations.

It was while on his way to this place of detention that he heard Mrs. Arnot's voice, and encountered her eyes and those of Laura Romeyn. His first impulse was to end both his suffering and himself by some desperate act, but he was powerless even to harm himself.

The limit of endurance, however had been reached. The very worst that he could imagine had befallen him. Laura Romeyn had looked upon his unutterable shame and disgrace. From a quivering and almost agonizing sensibility to his situation he reacted into sullen indifference. He no longer saw the sun shining in the sky, nor the familiar sights of the street; he no longer heard nor heeded the jeering rabble that came tramping after. He became for the time scarcely more than a piece of mechanism, that barely retained the power of voluntary motion, but had lost ability to feel and think. When, at last, he entered his narrow cell, eight feet by eight, the wish half formed itself in his mind that it was six feet by two, and that he might hide in it forever.

He sat down on the rough wooden couch which formed the only furniture of the room, and buried his face in his hands, conscious only of a dull, leaden weight of pain. He made no effort to obtain legal counsel or to communicate his situation to his mother. Indeed, he dreaded to see her, and he felt that he could not look his sisters in the face again. The prison cell seemed a refuge from the terrible scorn of the world, and his present impulse was to cower behind its thick walls for the rest of his life.

CHAPTER XIV

MR. ARNOT'S SYSTEM WORKS BADLY

MR. ARNOT was so disturbed by his wife's visit that he found it impossible to return to the routine of business, and, instead of maintaining the cold, lofty bearing of a man whose imperious will awed and controlled all within its sphere, he fumed up and down his office like one who had been caught in the toils himself. In the morning it had seemed that there could not have been a fairer opportunity to vindicate his iron system, and make it irresistible. The offending subject in his business realm should receive due punishment, and all the rest be taught that they were governed by inexorable laws, which would be executed with the certainty and precision with which the wheels moved in a great factory under the steady impulse of the motor power. But the whole matter now bade fair to end in a tangled snarl, whose final issue no one could foretell.

He was sensitive to public opinion, and had supposed that his course would be upheld and applauded, and he be commended as a conservator of public morals. He now feared, however, that he would be portrayed as harsh, grasping, and unfeeling. It did not trouble him that he was so, but that he would be made to appear so.

But his wife's words in reference to the withdrawal of her large property from his business was a far more serious consideration. He had learned how resolute and unswerving she could be in matters of conscience, and he knew that she was not in the habit of making idle threats in moments of irritation. If, just at this time, when he was widely ex-

tending his business, she should demand a separate invest-
ment of her means, it would embarrass and cripple him in
no slight degree. If this should be one of the results of his
master-stroke, he would have reason to curse his brilliant
policy all his days. He would now be only too glad to
get rid of the Haldane affair on any terms, for thus far it
had proved only a source of annoyance and mortification.
He was somewhat consoled, however, when his confidential
clerk returned and intimated that the examination before
the justice had been brief; that Haldane had eagerly stated
his case to the justice, but when that dignitary remarked
that it was a clear case of embezzlement, and that he would
have to commit the prisoner unless some one went security
for his future appearance, the young fellow had grown sullen and answered, "Send me to jail then; I have no friends
in this accursed city."

To men of the law and of sense the case was as clear as
daylight.

But Mr. Arnot was not by any means through with his
disagreeable experiences. He had been a manufacturer sufficiently long to know that when a piece of machinery is set
in motion, not merely the wheels nearest to one will move,
but also others that for the moment may be out of sight.
He who proposes to have a decided influence upon a fellow-
creature's destiny should remember our complicated relations, for he cannot lay his strong grasp upon one life without becoming entangled in the interests of many others.

Mr. Arnot was finding this out to his cost, for he had
hardly composed himself to his writing again before there
was a rustle of a lady's garments in the outer office, and a
hasty step across the threshold of his private *sanctum*.
Looking up, he saw, to his dismay, the pale, frightened
face of Mrs. Haldane.

"Where is Egbert?—where is my son?" she asked
abruptly.

At that moment Mr. Arnot admitted to himself that he
had never been asked so embarrassing a question in all his

life. Before him was his wife's friend, a lady of the highest social rank, and she was so unmistakably a lady that he could treat her with only the utmost deference. He saw with alarm himself the mother's nervous and trembling apprehension, for there was scarcely anything under heaven that he would not rather face than a scene with a hysterical woman. If this was to be the climax of his policy he would rather have lost the thousand dollars than have had it occur. Rising from his seat, he said awkwardly:

"Really, madam, I did not expect you here this morning."

"I was on my way to New York, and decided to stop and give my son a surprise. But this paper—this dreadful report—what does it mean?"

"I am sorry to say, madam, it is all too true," replied Mr. Arnot uneasily. "Please take a chair, or perhaps it would be better for you to go at once to our house and see Mrs. Arnot," he added, now glad to escape the interview on any terms.

"What is too true?" she gasped.

"I think you had better see Mrs. Arnot; she will explain," said the unhappy man, who felt that his system was tumbling in chaos about his ears. "Let me assist you to your carriage."

"Do you think I can endure the suspense of another moment? In mercy speak—tell me the worst!"

"Well," said Mr. Arnot, with a shiver like that of one about to plunge into a cold bath, "I suppose you will learn sooner or later that your son has committed a very wrong act. But," he added hastily, on seeing Mrs. Haldane's increasing pallor, "there are extenuating circumstances—at least, I shall act as if there were."

"But what has he done—where is he?" cried the mother in agony. Then she added in a frightened whisper, "But the matter can be hushed up—there need be no publicity —oh, that would kill me! Please take steps—"

"Mr. Arnot," said a young man just entering, and speaking in a piping, penetrating voice, "I represent the 'Evening Spy.' I wish to obtain from you for publication the particulars of this disgraceful affair." Then, seeing Mrs. Haldane, who had dropped her veil, and was trembling violently, he added, "I hope I am not intruding; I—"

"Yes, sir, you are intruding," said Mr. Arnot harshly.

"Then, perhaps, sir, you will be so kind as to step outside for a moment. I can take down your words rapidly, and—"

"Step outside yourself, sir. I have nothing whatever to say to you."

"I beg you to reconsider that decision, sir. Of course, a full account of the affair must appear in this evening's 'Spy.' It will be your own fault if it is not true in all respects. It is said that you have acted harshly in the matter —that it was young Haldane's first offence, and—"

"Leave my office!" thundered Mr. Arnot.

The lynx-eyed reporter, while speaking thus rapidly, had been scrutinizing the veiled and trembling lady, and he was scarcely disappointed that she now rose hastily, and threw back her veil as she said eagerly:

"Why must the whole affair be published? You say truly that his offence, whatever it is, is his first. Surely the editor of your paper will not be so cruel as to blast a young man forever with disgrace!"

"Mrs. Haldane, I presume," said the reporter, tracing a few hieroglyphics in his note-book.

"Yes," continued the lady, speaking from the impulse of her heart, rather than from any correct knowledge of the world, "and I will pay willingly any amount to have the whole matter quietly dropped. I could not endure anything of this kind, for I have no husband to shelter me, and the boy has no father to protect him."

Mr. Arnot groaned in spirit that he had not considered this case in any of its aspects save those which related to his business. He had formed the habit of regarding all other considerations as unworthy of attention, but here, certainly, was a most disagreeable exception.

"You touch my feelings deeply," said the reporter, in a tone that never for a second lost its professional cadence, "but I much regret that your hopes cannot be realized. Your son's act could scarcely be kept a secret after the fact —known to all—that he has been openly dragged to prison through the streets," and the gatherer of news and sensations kept an eye on each of his victims as he made this statement. A cabalistic sign in his note-book indicated the visible wincing of the enraged and half-distracted manufacturer, whose system was like an engine off the track, hissing and helpless; and a few other equally obscure marks suggested to the initiated the lady's words as she half shrieked:

"My son dragged through the streets to prison! By whom—who could do so dreadful?"—and she sank shudderingly into a chair, and covered her face with her hands, as if to shut out a harrowing vision.

"I regret to say, madam, that it was by a policeman," added the reporter.

"And thither a policeman shall drag you, if you do not instantly vacate these premises!" said Mr. Arnot, hoarse with rage.

"Thank you for your courtesy," answered the reporter, shutting his book with a snap like that of a steel trap. "I have now about all the points I wish to get here. I understand that Mr. Patrick M'Cabe is no longer under any obligations to you, and from him I can learn additional particulars. Good-morning."

"Yes, go to that unsullied source of truth, whom I have just discharged for lying and disobedience. Go to perdition, also, if you please; but take yourself out of my office," said Mr. Arnot recklessly, for he was growing desperate from the unexpected complications of the case. Then he summoned one of his clerks, and said in a tone of authority, "Take this lady to my residence, and leave her in the care of Mrs. Arnot."

Mrs. Haldane rose unsteadily, and tottered toward the door.

"No," said she bitterly; "I may faint in the street, but I will not go to your house."

"Then assist the lady to her carriage;" and Mr. Arnot turned the key of his private office with muttered imprecations upon the whole wretched affair.

"Whither shall I tell the man to drive?" asked the clerk, after Mrs. Haldane had sunk back exhausted on the seat.

The lady put her hand to her brow, and tried to collect her distracted thoughts, and, after a moment's hesitation, said:

"To the prison."

The carriage containing Mrs. Haldane stopped at last before the gloomy massive building, the upper part of which was used as a court-room and offices for city and county officials, while in the basement were constructed the cells of the prison. It required a desperate effort on the part of the timid and delicate lady, who for years had almost been a recluse from the world, to summon courage to alight and approach a place that to her abounded in many and indefinite horrors. She was too preoccupied to observe that another carriage had drawn up to the entrance, and the first intimation that she had of Mrs. Arnot's presence occurred when that lady took her hand in the shadow of the porch, and said:

"Mrs. Haldane, I am greatly surprised to see you here; but you can rely upon me as a true friend throughout this trial. I shall do all in my power to—"

After the first violent start caused by her disturbed nervous condition, Mrs. Haldane asked, in a reproachful and almost passionate tone:

"Why did you not prevent—" and then she hesitated, as if she could not bring herself to utter the concluding words.

'I could not; I did not know; but since I heard I have been doing everything in my power."

"It was your husband who—"

"Yes," replied Mrs. Arnot, sadly, completing in thought her friend's unfinished sentence. "But I had no part in the act, and no knowledge of it until a short time since. I am now doing all I can to procure your son's speedy release. My husband's action has been perfectly legal, and we, who would temper justice with mercy, must do so in a legal way. Permit me to introduce you to my friend, Mr. Melville. He can both advise us and carry out such arrangements as aré necessary;" and Mrs. Haldane saw that Mrs. Arnot was accompanied by a gentleman, whom in her distress she had not hitherto noticed.

The janitor now opened the door, and ushered them into a very plain apartment, used both as an office and reception-room. Mrs. Haldane was so overcome by her emotion that her friend led her to a chair, and continued her reassuring words in a low voice designed for her ears alone:

"Mr. Melville is a lawyer, and knows how to manage these matters. You may trust him implicitly. I will give security for your son's future appearance, should it be necessary, and I am quite satisfied it will not be, as my husband has promised me that he will not prosecute if the money is refunded."

"I would have paid ten times the amount—anything rather than have suffered this public disgrace," sobbed the poor woman, who, true to her instincts and life-long habit of thought, dwelt more upon the consequent shame of her son's act than its moral character.

"Mr. Melville says he will give bail in his own name for me," resumed Mrs. Arnot, "as, of course, I do not wish to appear to be acting in opposition to my husband. Indeed, I am not, for he is willing that some such an arrangement should be made. He has very many in his employ, and feels that he must be governed by rigid rules. Mr. Melville assures me that he can speedily effect Egbert's release. Perhaps it will save you pain to go at once to our house and meet your son there."

"No," replied the mother, rising, "I wish to see him at

once. I *do* appreciate *your* kindness, but I cannot go to the place which shelters your husband. I can never forgive him. Nor can I go to a hotel. I would rather stay in this prison until I can hide myself and my miserable son in our own home. Oh, how dark and dreadful are God's ways! To think that the boy that I had brought up in the Church, as it were, should show such unnatural depravity!" Then, stepping to the door, she said to the under-sheriff in waiting, "Please take me to my son at once, if possible."

"Would you like me to go with you?" asked Mrs. Arnot, gently.

"Yes, yes! for I may faint on the way. Oh, how differently this day is turning out from what I expected! I was in hopes that Egbert could meet me in a little trip to New York, and I find him in prison!"

CHAPTER XV

HALDANE'S RESOLVE

IT WAS not in accordance with nature nor with Haldane's peculiar temperament that he should remain long under a stony paralysis of shame and despair. Though tall and manlike in appearance, he was not a man. Boyish traits and impulses still lingered; indeed, they had been fostered and maintained longer than usual by a fond and indulgent mother. It was not an evidence of weakness, but rather a wholesome instinct of nature, that his thoughts should gradually find courage to go to that mother as his only source of comfort and help. She, at least, would not scorn him, and with her he might find a less dismal refuge than his narrow cell, should it be possible to escape imprisonment. If it were not, he was too young and unacquainted with misfortune not to long for a few kind words of comfort.

He did not even imagine that Mrs. Arnot, the wife of his employer, would come near him in his deep disgrace. Even the thought of her kindness and his requital of it now stung him to the quick, and he fairly writhed as he pictured to himself the scorn that must have been on Laura's face as she saw him on his way to prison like a common thief.

As he remembered how full of rich promise life was but a few days since, and how all had changed even more swiftly and unexpectedly than the grotesque events of a horrid dream, he bowed his head in his hands and sobbed like a grief-stricken child.

"O mother, mother," he groaned, "if I could only hear

your voice and feel your touch, a little of this crushing weight might be lifted off my heart!"

Growing calmer after a time, he was able to consider his situation more connectedly, and he was about to summon the sheriff in charge of the prison, that he might telegraph his mother, when he heard her voice as, in the company of that official, she was seeking her way to him.

He shrank back in his cell. His heart beat violently as he heard the rustle of her dress. The sheriff unlocked the grated iron door which led to the long, narrow corridor into which the cells opened, and to which prisoners had access during the day.

"He's in that cell, ladies," said the officer's voice, and then, with commendable delicacy, withdrew, having first ordered the prisoners in his charge to their cells.

"Lean upon my arm," urged a gentle voice, which Haldane recognized as that of Mrs. Arnot.

"O, this is awful!" moaned the stricken woman; "this is more than *I* can endure."

The pronoun she used threw a chill on the heart of her son, but when she tottered to the door of his cell he sprang forward with the low, appealing cry:

"Mother!"

But the poor gentlewoman was so overcome that she sank down on a bench by the door, and, with her face buried in her hands, as if to shut out a vision that would blast her, she rocked back and forth in anguish, as she groaned:

"O Egbert, Egbert! you have disgraced me, you have disgraced your sisters, you have disgraced yourself beyond remedy. O God! what have I done to merit this awful, this overwhelming disaster?"

With deep pain and solicitude Mrs. Arnot watched the young man's face as the light from the grated window fell upon it. The appeal that trembled in his voice had been more plainly manifest in his face, which had worn an eager and hopeful expression, and even suggested the spirit of the little child when in some painful emergency it turns to its first and natural protector.

But most marked was the change caused by the mother's lamentable want of tact and self-control, for that same face became stony and sullen. Instead of showing a spirit which deep distress and crushing disaster had made almost child-like in its readiness to receive a mother's comfort once more, he suddenly became, in appearance, a hardened criminal.

Mrs. Arnot longed to undo by her kindness the evil which her friend was unwittingly causing, but could not come between mother and son. She stooped down, how-ever, and whispered:

"Mrs. Haldane, speak kindly to your boy. He looked to you for sympathy. Do not let him feel that you, like the world, are against him."

"O no," said Mrs. Haldane, her sobs ceasing somewhat, "I mean to do my duty by him. He shall always have a good home, but oh! what a blight and a shadow he has brought to that home! That I should have ever lived to see this day! O Egbert, Egbert! your sisters will have to live like nuns, for they can never even go out upon the street again; and to think that the finger of scorn should be pointed after you in the city were your father made our name so honorable!"

"It never shall be," said Haldane coldly. "You have only to leave me in prison to be rid of me a long time."

"Leave you, in prison!" exclaimed his mother; "I would as soon stay here myself. No; through Mrs. Arnot's kind-ness, arrangements are made for your release. I shall then take you to our miserable home as soon as possible."

"I am not going home."

"Now, this is too much! What will you do?"

"I shall remain in this city," he replied, speaking from an angry impulse. "It was here I fell and covered myself with shame, and I shall here fight my way back to the position I lost. The time shall come when you will no longer say I'm a disgrace to you and my sisters. My heart was breaking, and the first word you greet me with is 'disgrace'; and if I went home, disgrace would always be in your mind, if not upon your tongue. I should have the word and thought kept before me till I went mad. If I go home all my old acquaintances would sneer at me as a meanspirited cur, whose best exploit was to get in jail, and when his mother obtained his release he could do nothing more manly than hide behind her apron the rest of his days. As far as I can judge, you and my sisters would have no better opinion of me. I have been a wicked fool, I admit, but I was not a deliberate thief. I did hope for a little comfort from you. But since all the world is against me, I'll face and fight the world. I have been dragged through these streets, the scorn of every one, and I will remain in this city until I compel the respect of its proudest citizen."

The moment he ceased his passionate utterance, Mrs. Arnot said kindly and gravely:

"Egbert, you are mistaken. There was no scorn in my eyes, but rather deep pity and sorrow. While your course has been very wrong, you have no occasion to despair, and as long as you will try to become a true man you shall have my sympathy and friendship. You do not understand your mother. She loves you as truly as ever, and is willing to make any sacrifice for you. Only, her fuller knowledge of the world makes her realize more truly than you yet can the consequences of your act. The sudden shock has overwhelmed her. Her distress shows how deeply she is wounded, and you should try to comfort her by a lifetime of kindness."

"The best way I can comfort her is by deeds that will wipe out the memory of my disgrace; and," he continued, his impulsive, sanguine spirit kindling with the thought and prospect, "I will regain all and more than I have lost. The time shall come when neither she nor my sisters will have occasion to blush for me, nor to seclude themselves from the world because of their relation to me."

"I should think my heart was sufficiently crushed and

broken already,'' Mrs. Haldane sobbed, ''without your adding to its burden by charging me with being an unnatural
mother. I cannot understand how a boy brought up as
religiously as you have been can show such strange depravity. The idea that a child of mine could do anything
which would bring him to such a place as this!''

His mother's words and manner seemed to exasperate
her son beyond endurance, and he exclaimed passionately:

''Well, curse it all! I am here. What's the use of harp-
ing on that any longer? Can't you listen when I say I want
to retrieve myself? As to my religious bringing up, it never
did me a particle of good. If you had whipped my infernal
nonsense out of me, and made me mind when I was little—
There, there, mother,'' he concluded more considerately, as
she began to grow hysterical under his words, ''do, for God's
sake, be more composed! We can't help what has happened
now. I'll either change the world's opinion of me, or else
get out of it.''

''How can I be composed when you talk in so dreadful
a manner? You can't change the world's opinion. It never
forgives and never forgets. It's the same as if you had said,
I'll either do what is impossible or throw away my life!''

''My dear Mrs. Haldane,'' said Mrs. Arnot, gently but
firmly, ''your just and natural grief is such that you cannot
now judge correctly and wisely concerning this matter.
The emergency is so unexpected and so grave that neither
you nor your son should form opinions or make resolves
until there has been time for calmer thought. Let me take
you home with me now, and as soon as Egbert is released
he can join you there.''

''No, Mrs. Arnot,'' said Haldane decidedly; ''I shall
never enter your parlor again until I can enter it as a gentleman—as one whom your other guests, should I meet
them, would recognize as a gentleman. Your kindness is
as great as it is unexpected, but I shall take no mean
advantage of it.''

''Well, then,'' said Mrs. Arnot with a sigh, ''nothing

can be gained by prolonging this painful interview. We are detaining Mr. Melville, and delaying Egbert's release. Come, Mrs. Haldane; I can take you to the private entrance of a quiet hotel, where you can be entirely secluded until you are ready to return home. Egbert can come there as soon as the needful legal forms are complied with.''

"No," said the young man with his former decision, "mother and I must take leave of each other here. Mother wants no jail-birds calling on her at the hotel. When I have regained my social footing—when she is ready to take my arm and walk up Main street of this city—then she shall see me as often as she wishes. It was my own cursed folly that brought me to the gutter, and if mother will pay the price of my freedom, I will alone and unaided make my way back among the highest and proudest."

"I sincerely hope you may win such a position," said Mrs. Arnot gravely, "and it is not impossible for you to do so, though I wish you would make the attempt in a different spirit; but please remember that these considerations do not satisfy and comfort a mother's heart. You should think of all her past kindness; you should realize how deeply you have now wounded her, and strive with tenderness and patience to mitigate the blow."

"Mother, I am sorry, more sorry than you can ever know," he said, advancing to her side and taking her hand, "and I have been bitterly punished; but I did not mean to do what I did; I was drunk—''

"Drunk!" gasped the mother, "merciful Heaven!"

"Yes, drunk—may the next drop of wine I take choke me!—and I did not know what I was doing. But do not despair of me. I feel that I have it in me to make a man yet. Go now with Mrs. Arnot, and aid in her kind efforts to procure my release. When you have succeeded, return home, and think of me as well as you can until I make you think better," and he raised and kissed her with something like tenderness, and then placed within Mrs. Arnot's arm the hand of the poor weak woman, who had become so faint

and exhausted from her conflicting emotions that she submitted to be led away after a feeble remonstrance.

Mrs. Arnot sent Mr. Melville to the prisoner, and also
the food she had brought. She then took Mrs. Haldane to
a hotel, where, in the seclusion of her room, she could have
every attention and comfort. With many reassuring words
she promised to call later in the day, and if possible bring
with her the unhappy cause of the poor gentlewoman's
distress.

CHAPTER XVI

THE IMPULSES OF WOUNDED PRIDE

THAT which at first was little more than an impulse, caused by wounded pride, speedily developed into a settled purpose, and Haldane would leave his prison cell fully bent on achieving great things. In accordance with a tendency in impulsive natures, he reacted from something like despair into quite a sanguine and heroic mood. He would "face and fight the world, ay, and conquer it, too." He would go out into the streets which had witnessed his disgrace, and, penniless, empty-handed, dowered only with shame, he would prove his manhood by winning a position that would compel respect and more than respect.

Mrs. Arnot, who returned immediately to the prison, was puzzled to know how to deal with him. She approved of his resolution to remain in Hillaton, and of his purpose to regain respect and position on the very spot, as it were, where, by his crime and folly, he had lost both. She was satisfied that such a course promised far better for the future than a return to his mother's luxurious home. With all its beauty and comfort it would become to him almost inevitably a slough, both of "despond" and of dissipation—dissipation of the worst and most hopeless kind, wherein the victim's ruling motive is to get rid of self. The fact that the young man was capable of turning upon and facing a scornful and hostile world was a good and hopeful sign. If he had been willing to slink away with his mother, bent only on escape from punishment and on the continuance of animal enjoyment, Mrs. Arnot would have felt that his nature was not sufficiently leavened with manhood to give hope of reform.

But while his action did suggest hope, it also contained elements of discouragement. She did not find fault with what he proposed to do, but with the spirit in which he was entering on his most difficult task. His knowledge of the world was so crude and partial that he did not at all realize the herculean labor that he now became eager to attempt; and he was bent on accomplishing everything in a way that would minister to his own pride, and proposed to be under obligations to no one.

Mrs. Arnot, with her deep and long experience, knew how vitally important it is that human endeavor should be supplemented by divine aid, and she sighed deeply as she saw that the young man not only ignored this need, but did not even seem conscious of it. Religion was to him a matter of form and profession, to which he was utterly indifferent. The truth that God helps the distressed as a father helps and comforts his child, was a thought that then made no impression on him whatever. God and all relating to him were abstractions, and he felt that the emergency was too pressing, too imperative, for considerations that had no practical and immediate bearing upon his present success.

Indeed, such was his pride and self-confidence, that he refused to receive from Mrs. Arnot, and even from his mother, anything more than the privilege of going out empty-handed into the city which was to become the arena of his future exploits.

He told Mrs. Arnot the whole story, and she had hoped that she could place his folly and crime before him in its true moral aspects, and by dealing faithfully, yet kindly, with him, awaken his conscience. But she had the tact to discover very soon that such effort was now worse than useless. It was not his conscience, but his pride, that had been chiefly wounded. He felt his disgrace, his humiliation, in the eyes of men almost too keenly, and he was consumed with desire to regain society's favor. But he did not feel his sin. To God's opinion of him he scarcely gave a thought. He regarded his wrong act in the light of a sudden and grave misfortune rather than as the manifestation of a foul and inherent disease of his soul. He had lost his good name as a man loses his property, and believed that he, in his own strength, and without any moral change, could regain it.

When parting at the prison, Mrs. Arnot gave him her hand, and said:

"I trust that your hopes may be realized, and your efforts meet with success; but I cannot help warning you that I fear you do not realize what you are attempting. The world is not only very cold, but also suspicious and wary in its disposition toward those who have forfeited its confidence. I cannot learn that you have any definite plans or prospects. I have never been able to accomplish much without God's help. You not only seem to forget your need of Him, but you are not even willing to receive aid from me or your own mother. I honor and respect you for making the attempt upon which you are bent, but I fear that pride rather than wisdom is your counsellor in carrying out your resolution; and both God's word and human experience prove that pride goes but a little way before a fall."

"I have reached a depth," replied Haldane, bitterly, "from whence I cannot fall; and it will be hereafter some consolation to remember that I was not lifted out of the mire, but that I got out. If I cannot climb up again it were better I perished in the gutter of my shame."

"I am sorry, Egbert, that you cut yourself off from the most hopeful and helpful relations which you can ever sustain. A father helps his children through their troubles, and so God is desirous of helping us. There are some things which we cannot do alone—it is not meant that we should. God is ever willing to help those who are down, and Christians are not worthy of the name unless they are also willing. It is our duty to make every effort of which

we ourselves are capable; but this is only half our duty.
Since our tasks are beyond our strength and ability, we are
equally bound to receive such human aid as God sends us,
and, chief of all, to ask daily, and sometimes hourly, that
His strength be made perfect in our weakness. But there
are some lessons which are only learned by experience. I
shall feel deeply grieved if you do not come or send for
me in any emergency or time of special need. In parting,
I have one favor to ask, and I think I have a right to ask
it. I wish you to go and see your mother, and spend at
least an hour with her before she returns home. As a matter of manly duty, be kind and gentle. Remember how
deeply you have wounded her, and that you are under the
most sacred obligations to endure patiently all reproaches
and expressions of grief. If you will do this you will do
much to regain my respect, and it will be a most excellent
step toward a better life. You can gain society's respect
again only by doing your duty, and nothing can be duty
more plainly than this."

After a moment's hesitation he said, "I do not think an
interview with mother now will do either of us any good;
but, as you say, you have a right to ask this, and much
more, of me. I will go to her hotel and do the best I can;
but somehow mother don't understand human nature—or,
at least, my nature—and when I have been doing wrong she
always makes me feel like doing worse."

"If you are to succeed in your endeavor you are not to
act as you feel. *You are to do right.* Remember that in your
effort to win the position you wish in this city, you start
with at least one friend to whom you can always come.
Good-by," and Mrs. Arnot returned home weary and sad
from the day's unforeseen experiences.

In answer to Laura's eager questioning, she related what
had happened quite fully, veiling only that which a delicate
regard for others would lead her to pass in silence. She
made the young girl womanly by treating her more as a
woman and a companion than as a child. In Mrs. Arnot's

estimation her niece had reached an age when her innocence and simplicity could not be maintained by efforts to keep her shallow and ignorant, but by revealing to her life in its reality, so that she might wisely and gladly choose the good from its happy contrast with evil and its inevitable suffering.

The innocence that walks blindly on amid earth's snares and pitfalls is an uncertain possession; the innocence that recognizes evil, but turns from it with dread and aversion, is priceless.

Mrs. Arnot told Laura the story of the young man's folly substantially as he had related it to her, but she skilfully showed how one comparatively venial thing had led to another, until an act had been committed which might have resulted in years of imprisonment.

"Let this sad and miserable affair teach you," said she, "that we are never safe when we commence to do wrong or act foolishly. We can never tell to what disastrous lengths we may go when we leave the path of simple duty."

While she mentioned Haldane's resolution to regain, if possible, his good name and position, she skilfully removed from the maiden's mind all romantic notions concerning the young man and her relation to his conduct.

Laura's romantic nature would always be a source both of strength and weakness. While, on the one hand, it rendered her incapable of a sordid and calculating scheme of life, on the other, it might lead to feeling and action prejudicial to her happiness. Mrs. Arnot did not intend that she should brood over Haldane until her vivid imagination should weave a net out of his misfortunes which might insnare her heart. It was best for Laura that she should receive her explanations of life in very plain prose, and the picture that her aunt presented of Haldane and his prospects was prosaic indeed. He was shown to be but an ordinary young man, with more than ordinarily bad tendencies. While she commended his effort in itself, she plainly stated how wanting it was in the true elements of success, and how great were her fears that it would meet with utter failure.

Thus the affair ended, as far as Laura was concerned, in a sincere pity for her premature lover, and a mild and natural interest in his future welfare—but nothing more.

Mr. Arnot uttered an imprecation on learning that his wife had gone security for Haldane. But when he found that she had acted through Mr. Melville, in such a way that the fact need not become known, he concluded to remain silent concerning the matter. He and his wife met at the dinner-table that evening as if nothing unusual had occurred, both having concluded to ignore all that had transpired, if possible. Mrs. Arnot saw that her husband had only acted characteristically, and, from his point of view, correctly. Perhaps his recent experience would prevent him from being unduly harsh again should there ever be similar cause, which was quite improbable. Since it appeared that she could minister to his happiness in no other way save through her property, she decided to leave him the one meagre gratification of which he was capable.

The future in its general aspects may here be anticipated by briefly stating that the echoes of the affair gradually died away. Mr. Arnot, on the receipt of a check for one thousand dollars from Mrs. Haldane's lawyer, was glad to procure Mr. Melville's release from the bond for which his wife was pledged, by assuring the legal authorities that he would not prosecute. The superior young man, who made free drinks the ambition of his life, had kept himself well informed, and on learning of the order for his arrest left town temporarily for parts unknown. The papers made the most of the sensation, to the disgust of all concerned, but reference to the affair soon dwindled down to an occasional paragraph. The city press concluded editorially that the great manufacturer had been harsh only seemingly, for the sake of effect, and with the understanding that his wife would show a little balancing kindness to the culprit and his aristocratic mother. That Haldane should still remain in the city was explained on the ground that he was ashamed to go home, or that he was not wanted there.

CHAPTER XVII

AT ODDS WITH THE WORLD

HALDANE kept his promise to spend an hour with his mother. While he told her the truth concerning his folly, he naturally tried to place his action in the best light possible. After inducing her to take some slight refreshment, he obtained a close carriage, and saw her safely on the train which would convey her to the city wherein she resided. During the interview she grew much more composed, and quite remorseful that she had not shown greater consideration for her son's feelings, and she urged and even entreated him to return home with her. He remained firm, however, in his resolution, and would receive from her only a very small sum of money, barely enough to sustain him until he could look around for employment.

His mother shared Mrs. Arnot's distrust, greatly doubting the issue of his large hopes and vague plans; but she could only assure him that her home, to which she returned crushed and disconsolate, was also his.

But he felt that return was impossible. He would rather wander to the ends of the earth than shut himself up with his mother and sisters, for he foresaw that their daily moans and repinings would be daily torture. It would be even worse to appear among his old acquaintances and companions, and be taunted with the fact that his first venture from home ended in a common jail. The plan of drifting away to parts unknown, and of partially losing his identity by changing his name, made a cold, dreary impression upon him, like the thought of annihilation, and thus his purpose of remaining in Hillaton, and winning victory on the very ground of his defeat, grew more satisfactory.

But he soon began to learn how serious, how disheartening, is the condition of one who finds society arrayed against him.

It is the fashion to inveigh against the "cold and pitiless world"; but the world has often much excuse for maintaining this character. As society is now constituted, the consequences of wrong-doing are usually terrible and greatly to be dreaded; and all who have unhealthful cravings for forbidden things should be made to realize this. Society very naturally treats harshly those who permit their pleasures and passions to endanger its very existence. People who have toilsomely and patiently erected their homes and placed therein their treasures do not tolerate with much equanimity those who appear to have no other calling than that of recklessly playing with fire. The well-to-do, conservative world has no inclination to make things pleasant for those who propose to gratify themselves at any and every cost; and if the culprit pleads, "I did not realize—I meant no great harm," the retort comes back, "But you do the harm; you endanger everything. If you have not sense or principle enough to act wisely and well, do not expect us to risk our fortunes with either fools or knaves." And the man or the woman who has preferred pleasure or passing gratification or transient advantage to that priceless possession, a good name, has little ground for complaint. If society readily condoned those grave offences which threaten chaos, thousands who are now restrained by salutary fear would act out disastrously the evil lurking in their hearts. As long as the instinct of self-preservation remains, the world will seem cold and pitiless.

But it often is so to a degree that cannot be too severely condemned. The world is the most soulless of all corporations. In dealing with the criminal or unfortunate classes it generalizes to such an extent that exceptional cases have little chance of a special hearing. If by any means, however, such a hearing can be obtained, the world is usually just, and often quite generous. But in the main it says to all: "Keep your proper places in the ranks. If you fall out, we must leave you behind; if you make trouble, we must abate you as a nuisance." This certainty has the effect of keeping many in their places who otherwise would drop out and make trouble, and is, so far, wholesome. And yet, in spite of this warning truth, the wayside of life is lined with those who, for some reason, have become disabled and have fallen out of their places; and miserably would many of them perish did not the Spirit of Him who came "to seek and save the lost" animate true followers like Mrs. Arnot, leading them likewise to go out after the lame, the wounded, and the morally leprous.

Haldane was sorely wounded, but he chose to make his appeal wholly to the world. Ignoring Heaven, and those on earth representing Heaven's forgiving and saving mercy, he went out alone, in the spirit of pride and self-confidence, to deal with those who would meet him solely on the ground of self-interest. How this law works against such as have shown themselves unworthy of trust, he at once began to receive abundant proof.

He returned to the hotel whence he had just taken his mother, but the proprietor declined to give him lodgings. It was a house that cherished its character for quietness and eminent respectability, and a young gambler and embezzler just out of prison would prove an ill-omened guest. On receiving a cold and peremptory refusal to his application, and in the presence of several others, Haldane stalked haughtily away; but there was misgiving and faintness at his heart. Such a public rebuff was a new and strange experience.

With set teeth and lips compressed he next resolved to go to the very hotel where he had committed his crime, and from that starting-point fight his way up. He found the public room more than usually well filled with loungers, and could not help discovering, as he entered, that he was the subject of their loud and unsavory conversation. The "Evening Spy" had just been read, and all were very busy discussing the scandal. As the knowledge of his presence and identity was speedily conveyed to one and another in loud whispers, the noisy tongues ceased, and the young man found himself the centre of an embarrassing amount of observation. But he endeavored to give the idlers a defiant and careless glance as he walked up to the proprietor and asked for a room.

"No, sir!" replied that virtuous individual, with sharp emphasis; "you have had a room of me once too often. It's not my way to ·have gamblers, bloats, and jail-birds hanging around my place—'not if the court knows herself; and she thinks she does.' You've done all you could to give my respectable, first-class house the name of a low gambling hell. The evening paper even hints that some one connected with the house had a hand in your being plucked. You've damaged me hundreds of dollars, and if you ever show your face within my doors again I'll have you arrested."

Haldane was stung to the quick, and retorted vengefully:

"Perhaps the paper is right. I was introduced to the blacklegs in your bar-room, and by a scamp who was a habitual lounger here. They got their cards of you, and, having made me drunk, and robbed me in one of your rooms, they had no trouble in getting away."

"Do you make any such charge against me?" bellowed the landlord, starting savagely forward.

"I say, as the paper says, *perhaps*," replied Haldane, standing his ground, but quivering with rage. "I shall give you no ground for a libel suit; but if you will come out in the street you shall have all the satisfaction you want; and if you lay the weight of your finger on me here, I'll damage you worse than I did last night."

"How dare you come here to insult me?" said the landlord, but keeping now at a safe distance from the incensed youth. "Some one, go for a policeman, for the fellow is out of jail years too soon."

"I did not come here to insult you, I came, as every one has a right to come, to ask for a room, for which I meant to pay your price, and you insulted me."

"Well, you can't have a room."

"If you had quietly said that and no more in the first place, there would have been no trouble. But I want you and every one else to understand that I won't be struck, if I am down;" and he turned on his heel and strode out of the house, followed by a volley of curses from the enraged landlord and the bartender, who had smirked so agreeably the evening before.

A distorted account of this scene—published in the "Courier" the following day, in connection with a detailed account of the whole miserable affair—added considerably to the ill repute that already burdened Haldane; for it was intimated that he was as ready for a street brawl as for any other species of lawlessness.

The "Courier," having had the nose of its representative demolished by Haldane, was naturally prejudiced against him; and, influenced by its darkly-colored narrative, the citizens shook their heads over the young man, and concluded that he was a dangerous character, who had become unnaturally and precociously depraved; and there was quite a general hope that Mr. Arnot would not fail to prosecute, so that the town might be rid of one who promised to continue a source of trouble.

The "Spy," a rival paper, showed a tendency to dwell on the extenuating circumstances. But it is so much easier for a community to believe evil rather than good of a person, that mere excuses and apologies, and the suggestion that the youth had been victimized, had little weight. Besides, the world shows a tendency to detest weak fools even more than knaves.

After his last bitter experience Haldane felt unwilling to

venture to another hotel, and he endeavored to find a quiet boarding-place; but as soon as he mentioned his name, the keepers, male and female, suddenly discovered that they had no rooms. Night was near, and his courage was beginning to fail him, when he at last found a thrifty gentlewoman who gave far more attention to her housewifely cares than to the current news. She readily received the well-dressed stranger, and showed him to his room. Haldane did not hide his name from her, for he resolved to spend the night in the street before dropping a name which now seemed to turn people from him as if contagion lurked in it, and he was relieved to find that, as yet, it had to her no disgraceful associations. He was bent on securing one good night's rest, and so excused himself from going down to supper, lest he should meet some one that knew him. After nightfall he slipped out to an obscure restaurant for his supper.

His precaution, however, was vain, for on his return to his room he encountered in a hallway one of the loungers who had witnessed the recent scene at the hotel. After a second's stare the man passed on down to the shabby-genteel parlor, and soon whist, novels, and papers were dropped, as the immaculate little community learned of the contaminating presence beneath the same roof with themselves.

"A man just out of prison! A man merely released on bail, and who would certainly be convicted and tried!"

With a virtue which might have put "Cæsar's wife" to the blush, sere and withered gentlewomen pursed up their mouths, and declared that they could not sleep in the same house with such a disreputable person. The thrifty landlady, whose principle of success was the concentration of all her faculties on the task of satisfying the digestive organs of her patrons, found herself for once at fault, and she was quite surprised to learn what a high-toned class of people she was entertaining.

But, then, "business is business." Poor Haldane was

but one uncertain lodger, and here were a dozen or more "regulars" arrayed against him. The sagacious woman was not long in climbing to the door of the obnoxious guest, and her very knock said, "What are you doing here?"

Haldane's first thought was, "She is a woman; she will not have the heart to turn me away." He had become so weary and disheartened that his pride was failing him, and he was ready to plead for the chance of a little rest. Therefore he opened the door, and invited the landlady to enter in the most conciliating manner. But no such poor chaff would be of any avail with one of Mrs. Gruppins' experience, and looking straight before her, as if addressing no one in particular, she said sententiously:

"I wish this room vacated within a half-hour."

"If you have the heart of a woman you will not send me out this rainy night. I am weary and sick in body and mind. I wouldn't turn a dog out in the night and storm."

"You ought to be ashamed of yourself, sir," said Mrs. Gruppins, turning on him indignantly; "to think that you should take advantage of a poor and defenceless widow, and me so inexperienced and ignorant of the wicked world."

"I did not take advantage of your ignorance. I told you who I was, and am able to pay for the room. In the morning I will leave your house, if you have so much objection to my remaining."

"Why shouldn't I object? I never had such as you here before. All my boarders"—she added in a louder tone, for the benefit of those who were listening at the foot of the stairs—"all my boarders are peculiarly respectable people, and I would not have them scandalized by your presence here another minute if I could help it."

"How much do I owe you?" asked Haldane, in a tone that was harsh from its suppressed emotion.

"I don't want any of your money—I don't want anything to do with people who are lodged at the expense of

the State.   If you took money last night, there is no telling what you will take to-night."

Haldane snatched his hat and rushed from the house,
overwhelmed with a deeper and more terrible sense of
shame and degradation than he had ever imagined possible.   He had become a pariah, and in bitterness of heart
was realizing the truth.

CHAPTER XVIII

THE WORLD'S VERDICT—OUR KNIGHT A CRIMINAL

A FEW moments before his interview with the thrifty and respectable Mrs. Gruppins, Haldane had supposed himself too weary to drag one foot after the other in search of another resting-place; and therefore his eager hope that that obdurate female might not be gifted with the same quality of "in'ards" which Pat M'Cabe ascribed to Mr. Arnot. He had, indeed, nearly reached the limit of endurance, for had he been in his best and most vigorous condition, a day which taxed so terribly both body and mind would have drained his vitality to the point of exhaustion. As it was, the previous night's debauch told against him like a term of illness. He had since taken food insufficiently and irregularly, and was, therefore, in no condition to meet the extraordinary demands of the ordeal through which he was passing. Mental distress, moreover, is far more wearing than physical effort, and his anguish of mind had risen several times during the day almost to frenzy.

In spite of all this, the sharp and pitiless tongue of Mrs. Gruppins goaded him again to the verge of desperation, and he strode rapidly and aimlessly away, through the night and storm, with a wilder tempest raging in his breast. But the gust of feeling died away as suddenly as it had arisen, and left him ill and faint. A telegraph pole was near, and he leaned against it for support.

"Move on," growled a passing policeman.

"Will you do me a kindness?" asked Haldane; "I am

poor and sick—a stranger.   Tell me where I can hire a bed
for a small sum."

The policeman directed him down a side street, saying,
"You can get a bed at No. 13, and no questions asked."

There was unspeakable comfort in the last assurance,
for it now seemed that he could hope to find a refuge only
in places where "no questions were asked."

With difficulty the weary youth reached the house, and
by paying a small extra sum was able to obtain a wretched
little room to himself; but never did storm-tossed and endangered sailors enter a harbor's quiet waters with a greater
sense of relief than did Haldane as he crept up into this
squalid nook, which would at least give him a little respite
from the world's terrible scorn.

What a priceless gift for the unhappy, the unfortunate
—yes, and for the guilty—is sleep! Many seem to think of
the body only as a clog, impeding mental action—as a weight,
chaining the spirit down. Were the mind, in its activity,
independent of the body—were the wounded spirit unable
to forget its pain—could the guilty conscience sting inces-
santly—then the chief human industry would come to be
the erection of asylums for the insane. But by an unfathomable mystery the tireless regal spirit has been
blended with the flesh and blood of its servant, the body.
In heaven, where there is neither sin nor pain, even the
body becomes spiritual; but on earth, where it so often
happens, as in the case of poor Haldane, that to think and
to remember is torture, it is a blessed thing that the body,
formed from the earth, often becomes heavy as earth, and
rests upon the spirit for a few hours at least, like the clods
with which we fill the grave.

The morning of the following day was quite well advanced when Haldane awoke from his long oblivion, and,
after regaining consciousness, he lay a full hour longer trying to realize his situation, and to think of some plan by
which he might best recover his lost position. As he recalled all that had occurred he began to understand the

extreme difficulty of his task, and he even queried whether
it were possible for him to succeed. If the respectable would
not even give him shelter, how could he hope that they would
employ and trust him?

After he had partaken of quite a hearty breakfast, however, his fortunes began to wear a less forbidding aspect.
Endowed with youth, health, and, as he believed, with
more than usual ability, he felt that there was scarcely
occasion for despair. Some one would employ him—some
one would give him another chance. He would take any
respectable work that would give him a foothold, and by
some vague, fortunate means, which the imagination of
the young always supplies, he would achieve success that
would obliterate the memory of the past. Therefore, with
flashes of hope in his heart, he started out to seek his fortune, and commenced applying at the various stores and
offices of the city.

So far from giving any encouragement, people were
much surprised that he had the assurance to ask to be
employed and trusted again. The majority dismissed him
coldly and curtly. A few mongrel natures, true to themselves, gave a snarling refusal. Then there were jovial
spirits who must have their jest, even though the sensitive
subject of it was tortured thereby—men who enjoyed quiz-
zing Haldane before sending him on, as much as the old
inquisitors relished a little recreation with hot pincers and
thumb-screws. There were also conscientious people,
whose worldly prudence prevented them from giving employment to one so damaged in character, and yet who felt
constrained to give some good advice. To this, it must be
confessed, Haldane listened with very poor grace, thus ex-
tending the impression that he was a rather hopeless subject.

"Good God!" he exclaimed, interrupting an old gentleman who was indulging in some platitudes to the effect that
the "way of the transgressor is hard"—"I would rather
black your boots than listen to such talk. What I want
is work—a chance to live honestly. What's the use of tell-

ing a fellow not to go to the devil, and then practically send him to the devil ?''

The old gentleman was somewhat shocked and offended, and coldly intimated that he had no need of the young man's services.

A few spoke kindly and seemed truly sorry for him, but they either had no employment to give, or, on business principles, felt that they could not introduce among their other assistants one under bonds to appear and be tried for a State-prison offence that was already the same as proved.

After receiving rebuffs, and often what he regarded as insults, for hours, the young man's hope began to fail him utterly. His face grew pale and haggard, not only from fatigue, but from that which tells disastrously almost as soon upon the body as upon the mind—discouragement. He saw that he had not yet fully realized the consequences of his folly. The deep and seemingly implacable resentment of society was a continued surprise. He was not conscious of being a monster of wickedness, and it seemed to him that after his bitter experience he would rather starve than again touch what was not his own.

But the trouble is, the world does not give us much credit for what we think, feel, and imagine, even if aware of our thoughts. It is what we *do* that forms public opinion; and it was both natural and just that the public should have a very decided opinion of one who had recently shown himself capable of gambling, drunkenness, and practical theft.

And yet the probabilities were that if some kind, just man had bestowed upon Haldane both employment and trust, with a chance to rise, his bitter lesson would have made him scrupulously careful to shun his peculiar temptations from that time forward. But the world usually regards one who has committed a crime as a criminal, and treats him as such. It cannot, if it would, nicely calculate the hidden moral state and future chances. It acts on sound generalities, regardless of the exceptions; and thus it often happens that men and women who at first can scarcely understand the world's adverse opinion, are disheartened by it, and at last come to merit the worst that can be said or thought.

As, at the time of his first arrest, Haldane had found his eyes drawn by a strange, cruel fascination to every scornful or curious face upon the street, so now he began to feel a morbid desire to know just what people were saying and thinking of him. He purchased both that day's papers and those of the previous day, and, finding a little out-of-the-way restaurant kept by a foreigner, he "supped full with"—what were to him emphatically—"horrors"; the dinner and supper combined, which he had ordered, growing cold, in the meantime, and as uninviting as the place in which it was served.

His eyes dwelt longest upon those sentences which were the most unmercifully severe, and they seemed to burn their way into his very soul. Was he in truth such a miscreant as the "Courier" described? Mrs. Arnot had not shrunk from him as from contamination; but she was different from all other people that he had known; and he now remembered, also, that even she always referred to his act in a grave, troubled way, as if both its character and consequences were serious indeed.

There was such a cold, leaden despondency burdening his heart that he felt that he must have relief of some kind. Although remembering his rash invocation of fatal consequences to himself should he touch again that which had brought him so much evil, he now, with a reckless oath, muttered that he "needed some liquor, and would have it."

Having finished a repast from which he would have turned in disgust before his fortunes had so greatly altered, and having gained a little temporary courage from the more than doubtful brandy served in such a place, he obtained permission to sit by the fire and smoke away the blustering evening, for he felt no disposition to face the world again that day. The German proprietor and his beer-drinking patrons paid no attention to the stranger, and as he sat off on one side by himself at a table, with a mug of lager before him, he was practically as much alone, and as lonely, as if in a desert.

In a dull, vague way it occurred to him that it was very fitting that those present should speak in a foreign and unknown tongue, and act and look differently from all classes of people formerly known to him. He was in a different world, and it was appropriate that everything should appear strange and unfamiliar.

Finding that he could have a room in this same little, dingy restaurant-hotel, where he had obtained his supper, he resolved that he would torture himself no more that night with thoughts of the past or future, but slowly stupefy himself into sleep.

CHAPTER XIX

THE WORLD'S BEST OFFER—A PRISON

AFTER a walk in the sweet April sunshine the following morning, a hearty breakfast, and a general rallying of the elastic forces of youth, Haldane felt that he had not yet reached the "brink of dark despair."

Indeed, he had an odd sense of pride that he had survived the ordeal of the last two days, and still felt as well as he did. Although it was but an Arab's life, in which every man's hand seemed against him, yet he still lived, and concluded that he could continue to live indefinitely.

He did not go out again, as on the previous day, to seek employment, but sat down and tried to think his way into the future somewhat.

The first question that presented itself was, Should he in any contingency return home to his mother?

He was not long in deciding adversely, for it seemed to him to involve such a bitter mortification that he felt he would rather starve.

Should he send to her for money?

That would be scarcely less humiliating, for it was equivalent to a confession that he could not even take care of himself, much less achieve all the brave things he had intimated. He was still more averse to going to Mrs. Arnot for what would seem charity to her husband and to every one else who might hear of it. The probability, also, that Laura would learn of such an appeal for aid made him scout the very thought.

Should he go away among strangers, change his name,

and commence life anew, unburdened by the weight which now dragged him down?

The thought of cutting himself off utterly from all whom he knew, or who cared for him, caused a cold, shivering sense of dread. It would, also, be a confession of defeat, an acknowledgment that he could not accomplish what he had promised to himself and to others. He had, moreover, sufficient forethought to perceive that any success which he might achieve elsewhere, and under another name, would be such a slight and baseless fabric that a breath from one who now knew him could overturn it. He might lead an honorable life for years, and yet no one would believe him honorable after discovering that he was living under an *alias* and concealing a crime. If he could build himself up in Hillaton he would be founded on the rock of truth, and need fear no disastrous reverses from causes against which he could not guard.

Few can be more miserable than those who hold their fortunes and good name on sufferance—safe only in the power and disposition of others to keep some wretched secret; and he is but little better off who fears that every stranger arriving in town may recognize in his face the features of one that, years before, by reason of some disgraceful act, fled from himself and all who knew him. The more Haldane thought upon the scheme of losing his identity, and of becoming that vague, and, as yet, unnamed stranger, who after years of exile would still be himself, though to the world not himself, the less attractive it became.

He finally concluded that, as he had resolved to remain in Hillaton, he would keep his resolution, and that, as he had plainly stated his purpose to lift himself up by his own unaided efforts, he would do so if it were possible; and if it were not, he would live the life of a laborer—a tramp, even—rather than "skulk back," as he expressed it, to those who were once kindred and companions.

"If I cannot walk erect to their front doors, I will never crawl around to the back entrances. If I ever must take alms to keep from starving, it will be from strangers. I shall never inflict myself as a dead weight and a painfully tolerated infamy on any one. I was able to get myself into this disgusting slough, and if I haven't brains and pluck enough to get myself out, I will remain at this, my level, to which I have fallen.''

Thus pride still counselled and controlled, and yet it was a kind of pride that inspires something like respect. It proved that there was much good metal in the crude, misshapen ore of his nature.

But the necessity of doing something was urgent, for the sum he had been willing to receive from his mother was small, and rapidly diminishing.

Among the possible activities in which he might engage, that of writing for papers and magazines occurred to him, and the thought at once caught and fired his imagination. The mysteries of the literary world were the least known to him, and therefore it offered the greatest amount of vague promise and indefinite hope. Here a path might open to both fame and fortune. The more he dwelt on the possibility the more it seemed to take the aspect of probability. Under the signature of E. H. he would write thrilling tales, until the public insisted upon knowing the great unknown. Then he could reverse present experience by scorning those who had scorned him. He recalled all that he had ever read about genius toiling in its attic until the world was compelled to recognize and do homage to the regal mind. He would remain in seclusion also; he would burn midnight oil until he should come to be known as Haldane the brilliant writer instead of Haldane the gambler, drunkard, and thief.

All on fire with his new project, he sallied forth to the nearest news-stand, and selected two or three papers and magazines, whose previous interest to him and known popularity suggested that they were the best mediums in which he could rise upon the public as a literary star, all the more attractive because unnamed and unknown.

His next proceeding indicated a commendable amount of shrewdness, and proved that his roseate visions resulted more from ignorance and inexperience than from innate foolishness. He carefully read the periodicals he had bought, in the hope of obtaining hints and suggestions from their contents which would aid him in producing acceptable manuscripts. Some of the sketches and stories appeared very simple, the style flowing along as smoothly and limpidly as a summer brook through the meadows. He did not see why he could not write in a similar vein, perhaps more excitingly and interestingly. In his partial and neglected course of study he had not given much attention to *belles-lettres*, and was not aware that the simplicity and lucid purity of thought which made certain pages so easily read were produced by the best trained and most cultured talent existing among the regular contributors.

He spent the evening and the greater part of a sleepless night in constructing a crude plot of a story, and, having procured writing materials, hastened through an early breakfast, the following morning, in his eagerness to enter on what now seemed a shining path to fame.

He sat down and dipped his pen in ink. The blank, white page was before him, awaiting his brilliant and burning thoughts; but for some reason they did not and would not come. This puzzled him. He could dash off a letter, and write with ease a plain business statement. Why could he not commence and go on with his story?

"How do those other fellows commence?" he mentally queried, and he again carefully read and examined the opening paragraphs of two or three tales that had pleased him. They seemed to commence and go forward very easily and naturally. Why could not he do the same?

To his dismay he found that he could not. He might as well have sat down and hoped to have deftly and skilfully constructed a watch as to have imitated the style of the stories that most interested him, for he had never formed even the power, much less the habit, of composition.

After a few labored and inconsequential sentences, which seemed like crude ore instead of the molten, burning metal of thought left to cool in graceful molds, he threw aside his pen in despair.

After staring despondently for a time at the blank page, which now promised to remain as blank as the future then seemed, the fact suddenly occurred to him that even genius often spurred its flagging or dormant powers by stimulants. Surely, then, he, in his pressing emergency, had a right to avail himself of this aid. A little brandy might awaken his imagination, which would then kindle with his theme.

At any rate, he had no objection to the brandy, and with this inspiration he again resumed his pen. He was soon astonished and delighted with the result, for he found himself writing with ease and fluency. His thoughts seemed to become vivid and powerful, and his story grew rapidly. As body and mind flagged, the potent genii in the black bottle again lifted and soared on with him until the marvellous tale was completed.

He decided to correct the manuscript on the following day, and was so complacent and hopeful over his performance that he scarcely noted that he was beginning to feel wretchedly from the inevitable reaction. The next day, with dull and aching head he tried to read what he had written, but found it dreary and disappointing work. His sentences and paragraphs appeared like clouds from which the light had faded; but he explained this fact to himself on the ground of his depressed physical state, and he went through his task with dogged persistence.

He felt better on the following day, and with the aid of the bottle he resolved to give his inventive genius another flight. On this occasion he would attempt a longer story— one that would occupy him several days—and he again stimulated himself up to a condition in which he found at least no lack of words. When he attained what he supposed was his best mood, he read over again the work of the preceding day, and was delighted to find that it now glowed with prismatic hues. In his complacence he at once despatched it to the paper for which it was designed.

Three or four days of alternate work and brooding passed, and if various and peculiar moods prove the possession of genius, Haldane certainly might claim it. Between his sense of misfortune and disgrace, and the fact that his funds were becoming low, on one hand, and his towering hopes and shivering fears concerning his literary ventures, on the other, he was emphatically in what is termed "a state of mind" continuously. These causes alone were sufficient to make mental serenity impossible; but the after-effects of the decoction from which he obtained his inspiration were even worse, and after a week's work the thought occurred to him more than once that if he pursued a literary life, either his genius or that which he imbibed as its spur would consume him utterly.

By the time the first two stories were finished he found that it would be necessary to supplement the labors of his pen. He would have to wait at least a few days before he could hope for any returns, even though he had urged in his accompanying notes prompt acceptance and remittance for their value.

He went to the office of the "Evening Spy," the paper which had shown some lenience toward him, and offered his services as writer, or reporter; and, although taught by harsh experience not to hope for very much, he was a little surprised at the peremptory manner in which his services were declined. His face seemed to ask an explanation, and the editor said briefly:

"We did not bear down very hard on you—it's not our custom; but both inclination and necessity lead us to require that every one and everything connected with this paper should be eminently respectable and deserving of respect. Good-morning, sir."

Haldane's pre-eminence consisted only in his lack of respectability; and after the brave visions of the past week, based on his literary toil, this cool, sharp-cut statement of society's opinion quenched about all hope of ever rising by first gaining recognition and employment among those whose position was similar to what his own had been. As he plodded his way back to the miserable little foreign restaurant, his mind began to dwell on this question:

"Is there any place in the world for one who has committed a crime, save a prison?"

CHAPTER XX

MAIDEN AND WOOD-SAWYER

B EFORE utterly abandoning all hope of finding employment that should in some small degree preserve an air of respectability, Haldane resolved to give up one more day to the search, and on the following morning he started out and walked until nightfall. He even offered to take the humblest positions that would insure him a support and some recognition; but the record of his action while in Mr. Arnot's employ followed him everywhere, creating sufficient prejudice in every case to lead to a refusal of his application. Some said "No" reluctantly and hesitatingly, as if kindly feelings within took the young man's part; but they said it, nevertheless.

For the patient resolution with which he continued to apply to all kinds of people and places, hour after hour, in spite of such disheartening treatment, he deserved much praise; but he did not receive any; and at last, weary and despondent, he returned to his miserable lodgings. He was so desperately depressed in body and mind that the contents of the black bottle seemed his only resource.

Such a small sum now remained that he felt that something must be done instantly. He concluded that his only course now was to go out and pick up any odd bits of work that he could find. He hoped that by working half the time he might make enough to pay for his board at his present cheap lodging-place. This would leave him time to continue his writing, and in the course of a week more he would certainly hear from the manuscripts already forwarded. On these he now built nearly all his hope. If they were well received and paid for, he considered his fortunes substantially restored, and fame almost a certainty in the future. If he could only produce a few more manuscripts, and bridge over the intervening time until he could hear from them, he felt that his chief difficulties would be past.

Having decided to do a laborer's work, he at once resolved to exchange his elegant broadcloth for a laborer's suit, and he managed this transfer so shrewdly that he obtained quite a little sum of money in addition.

It was well that he did replenish his finances somewhat, for his apparently phlegmatic landlord was as wary as a veteran mouser in looking after his small interests. He had just obtained an inkling as to Haldane's identity, and, while he was not at all chary concerning the social and moral standing of his few uncertain lodgers, he proposed henceforth that all transactions with the suspicious stranger should be on a strictly cash basis.

It was the busy spring-time, and labor was in great demand. Haldane wandered off to the suburbs, and, as an ordinary laborer, offered his services in cleaning up yards, cutting wood, or forking over a space of garden ground. His stalwart form and prepossessing appearance generally secured him a favorable answer, but before he was through with his task he often received a sound scolding for his unskilful and bungling style of work. But he in part made up by main strength what he lacked in skill, and after two or three days he acquired considerable deftness in his unwonted labors, and felt the better for them. They counteracted the effects of his literary efforts, or, more correctly, his means of inspiration in them.

Thus another week passed, of which he gave three days to the production of two or three more brief manuscripts, and during the following week he felt sure that he would hear from those first sent.

He wrote throughout the hours of daylight on Sunday,

scarcely leaving his chair, and drank more deeply than usual. In consequence, he felt wretchedly on Monday, and, therefore, strolled off to look for some employment that would not tax his aching head. Hitherto he had avoided all localities where he would be apt to meet those who knew him; and by reason of his brief residence in town there were comparatively few who were familiar with his features. He now recalled the fact that he had often seen from his window, while an inmate of Mrs. Arnot's home, quite a collection of cottages across a small ravine that ran a little back of that lady's residence. He might find some work among them, and he yielded to the impulse to look again upon the place where such rich and abundant happiness had once seemed within his grasp.

For several days he had been conscious of a growing desire to hear from his mother and Mrs. Arnot, and often found himself wondering how they regarded his mysterious disappearance, or whether reports of his vain inquiry for work had reached them.

With a pride and resolution that grew obstinate with time and failure, he resolved that he would not communicate with them until he had something favorable to tell; and he hoped, and almost believed, that before many days passed, he could address to them a literary weekly paper in which they would find, in prominent position, the underscored initials of E. H. Until he could be preceded by the first flashes of fame he would remain in obscurity. He would not even let Mrs. Arnot know where he was hiding, so that she might send to him his personal effects left at her house. Indeed, he had no place for them now, and was, besides, more morbidly bent than ever on making good the proud words he had spoken. If, in the face of such tremendous odds he could, alone and unaided, with nothing but his hands and brain, win again all and more than he had lost, he could compel the respect and admiration of those who had witnessed his downfall and consequent victorious struggle.

Was the girl who had inspired his sudden, and, as he had supposed, "undying" passion, forgotten during these trying days? Yes, to a great extent. His self-love was greater than his love for Laura Romeyn. He craved intensely to prove that he was no longer a proper object of her scorn. She had rejected him as a slave to "disgusting vices," and such he had apparently shown himself to be; but now he would have been willing to have dipped his pen in his own blood, and have written away his life, if thereby he could have filled her with admiration and regret. Although he scarcely acknowledged it to himself, perhaps the subtlest and strongest impulse to his present course was the hope of teaching her that he was not what she now regarded him. But he was not at that time capable of a strong, true affection for any one, and thoughts of the pretty maiden wounded his pride more than his heart.

After arriving at the further bank of the ravine, back of Mrs. Arnot's residence, he sat down for a while, and gave himself up to a very bitter revery. There, in the bright spring sunshine, was the beautiful villa which might have been a second home to him. The gardener was at work among the shrubbery, and the sweet breath of crocuses and hyacinths was floated to him on the morning breeze. There were the windows of his airy, lovely room, in comparison with which the place in which he now slept was a kennel. If he had controlled and hidden his passion, if he had waited and wooed patiently, skilfully, winning first esteem and friendship, and then affection, yonder garden paths might have witnessed many happy hours spent with the one whom he loved as well as he could love any one save himself. But now—and he cursed himself and his folly.

Poor fellow! He might as well have said, "If I had not been myself, all this might have been as I have imagined." He had acted naturally, and in accordance with his defective character; he had been himself, and that was the secret of all his troubles. He sprang up, exclaiming in anger:

"Mother made a weak fool of me, and I was willing to be a fool. Now we are bothing reaping our reward."

He went off among the cottages looking for employment, but found little encouragement. The people were, as a general thing, in humble circumstances, and did their work among themselves. But at last he found, near the ravine, a small dwelling standing quite apart from any others, before which a load of wood had been thrown. The poor woman whose gateway it obstructed was anxious to have it sawed up and carried to her little wood-shed, but was disposed to haggle about the price.

"Give me what you please," said Haldane, throwing off his coat; "I take the job;" and in a few moments the youth who had meditated indefinite heights of "gloomy grandeur" appeared—save to the initiated—as if he had been born a wood-sawyer.

He was driving his saw in the usual strong, dogged manner in which he performed such tasks, when a light step caused him to look up suddenly, and he found himself almost face to face with Laura Romeyn. He started violently; the blood first receded from his face, and then rushed tumultuously back. She, too, seemed much surprised and startled, and stopped hesitatingly, as if she did not know what to do. But Haldane had no doubt as to his course. He felt that he had no right to speak to her, and that she might regard it as an insult if he did; therefore he bent down to his work again with a certain proud humility which Laura, even in her perturbation, did not fail to notice.

In her diffidence and confusion she continued past him a few steps, and, although he expected nothing less, the fact that she did not recognize or speak to him cut to his heart with a deeper pain than he had yet suffered. With a gesture similar to that which he made when she saw him on the way to prison, he dashed his hat down over his eyes, and drove his saw through the wood with savage energy.

She looked at him doubtfully for a moment, then yield-

ing to her impulse, came to his side. His first intimation
of her presence was the scarcely heard tones of her voice
mingling with the harsh rasping of the saw.

"Will you not speak to me, Mr. Haldane?" she asked.

He dropped his saw, stood erect, trembled slightly, but
did not answer or even raise his eyes to her face. His pain
was so great he was not sure of his self-control.

"Perhaps," she added timidly, "you do not wish me to
speak to you."

"I now have no right to speak to you, Miss Romeyn,"
he answered in a tone which his suppressed feelings rendered constrained and almost harsh.

"But I feel sorry for you," said she quickly, "and so
does my aunt, and she greatly—"

"I have not asked for your pity," interrupted Haldane,
growing more erect and almost haughty in his bearing,
quite oblivious for a moment of his shirt-sleeves and buck-
saw. What is more, he made Laura forget them also, and
his manner embarrassed her greatly. She was naturally
gentle and timid, and she deferred so far to his mood that
one would have thought that she was seeking to obtain
kindness rather than to confer it.

"You misunderstand me," said she: "I do respect you
for the brave effort you are making. I respect you for
doing this work. You cannot think it strange, though,
that I am sorry for all that has happened. But I did not
intend to speak of myself at all—of Mrs. Arnot rather,
and your mother. They do not know where to find you,
and wish to see and hear from you very much. Mrs. Arnot
has letters to you from your mother."

"The time shall come—it may not be so very far distant,
Miss Romeyn—when it will be no condescension on your
part to speak to me," said Haldane loftily, ignoring all that
related to Mrs. Arnot and his mother, even if he heard it.

"I do not feel it to be condescension now," replied
Laura, with almost the frank simplicity of a child. "I cannot help feeling sympathy for you, even though you are

too proud to receive it." Then she added, with a trace of dignity and maidenly pride, "Perhaps when you have realized your hopes, and have become rich or famous, I may not choose to speak to you. But it is not my nature to turn from any one in misfortune, much less any one whom I have known well."

He looked at her steadily for a moment, and his lip quivered slightly with his softening feeling.

"You do not scorn me, then, like the rest of the world," said he in a low tone.

Tears stood in the young girl's eyes as she answered, "Mr. Haldane, I do feel deeply for you; I know you have done very wrong, but that only makes you suffer more."

"How can you overlook the wrong of my action? Others think I am not fit to be spoken to," he asked, in a still lower tone.

"I do not overlook the wrong," said she, gravely; "it seems strange and terrible to me; and yet I do feel sorry for you, from the depths of my heart, and I wish I could help you."

"You have helped me," said he, impetuously; "you have spoken the first truly kind word that has blessed me since I bade mother good-by. I was beginning to hate the hard-hearted animals known as men and women. They trample me down like a herd of buffaloes."

"Won't you go with me and see Mrs. Arnot? She has letters for you, and she greatly wishes to see you."

He shook his head.

"Why not?"

"I have the same as made a vow that I will never approach any one to whom I held my old relations until I regain at least as good a name and position as I lost. I little thought we should meet soon again, if ever, and still less that you would speak to me as you have done."

"I had been taking some delicacies from auntie to a poor sick woman, and was just returning," said Laura, blushing slightly. "I think your vow is very wrong. Your pride brings grief to your mother, and pain to your good friend, Mrs. Arnot.''

''I cannot help it,'' said he, in a manner that was gloomy and almost sullen; ''I got myself into this slough, and I intend to get myself out of it. I shall not take alms from any one.''

''A mother cannot give her son alms,'' said Laura simply.

''The first words my mother said to me when my heart was breaking were, 'You have disgraced me.' When I have accomplished that which will honor her I will return.''

''I know from what auntie said that your mother did not mean any unkindness, and you surely know that you have a friend in Mrs. Arnot.''

''Mrs. Arnot *has* been a true friend, and no small part of my punishment is the thought of how I have requited her kindness. I reverence and honor her more than any other woman, and I did not know that you were so much like her. You both seem different from all the rest of the world. But I shall take no advantage of her kindness or yours.''

''Mr. Haldane,'' said Laura gravely, but with rising color, ''I am not a woman. In years and feelings I am scarcely more than a child. It may not be proper or conventional for me to stop and talk so long to you, but I have acted from the natural impulse of a young girl brought up in a secluded country home. I shall return thither to-morrow, and I am glad I have seen you once more, for I wished you to know that I did feel sorry for you, and that I hoped you might succeed. I greatly wish you would see Mrs. Arnot, or let me tell her where she can see you, and send to you what she wishes. She has heard of you once or twice, but does not know where to find you. Will you not let me tell her?''

He shook his head decidedly.

''Well, then, good-by,'' said she kindly, and was about to depart.

"Wait," he said hastily; "will you do me one small favor?"

"Yes, if I ought."

"This is my father's watch and chain," he continued, taking them off. "They are not safe with me in my present life. I do not wish to have it in my power to take them to a pawnshop. I would rather starve first, and yet I would rather not be tempted. I can't explain. You cannot and should not know anything about the world in which I am living. Please give these to Mrs. Arnot, and ask her to keep them till I come for them; or she can send them, with the rest of my effects, to my mother. I have detained you too long already. Whatever may be my fate, I shall always remember you with the deepest gratitude and respect."

There was distress in Laura's face as he spoke; but she took the watch and chain without a word, for she saw that he was fully resolved upon his course.

"I know that Mrs. Arnot will respect my wish to remain in obscurity until I can come with a character differing from that which I now bear. Your life would be a very happy one, Miss Romeyn, if my wishes could make it so;" and the wood-sawyer bowed his farewell with the grace and dignity of a gentleman, in spite of his coarse laborer's garb. He then resumed his work, to the great relief of the woman, who had caught glimpses of the interview from her window, wondering and surmising why the "young leddy from the big house" should have so much to say to a wood-sawyer.

"If she had a-given him a tract upon leavin', it would a-seemed more nateral like," she explained to a crony the latter part of the day.

Mrs. Arnot did respect Haldane's desire to be left to himself until he came in the manner that his pride dictated; but, after hearing Laura's story, she cast many a wistful glance toward the one who, in spite of his grave faults and weaknesses, deeply interested her, and she sighed:

"He must learn by hard experience."

"Did I do wrong in speaking to him, auntie?" Laura asked.

"I do not think so. Your motive was natural and kindly; and yet I would not like you to meet him again until he is wholly different in character, if that time ever comes."

CHAPTER XXI

MAGNANIMOUS MR. SHRUMPF

AFTER the excitement caused by his unexpected interview with Laura subsided, and Haldane was able to think it over quietly, it seemed to him that he had burned his ships behind him. He must now make good his proud words, for to go "crawling back" after what he had said to-day, and, of all persons, to the one whose opinion he most valued—this would be a humiliation the thought of which even he could not endure.

Having finished his task, he scarcely glanced at the pittance which the woman reluctantly gave him, and went straight to the city post-office. He was so agitated with conflicting hopes and fears that his voice trembled as he asked if there were any letters addressed to E. H., and he was so deeply disappointed that he was scarcely willing to take the careless negative given. He even went to the express office, in the vague hope that the wary editors had remitted through them; and the leaden weight of despondency grew heavier at each brisk statement:

"Nothing for E. H."

He was so weary and low-spirited when he reached his dismal lodgings that he felt no disposition either to eat or drink, but sat down in the back part of the wretched, musty saloon, and, drawing his hat over his eyes, he gave himself up to bitter thoughts. With mental imprecations he cursed himself that he had not better understood the young girl who once had been his companion. Never before had she seemed so beautiful as to-day, and she had revealed a forming character as lovely as her person. She *was* like Mrs. Arnot—the woman who seemed to him perfect—and what more could he say in her praise? And yet his folly had placed between them an impassable gulf. He was not misled by her kindness, for he remembered her words, and now believed them, "If I ever love a man he will be one that I can look up to and respect." If he could only have recognized her noble tendencies he might have resolutely set about becoming such a man. If his character had been pleasing to her, his social position would have given him the right to have aspired to her hand. Why had he not had sufficient sense to have realized that she was young—much too young to understand his rash, hasty passion? Why could he not have learned from her pure, delicate face that she might possibly be won by patient and manly devotion, but would be forever repelled from the man who wooed her like a Turk?

In the light of experience he saw his mistakes. From his present depth he looked up, and saw the inestimable vantage ground which he once possessed. In his deep despondency he feared he never would regain it, and that his hopes of literary success would prove delusive.

Regret like a cold, November wind, swept through all his thoughts and memories, and there seemed nothing before him but a chill winter of blight and failure that would have no spring.

But he was not left to indulge his miserable mood very long, for his mousing landlord—having finally learned who Haldane was, and all the unfavorable facts and comments with which the press had abounded—now concluded that he could pounce upon him in such a way that something would be left in his claws before the victim could escape.

That very morning Haldane had paid for his board to date, but had thoughtlessly neglected to have a witness or take a receipt. The grizzled grimalkin who kept the den, and thrived as much by his small filchings as from his small profits, had purred to himself, "Very goot, very goot," on learning that Haldane's word would not be worth much with the public or in court; and no yellow-eyed cat ever waited and watched for his prey with a quieter and cooler deliberation than did Weitzel Shrumpf, the host of the dingy little hotel.

After Haldane appeared he delayed until a few cronies whom he could depend upon had dropped in, and then, in an off-hand way, stepped up to the despondent youth, and said:

"I zay, mister, you been here zwei week; I want you bay me now."

"What do you means:" asked Haldane, looking up with an uncomprehending stare.

"Dis is vot I mean; you buts me off long nuff. I vants zwei weeks' bort."

"I paid you for everything up to this morning, and I have had nothing since."

"O, you have baid me—strange I did not know. Vill you bays now ven I does know?"

"I tell you I have paid you!" said Haldane, starting up.

"Vel, vell, show me der receipt, an I says not von vort against him."

"You did not give me a receipt."

"No, I thinks not—not my vay to give him till I gits de moneys."

"You are an unmitigated scoundrel. I won't pay you another cent."

"Lock dat door, Carl," said the landlord, coolly, to one of his satellites. "Now, Mister Haldane, you bays, or you goes to jail. You has been dare vonce, and I'll but you dare dis night if you no bays me."

"Gentlemen, I appeal to you to prevent this downright villany," cried Haldane.

"I sees no villany," said one of the lookers-on, stolidly. "You shows your receipt, and he no touch you."

"I neglected to take a receipt. I did not know I was dealing with a thief."

"Ho, ho, ho!" laughed the landlord; "he tinks I vas honest like himself, who vas jus' out of jail!"

"I won't pay you twice," said Haldane doggedly.

"Carl, call de policeman, den."

"Wait a moment; your rascality will do you no good, and may get you into trouble. I have very little money left."

"Den you can leave your vatch till you brings de money."

"Ah, thank Heaven! that is safe, and beyond your clutches."

"In a pawnshop? or vas he stolen, like de tousand dollar, and you been made give him up?"

Haldane had now recovered himself sufficiently to realize that he was in an ugly predicament. He was not sufficiently familiar with the law to know how much power his persecutor had, but feared, with good reason, that some kind of a charge could be trumped up which would lead to his being locked up for the night. Then would follow inevitably another series of paragraphs in the papers, deepening the dark hues in which they had already portrayed his character. He could not endure the thought that the last knowledge of him that Laura carried away with her from Hillaton should be that he was again in jail, charged with trying to steal his board and lodging from a poor and ignorant foreigner; for he foresaw that the astute Shrumpf, his German landlord, would appear in the police court in the character of an injured innocent. He pictured the disgust upon her face as she saw his name in the vile connection which this new arraignment would occasion, and he felt that he must escape it if possible. Although enraged at Shrumpf's false charge, he was cool enough to remember that he had nothing to oppose to it save his own unsupported word; and what was that worth in Hillaton? The public would even be inclined to believe the opposite of what he affirmed. Therefore, by a great effort, he regained his self-control, and said firmly and quietly:

"Shrumpf, although you know I have paid you, I am yet in a certain sense within your power, since I did not take your receipt. I have not much money left, but after I have taken out fifty cents for my supper and bed you can take all the rest. My watch is in the hands of a friend, and you can't get that, and you can't get any more than I have by procuring my arrest; so take your choice. I don't want to have trouble with you, but I won't go out penniless and spend the night in the street, and if you send for a policeman I will make you all the trouble I can, and I promise you it will not be a little."

Herr Shrumpf, conscious that he was on rather delicate ground, and remembering that he was already in bad odor with the police authorities, assumed a great show of generosity.

"I vill not be tough," he said, "ven a man's boor and does all vat he can; I knows my rights, and I stands up for him, but ven I gits him den I be like von leetle lamb. I vill leave you tree quarter dollar, and you bays der rest vat you have, and ve says nothing more 'bout him."

"You are right—the least said the better about this transaction. I've been a fool, and you are a knave, and that is all there is to say. Here are seventy-five cents, which I keep, and there are four dollars, which is all I have—every cent. Now unlock your door and let me out."

"I tinks you has more."

"You can search my pockets if you wish. If you do, I call upon these men present to witness the act, for, as I have said, if you go beyond a certain point I will make you trouble, and justly, too."

"Nah, nah! vat for I do so mean a ting? You but your hand in my bocket ven you takes my dinners, my lagers, and my brandies, but I no do vat no shentlemens does. You can go, and ven you brings de full moneys for zwei weeks' bort I gives you receipt for him."

Haldane vouchsafed no reply, but hastened away, as a fly would escape from a spider's web. The episode, intensely disagreeable as it was, had the good effect of arousing him out of the paralysis of his deep despondency. Besides, he could not help congratulating himself that he had avoided another arrest and all the wretched experience which must have followed.

He concluded that there was no other resource for him that night save "No. 13," the lodging-house in the side street where "no questions were asked"; and, having stolen into another obscure restaurant, he obtained such a supper as could be had for twenty-five cents. He then sought his former miserable refuge, and, as he could not pay extra for a private room on this occasion—for he must keep a little money for his breakfast—there was nothing for him, therefore, but to obtain what rest he could in a large, stifling room, half filled with miserable waifs like himself. He managed to get a bed near a window, which he raised slightly, and fatigue soon brought oblivion.

CHAPTER XXII

A MAN WHO HATED HIMSELF

THE light of the following day brought little hope or courage; but Haldane started out, after a meagre breakfast, to find some means of obtaining a dinner and a place to sleep. He was not as successful as usual, and noon had passed before he found anything to do.

As he was plodding wearily along through a suburb he heard some one behind a high board fence speaking so loudly and angrily that he stopped to listen, and was not a little surprised to find that the man was talking to himself. For a few moments there was a sound of a saw, and when it ceased, a harsh, querulous voice commenced again:

"A·a·h"—it would seem that the man thus given to soliloquy often began and finished his sentences with a vindictive and prolonged guttural sound like that here indicated —"Miserable hand at sawin' wood! Why don't you let some one saw it that knows how? Tryin' to save a half dollar, when you know it'll give you the rheumatiz, and cost ten in doctor bills! 'Nother thing; it's mean—mean as dirt. You know there's poor devils who need the work, and you're cheatin' 'em out of it. But it's just like yer! A·a·h!" and then the saw began again.

Haldane was inclined to believe that this irascible stranger was as providential as the croaking ravens that fed the prophet, and he promptly sought the gate and entered. An old man looked up in some surprise. He was short in stature and had the stoop of one who is bending under the weight of years and infirmities. His features

were as withered and brown as a russet apple that had been
kept long past its season, and his head was surmounted by
a shock of white locks that bristled out in all directions, as
if each particular hair was on bad terms with its neighbors.
Curious seams and wrinkles gave the continuous impression
that the old gentleman had just swallowed something very
bitter, and was making a wry face over it. But Haldane
was in no mood for the study of physiognomy and character, however interesting a subject he might stumble upon,
and he said:

"I am looking for a little work, and with your permission I will saw that wood for whatever you are willing
to pay."

"That won't be much."

"It will be enough to get a hungry man a dinner."

"Haven't you had any dinner?"

"No."

"Why didn't you ask for one, then?"

"Why should I ask you for a dinner?"

"Why shouldn't you? If I be a tight-fisted man, I'm
not mean enough to refuse a hungry man."

"Give me some work, and I can buy my dinner."

"What's your name?"

"Egbert Haldane."

"Ah ha! That name's been in the papers lately."

"Yes, and *I* have been in jail."

"And do you expect me to have a man around that's
been in jail?"

"No; I don't expect any humanity from any human
being that knows anything about me. I am treated as if
I were the devil himself, and hadn't the power or wish to
do anything save rob and murder. The public should keep
such as I am in prison the rest of our lives, or else cut our
throats. But this sending us out in the world to starve,
and to be kicked and cuffed during the process, is scarcely
in keeping with the Bible civilization they are always boast-
ing of."

He spoke recklessly and bitterly, and his experience made his words appear to him only too true. But his shrivelled and shrunken auditor grinned appreciatively, and said, with more than his usual vindictive emphasis:

"A-a-h! that's the right kind of talk. Now you're gittin' past all this make-believin' to the truth. We're a cussed mean set—we folk who go to church and read the Bible, and then do just what the devil tells us, a-helpin' him along all the time. Satan's got a strong grip on you, from all I hear, and we're all a-helpin' him keep it. You've gone half way to the devil, and all the good people tell you to go the rest of the way, for they won't have anything to do with you. Hain't that the way?"

"Oh, no," said Haldane with a bitter sneer; "some of the good people to whom you refer put themselves out so far as to give me a little advice."

"What was it wuth to you? Which would you ruther —some good advice from me, or the job of sawin' the wood there?"

"Give me the saw—no matter about the advice," said Haldane, throwing off his coat.

"A-a-h! wasn't I a fool to ask that question? Well, I don't belong to the good people, so go ahead—I don't s'pose you know much about sawin' wood, bro't up as you've been; but you can't do it wuss than me. I don't belong to any one. What I was made for I can't see, unless it is to be a torment to myself. Nobody can stand me. I can't stand myself. I've got a cat and dog that will stay with me, and sometimes I'll git up and kick 'em jest for the chance of cussin' myself for doin' it."

"And yet you are the first man in town that has shown me any practical kindness," said Haldane, placing another stick on his saw-buck.

"Well, I kinder do it out o' spite to myself. There's somethin' inside of me sayin' all the time, 'Why are you spendin' time and money on this young scapegrace? It'll end in your havin' to give him a dinner, for you can't be so blasted mean as to let him go without it, and yet all the time you're wishin' that you needn't do it.' "

"Well, you need not," said Haldane.

"Yes, I must, too."

"All I ask of you is what you think that work is worth."

"Well, that ain't all I ask of my confounded old self. Here, you're hungry you say—s'pose you tell the truth sometimes; here you're down, and all the respectable people sittin' down hard on you; here you are in the devil's clutches, and he's got you half way toward the brimstone, and I'm grudgin' you a dinner, even when I know I've got to give it to you. That's what I call bein' mean and a fool both. A-a-h!"

Haldane stopped a moment to indulge in the first laugh he had enjoyed since his arrest.

"I hope you will pardon me, my venerable friend," said he; "but you have a rather strangely honest way of talking."

"I'm old, but I ain't venerable. My name is Jeremiah Growther," was the snarling reply.

"I'm fraid you have too much conscience, Mr. Growther. It won't let you do comfortably what others do as a matter of course."

"I've nothin' to do with other people. I know what's right, and I'm all the time hatin' to do it. That's the mean thing about me which I can't stand. A-a-h!"

"I'm sorry my coming has made you so out of sorts with yourself."

"If it ain't you it's somethin' else. I ain't more out of sorts than usual."

"Well, you'll soon be rid of me—I'll be through in an hour."

"Yes, and here it is the middle of the afternoon, and you haven't had your dinner yet, and for all I know, no breakfast nuther. I was precious careful to have both of mine, and find it very comfortable standin' here a-growlin' while you're workin' on an empty stomach. But it's just like me. A-a-h! I'll call you in a few minutes, and I won't pay you a cent unless you come in;" and the old man started for the small dilapidated cottage which he shared with the cat and dog that, as he stated, managed to worry along with him.

But he had not taken many steps before he stumbled slightly against a loose stone, and he stopped for a moment, as if he could find no language equal to the occasion, and then commenced such a tirade of abuse with his poor weazened little self as its object, that one would naturally feel like taking sides with the decrepit body against the vindictive spirit. Haldane would have knocked a stranger down had he said half as much to the old gentleman, who seemed bent on befriending him after his own odd fashion. But the irate old man finished his objurgation with the words:

"What's one doin' above ground who can't lift his foot over a stone only an inch high? A-a-h!" and then he went on, and disappeared in the house, from the open door of which not long after came the savory odor of coffee.

Partly to forget his miserable self in his employer's strange manner, and partly because he was almost faint from hunger, Haldane concluded to accept this first invitation to dine out in Hillaton, resolving that he would do his queer host some favor to make things even.

"Come in," shouted Mr. Growther a few minutes later.

Haldane entered quite a large room, which presented an odd aspect of comfort and disorder.

"There's a place to wash your hands, if you think it's wuth while. I don't often, but I hope there's few like me," said the busy host, lifting the frying-pan from some coals, and emptying from it a generous slice of ham and three or four eggs on a platter.

"I like your open fire-place," said Haldane, looking curiously around the hermitage as he performed his ablutions.

"That's a nuther of my weaknesses. I know a stove

would be more convenient and economical, but I hate all improvements."

"One would think, from what you said, your cat and dog had a hard time of it; but two more sleek, fat, and lazy animals I never saw."

"No thanks to me. I s'pose they've got clear consciences."

As the table began to fairly groan with good things, Haldane said:

"Look here, Mr. Growther, are you in the habit of giving disreputable people such a dinner as that?"

"If it's good enough for me, it's good enough for you," was the tart reply.

"O, I'm not finding fault; I only wanted you to know that I would be grateful for much less."

"I'm not doin' it to please you, but to spite myself."

"Have your own way, of course," said Haldane, laughing; "it's a little odd, though, that your spite against yourself should mean so much practical kindness to me."

"Hold on!" cried his host, as Haldane was about to attack the viands; "ain't you goin' to say grace?"

"Well," said the young man, somewhat embarrassed, "I would rather you would say it for me."

"I might as well eat your dinner for you."

"Mr. Growther, you are an unusually honest man, and I think a kind one; so I am not going to act out any lies before you. Although your dinner is the best one I have seen for many a long day, or am likely to see, yet, to tell you the truth, I could swear over it easier than I could pray over it."

"A-a-h! that's the right spirit; that's the way I ought to feel. Now you see what a mean hypocrite I am. I'm no Christian—far from it—and yet I always have a sneakin' wish to say grace over my victuals. As if it would do anybody any good! If I'd jest swear over 'em, as you say, then I would be consistent."

"Are you in earnest in all this strange talk?"

"Yes, I am; I hate myself."

"Why?"

"Because I know all about myself. A-a-h!"

"How many poor, hungry people have you fed since the year opened?"

"Your question shows me jest what I am. I could tell you within three or four. I found myself a-countin' of 'em up and a-gloryin' in it all the tother night, takin' credit to myself for givin' away a few victuals after I had had plenty myself. Think of a man gittin' self-righteous over givin' to some poor fellow-critters what he couldn't eat himself! If that ain't meanness, what is it? A-a-h!"

"But you haven't told me how many you have fed."

"No, and I ain't a-goin' to—jest to spite myself. I want to tell you, and to take credit for it, but I'll head myself off this time."

"But you could eat these things which you are serving to me—if not to-day, why, then to-morrow."

"To-morrow's income will provide for to-morrow. The Lord shows he's down on this savin' and hoardin' up of things, for he makes 'em get musty right away; and if anything spiles on my hands I'm mad enough to bite myself in two."

"But if you treat all stragglers as you do me, you do not give away odds and ends and what's left over. This coffee is fine old Java, and a more delicate ham I never tasted."

"Now you hit me twice. I will have the best for myself, instead of practicin' self-denial and economy. Then I'm always wantin' to get some second-hand victuals to give away, but I daresn't. You see I read the Bible sometimes, and it's the most awfully oncomfortable book that ever was written. You know what the Lord says in it—or you ought to—about what we do for the least of these his brethren; that means such as you, only you're a sort of black sheep in the family; and if words have any sense at all, the Lord takes my givin' you a dinner the same as if I gave it to him. Now s'pose the Lord came to my house, as he did to Mary

and Martha's, and I should git him up a slimpsy dinner of
second-hand victuals, and stand by a-chucklin' that I had
saved twenty-five cents on it, wouldn't that be meanness
itself? Some time ago I had a ham that I couldn't and
wouldn't eat, and they wouldn't take it back at the store,
so I got some of the Lord's poor brethren to come to dinner,
and I palmed it off on them. But I had to cuss myself the
whole evenin' to pay up for it! A-a-h!"

"By Jove!" cried Haldane, dropping his knife and fork,
and looking admiringly at his host, who stood on the hearth,
running his fingers through his shock of white hair, his
shriveled and bristling aspect making a marked contrast
with his sleek and lazy cat and dog—"by Jove, you are
that I call a Christian!"

"Now, look here, young man," said Mr. Growther,
wrathfully, "though you are under no obligations to me,
you've got no business makin' game of me and callin'
me names, and I won't stand it. You've got to be civil and
speak the truth while you're on my premises, whether you
want to or no."

Haldane shrugged his shoulders, laughed, and made haste
with his dinner, for with such a gusty and variable host he
might not get a chance to finish it. As he glanced around
the room, however, and saw how cosey and inviting it might
be made by a little order and homelike arrangement, he
determined to fix it up according to his own ideas, if
he could accomplish it without actually coming to blows
with the occupant.

"Who keeps house for you?" he asked.

"Didn't I tell you nobody could stand me!"

"Will you stand me for about half an hour while I fix
up this room for you?"

"No!"

"What will you do if I attempt it?"

"I'll set the dog on you."

"Nothing worse?" asked Haldane, with a laughing
glance at the lazy cur.

"You might take something."

An expression of sharp pain crossed the young man's face; the sunshine faded out of it utterly, and he said in a cold, constrained voice, as he rose from the table:

"Oh, I forgot for a moment that I am a thief in the world's estimation."

"That last remark of mine was about equal to a kick, wasn't it?"

"A little worse."

"Ain't you used to 'em yet?"

"I ought to be."

"Why, do many speak out as plain as that?"

"They act it out just as plainly. Since you don't trust me, you had better watch me, lest I put some cord-wood in my pocket."

"What do you want to do?"

"If the world is going to insist upon it that I am a scoundrel to the end of the chapter, I want to find some deep water, and get under it," was the reckless reply.

"A-a-h! Didn't I say we respectable people and the devil was in partnership over you? He wants to get you under deep water as soon as possible, and we're all a-helpin' him along. Young man, I *am* afraid of you, like the rest, and it seems to me that I think more of my old duds here than of your immortal soul that the devil has almost got. But I'm goin' to spite him and myself for once. I'm goin' down town after the evenin' paper, and, instead of lockin' up, as I usually do, I shall leave you in charge. I know it's risky, and I hate to do it, but it seems to me that you ought ter have sense enough to know that if you take all I've got you would be jest that much wuss off;" and before Haldane could remonstrate or reply he took a curiously twisted and gnarled cane that resembled himself and departed.

CHAPTER XXIII

MR. GROWTHER BECOMES GIGANTIC

HALDANE was so surprised at Mr. Growther's unexpected course that the odd old man was out of the gate before the situation was fully realized. His first impulse was to follow, and say that he would not be left alone in circumstances that might compromise him; but a second thought assured him that he was past being compromised. So he concluded to fall in with his host's queer humor, and try to prove himself worthy of trust. He cleared away his dinner with as much deftness as could be expected of one engaging in an unusual task, and put everything in its place, or what should be its place. He next found a broom, and commenced sweeping the room, which unwonted proceeding aroused the slumbering cat and dog, and they sat up and stared at the stranger with unfeigned astonishment.

The cat looked on quietly and philosophically, acting on the generally received principle of the world, of not worrying until her own interests seemed threatened. But the dog evidently thought of the welfare of his absent master, and had a vague troubled sense that something was wrong. He waddled up to the intruder, and gravely smelled of him. By some canine casuistry he arrived at the same conclusion which society had reached—that Haldane was a suspicious character, and should be kept at arm's-length. Indeed, the sagacious beast seemed to feel toward the unfortunate youth precisely the same impulse which had actuated all the prudent citizens in town—a desire to be rid of him, and to have

nothing to do with him. If Haldane would only take himself off to parts unknown, to die in a gutter, or to commit
a burglary, that he might, as it were, break into jail again,
and so find a refuge and an abiding-place, the faithful dog,
believing his master's interests no longer endangered, would
have resumed his nap with the same complacence and sense
of relief which scores of good people had felt as they saw
Mr. Arnot's dishonored clerk disappearing from their premises, after their curt refusal of his services. The community's thoughts and wary eyes followed him only sufficiently
long to be sure that he committed no further depredations,
and then he was forgotten, or remembered only as a
danger, or an annoyance, happily escaped. What was to
become of this drifting human atom appeared to cause no
more solicitude in town than Mr. Growther's dog would
feel should he succeed in growling the intruder out of the
house; for, being somewhat mystified, and not exactly sure
as to his master's disposition toward the stranger, he concluded to limit his protest to a union of his voice with what
might be termed society's surly and monotonous command,
"Move on."

Haldane tried to propitiate this mild and miniature Cer-
berus with a dainty piece of ham, but was rewarded only
by a disdainful sniff and angrier snarl. The politic cat,
however, with wary glances at the dog and the stranger,
stole noiselessly to the meat, seized it, and retreated quickly
to her recognized corner of the hearth; but when the youth,
hoping that the morsel might lead to a friendly acquaintance, offered a caress, her back and tail went up instantly,
and she became the embodiment of repellant conservatism.
He looked at her a moment, and then said, with a bitter
laugh:

"If you could be transformed into a woman, as the old
fairy tale goes, you would make an excellent wife for Weitzel Shrumpf, while the snarling dog represents the respectable portion of the community, that will have nothing to
do with me whatever. When my pen, however, has brought

name and fame, the churlish world will be ready to fawn, and forget that it tried to trample me into the mire of the street until I became a part of it. Curses on the world! I would give half my life for the genius of a Byron, that I migt heap scorn on society until it writhed under the intolerable burden. Oh that I had a wit as keen and quick as the lightning, so that I might transfix and shrivel up the well-dressed monsters that now shun me as if I had a contagion!"

From a heart overflowing with bitterness and impotent protest against the condition to which his own act had reduced him, Haldane was learning to indulge in such bitter soliloquy with increasing frequency. It is ever the tendency of those who find themselves at odds with the world, and in conflict with the established order of things, to inveigh with communistic extravagance against the conservatism and wary prudence which they themselves would have maintained had all remained well with them. The Haldane who had meditated "gloomy grandeur" would not have looked at the poor, besmirched Haldane who had just accepted what the world would regard as charity. The only reason why the proud, aristocratic youth could tolerate and make excuse for the disreputable character who was glad to eat the dinner given by Jeremiah Growther, was that this same ill-conditioned fellow was himself. Thus every bitter thing which he said against society was virtually self-condemnation. And yet his course was most natural, for men almost invariably forget that their views change with their fortunes. Thousands will at once form a positive opinion of a subject from its aspect seen at their standpoint, where one will walk around and scan it on all sides.

Either to spite himself, or to show his confidence in one whom others regarded as utterly unworthy of trust, Mr. Growther remained away sufficiently long for Haldane to have made up a bundle of all the valuables in the house, and have escaped. The young man soon discovered that there were valuables, but anything like vulgar theft never entered his mind. That people should believe him capable of acting the part of a common thief was one of the strange things in his present experience which he could not understand.

Finally, to the immense relief of the honest and conservative dog, that had growled himself hoarse, Haldane gave the room its finishing touches, and betook himself to the woodpile again. The cat watched his departure with philosophic composure. Like many fair ladies, she had thought chiefly of herself during the interview with the stranger, from whom she had managed to secure a little agreeable attention without giving anything in return; and, now that it was over, she complacently purred herself to sleep, with nothing to regret.

"Hullo! you're here yet, eh!" said Mr. Growther, entering the gate.

"Can you name any good reason why I should not be here?" asked Haldane, somewhat nettled.

"No, but I could plenty of bad reasons."

"Keep them to yourself then," said the young man, sullenly resuming his work.

"You talk as if you was an honest man," growled the old gentleman, hobbling into the house.

Sitting down in his stout oak chair to rest himself, he stared in silence for a time at the changes that Haldane had wrought. At last he commenced:

"Now, Jeremiah Growther, I hope you can see that you are a perfect pig! I hope you can see that dirt and confusion are your nateral elements; and you had to live like a pig till a boy just out of jail came to show you what it was to live like a decent human. But you've been showed before, and you'll get things mixed up to-morrow. A-a-h!

"Where's that young fellow goin' to sleep to-night? That's none o' your business. Yes, 'tis my business, too. I'm always mighty careful to know where I'm goin' to sleep, and if I don't sleep well my cat and dog hear from

me the next day. You could be mighty comfortable to-
night in your good bed with this young chap sittin' on a
curb-stun in the rain; but I be hanged if you shall be. It's
beginnin' to rain now—it's goin' to be a mean night—mean
as yourself—a cold, oncomfortable drizzle; just such a night
as makes these poor homeless devils feel that since they are
half under water they might as well go down to the river and
get under altogether. P'raps they do it sometimes in the
hope of finding a warm, dry place somewhere. Dreadful
suddint change for 'em, though! And it's we respectable,
comfortable people that's to blame for these suddint changes
half the time.

"You know that heady young chap out there will go to
the bad if somebody don't pull him up. You know that it
would be mean as dirt to let him go wanderin' off to-night
with only fifty cents in his pocket, tryin' to find some place
to put his head in out of the storm; and yet you want to git
out of doin' anything more for him. You're thinkin' how
much more comfortable it will be to sit dozin' in your chair,
and not have any stranger botherin' round. But I'll head
you off agin in spite of your cussed, mean, stingy, selfish,
old, shrivelled-up soul, that would like to take its case even
though the hull world was a-groanin' outside the door.
A-a-h!"

Having made it clear to the perverse Jeremiah Growther
—against whom he seemed to hold such an inveterate spite—
what he must do, he arose and called to Haldane:

"What are you doin' out there in the rain?"

"I'll be through in a few minutes."

"I don't want the rest done till mornin'."

"It will pay neither of us for me to come back here to do
what's left."

"It may pay you, and as to its payin' me, that's my business."

"Not altogether—I wish to do my work on business principles; I haven't got down to charity yet."

"Well, have your own way, then; I s'pose other folks

have a right to have it as well as myself, sometimes. Come in soon as you are through."

By the time Haldane finished his task the clouds had settled heavily all around the horizon, hastening forward an early and gloomy twilight, and the rain was beginning to fall steadily. His mood comported with the aspect of sky and earth, and weariness, the fast ally of despondency, aided in giving a leaden hue to the future and a leaden weight to his thoughts. The prospect of trudging a mile or more through the drenching rain to his previous squalid resting-place at No. 13, whose only attraction consisted in the fact that no questions were asked, was so depressing that he decided to ask Mr. Growther for permission to sleep in the corner of his woodshed.

"Come in," shouted Mr. Growther, in response to his knock at the door.

"I'm through," said Haldane laconically.

"Well, I ain't," replied Mr. Growther; "you wouldn't mind taking that cheer till I am, would you?"

Haldane found the cushioned armchair and the genial fire exceedingly to his taste, and he felt that in such comfortable quarters he could endure hearing the old man berate himself or any one else for an hour or more.

"Where are you goin' to sleep to-night?" asked his quaint-visaged host.

"That is a problem I had been considering myself," answered Haldane, dubiously. "I had about concluded that, rather than walk back through the rain to the wretched place at which I slept last night, I would ask for the privilege of sleeping in your wood-shed. It wouldn't be much worse than the other place, or any place in which I could find lodging if I were known. Since I did not steal your silver I suppose you can trust me with your wood."

"Yet they say your folks is rich."

"Yes, I can go to as elegant a house as there is in this city."

"Why in thunder don't you go there, then?"

"Because I would rather be in your wood-shed and other places like it for the present."

"I can't understand that."

"Perhaps not, but there are worse things than sleeping hard and cold. There are people who suffer more through their minds than their bodies. I am not going back among my former acquaintances till I can go as a gentleman."

The old man looked at him approvingly a moment, and then said sententiously:

"Well, you may be a bad cuss, but you ain't a mean one."

Haldane laughed outright. "Mr. Growther," said he, "you do me honor. I foresee you will trust me with your wood-pile to-night."

"No I won't nuther. You might not take my wood, but you would take cold, and then I'd have to nuss you and pay doctor's bills, and bother with you a week or more. I might even have your funeral on my hands. You needn't think you're goin' to get me into all this trouble, fur I'm one that hates trouble, unless it's fur myself; and, if I do say it, it's askin' a little too much of me, almost a stranger, to 'tend to your funeral. I don't like funerals—never did—and I won't have nothin' to do with yours. There's a room right upstairs here, over the kitchen, where you can sleep without wakin' up the hull neighborhood a coughin' before mornin'. Now don't say nothin' more about it. I'm thinkin' of myself plaguy sight more'n I am of you. If I could let you go to the dogs without worryin' about it, I'd do it quick enough; but I've got a miserable, sneakin' old conscience that won't stand right up and make me do right, like a man; but when I want to do somethin' mean it begins a gnawin' and a gnawin' at me till I have to do what I oughter for the sake of a little peace and comfort. A-a-h!"

"Your uncomfortable conscience seems bent on making me very comfortable; and yet I pledge you my word that I will stay only on one condition, and that is, that you let me get supper and breakfast for you, and also read the paper aloud this evening. I can see that you are tired and lame from your walk. Will you agree?"

"Can't very well help myself. These easterly storms allers brings the rheumatiz into my legs. About all they are good fur now is to have the rheumatiz in 'em. So set plates for two, and fire ahead."

Haldane entered into his tasks with almost boyish zest. "I've camped out in the woods, and am considerable of a cook," said he. "You shall have some toast browned to a turn, to soak in your tea, and then you shall have some more with hot cream poured over it. I'll shave the smoked beef so thin that you can see to read through it."

"Umph! I can't see after dark any more than an old hen."

"How did you expect to read the paper then?" asked Haldane, without pausing in his labors.

"I only read the headin's. I might as well make up the rest as the editors, fur then I can make it up to suit me. It's all made up half the time, you know."

"Well, you shall hear the editors' yarns to-night then, by way of variety."

The old man watched the eager young fellow as he bustled from the cupboard to the table, and from the store-closet to the fireplace, with a kindly twinkle in his small eyes, from which the deep wrinkles ran in all directions and in strange complexity. There could scarcely be a greater contrast than that between the headstrong and stalwart youth and the withered and eccentric hermit; but it would seem that mutual kindness is a common ground on which all the world can meet and add somewhat to each other's welfare.

The sound hard wood which Haldane had just sawn into billets blazed cheerily on the hearth, filling the quaint old kitchen with weird and flickering lights and shades. Mr. Growther was projected against the opposite wall in the aspect of a benevolent giant, and perhaps the large, kindly, but unsubstantial shadow was a truer type of the man than the shrivelled anatomy with which the town was familiar. The conservative dog, no longer disquieted by doubts and fears, sat up and blinked approvingly at the preparation for supper. The politic cat, now satisfied that any attentions to the stranger would not compromise her, and might lead to another delicate morsel, fawned against his legs, and purred as affectionately as if she had known him all her life and would not scratch him instantly if he did anything displeasing to her.

Take it altogether, it was a domestic scene which would have done Mrs. Arnot's heart good to have witnessed; but poor Mrs. Haldane would have sighed over it as so utterly unconventional as to be another proof of her son's unnatural tastes. In her estimation he should spend social evenings only in aristocratic parlors; and she mourned over the fact that from henceforth he was excluded from these privileged places of his birthright, with a grief only less poignant than her sorrow over what seemed to her a cognate truth, that his course and character also excluded him from heaven.

CHAPTER XXIV

HOW PUBLIC OPINION IS OFTEN MADE

"I DON'T s'pose there's any use of two such reprobates as us thinkin' about sayin' grace," said Mr. Growther, taking his place at the head of the table; "and yet, as I said, I allers have a sneakin' wish jest to go through the form; so we'll all begin in the same way—cat and dog and God's rational critters. Howsomever, they don't know no better, and so their consciences is clear. I'll own up this toast is good, if I am eatin' it like a heathen. If you can't find anything else to do, you can take to cookin' for a livin'."

"No one in town, save yourself, would trust me in their kitchen."

"Well, it does seem as if a man had better lose everything rather than his character," said Mr. Growther thoughtfully.

"Then it seems a pity a man can lose it so cursed easily," added Haldane bitterly, "for, having lost it, all the respectable and well-to-do would rather one should go to the devil a thousand times than give him a chance to win it back again."

"You put it rather strong—rather strong," said the old man, shaking his head; "for some reason or other I am not as mad at myself and everything and everybody to-night as usual, and I can see things clearer. Be honest now. A month ago you belonged to the rich, high-flyin' class. How much then would you have had to do with a young

fellow of whom you knew only four things—that he gam-
bled, got drunk, 'bezzled a thousand dollars, and had been
in jail? That's all most people in town know about
you.''

Haldane laid down his knife and fork and fairly
groaned.

"I know the plain truth is tough to hear and think about,
and I'm an old brute to spile your supper by bringing it up.
I hope you won't think I'm trying to save some victuals by
doin' it. And yet it's the truth, and you've got to face
it. But face it to-morrow—face it to-morrow; have a comfortable time to-night.''

"Your statement of the case is perfectly bald," said Haldane, with a troubled brow; "there are explanatory and
excusing circumstances.''

"Yes, no doubt; but the world don't take much account
of them. When one gits into a scrape, about the only question asked is, What did he *do?* And they all jump to the
conclusion that if he did it once he'll do it agin. Lookin'
into the circumstances takes time and trouble, and it isn't
human nature to bother much about other people.''

"What chance is there, then, for such as I am?''

The old man hitched uneasily on his chair, but at last,
with his characteristic bluntness said, "Hanged if I know!
They say that them that gits down doesn't very often git
up again. Yet I know they do sometimes.''

"What would you do if you were me?''

"Hanged if I know that either! Sit down and cuss myself to all eternity, like enough. I feel like doin' it sometimes as it is. A-a-h!''

"I think I know a way out of the slough," said Haldane
more composedly—his thoughts recurring to his literary
hopes—"and if I do, you will not be sorry.''

"Of course I won't be sorry. A man allers hates one
who holds a mortgage against him which is sure to be fore-
closed. That's the way the devil's got me, and I hate him
about as bad as I do myself, and spite him every chance I

git. Of course, I'll be glad to see you git out of his clutches; but he's got his claws in you deep, and he holds on to a feller as if he'd pull him in two before he'll let go."

"Mr. Growther, I don't want to get into a quarrel with you, for I have found that you are very touchy on a certain point; but I cannot help hinting that you are destined to meet a great disappointment when through with your earthly worry. I wish my chances were as good as yours."

"Now you are beginnin' to talk foolishly. I shall never be rid of myself, and so will never be rid of my worry."

"Well, well, we won't discuss the question; it's too deep for us both; but in my judgment it will be a great piece of injustice if you ever find a warmer place than your own hearthstone."

"That's mighty hot, sometimes, boy; and, besides, your judgment hasn't led you very straight so far," said the old man testily. "But don't talk of such things. I don't want to come to 'em till I have to."

"Suppose I should become rich and famous, Mr. Growther," said Haldane, changing the subject; "would you let me take a meal with you then?"

"That depends. If you put on any airs I wouldn't."

"Good for you!"

"Oh, I'd want to make much of you, and tell how I helped you when you was down, and so git all the reflected glory I could out of you. I've learned how my sneakin' old speret pints every time; but I'll head it off, and drive it back as I would a fox into its hole."

In spite of some rather harrowing and gloomy thoughts on the part of two of them, the four inmates of the cottage made a very comfortable supper; for Mr. Growther always insisted that since his cat and dog could "stand him," they should fare as well as he did.

Having cleared the table, Haldane lighted a candle—kerosene lamps were an abomination that Mr. Growther would not abide—and began reading aloud the "Evening Spy." The old gentleman half listened and half dozed, pricking up his ears at some tale of trouble or crime, and almost snoring through politics and finance. At last he was half startled out of his chair by a loud, wrathful oath from Haldane.

"Look here, young man," he said; "the devil isn't so far off from either of us that you need shout for him."

"True, indeed! he isn't far off, and he has everything his own way in this world. Listen to this"—and he read with sharp, bitter emphasis the following editorial paragraph, headed "Unnatural Depravity":

"Being ever inclined to view charitably the faults and failings of others, and to make allowance for the natural giddiness of youth, we gave a rather lenient estimate, not of the crime committed by Mr. Arnot's clerk, Egbert Haldane, but of the young man himself. It would seem that our disposition to be kindly led us into error, for we learn from our most respectable German contemporary, published in this city, that this same unscrupulous young fraud has been guilty of the meanness of taking advantage of a poor foreigner's ignorance of our language. Having found it impossible to obtain lodgings among those posted in the current news of the day, and thus to impose on any one to whom he was known, he succeeded in obtaining board of a respectable German, and ran up as large a bill as possible at the bar, of course. When the landlord of the hotel and restaurant at last asked for a settlement, this young scapegrace had the insolence to insist that he had paid every cent of his bill, though he had not a scrap of paper or proof to support his assertion. Finding that this game of bluster would not succeed, and that his justly incensed host was about to ask for his arrest, he speedily came down from his high and virtuous mood, and compromised by pretending to offer all the money he had.

"This was undoubtedly a mere pretence, for he had worn a valuable watch in the morning, and had parted with it during the day. Though the sum he apparently had upon his person was scarcely half payment, the kind-hearted German took him at his word, and also left him seventy-five cents to procure lodgings elsewhere. In what rôle of crime he will next appear it is hard to guess; but it seems a pity that Mr. Arnot did not give him the full bene-fit of the law, for thus the community would have been rid, for a time at least, of one who can serve his day and genera-tion better at breaking stone under the direction of the State than by any methods of his own choosing. He is one of those phenomenal cases of unnatural depravity; for, as far as we can learn, he comes from a home of wealth, refine-ment, and even Christian culture. We warn our fellow-citizens against him."

"A-a-a-h!" ejaculated Mr. Growther, in prolonged and painful utterance, as if one of his teeth had just been drawn. "Now that is tough! I don't wonder you think Satan had a finger in that pie. Didn't I tell you the ed-itors made up half that's in the papers? I don't know what started this story. There's generally a little begin-ning, like the seed of a big flauntin' weed; but I don't be-lieve you did so mean a thing. In fact, I don't think I'm quite mean enough to have done it myself."

"You, and perhaps one other person, will be the only ones in town, then, who will not believe it against me. I know I've acted wrong and like a fool; but what chance has a fellow when he gets credit for evil only, and a hun-dred-fold more evil than is in him? Curse it all! since every one insists that I have gone wholly over to the devil, I might as well go."

"That's it, that's it! we're all right at his elbow, a-helpin' him along. But how did this story start? The scribbler in the German paper couldn't have spun it, like a spider, hully out of his own in'ards."

Haldane told him the whole story, sketching the "kind-hearted German" in his true colors.

At its conclusion Mr. Growther drew a long, meditative

breath, and remarked sententiously, "Well, I've allers heard that 'sperience was an awfully dear school; but we do learn in it. I'll bet my head you will never pay another dollar without takin' a receipt."

"What chance will I ever have to make another dollar? They have raised a mad-dog cry against me, and I shall be treated as if I were a dog."

"Why don't you go home, then?"

"I'll go to the bottom of the river first."

"That would suit the devil, the crabs, and the eels," remarked Mr. Growther.

"Faugh! crabs and eels!" exclaimed Haldane with a shudder of disgust.

"That's all you'd find at the bottom of the river, except mud," responded Mr. Growther, effectually quenching all tragic and suicidal ideas by his prosaic statement of the facts. "Young man," he continued, tottering to his feet, "I s'pose you realize that you are in a pretty bad fix. I ain't much of a mother at comfortin'. When I feel most sorry for any one I'm most crabbed. It's one of my mean ways. If there's many screws loose in you, you will go under. If you are rash, or cowardly, or weak—that is, ready to give up-like—you will make a final mess of your life; but if you fight your way up you'll be a good deal of a man. Seems to me if I was as young and strong as you be, I'd pitch in. I'd spite myself; I'd spite the devil; I'd beat the world; I'd just grit my teeth, and go fur myself and everything else that stood in my way, and I'd whip 'em all out, or I'd die a-fightin'. But I've got so old and rheumatic that all I can do is cuss. A-a-h!"

"I will take your advice—I will fight it out," exclaimed the excitable youth with an oath. Between indignation and desperation he was thoroughly aroused. He already cherished only revenge toward the world, and he was catching the old man's vindictive spirit toward himself.

Mr. Growther seemed almost as deeply incensed as his guest at the gross injustice of the paragraph, which, nevertheless, would be widely copied, and create public opinion, and so double the difficulties in the young man's way; and he kept up as steady a grumble and growl as had his sorely disquieted dog in the afternoon. But Haldane lowered at the fire for a long time in silence.

"Well," concluded the quaint old cynic, "matters can't be mended by swearin' at 'em, is advice I often give myself, but never take. I s'pose it's bed-time. To-morrow we will take another squint at your ugly fortunes, and see which side pints toward daylight. Would you mind readin' a chapter in the Bible first?"

"What have I to do with the Bible?"

"Well, the Bible has a good deal to say about you and most other people."

"Like those who pretend to believe it, it has nothing good to say about me. I've had about all the hard names I can stand for one night."

"Read where it hits some other folks, then."

"Oh, I will read anywhere you like. It's a pity if I can't do that much for perhaps the only one now left in the world who would show me a kindness."

"That's a good fellow. There's one chapter I'd like to hear to-night. The words come out so strong and hearty-like that they generally express just my feelin's. Find the twenty-third chapter of Matthew, and read where it says, 'Woe unto you, scribes and Pharisees, hypocrites.'"

Haldane read the chapter with much zest, crediting all its denunciation to others, in accordance with a very general fashion. When he came to the words, "Ye serpents, ye generation of vipers," the old man fairly rubbed his hands together in his satisfaction, exclaiming:

"That's it! that's genuine! that's telling us sleek, comfortable sinners the truth without mincin'! No smooth, deludin' lies in that chapter. That's the way to talk to people who don't want their right hand to know what cussedness their left hand is up to. Now, Jeremiah Growther, the next time you want to do a mean thing that you wouldn't have all the town know, just remember what a wrigglin' snake in the grass you are."

With this personal exhortation Mr. Growther brought the evening to a close, and, having directed Haldane to his comfortable quarters, hobbled and mumbled off to an adjoining room, and retired for the night. The dying fire revealed for a time the slumbering cat and dog, but gradually the quaint old kitchen faded into a blank of darkness.

CHAPTER XXV

A PAPER PONIARD

THROUGHOUT an early breakfast Mr. Growther appeared to be revolving some subject in his mind, and his question, at last, was only seemingly abrupt, for it came at the end of quite a long mental altercation, in which, of course, he took sides against himself.

"I say, young man, do you think you could stand me?"

"What do you mean?" asked Haldane.

"Well, before you say no, you ought to realize all the bearin's of the case. The town is down on you. Respectable people won't have nothin' to do with you, any more than they would walk arm in arm with the charcoal-man in their Sunday toggery. I aren't respectable, so you can't blacken me. I've showed you I'm not afraid to trust you. You can't sleep in the streets, you can't eat pavin'-stuns and mud, and you won't go home. This brings me to the question again: Can you stand me? I warn you I'm an awful oncomfortable customer to live with; I won't take any mean advantage of you in this respect, and, what's more, I don't s'pose I'll behave any better for your sake or anybody else's. I'm all finished and cooled off, like an old iron casting, and can't be bent or made over in any other shape. You're crooked enough, the Lord knows; but you're kind o' limber yet in your moral jints, and you may git yourself in decent shape if you have a chance. I've taken a notion to give you a chance. The only question is, Can you stand me?"

"It would be strange if I could not stand the only man

in Hillaton who has shown a human and friendly interest in me. But the thing I can't stand is taking charity."

"Who's asked you to take charity?"

"What else would it be—my living here on you?"

"I can open a boardin'-house if I want to, can't I? I have a right to lend my own money, I s'pose. You can open a ledger account with me to a penny. What's more, I'll give you a receipt every time," added the old man, with a twinkle in his eye; "you don't catch me gettin' into the papers as 'kind-hearted' Mr. Growther."

"Mr. Growther, I can scarcely understand your kindness to me, for I have no claim on you whatever. As much as I would like to accept your offer, I scarcely feel it right to do so. I will bring discredit to you with certainty, and my chances of repaying you seem very doubtful now."

"Now, look here, young man, I've got to take my choice 'twixt two evils. On one side is you. I don't want you botherin' round, seein' my mean ways. For the sake of decency I'll have to try to hold in a little before you, while before my cat and dog I can let out as I please; so I'd rather live alone. But the tother side is a plaguy sight worse. If I should let you go a-wanderin' off you don't know where, the same as if I should start my dog off with a kick, knowin' that every one else in town would add a kick or fire a stun, I couldn't sleep nights or enjoy my vittels. I'd feel so mean that I should jest set and cuss myself from mornin' till night. Look here, now; I couldn't stan' it," concluded Mr. Growther, overcome by the picture of his own wretchedness. "Let's have no more words. Come back every night till you can do better. Open an account with me. Charge what you please for board and lodgin', and pay all back with lawful interest, if it'll make you sleep better." And so it was finally arranged.

Haldane started out into the sun-lighted streets of the city as a man might sally forth in an enemy's country, fearing the danger that lurked on every side, and feeling that his best hope was that he might be unnoted and unknown.

He knew that the glance of recognition would also be a glance of aversion and scorn, and, to his nature, any manifestation of contempt was worse than a blow. He now clung to his literary ventures as the one rope by which he could draw himself out of the depths into which he had fallen, and felt sure that he must hear from some of his manuscripts within a day or two. He went to the post-office in a tremor of anxiety only to hear the usual response, "Nothing for E. H."

With heavy steps and a sinking heart he then set out in his search for something to do, and after walking weary miles he found only a small bit of work, for which he received but small compensation. He returned despondently in the evening to his refuge at Mr. Growther's cottage, and his quaint good Samaritan showed his sympathy by maintaining a perpetual growl at himself and the "disjinted world" in general. But Haldane lowered at the fire and said little.

Several successive days brought disappointment, discouragement, and even worse. The slanderous paragraph concerning his relations with Mr. Shrumpf was copied by the *Morning Courier*, with even fuller and severer comment. Occasionally upon the street and in his efforts to procure employment, he was recognized, and aversion, scorn, or rough dismissal followed instantly.

For a time he honestly tried to obtain the means of livelihood, but this became more and more difficult. People of whom he asked employment naturally inquired his name, and he was fairly learning to hate it from witnessing the malign changes in aspect and manner which its utterance invariably produced. The public had been generally warned against him, and to the natural distrust inspired by his first crime was added a virtuous indignation at the supposed low trickery in his dealing with the magnanimous Mr. Shrumpf, "the poor but kind-hearted German." Occasionally, that he might secure a day's work in full or in part, he was led to suppress his name and give an *alias*.

He felt as if he had been caught in a swift black torrent that was sweeping him down in spite of all that he could do; he also felt that the black tide would eventually plunge him into an abyss into which he dared not look. He struggled hard to regain a footing, and clutched almost desperately at everything that might impede or stay his swift descent; but seemingly in vain.

His mental distress was such that he was unable to write, even with the aid of stimulants; and he also felt that it was useless to attempt anything further until he heard from the manuscripts already in editorial hands. But the ominous silence in regard to them remained unbroken. As a result, he began to give way to moods of the deepest gloom and despondency, which alternated with wild and reckless impulses.

He was growing intensely bitter toward himself and all mankind. Even the image of his kind friend, Mrs. Arnot, began to merge itself into merely that of the wife of the man who had dealt him a blow from which he began to fear he would never recover. He was too morbid to be just to any one, even himself, and he felt that she had deserted and turned against him also, forgetting that he had given her no clew to his present place of abode, and had sent a message indicating that he would regard any effort to discover him as officious and intrusive. He quite honestly believed that by this time she had come to share in the general contempt and hostility which is ever cherished toward those whom society regards as not only depraved and vile, but also dangerous to its peace. It seemed as if both she and Laura had receded from him to an immeasurable distance, and he could not think of either without almost gnashing his teeth in rage at himself, and at what he regarded as his perverse and cruel fate. At times he would vainly endeavor to banish their images from his mind, but more often would indulge in wild and impossible visions of coming back to them in a dazzling halo of literary glory, and of overwhelming them with humiliation that they were so slow to recognize the genius which smouldered for weeks under their very eyes.

But his dreams were in truth "baseless fabrics," for at last there came a letter addressed to "E. H.," with the name of a popular literary paper printed upon it. He clutched it with a hand that shook in his eagerness, and walked half a mile before finding a nook sufficiently secluded in which to open the fateful missive. There were moments as he hastened through the streets when the crumpled letter was like a live coal in his hand; again it seemed throbbing with life, and he held it tighter, as though it might escape. With a chill at heart he also admitted that this bit of paper might be a poniard that would stab his hope and so destroy him.

He eventually entered a half-completed dwelling, which some one had commenced to build but was not able to finish.

It was a wretched, prosaic place, that apparently had lost its value even to the owner, and had become to the public at large only an unsightly blot upon the street. There was no danger of his being disturbed here, for the walls were not sufficiently advanced to have ears, and even a modern ghost would scorn to haunt a place whose stains were not those of age, and whose crumbling ruins resulted only from superficial and half-finished work. Indeed, the prematurely old and abortive house had its best counterpart in the young man himself, who stole into one of its small, unplastered rooms with many a wary glance, as though it were a treasure-vault which he was bent on plundering.

Feeling at last secure from observation, he tremblingly opened the letter, which he hoped contained the first instalment of wealth and fame. It was, indeed, from the editor of the periodical, and, remembering the avalanche of poetry and prose from beneath which this unfortunate class must daily struggle into life and being, it was unusually kind and full; but to Haldane it was cruel as death

—a Spartan short-sword, only long enough to pierce his heart. It was to the following effect:

E. fl.—DEAR SIR: It would be easier to throw your communication into the waste-basket than thus to reply; and such, I may add, is the usual fate of productions like yours. But something in your letter accompanying the MSS. caught my attention, and induced me to give you a little good advice, which I fear you will not take, however. You are evidently a young and inexperienced man, and I gather from your letter that you are in trouble of some nature, and, also, that you are building hopes, if not actually depending, upon the crude labors of your pen. Let me tell you frankly at once that literature is not your forte. If you have sent literary work to other parties like that inclosed to me you will never hear from it again. In the first place, you do not write correctly; in the second, you have nothing to say. We cannot afford to print words merely—much less pay for them. What is worse, many of your sentences are so unnatural and turgid as to suggest that you sought in stimulants a remedy for paucity of ideas. Take friendly advice. Attempt something that you are capable of doing, and build your hopes on *that*. Any honest work—even sawing wood—well done, is better than childish efforts to perform what, to us, is impossible. Before you can do anything in the literary world it is evident that years of culture and careful reading would be necessary. But, as I have before said, your talents do not seem to lie in this direction. Life is too precious to be wasted in vain endeavor; and that reminds me that I have spent several moments, and from the kindliest motives, in stating to you facts which you may regard as insults. But were the circumstances the same I would give my own son the same advice. Do not be discouraged; there is plenty of other work equally good and useful as that for which you seem unfitted.   Faithfully yours,   —— ——

CHAPTER XXVI

A SORRY KNIGHT

THE writer has known men to receive mortal wounds in battle, of which, at the moment, they were scarcely conscious. The mind, in times of grand excitement, has often risen so far superior to the material body that only by trickling blood or faintness have persons become aware of their injuries. But "a wounded spirit, who can bear?" and when did hope, self-love, or pride, ever receive home-thrusts unconsciously?

The well-meaning letter, written by the kindly editor, and full of wholesome advice, cut like a surgeon's knife in some desperate case when it is a question whether the patient can endure the heroic treatment necessary. Haldane's stilted and unnatural tales had been projected into being by such fiery and violent means that they might almost be termed volcanic in their origin; but the fused mass which was the result, resembled scoria or cinders rather than fine metal shaped into artistic forms. Although his manuscripts could have been sold in the world's market only by the pound, he had believed, or, at least, strongly hoped otherwise, like so many others, who, with beating hearts, have sent the children of their brains out to seek their fortunes with no better results.

The unbroken and ominous silence or the returned manuscript is a severe disappointment even to those who from safe and happy homes have sought to gain the public ear, and whose impelling motive toward literature is scarcely more than an impulse of vanity. But to Haldane the letter, which in giving the editorial estimate of one of his stories revealed the fate of all the others, brought far more than a mere disappointment. It brought despair and the recklessness and demoralization which inevitably follow. The public regarded him as a depraved, commonplace vagabond, eminent only in his capacity for evil and meanness, and he now inclined strongly to the same view of himself. True self-respect he had never possessed, and his best substitute, pride, at last gave way. He felt that he was defeated for life, and the best that life could now offer was a brief career of sensual pleasure. Mrs. Arnot and Laura Romeyn were so far removed from him as the stars; it was torment to think of them, and he would blot out their memory and the memory of all that he had hoped for, with wine and excitement. It seemed to him that the world said to him with united voice, "Go to the devil," and then made it impossible for him to do otherwise.

Since he was defeated—since all his proud assurances to his mother that he would, alone and unaided, regain his lost good name and position in society, had proved but empty boasts—he would no longer hide the fact from her, not in the hope of being received at home as a repentant prodigal (even the thought of such a course was unendurable), but with the purpose of obtaining from her the means of entering upon a life of vicious pleasure.

The young man's father—impelled both by his strong attachment for his wife, and also by the prudent forethought with which men seek to protect and provide for those they love, long after they have passed away from earthly life—had left his property wholly in trust to his wife, associating with her one or two other chosen counsellors. As long as she lived and remained unmarried she controlled it, the husband trusting to her affection for her children to make suitable provision for them. He had seen with prophetic anxiety the mother's fond indulgence of their only son, and the practical man dreaded the consequences. He there-

fore. communicated to her verbally, and also embodied in
his will, his wish that his son should have no control over
the principal of such portion of the estate as would eventually fall to him until he had established a character that
secured the confidence of all good men, and satisfied the
judgment of the cautious co-executors. The provisions of
the will still further required that, should the young man
prove erratic and vicious, his income should be limited in
such ways as would, as far as possible, curb excess.

Haldane knew all this, and in the days of his confidence
in himself and his brilliant future had often smiled at these
"absurd restrictions." The idea that there would ever be
any reason for their enforcement was preposterous, and
the thought of his fond, weak mother refusing anything
that he demanded, was still further out of the range of
possibility.

The wretched youth now sank into a far lower depth than
he had ever yet reached. He deliberately resolved to take
advantage of that mother's weakness, and for the basest
ends. While under the influence of hope and pride, he had
resolved to receive no assistance even from her, so that he
might wholly claim the credit of regaining all that he had
lost; but now, in the recklessness of despair, he proposed
not only to ask for all the money he could obtain, but, if
necessary, extort it by any means in his power.

He and the forlorn place of his bitter revery grew more
and more into harmony. The small, half-finished apartment
of the ruinous new house became more truly the counterpart of his life. It was bare; it was unsightly from the
débris of its own discolored and crumbling walls. The possibility of sweet home scenes had passed from it, and it had
become a place in which an orgy might be hidden, or some
revolting crime committed. To precisely this use Haldane
put his temporary refuge before leaving it; for excesses and
evil deeds that the mind has deliberately resolved upon are
virtually accomplished facts as far as the wrong-doer is concerned. Before leaving his dingy hiding-place Haldane had

in the depths of his soul been guilty of drunkenness and all kinds of excess. He also purposed unutterable baseness toward the widowed mother whom, by every principle of true manhood, he was bound to cherish and shield; and he had in volition more certainly committed the act of self-destruction than does the poor wretch who, under some mad, half-insane impulse, makes permanent by suicide the evils a little fortitude and patient effort might have remedied. There is no self-murder so hopeless and wicked as that of deliberate sin against one's own body and soul.

No man becomes a saint or villain in an hour or by a single step; but there are times when evil tendencies combine with adverse influences and circumstances to produce sudden and seemingly fatal havoc in character. As the world goes, Haldane was a well-meaning youth, although cursed with evil habits and tendencies, when he entered the isolated, half-finished house. He was bad and devilish when he came out upon the street again, and walked recklessly toward the city, caring not who saw or recognized him. In the depths of his heart he had become an enemy to society, and, so far from hoping to gain its respect and good-will, he defied and intended to outrage it to the end of life.

A man in such a mood gravitates with almost certainty toward the liquor-saloon, and Haldane naturally commenced drinking at the various dens whose doors stood alluringly open. His slender purse did not give him the choice of high-priced wines, and to secure the mad excitement and oblivion he craved, only fiery compounds were ordered—such as might have been distilled in the infernal regions to accomplish infernal results; and they soon began to possess him like a legion of evil spirits.

If Shakespeare characterized the "invisible spirit of wine" as a "devil" in the unsophisticated days of old, when wine was wine, and not a hell-broth concocted of poisonous drugs, what unspeakable fiends must lurk in the grimy bottles whose contents, analyzed and explained, would appall some, at least, of the stolid and stony-hearted venders!

Haldane soon felt himself capable of any wickedness, any crime. He became a human volcano, that might at any moment pass into a violent and murderous action, regardless of consequences—indeed, as utterly incapable of foreseeing and realizing them as the mountain that belches destruction on vineyard and village.

We regard ourselves as a civilized and Christian people, and yet we tolerate on every corner places where men are transformed into incarnate devils, and sent forth to run amuck in our streets, and outrage the helpless women and children in their own homes. The naked inhabitants of Dahomey could do no worse in this direction.

But Haldane was not destined to end his orgy in the lurid glare of a tragedy, for, as the sun declined, the miserable day was brought to a wretched and fitting close. Unconsciously he had strayed to the saloon on whose low steps Messrs. Van Wink and Ketchem had left him on the memorable night from which he dated his downfall. Of course he did not recognize the place, but there was one within that associated him inseparably with it, and also with misfortunes of his own. As Haldane leaned unsteadily against the bar a seedy-looking man glared at him a moment, and then stepped to his side, saying:

"I'll take a few dhrinks wid ye. Faix! after all the trouble ye've been to me ye oughter kape me in dhrink the year."

Turning to the speaker, the young man recognized Pat M'Cabe, whom he also associated with his evil fortunes, and toward whom he now felt a strong vindictiveness, the sudden and unreasoning anger of intoxication. In reply, therefore, he threw the contents of his glass into Pat's face, saying with a curse:

"That is the way I drink with such as you."

Instantly there was a bar-room brawl of the ordinary brutal type, from whose details we gladly escape. Attracted by the uproar, a policeman was soon on hand, and both the combatants were arrested and marched off to the nearest police station. Bruised, bleeding, disheveled, and with rent garments, Haldane again passed through the streets as a criminal, with the rabble hooting after him. But now there was no intolerable sense of shame as at first. He had become a criminal at heart; he had deliberately and consciously degraded himself, and his whole aspect had come to be in keeping with his character.

It may be objected that the transformation had been too rapid. It had not been rapid. His mother commenced preparing him for this in the nursery by her weak indulgence. She had sown the seeds of which his present actions were the legitimate outgrowth. The weeds of his evil nature had been unchecked when little, and now they were growing so rank as to overshadow all.

Multitudes go to ruin who must trace their wrong bias back to cultivated and even Christian homes.

CHAPTER XXVII

GOD SENT HIS ANGEL

THE mad excitement of anger and drunkenness was speedily followed by stupor, and the night during which Haldane was locked up in the station-house was a blank. The next morning he was decidedly ill as the result of his debauch; for the after-effects of the vile liquor he had drank was such as to make any creature save rational man shun it in the future with utter loathing.

But the officers of the law had not the slightest consideration for his aching head and jarring nerves. He was hustled off to the police court with others, and he now seemed in harmony with the place and company.

Pat M'Cabe was a veteran in these matters, and had his witnesses ready, who swore to the truth, and anything else calculated to assist Pat, their crony, out of his scrape. Unfortunately for Haldane, the truth was against him, and he remained sullen and silent, making no defence. The natural result, therefore, of the brief hearing, was his committal to the common jail for ten days, and the liberation of Pat, with a severe reprimand.

Thus, after the lapse of a few brief weeks, Haldane found himself in the same cell whence he had gone out promising and expecting to accomplish so much. He could not help recalling his proud words to his mother and Mrs. Arnot as he looked around the bare walls, and he was sufficiently himself again to realize partially how complete and disgraceful had been his defeat. But such was his mood that it could find no better expression than a malediction upon himself and the world in general. Then, throwing himself upon his rude and narrow couch, he again resigned himself to his stupor, from which he had been aroused to receive his sentence.

It was late in the afternoon when he awoke, and his cell was already growing dusky with the coming night. It was a place congenial to shadows, and they came early and lingered till the sun was high.

But as Haldane slowly regained full consciousness, and recalled all that had transpired, he felt himself to be under a deeper shadow than the night could cast. The world condemned him, and he deserved condemnation; but he was also deserving of pity. Scarcely more than twenty, he had seemingly spoiled his life utterly. It was torment to remember the past, and the future was still darker; for his outraged physical nature so bitterly resented its wrongs by racking pains that it now seemed to him that even a brief career of sensual gratification was impossible, or so counterbalanced with suffering as to be revolting. Though scarcely more than across the threshold of life, existence had become an unmitigated evil. Had he been brought up in an atmosphere of flippant scepticism he would have flung it away as he would a handful of nettles; but his childish memory had been made familiar with that ancient Book whose truths, like anchors, enable many a soul on the verge of wreck to outride the storm. He was too well acquainted with its teachings to entertain for a moment the shallow theory that a man can escape the consequences of folly, villany, and unutterable baseness by merely ceasing to breathe.

He could not eat the coarse food brought to him for supper, and his only craving was for something to quench his feverish thirst. His long lethargy was followed by corresponding sleeplessness and preternatural activity of brain. That night became to him like the day of judgment; for it seemed as if his memory would recall everything he had ever done or said, and place all before him in the most dreary and discouraging aspect.

He saw his beautiful and aristocratic home, which he had forfeited so completely that the prison would be more endurable than the forced and painful toleration of his presence, which was the best he could hope for from his mother and sisters; and he felt that he would much rather stay where he was for life than again meet old neighbors and companions. But he now saw how, with that home and his father's honored name as his vantage ground, he might have made himself rich and honored.

The misspent days and years of the past became like so many reproachful ghosts, and he realized that he had idled away the precious seed-time of his life, or, rather, had been busy sowing thorns and nettles, that had grown all too quickly and rankly. Thousands had been spent on his education; and yet he was oppressed with a sense of his ignorance and helplessness. Rude contact with the world had thoroughly banished self-conceit, and he saw that his mind was undisciplined and his knowledge so superficial and fragmentary as to be almost useless. The editor of the paper whose columns he had hoped to illumine told him that he could not even write correctly.

While in bitterness of soul he cursed himself for his wasted life, he knew that he was not wholly to blame. Indeed, in accordance with a trait as old as fallen man, he sought to lay the blame on another. He saw that his own folly had ever found an ally in his mother's indulgence, and that, instead of holding him with a firm yet gentle hand to his tasks and duties, she had been the first to excuse him from them and to palliate his faults. Instead of recalling her fond and blind idolatry with tenderness, he felt like one who had been treacherously poisoned with a wine that was sweet while it rested on the palate, but whose after-taste is vile, and whose final effect is death.

There is no memory that we cherish so sacredly and tenderly as that of our parents' kind and patient love. It often softens the heart of the hardened man and abandoned woman when all other influences are powerless. But when love degenerates into idolatry and indulgence, and those to whom the child is given as a sacred trust permit it to grow awry, and develop into moral deformity, men and women, as did Haldane, may breathe curses on the blindness and weakness that was the primal cause of their life-failure. Throughout that long and horrible night he felt only resentment toward his mother, and cherished no better purpose toward her than was embodied in his plan to wring from her, even by methods that savored of blackmail, the means of living a dissipated life in some city where he was unknown, and could lose himself in the multitude.

But the ten days of enforced seclusion and solitude that must intervene seemed like an eternity. With a shudder he thought of the real eternity, beyond, when the power to excite or stupefy his lower nature would be gone forever. That shadow was so dark and cold that it seemed to chill his very soul, and by a resolute effort of will he compelled his mind to dwell only on the immediate future and the past.

Day at last dawned slowly and dimly in his cell, and found him either pacing up and down like some wild creature in its cage, turning so often by reason of the limited space as to be almost dizzy, or else sitting on his couch with his haggard face buried in his hands.

After fighting all night against the impulse to think about Mrs. Arnot and her niece, he at last gave up the struggle, and permitted his mind to revert to them. Such thoughts were only pain now, and yet for some reason it seemed as if his mind were drawn irresistibly toward them. He felt that his deep regret was as useless and unavailing as the November wind that sweeps back and forth the withered and fallen leaves. His whole frame would at times tremble with gusts of remorseful passion, and again he would sigh long and drearily.

He now realized what a priceless opportunity he had lost. It was once his privilege to enter Mrs. Arnot's beautiful home assured of welcome. She had been deeply interested in him for his mother's sake, and might have become so for his own. He had been privileged to meet Laura Romeyn as her equal, at least in social estimation, and he might have made himself worthy of her esteem, and possibly of her affection. He saw that he had foolishly clamored, like a spoiled child, for that which he could only hope to possess by patient waiting and manly devotion; and now, with a regret that was like a serpent's tooth, he felt that such devotion might have been rewarded.

But a few months ago, whose life had been more rich with promise than his, or to whom had been given a better vantage-ground? And yet he had already found the lowest earthly perdition possible, and had lost hope of anything better.

In his impotent rage and despair he fairly gnashed his teeth and cursed himself, his fate, and those who had led to his evil fortunes. Then, by a natural revulsion of feeling, he sobbed like a child that has lost its way and can discover no returning path, and whose heart the darkness of the fast-approaching night fills with unutterable dread.

He was a criminal—in his despair he never hoped to be anything else—but he was not a hardened criminal and was still capable of wishing to be different. In the memory of his bitter experience a pure and honorable life now appeared as beautiful as it was impossible. He had no expectation, however, of ever living such a life, for pride, the corner-stone of his character, had given way, and he was too greatly discouraged at the time to purpose reform even in the future. Without the spur and incentive of hope we become perfectly helpless in evil; therefore all doctrines and philosophies which tend to quench or limit hope, or which are bounded by the narrow horizon of time and earth, are, in certain emergencies, but dead weights, dragging down the soul.

At last, from sheer exhaustion, he threw himself on his couch, and fell into a troubled sleep, filled with broken and distorted visions of the scenes that had occupied his waking hours. But he gradually became quieter, and it appeared in his dream as if he saw a faint dawning in the east which grew brighter until a distinct ray of light streamed from an infinite distance to himself. Along this shining pathway an angel seemed approaching him. The vision grew so distinct and real that he started up and saw Mrs. Arnot sitting in the doorway, quietly watching him. Confused and oblivious of the past, he stepped forward to speak to her with the natural instinct of a gentleman. Then the memory of all that had occurred rolled before him like a black torrent, and he shrank back to his couch and buried his face in his hands. But when Mrs. Arnot came and placed her hand on his shoulder, saying gently, but very gravely, "Egbert, since you would not come to me I have come to you," he felt that his vision was still true, and that God had sent his angel.

CHAPTER XXVIII

FACING THE CONSEQUENCES

A YOUNG man of Haldane's age is capable of despairing thoughts, and even of desperate moods, of quite extended continuance; but it usually requires a long lifetime of disaster and sin to bury hope so deep that the stone of its sepulchre is not rolled away as the morning dawns. Haldane had thought that his hope was dead; but Mrs. Arnot's presence, combined with her manner, soon made it clear, even to himself, that it was not; and yet it was but a weak and trembling hope, scarcely assured of its right to exist, that revived at her touch and voice. His heart both clung to and shrank from the pure, good woman who stood beside him.

He trembled, and his breast heaved convulsively for a few moments, and she quietly waited until he should grow more calm, only stroking his bowed head once or twice with a slight and reassuring caress. At last he asked in a low, hoarse voice:

"Do you know why I am here?"

"Yes, Egbert."

"And yet you have come in kindness—in mercy, rather."

"I have come because I am deeply interested in you."

"I am not worthy—I am not fit for you to touch."

"I am glad you feel so."

"Then why do you come?"

"Because I wish to help you to become worthy."

"That's impossible. It's too late."

"Perhaps it is. That is a question for you alone to decide; but I wish you to think well before you do decide it."

"Pardon me, Mrs. Arnot," he said emphatically, raising his head, and dashing away bitter tears; "the world has decided that question for me, and all have said in one harsh, united voice, 'You shall not rise.' It has ground me under its heel as vindictively as if I were a viper. You are so unlike the world that you don't know it. It has given me no chance whatever."

"Egbert, what have you to do with the world?"

"God knows I wanted to recover what I had lost," he continued in the same rapid tone. "God knows I left this cell weeks since with the honest purpose of working my way up to a position that would entitle me to your respect, and change my mother's shame into pride. But I found a mad-dog cry raised against me. And this professedly Christian town has fairly hunted me back to this prison."

Mrs. Arnot sighed deeply, but after a moment said, "I do not excuse the Christian town, neither can I excuse you."

"You too, then, blame me, and side against me."

"No, Egbert, I side with you, and yet I blame you deeply; but I pity you more."

He rose, and paced the cell with his old, restless steps. "It's no use," he said; "the world says, 'Go to the devil,' and gives me no chance to do otherwise."

"Do you regard the world—whatever you may mean by the phrase—as your friend?"

"Friend!" he repeated, with bitter emphasis.

"Why, then, do you take its advice? I did not come here to tell you to go to perdition."

"But if the world sets its face against me like a flint, what is there for me to do but to remain in prison or hide in a desert, unless I do what I had purposed, defy it and strike back, though it be only as a worm that tries to sting the foot that crushes it."

"Egbert, if you should die, the world would forget that you had ever existed, in a few days."

"Certainly. It would give me merely a passing thought as of a nuisance that had been abated."

"Well, then, would it not be wise to forget the world for a little while? You are shut away from it for the present, and it cannot molest you. In the meantime you can settle some very important personal questions. The world has power over your fate only as you give it power. You need not lie like a helpless worm in its path, waiting to be crushed. Get up like a man, and take care of yourself. The world may let you starve, but it cannot prevent you from becoming good and true and manly; if you do become so, however, rest assured the world will eventually find a place for you, and, perhaps, an honored place. But be that as it may, a good Christian man is sustained by something far more substantial than the world's breath."

Out of respect for Mrs. Arnot, Haldane was silent. He supposed that her proposed remedy for his desperate troubles was that he should "become a Christian," and to this phrase he had learned to give only the most conventional meaning.

"Becoming a Christian," in his estimation, was the making of certain professions, going through peculiar and abnormal experiences, and joining a church, the object of all this being to escape a "wrath to come" in the indefinite future. To begin with, he had not the slightest idea how to set in motion these spiritual evolutions, had he desired them; and to his intense and practical nature the whole subject was as unattractive as a library of musty and scholastic books. He wanted some remedy that applied to this world, and would help him now. He did not associate Mrs. Arnot's action with Christian principle, but believed it to be due to the peculiar and natural kindness of her heart. Christians in general had not troubled themselves about him, and, as far as he could judge, had turned as coldly from him as had others. His mother had always been regarded as an eminently religious woman, and yet he knew that she was morbidly sensitive to the world's opinion and society's verdict.

From childhood he had associated religion with numerous Sunday restraints and the immaculate mourning-dress which seemed chiefly to occupy his mother's thoughts during the hour preceding service. He had no conception of a faith that could be to him what the Master's strong sustaining hand was to the disciple who suddenly found himself sinking in a stormy sea.

It is not strange that the distressed in body or mind turn away from a religion of dreary formalities and vague, uncomprehended mental processes. Instant and practical help is what is craved; and just such help Christ ever gave when he came to manifest God's will and ways to men. By whose authority do some religious teachers now lead the suffering through such a round-about, intricate, or arid path of things to be done and doctrines to be accepted before bringing them to Christ?

But when a mind has become mystified with preconceived ideas and prejudices, it is no easy task to reveal to it the truth, however simple. Mrs. Arnot had come into the light but slowly herself, and she had passed through too many deep and prolonged spiritual experiences to hope for any immediate and radical change in Haldane. Indeed, she was in great doubt whether he would ever receive the faithful words she proposed speaking to him; and she fully believed that anything he attempted in his own strength would again end in disheartening failure.

"Egbert," she said gently, but very gravely, "have you fully settled it in your own mind that I am your friend and wish you well?"

"How can I believe otherwise, since you are here, and speaking to me as you do?"

"Well, I am going to test your faith in me and my kindness. I am going to speak plainly, and perhaps you may think even harshly. You are very sick, and if I am to be your physician I must give you some sharp, decisive treatment. Will you remember through it all that my only motive is to make you well?"

"I will try to."

"You have kept away from me a long time. Perhaps when released from this place you will again avoid me, and I may never have another opportunity like the present. Now, while you have a chance to think, I am going to ask you to face the consequences of your present course. Within an hour after passing out of this cell you will have it in your power to trample on your better nature and stupefy your mind. But now, if you will, you have a chance to use the powers God has given you, and settle finally on your plan of life."

"I have already trampled on my manhood—what is worse, I have lost it. I haven't any courage or strength left."

"That can scarcely be true of one but little more than twenty. You are to be here in quietness for the next ten days, I learn. It is my intention, so far as it is in my power to bring it about, that you deliberately face the consequences of your present course during this time. By the consequences I do not mean what the world will think of you, but, rather, the personal results of your action—what you must suffer while you are in the world, and what you must suffer when far beyond the world. Egbert, are you pleased with yourself? are you satisfied with yourself?"

"I loathe myself."

"You can get away from the world—you are away from it now, and soon you will be away from it finally—but you can never get away from yourself. Are you willing to face an eternal consciousness of defeat, failure, and personal baseness?"

He shuddered, but was silent.

"There is no place in God's pure heaven for the drunkard—the morally loathsome and deformed. Are you willing to be swept away among the chaff and the thorns, and to have, forever, the shameful and humiliating knowledge that you rightfully belong to the rubbish of the universe? Are you willing to have a sleepless memory tell you in every torturing way possible what a noble, happy man you

might have been, but would not be? Your power to drown
memory and conscience, and stupefy your mind, will last a
little while only at best. How are you going to endure the
time when you must remember everything and think of
everything? These are more important questions than
what the world thinks of you."

"Have you no pity?" he groaned.

"Yes, my heart overflows with pity. Is it not kindness
to tell you whither your path is leading? If I had the
power I would lay hold of you, and force you to come with
me into the path of life and safety," she answered, with a
rush of tears to her eyes.

Her sympathy touched him deeply, and disarmed her
words of all power to awaken resentment.

"Mrs. Arnot," he cried, passionately, "I did mean—I
did try—to do better when I left this place; but, between
my own accursed weakness and the hard-hearted world, I
am here again, and almost without hope."

"Egbert, though I did not discourage you at the time, I
had little hope of your accomplishing anything when you
left this cell some weeks since. You went out to regain
your old position and the world's favor, as one might look
for a jewel or sum of money he had lost. You can never
gain even these advantages in the way you proposed, and
if you enjoy them again the cause will exist, not in what
you do only, but chiefly in what you *are*. When you
started out to win the favor of society, from which you
had been alienated partly by misfortune, but largely
through your own wrong action, there was no radical
change in your character, or even in your controlling motives. You regretted the evil because of its immediate and
disagreeable consequences. I do not excuse the world's
harshness toward the erring; but, after all, if you can dis-
abuse your mind of prejudice you will admit that its action
is very natural, and would, probably, have been your own
before you passed under this cloud. Consider what the
world knows of you. It, after all, is quite shrewd in judg-

ing whom it may trust and whom it is safe to keep at arm's-length. Knowing yourself and your own weaknesses as you do, could you honestly recommend yourself to the confidence of any one? With your character unchanged, what guarantee have you against the first temptation or gust of passion to which you are subjected? You had no lack of wounded pride and ambition when you started out, but you will surely admit that such feelings are of little value compared with Christian integrity and manly principle, which render anything dishonorable or base impossible.

"I do not consider the world's favor worth very much, but the world's respect is, for it usually respects only what is respectable. As you form a character that you can honestly respect yourself, you will find society gradually learning to share in that esteem. Believe me, Egbert, if you ever regain the world's lost favor, which you value so highly, you will discover the first earnest of it in your own changed and purified character. The world will pay no heed to any amount of self-assertion, and will remain equally indifferent to appeals and upbraidings; but sooner or later it will find out just what you are in your essential life, and will estimate you accordingly. I have dwelt on this phase of your misfortune fully, because I see that it weighs so heavily on your heart. Can you accept my judgment in the matter? Remember, I have lived nearly three times as long as you have, and speak from ripe experience. I have always been a close observer of society, and am quite sure I am right. If you were my own son I would use the same words."

"Mrs. Arnot," he replied slowly, with contracted brow, "you are giving me much to think about. I fear I have been as stupid as I have been bad. My whole life seems one wretched blunder."

"Ah, if you will only *think*, I shall have strong hopes of you. But in measuring these questions do not use the inch rule of time and earth only. As I have said before, remember you will soon have done with earth forever, but never can you get away from God, nor be rid of yourself. You are on wretched terms with both, and will be, whatever happens, until your nature is brought into harmony with God's will.   We are so made, so designed in our every fibre, that evil tortures us like a diseased nerve; and it always will till we get rid of it.   Therefore, Egbert, remember—O that I could burn it into your consciousness—the best that you can gain from your proposed evil course is a brief respite in base and sensual stupefaction, or equally artificial and unmanly excitement, and then endless waking, bitter memories, and torturing regret.   Face this truth now, before it is too late.   Good-by for a time.   I will come again when I can; or you can send for me when you please;'' and she gave him her hand in cordial pressure.

He did not say a word, but his face was very white, and it was evident that her faithful words had opened a prospect that had simply appalled him.

CHAPTER XXIX

HOW EVIL ISOLATES

IF HALDANE had been left alone on an ice-floe in the Arctic Ocean he could scarcely have felt worse than he did during the remainder of the day after Mrs. Arnot's departure. A dreary and increasing sense of isolation oppressed him. The words of his visitor, "What have you to do with the world?" and "If you were dead it would forget you in a few days," repeated themselves over and over again. His vindictive feeling against society died out in the consciousness of his weakness and insignificance. What is the use of one's smiting a mountain with his fist? Only the puny hand feels the blow. The world became, under Mrs. Arnot's words, too large and vague a generality even to be hated.

In order to be a misanthrope one must also be an egotist, dwarfing the objects of his spite, and exaggerating the small atom that has arrayed itself against the universe. It is a species of insanity, wherein a mind has lost perception of the correct relationship between different existences. The poor hypochondriac who imagined himself a mountain was a living satire on many of his fellow-creatures, who differ only in being able to keep similar delusions to themselves.

Mrs. Arnot's plain, honest, yet kindly words had thrown down the walls of prejudice, and Haldane's mind lay open to the truth. As has been said, his first impression was a strange and miserable sense of loneliness. He saw what a slender hold he had upon the rest of humanity. The majority knew nothing of him, while, with few exceptions, those who were aware of his existence despised and detested him, and would breathe more freely if assured of his death. He instinctively felt that the natural affections of his mother and sisters were borne down and almost overwhelmed by his course and character. If they had any visitors in the seclusion to which his disgrace had driven them, his name would be avoided with morbid sensitiveness, and yet all would be as painfully conscious of him as if he were a corpse in the room, which by some monstrous necessity could not be buried. While they might shed natural tears, he was not sure but that deep in their hearts would come a sense of relief should they hear that he was dead, and so could not deepen the stain he had already given to a name once so respectable. He knew that his indifference and over-bearing manner toward his sisters had alienated them from him; while in respect to Mrs. Haldane, her aristocratic conventionality, the most decided trait of her character, would always be in sharp contest with her strong mother-love, and thus he would ever be only a source of disquiet and wretchedness whether present or absent. In view of the discordant elements and relations now existing, there was not a place on earth less attractive than his own home.

It may at first seem a contradiction to say that the thought of Mrs. Arnot gave him a drearier sense of isolation than the memory of all else. In her goodness she seemed to belong to a totally different world from himself and people in general. He had nothing in common with her. She seemed to come to him almost literally as an angel of mercy, and from an infinite distance, and her visits must, of necessity, be like those of the angels, few and far between, and, in view of his character, must soon cease. He shrank from her purity and nobility even while drawn toward her by her sympathy. He instinctively felt that in all her deep commiseration of him she could not for a moment tolerate the debasing evil of his nature, and that this evil, retained, would speedily and inevitably separate them forever. Could he be rid of it? He did not know. He could not then see how. In his weakness and despondency it seemed inwrought with every fibre of his being, and an essential part of himself. As for Laura, she was like a bright star that had set, and was no longer above his dim horizon.

As he felt himself thus losing his hold on the companionship and remembrance of others, he was thrown back upon himself, and this led him to feel with a sort of dreary foreboding that it would be a horrible thing thus to be chained forever to a self toward which the higher faculties of his soul must ever cherish only hatred and loathing. Even now he hated himself—nay, more, he was enraged with himself—in view of the folly of which he had been capable. What could be worse than the endless companionship of the base nature which had already dragged him down so low?

As the hours passed, the weight upon his heart grew heavier, and the chill of dread more unendurable. He saw his character as another might see it. He saw a nature to which, from infancy, a wrong bias had been given, made selfish by indulgence, imperious and strong only in carrying out impulses and in gratifying base passions, but weak as water in resisting evil and thwarting its vile inclinations. The pride and hope that had sustained him in what he regarded as the great effort of his life were gone, and he felt neither strength nor courage to attempt anything further. He saw himself helpless and prostrate before his fate, and yet that fate was so terrible that he shrank from it with increasing dread.

What could he do? Was it possible to do anything? Had he not lost his footing? If a man is caught in the rapids, up to a certain point his struggle against the tide is full of hope, but beyond that point no effort can avail. Had he not been swept so far down toward the final plunge that grim despair were better than frantic but vain effort?

And yet he felt that he could not give himself up to the absolute mastery of evil without one more struggle. Was there any chance? Was he capable of making the needful effort?

Thus hopes and fears, bitter memories and passionate regrets, swept to and fro through his soul like stormy gusts. A painful experience and Mrs. Arnot's words were teaching the giddy, thoughtless young fellow what life meant, and were forcing upon his attention the inevitable questions connected with it which must be solved sooner or later, and which usually grow more difficult as the consideration of them is delayed, and they become complicated. As his cell grew dusky with its early twilight, as he thought of another long night whose darkness would be light compared with the shadow brooding on his prospects, his courage and endurance gave way.

With something of the feeling of a terror-stricken child he called the under-sheriff, and asked for writing materials. With a pencil he wrote hastily:

"MRS. ARNOT—I entreat you to visit me once more to-day. Your words have left me in torture. I cannot face the consequences and yet see no way of escape. It would be very cruel to leave me to my despairing thoughts for another night, and you are not cruel."

In despatching the missive he said, "I can promise that if this note is delivered to Mrs. Arnot at once, the bearer shall be well paid."

Moments seemed hours while he waited for an answer. Suppose the letter was not delivered—suppose Mrs. Arnot was absent. A hundred miserable conjectures flitted through his mind; but his confidence in his friend was such that even his morbid fear did not suggest that she would not come.

The lady was at the dinner-table when the note was handed to her, and after reading it she rose hastily and excused herself.

"Where are you going?" asked her husband sharply.

"A person in trouble has sent for me."

"Well, unless the *person* is in the midst of a surgical operation, he, she, or it, whichever this person may be, can wait till you finish your dinner."

"I am going to visit Egbert Haldane," said Mrs. Arnot quietly. "Jane, please tell Michael to come round with the carriage immediately."

"You visit the city prison at this hour! Now I protest. The young rake probably has the delirium tremens. Send our physician rather, if some one must go, though leaving him to the jailer and a strait-jacket would be better still."

"Please excuse me," answered his wife, with her hand on the door-knob; "you forget my relations to Mrs. Haldane; her son has sent for me."

"'Her relations to Mrs. Haldane!' As if she were not always at the beck and call of every beggar and criminal in town! I do wish I had a wife who was too much of a lady to have anything to do with this low scum."

A few moments later Mr. Arnot broke out anew with muttered complaint and invective, as he heard the carriage driven rapidly away.

As by the flickering light of a dip candle Mrs. Arnot saw Haldane's pale, haggard face, she did not regret that she had come at once, for a glance gave to her the evidence of a human soul in its extremity.

In facing these deep questions of life, some regard themselves as brave or philosophical. Perhaps it were nearer the truth to say they are stolid, and are staring at that which they do not understand and cannot yet realize. Where in history do we read—who from a ripe experience can give—an instance of a happy life developing under the deepening shadow of evil? Suppose one has seen high types of character and happiness, and was capable of appreciating them, but finds that he has cherished a sottish, beastly nature so long that it has become his master, promising to hold him in thraldom ever afterward;—can there be a more wretched form of captivity? The ogre of a debased nature drags the soul away from light and happiness—from all who are good and pure—to the hideous solitude of self and memory.

There are those who will be incredulous and even resentful in view of this picture, but it will not be the first time

that facts have been quarrelled with. It is *true* that many
are writhing and groaning in this cruel bondage, mastered
and held captive by some debasing appetite or passion,
perhaps by many. Sometimes, with a bitter, despairing
sorrow, of which superficial observers of life can have no
idea, they speak of these horrid chains; sometimes they
tug at them almost frantically. A few escape, but more are
dragged down and away—away from honorable companionships and friendships; away from places of trust, from walks
of usefulness and safety; away from parents, from wife and
children, until the awful isolation is complete, and the guilty
soul finds itself alone with the sin that mastered it, conscious
that God only will ever see and remember. Human friends
will forget—they must forget in order to obtain relief from
an object that has become morally too unsightly to be looked
upon; and in mercy they are so created that they can forget,
though it may be long before it is possible.

There are people who scout this awful mystery of evil.
They have beautiful little theories of their own, which they
have spun in the seclusion of their studies. They keep carefully within their shady, flower-bordered walks, and ignore
the existence of the world's dusty highways, in which so
many are fainting and being trampled upon. What they
do not see does not exist. What they do not believe is not
true. They cannot condemn too severely the lack of artistic
taste and liberal culture which leads any one to regard sin
as other than a theologian's phrase or a piquant element
in human life, which otherwise would be rather dull and
flavorless.

Mrs. Arnot was not a theorist, nor was she the elegant
lady, wholly given to the æsthetic culture that her husband
desired; she was a large-hearted woman, and she understood human life and its emergencies sufficiently well to
tremble with apprehension when she saw the face of Egbert
Haldane, for she felt that a deathless soul in its crisis—its
deepest spiritual need—was looking to her solely for help.

CHAPTER XXX

IDEAL KNIGHTHOOD

M RS. ARNOT again came directly to the youth and put her hand on his shoulder with motherly free- dom and kindliness. Beyond even the word of sympathy is the touch of sympathy, and it often conveys to the fainting heart a subtle power to hope and trust again which the materialist cannot explain. The Divine Phy- sician often touched those whom he healed. He laid his hand fearlessly on the leper from whom all shrank with inexpressible dread. The moral leper who trembled under Mrs. Arnot's hand felt that he was not utterly lost and be- yond the pale of hope, if one so good and pure could still touch him; and there came a hope, like a ray struggling through thick darkness, that the hand that caressed might rescue him.

"Egbert," said the lady gravely, "tell me what I can do for you."

"I cannot face the consequences," he replied in a low, shuddering tone.

"And do you only dread the consequences?" Mrs. Arnot asked sadly. "Do you not think of the evil which is the cause of your trouble?"

"I can scarcely separate the sin from the suffering. My mind is confused, and I am overwhelmed with fear and loneliness. All who are good and all that is good seemed to be slipping from me, and I should soon be left only to my miserable self. O, Mrs. Arnot, no doubt I seem to you like a weak, guilty coward. I seem so to myself. If it were danger or difficulty I had to face I would not fear; but this slow, inevitable, increasing pressure of a horrible fate, this seeing clearly that evil cuts me off from hope and all happiness, and yet to feel that I cannot escape from it—that I am too weak to break my chains—it is more than I can endure. I fear that I should have gone mad if you had not come. Do you think there is any chance for me? I feel as if I had lost my manhood."

Mrs. Arnot took the chair which the sheriff had brought on her entrance, and said quietly, "Perhaps you have, Egbert; many a man has lost what you mean by that term."

"You speak of it with a composure that I can scarcely understand," said Haldane, with a quick glance of inquiry. "It seems to me an irreparable loss."

"It does not seem so great a loss to me," replied Mrs. Arnot gently. "As your physician you must let me speak plainly again. It seems to me that what you term your manhood was composed largely of pride, conceit, ignorance of yourself, and inexperience of the world. You were liable to lose it at any time, just as you did, partly through your own folly and partly through the wrong of others. You know, Egbert, that I have always been interested in young men, and what many of them regard as their manhood is not of much value to themselves or any one else."

"Is it nothing to be so weak, disheartened, and debased that you lie prostrate in the mire of your own evil nature, as it were, and with no power to rise?" he asked bitterly.

"That is sad indeed."

"Well, that's just my condition—or I fear it is, though your coming has brought a gleam of hope. Mrs. Arnot," he continued passionately, "I don't know how to be different; I don't feel capable of making any persistent and successful effort. I feel that I have lost all moral force and courage. The odds are too great. I can't get up again."

"Perhaps you cannot, Egbert," said Mrs. Arnot very gravely; "it would seem that some never do—"

He buried his face in his hands and groaned.

"You have, indeed, a difficult problem to solve, and, looking at it from your point of view, I do not wonder that it seems impossible."

"Cannot you, then, give me any hope?"

"No, Egbert; *I* cannot. It is not in my power to make you a good man. You know that I would do so if I could."

"Would to God I had never lived, then," he exclaimed, desperately.

"Can you offer God no better prayer than that? Will you try to be calm, and listen patiently to me for a few moments? When I said *I* could not give you hope—*I* could not make you a good man—I expressed one of my strongest convictions. But I have not said, Egbert, that there is no hope, no chance, for you. On the contrary, there is abundant hope—yes, absolute certainty—of your achieving a noble character, if you will set about it in the right way. But as one of the first and indispensable conditions of success, I wish you to realize that the task is too great for you alone; too great with my help; too great if the world that seems so hostile should unite to help you; and yet neither I nor all the world could prevent your success if you went to the right and true source of help. Why have you forgotten God in your emergency? Why are you looking solely to yourself and to another weak fellow-creature like yourself?"

"You are in no respect like me, Mrs. Arnot, and it seems profanation even to suggest the thought."

"I have the same nature. I struggled vainly and almost hopelessly against my peculiar weaknesses and temptations and sorrows until I heard God saying, 'Come, my child, let us work together. It is my will you should do all you can yourself, and what you cannot do I will do for you.' Since that time I have often had to struggle hard, but never vainly. There have been seasons when my burdens grew so heavy that I was ready to faint; but after appealing to my heavenly Father, as a little child might cry for help, the crushing weight would pass away, and I became able to go on my way relieved and hopeful."

"I cannot understand it," said the young man, looking at her in deep perplexity.

"That does not prevent its being true. The most skilful physician cannot explain why certain beneficial effects follow the use of certain remedies; but when these effects become an .established fact of experience it were sensible to employ the remedy as soon as possible. One might suffer a great deal, and, perhaps, perish, while asking questions and waiting for answers. To my mind the explanation is very simple. God is our Creator, and calls himself our Father. It would be natural on general principles that he should take a deep interest in us; but he assures us of the profoundest love, employing our tenderest earthly ties to explain how he feels toward us. What is more natural than for a father to help a child? What is more certain, also, than that a wise father would teach a child to do all within his ability to help himself, and so develop the powers with which he is endowed? Only infants are supposed to be perfectly helpless."

"It would seem that what you say ought to be true, and yet I have always half-feared God—that is, when I thought about him at all. I have been taught that he was to be served; that he was a jealous God; that he was angry with the sinful, and that the prayers of the wicked were an abomination. I am sure the Bible says the latter is true, or something like it."

"It is true. If you set your heart on some evil course, or are deliberating some dishonesty or meanness, be careful how you make long or short prayers to God while wilfully persisting in your sin. When a man is robbing and cheating, though in the most legal manner—when he is gratifying lust, hate, or appetite, and *intends* to *continue* doing so—the less praying he does the better. An avowed infidel is more acceptable. But the sweetest music that reaches heaven is the honest cry for help to forsake sin; and the more sinful

the heart that thus cries out for deliverance the more welcome the appeal. Let me illustrate what I mean by your
own case. If you should go out from this prison in the
same spirit that you did once before, seeking to gain position and favor only for the purpose of gratifying your own
pride—only that self might be advantaged, without any
generous and disinterested regard for others, without any
recognition of the sacred duties you owe to God, and content with a selfish, narrow, impure soul—if, with such a
disposition, you should commence asking for God's help as
a means to these petty, miserable ends, your prayers would,
and with good reason, be an abomination to him. But if
you had sunk to far lower depths than those in which you
now find yourself, and should cry out for purity, for the
sonship of a regenerated character, your voice would not
only reach your divine Father's ear, but his heart, which
would yearn toward you with a tender commiseration that
I could not feel were you my only son."

The sincerity and earnestness of Mrs. Arnot's words
were attested by her fast-gathering tears.

"This is all new to me. But if God is so kindly disposed toward us—so ready to help—why does he not reveal
himself in this light more clearly? why are we so slow and
long in finding him out? Until you came he seemed
against me."

"We will not discuss this matter in general. Take your
own experience again. Perhaps it has been your fault, not
God's, that you misunderstood him. He tries to show how
he feels toward us in many ways, chiefly by his written
Word, by what he leads his people to do for us, and by
his great mind acting directly on ours. Has not the Bible
been within your reach? Have none of God's servants tried
to advise and help you? I think you must have seen some
such effort on my part when you were an inmate of my
home. I am here this evening as God's messenger to you.
All the hope I have of you is inspired by his disposition
and power to help you. You may continue to stand aloof

from him, declining his aid, just as you avoided your mother, and myself all these weeks when we were longing to help you; but if you sink, yours will be the fate of one who refuses to grasp the strong hand that is and ever has been seeking yours."

"Mrs. Arnot," said Haldane thoughtfully, "if all you say is true there is hope for me—there is hope for every one."

Mrs. Arnot was silent for a moment, and then said, with seeming abruptness:

"You have read of the ancient knights and their deeds, have you not?"

"Yes," was the wondering reply, "but the subject seems very remote."

"You are in a position to realize my very ideal of knightly endeavor."

"I, Mrs. Arnot! What can you mean?"

"Whether I am right or wrong I can soon explain what I mean. The ancient knight set his lance in rest against what seemed to him the wrongs and evils of the world. In theory he was to be without fear and without reproach—as pure as the white cross upon his mantle. But in fact the average knight was very human. His white cross was soon soiled by foreign travel, but too often not before his soul was stained with questionable deeds. It was a life of adventure and excitement, and abundantly gratifying to pride and ambition. While it could be idealized into a noble calling, it too often ended in a lawless, capricious career of self-indulgence. The cross on the mantle symbolized the heavy blows and sorrows inflicted on those who had the misfortune to differ in opinion, faith, or race with the knight, the steel of whose armor seemingly got into his heart, rather than any personal self-denial. Without any moral change on his own part, or being any way better than they, he could fight the infidel or those whose views differed from his with great zest.

"But the man who will engage successfully in a crusade

against the evil of his own heart must have the spirit of a true knight, for he attempts the most difficult and heroic task within the limits of human endeavor. It is comparatively easy to run a tilt against a fellow-mortal, or an external evil; but to set our lance in rest against a cherished sin, a habit that has become our second nature, and remorselessly ride it down—to grapple with a secret fault in the solitude of our own soul, with no applauding hands to spur us on, and fight and wrestle for weary months—years perhaps—this does require heroism of the highest order, and the man who can do it is my ideal knight.

"You inveigh against the world, Egbert, as if it were a harsh and remorseless foe, bent on crushing you; but you have far more dangerous enemies lurking in your own heart. If you could thoroughly subdue these with God's aid, you would at the same time overcome the world, or find yourself so independent of it as scarcely to care whether or no it gave you its favor. When you left this prison before, you sought in the wrong way to win the position you had lost. You were very proud of your former standing; but you had very little occasion to be, for you had inherited it. The deeds of others, not your own, had won it for you. If you had realized it, it gave you a great vantage, but that was all. If you had been content to have remained a conceited, commonplace man, versed only in the fashionable jargon and follies of the hour, and basing your claims on the wealth which you had shown neither the ability nor industry to win, you would never have had my respect.

"Well, to tell the truth, such shadows of men are respected by no one, not even themselves, even though they may commit no deed which society condemns. But if in this prison cell you set your face like a flint against the weaknesses and grave faults of your nature which have brought you here, and which would have made you anything but an admirable man had you retained your old position—if, with God as your fast ally, you wage unrelenting and successful war against all that is unworthy of a Christian manhood—I will not only respect, I will honor you. You will be one of my ideal knights."

As Mrs. Arnot spoke, Haldane's eyes kindled, and his drooping manner was exchanged for an aspect that indicated reviving hope and courage.

"I have lost faith in myself," he said slowly; "and as yet I have no faith in God; but after what you have said I do not fear him as I did. I have faith in you, however, Mrs. Arnot, and I would rather gain your respect than that of all the world. You know me now better than any one else. Do you truly believe that I could succeed in such a struggle?"

"Without faith in God you cannot. Even the ancient knight, whose success depended so much on the skill and strength of his arm, and the temper of his weapons and armor, was supposed to spend hours in prayer before attempting any great thing. But with God's help daily sought and obtained, you cannot fail. You can achieve that which the world cannot take from you—which will be a priceless possession after the world has forgotten you and you it—a noble character."

Haldane was silent several moments, then, drawing a long breath, he said, slowly and humbly:

"How I am to do this I do not yet understand; but if you will guide me, I will attempt it."

"This book will guide you, Egbert," said Mrs. Arnot, placing her Bible in his hands. "God himself will guide you if you ask sincerely. Good-night." And she gave him such a warm and friendly grasp of the hand as to prove that evil had not yet wholly isolated him from the pure and good.

CHAPTER XXXI

THE LOW STARTING-POINT

ON the afternoon of the following day Mrs. Arnot again visited Haldane, bringing him several letters from his mother which had been sent in her care; and she urged that the son should write at once in a way that would reassure the mother's heart.

In his better mood the young man's thoughts recurred to his mother with a remorseful tenderness, and he eagerly sought out the envelope bearing the latest date, and tore it open. As he read, the pallor and pain expressed in his face became so great that Mrs. Arnot was much troubled, fearing that the letter contained evil tidings.

Without a word he handed it to her, and also two inclosed paragraphs cut from newspapers.

"Do you think your mother would wish me to see it?" asked Mrs. Arnot, hesitatingly.

"I wish you to see it, and it contains no injunctions of secrecy. Indeed, she has been taking some very open and decided steps which are here indicated."

Mrs. Arnot read:

My Unnatural Son—Though you will not write me a line, you still make it certain that I shall hear from you, as the inclosed clippings from Hillaton papers may prove to you. You have forfeited all claim on both your sisters and myself. Our lawyer has been here to-day, and has shown me, what is only too evident, that money would be a curse to you—that you would squander it and disgrace yourself still more, if such a thing were possible. As the property is wholly in my hands, I shall arrange it in such a way that you shall never have a chance to waste it. If you will comply with the following conditions I will supply all that is essential to one of your nature and tastes. I stipulate that you leave Hillaton, and go to some quiet place where our name is not known, and that you there live so quietly that I shall hear of no more disgraceful acts like those herein described. I have given up the hope of hearing anything good. If you will do this I will pay your board and grant you a reasonable allowance. If you will not do this, you end all communication between us, and we must be as strangers until you can show an entirely different spirit. Yours in bitter shame and sorrow,

EMILY HALDANE.

The clippings were Mr. Shrumpf's version of his own swindle, and a tolerably correct account of the events which led to the present imprisonment.

"Will you accept your mother's offer?" Mrs. Arnot asked, anxiously, for she was much troubled as to what might be the effect of the unfortunate letter at this juncture.

"No!" he replied with sharp emphasis.

"Egbert, remember you have given your mother the gravest provocation."

"I also remember that she did her best to make me the fool I have been, and she might have a little more patience now. The truth is that mother's God was respectability, and she will never forgive me for destroying her idol."

"Read the other letters; there may be that in them which will be more reassuring."

"No, I thank you," he replied, bitterly; "I have had all that I can stand for one day. She believes the infernal lie which that scoundrel Shrumpf tells, and gives me no hearing;" and he related to Mrs. Arnot the true version of the affair.

She had the tact to see that his present perturbed condition was not her opportunity, and she soon after left him in a mood that promised little of good for the future.

But in the long, quiet hours that followed her departure his thoughts were busy. However much he might think that others were the cause of his unhappy plight, he had seen that he was far more to blame. It had been made still more clear that, even if he could shift this blame somewhat, he could not the consequences. Mrs. Arnot's words had given him a glimpse of light, and had revealed a path,

which, though still vague and uncertain, promised to lead
out of the present labyrinth of evil. During the morning
hours he had dared to hope, and even to pray, that he
might find a way of escape from his miserable self and the
wretched condition to which it had brought him.

For a long time he turned the leaves of Mrs. Arnot's
Bible, and here and there a text would flash out like a
light upon the clouded future, but as a general thing the
words had little meaning.

To his ardent and somewhat imaginative nature she had
presented the struggle toward a better life in the most attractive light. He was not asked to do something which
was vague and mystical; he was not exhorted to emotions
and beliefs of which he was then incapable, nor to forms and
ceremonies that were meaningless to him, nor to professions
equally hollow. On the contrary, the evils, the defects of
his own nature, were given an objective form, and he could
almost see himself, like a knight, with lance in rest, preparing to run a tilt against the personal faults which had done
him such injury. The deeper philosophy, that his heart
was the rank soil from which sprang these faults, like Cad-
mus' armed men, would come with fuller experience.

But in a measure he had understood and had been inspired by Mrs. Arnot's thought. Although from a weak
mother's indulgence and his own, from wasted years and
bad companionships, his life was wellnigh spoiled, he still
had sufficient mind to see that to fight down the clamorous
passions of his heart into subjection would be a grand and
heroic thing. If from the yielding mire of his present self
a noble and granite-like character could be built up, so
strongly and on such a sure foundation that it would stand
the shocks of time and eternity, it were worth every effort
of which human nature is capable. Until Mrs. Arnot had
spoken her wise and kind, yet honest words, he had felt
himself unable to stand erect, much less to enter on a
struggle which would tax the strongest.

But suppose God would deign to help, suppose it was

the divine purpose and practice to supplement the feeble efforts of those who, like himself, sought to ally their weakness to his strength, might not the Creator and the creature, the Father and the child, unitedly achieve what it were hopeless to attempt unaided?

Thoughts like these more or less distinctly had been thronging his mind during the morning, and though the path out of his degradation was obscure and uncertain, it had seemed the only way of escape. He knew that Mrs. Arnot would not consciously mock him with delusive hopes, and as she spoke her words seemed to have the ring and echo of truth. When the courage to attempt better things was reviving, it was sad that he should receive the first disheartening blow from his mother. Not that she purposed any such cruel stroke; but when one commences wrong in life one is apt to go on making mischief to the end. Poor Mrs. Haldane's kindness and severity had always been ill-timed.

For some hours, as will be seen, the contents of the mother's letter inspired only resentment and caused discouragement; but calmer thoughts explained the letter, and confirmed Mrs. Arnot's words, that he had given the "gravest provocation."

At the same time the young man instinctively felt that if he attempted the knightly effort that Mrs. Arnot had so earnestly urged, his mother could not help him much, and might be a hindrance. Her views would be so conventional, and she would be so impatient of any methods that were not in accordance with her ideas of respectability, that she might imperil everything should he yield to her guidance. If, therefore, he could obtain the means of subsistence he resolved to remain in Hillaton, where he could occasionally see Mrs. Arnot. She had been able to inspire the hope of a better life, and she could best teach him how such a life was possible.

The next day circumstances prevented Mrs. Arnot from visiting the prison, and Haldane employed part of the time in writing to his mother a letter of mingled reproaches and apologies, interspersed with vague hopes and promises of future amendment, ending, however, with the positive assurance that he would not leave Hillaton unless compelled to do so by hunger.

To Mrs. Haldane this letter was only an aggravation of former misconduct, and a proof of the unnatural and impracticable character of her son. The fact that it was written from a prison was hideous, to begin with. That, after all the pains at which she had been to teach him what was right, he could suggest that she was in part to blame for his course seemed such black ingratitude that his apologies and acknowledgments of wrong went for nothing. She quite overlooked the hope, expressed here and there, that he might lead a very different life in the future. His large and self-confident assurances made before had come to naught, and she had not the tact to see that he would make this attempt in a different spirit.

It was not by any means a knightly or even a manly letter that he wrote to his mother; it was as confused as his own chaotic moral nature; but if Mrs. Haldane had had a little more of Mrs. Arnot's intuition, and less of prejudice, she might have seen scattered through it very hopeful indications. But even were such indications much more plain, her anger, caused by his refusal to leave Hillaton, and the belief that he would continue to disgrace himself and her, would have blinded her to them. Under the influence of this anger she sat down and wrote at once:

Since you cast off your mother for strangers—since you attempt again what you have proved yourself incapable of accomplishing—since you prefer to go out of jail to be a vagrant and a criminal in the streets, instead of accepting my offer to live a respectable and secluded life where your shame is unknown, I wash my hands of you, and shall take pains to let it be understood that I am no longer responsible for you or your actions. You must look to strangers solely until you can conform your course to the will of the one you have so greatly wronged.

Haldane received this letter on the morning of the day which would again give him freedom. Mrs. Arnot had visited him from time to time, and had been pleased to find him, as a general thing, in a better and more promising mood. He had been eager to listen to all that she had to say, and he seemed honestly bent on reform. And yet, while hopeful, she was not at all sanguine as to his future. He occasionally gave way to fits of deep despondency, and again was over-confident, while the causes of these changes were not very apparent, and seemingly resulted more from temperament than anything else. She feared that the bad habits of long standing, combining with his capricious and impulsive nature, would speedily betray him into his old ways. She was sure this would be the case unless the strong and steady hand of God sustained him, and she had tried to make him realize the same truth. This he did in a measure, and was exceedingly distrustful; and yet he had not been able to do much more than hope God would help him—for to anything like trustful confidence he was still a stranger.

The future was very dark and uncertain. What he was to do, how he was to live, he could not foresee. Even the prison seemed almost a refuge from the world, out into which he would be thrown that day, as one might be cast from a ship, to sink or swim, as the case might be.

While eager to receive counsel and advice from Mrs. Arnot, he felt a peculiar reluctance to take any pecuniary assistance, and he fairly dreaded to have her offer it; still, it might be all that would stand between him and hunger.

After receiving his mother's harsh reply to his letter, his despondency was too great even for anger. He was ashamed of his weakness and discouragement, and felt that they were unmanly, and yet was powerless to resist the leaden depression that weighed him down.

Mrs. Arnot had promised to call just before his release, and when she entered his cell she at once saw that something was amiss. In reply to her questioning he gave her the letter just received.

After reading it Mrs. Arnot did not speak for some time, and her face wore a sad, pained look.

At last she said, "You both misunderstand each other; but, Egbert, you have no right to cherish resentment. Your mother sincerely believes your course is all wrong, and that it will end worse than before. I think she is mistaken. And yet perhaps she is right, and it will be easier for you to commence your better and reformed life in the seclusion which she suggests. I am sorry to say it to you, Egbert but I have not been able to find any employment for you such as you would take, or I would be willing to have you accept. Perhaps Providence points to submission to your mother's will."

"If so, then I lose what little faith I have in Providence," he replied impetuously. "It is here, in this city, that I have fallen and disgraced myself, and it is here I ought to redeem myself, if I ever do. Weeks ago, in pride and self-confidence, I made the effort, and failed miserably, as might have been expected. Instead of being a gifted and brilliant man, as I supposed, that had been suddenly brought under a cloud as much through misfortune as fault, I have discovered myself to be a weak, commonplace, illiterate fellow, strong only in bad passions and bad habits. Can I escape these passions and habits by going elsewhere? You have told me, in a way that excited my hope, of God's power and willingness to help such as I am. If he will not help me here, he will not anywhere; and if, with his aid, I cannot surmount the obstacles in my way here, what is God's promised help but a phrase which means nothing, and what are we but victims of circumstances?"

"Are you not reaching conclusions rather fast, Egbert? You forget that I and myriads of others have had proof of God's power and willingness to help. If wide and varied experience can settle any fact, this one has been settled. But we should ever remember that we are not to dictate the terms on which he is to help us."

"I do not mean to do this," said Haldane eagerly, "but

I have a conviction that I ought to remain in Hillaton. To tell you the truth, Mrs. Arnot, I am afraid to go elsewhere," he added in a low tone, while tears suffused his eyes. "You are the only friend in the universe that I am sure cares for me, or that I can trust without misgivings. To me God is yet but little more than a name, and one that heretofore I have either forgotten or feared. You have led me to hope that it might be otherwise some day, but it is not so yet, and I dare not go away alone where no one cares for me, for I feel sure that I would give way to utter despondency, and recklessness would follow as a matter of course."

"O Egbert," sighed Mrs. Arnot, "how weak you are, and how foolish, in trusting so greatly in a mere fellow-creature."

"Yes, Mrs. Arnot, 'weak and foolish.' Those two words now seem to sum up my whole life and all there is of me."

"And yet," she added earnestly, "if you will, you can still achieve a strong, and noble character. O that you had the courage and heroic faith in God to fight out this battle to the end! Should you do so, as I told you before, you would be my ideal knight. Heaven would ring with your praise, however unfriendly the world might be. I cannot conceive of a grander victory than that of a debased nature over itself. If you should win such a victory, Egbert—if, in addition, you were able, by the blessing of God on your efforts, to build up a strong, true character—I would honor you above other men, even though you remained a wood-sawyer all your days," and her dark eyes became lustrous with deep feeling as she spoke.

Haldane looked at her fixedly for a moment, and grew very pale. He then spoke slowly and in a low tone:

"To fail after what you have said and after all your kindness would be terrible. To continue my old vile self, and also remember the prospect you now hold out—what could be worse? And yet what I shall do, what I shall be,

God only knows. But in sending you to me I feel that he has given me one more chance."

"Egbert," she replied eagerly, "God will give you chances as long as you breathe. Only the devil will tell you to despair. He, *never*. Remember this should you grow old in sin. To tell you the truth, however, as I see you going out into the world so humbled, so self-distrustful, I have far more hope for you than when you first left this place, fully assured that you were, in yourself, sufficient for all your peculiar difficulties. And now, once more, good-by, for a time. I will do everything I can for you. I have seen Mr. Growther to-day, and he appears very willing that you should return to his house for the present. Strange old man! I want to know him better, for I believe his evil is chiefly on the outside, and will fall off some day, to his great surprise."

CHAPTER XXXII

A SACRED REFRIGERATOR

THE glare of the streets was intolerable to Haldane after his confinement, and he hastened through them, looking neither to the right hand nor to the left. A growl from Mr. Growther's dog greeted him as he entered, and the old man himself snarled:

"Well, I s'pose you stood me as long as you could, and then went to prison for a while for a change."

"You are mistaken, Mr. Growther; I went to prison because I deserved to go there, and it's very good of you to let me come back again."

"No, it ain't good of me, nuther. I want a little peace and comfort, and how could I have 'em while you was bein' kicked and cuffed around the streets? Here, I'll get you some dinner. I s'pose they only gave you enough at jail to aggravate your in'ards."

"No, nothing more, please. Isn't there something I can do? I've sat still long enough."

Mr. Growther looked at him a moment, and then said:

"Are you sayin' that because you mean it?"

"Yes."

"Would you mind helpin' me make a little garden? I know I ought to have done it long ago, but I'm one of those 'crastinating cusses, and rheumatic in the bargain."

"I'll make your garden on the one condition that you stand by and boss the job."

"O, I'm good at bossin', if nothing else. There ain't much use of plantin' anything, though, for every pesky bug and worm in town will start for my patch as soon as they hear on't."

"I suppose they come on the same principle that I do."

"They hain't so welcome—the cussed little varmints! Some on 'em are so blasted mean that I know I ought to be easier on 'em just out of feller feelin'. Them cut-worms now—if they'd only take a plant and satisfy their natural appetites on it, it would go a good ways, and the rest o' the plants would have a chance to grow out of harm's way; but the nasty little things will jest eat 'em off above the ground, as if they was cut in two by a knife, and then go on to anuther. That's what I call a mean way of gettin' a livin'; but there's lots of people like 'em in town, who spile more than they eat. Then there's the squash-bug. If it's his nater to eat up the vines I s'pose he must do it, but why in thunder must he smell bad enough to knock you over into the bargain? It's allers been my private opinion that the devil made these pests, and the Lord had nothin' to do with 'em. The idea that he should create a rose, and then a rose-bug to spile it, ain't reconcilable to what little reason I've got."

"Well," replied Haldane with a glimmer of a smile, "I cannot account for rose-bugs and a good many worse things. I notice, however, that in spite of all these enemies people manage to raise a great deal that's very nice every year. Suppose we try it."

They were soon at work, and Haldane felt the better for a few hours' exercise in the open air.

The next morning Mrs. Arnot brought some papers which she said a legal friend wished copied, and she left with them, inclosed in an envelope, payment in advance. After she had gone Haldane offered the money to Mr. Growther, but the old man only growled:

"Chuck it in a drawer, and the one of us who wants it first can have it."

For the next two or three weeks Mrs. Arnot, by the dint of considerable effort, kept up a supply of MSS., of which copies were required, and she supplemented the prices which the parties concerned were willing to pay. Her charitable and helpful habits were well known to her friends, and they often enabled her thus to aid those to whom she could not give money direct. But this uncertain employment would soon fail, and what her protégé was then to do she could not foresee. No one would trust him, and no one cared to have him about his premises.

But in the meantime the young man was thinking deeply for himself. He soon concluded not to make Mr. Growther's humble cottage a hiding-place; and he commenced walking abroad through the city after the work of the day. He assumed no bravado, but went quietly on his way like any other passer-by. The majority of those who knew who he was either ignored his existence, or else looked curiously after him, but some took pains to manifest their contempt. He could not have been more lonely and isolated if he were walking a desert.

Among the promises he had made Mrs. Arnot was that he would attend church, and she naturally asked him to come to her own.

"As you feel toward my husband, it will probably not be pleasant for you to come to our pew," she had said; "but I hope the time will come when bygones will be bygones. The sexton, however, will give you a seat, and our minister preaches excellent sermons."

Not long after, true to his word, the young man went a little early, as he wished to be as unobtrusive as possible. At the same time there was nothing furtive or cringing in his nature. As he had openly done wrong, he was now resolved to try as openly to do right, and let people ascribe whatever motive they chose.

But his heart misgave him as he approached the new elegant church on the most fashionable street. He felt that his clothes were not in keeping with either the place of worship or the worshippers.

Mr. Arnot's confidential clerk was talking with the sexton as he hesitatingly mounted the granite steps, and he saw that dignified functionary, who seemed in some way made to order with the church over which he presided, eye him askance while he lent an ear to what was evidently a bit of his history. Walking quietly but firmly up to the official, Haldane asked:

"Will you give me a seat, sir?"

The man reddened, frowned, and then said:

"Really, sir, our seats are generally taken Sunday mornings. I think you will feel more at home at our mission chapel in Guy street."

"And among the guys, why don't you add?" retorted Haldane, his old spirit flashing up, and he turned on his heel and stalked back to Mr. Growther's cottage.

"Short sermon to-day," said the old man starting out of a doze.

Haldane told him of his reception.

The wrinkles in the quaint visage of his host grew deep and complicated, as though he had tasted something very bitter, and he remarked sententiously:

"If Satan could he'd pay that sexton a whoppin' sum to stand at the door and keep sinners out."

"No need of the devil paying him anything; the well-dressed Christians see to that. As I promised Mrs. Arnot to come, I tried to keep my word, but this flunky's face and manner alone are enough to turn away such as I am. None but the eminently respectable need apply at that gate of heaven. If it were not for Mrs. Arnot I would believe the whole thing a farce."

"Is Jesus Christ a farce?" asked the practical Mr. Growther, testily. "What is the use of jumping five hundred miles from the truth because you've happened to run afoul of some of those Pharisees that he cussed?"

Haldane laughed and said, "You have a matter-of-fact way of putting things that there is no escaping. It will, probably, do me more good to stay home and read the Bible to you than to be at church."

The confidential clerk, who had remained gossiping in the vestibule, thought the scene he had witnessed worth mentioning to his employer, who entered with Mrs. Arnot not very long after, and lingered for a word or two. The man of business smiled grimly, and passed on. He usually attended church once a day, partly from habit and partly because it was the respectable thing to do. He had been known to remark that he never lost anything by it, for some of his most successful moves suggested themselves to his mind during the monotony of the service.

To annoy his wife, and also to gratify a disposition to sneer at the faults of Christians, Mr. Arnot, at the dinner, commenced to commend ironically the sexton's course.

"A most judicious man!" he affirmed. "Saint Peter himself at the gate could not more accurately strain out the saints from the sinners—nay, he is even keener-eyed than Saint Peter, for he can tell first-class from second-class saints. Though our church is not full, I now understand why we have a mission chapel. You may trust 'Jeems' to keep out all but the very first-class—those who can exchange silk and broadcloth for the white robe. But what on earth could have brought about such a speedy transition from jail to church on the part of Haldane?"

"I invited him," said Mrs. Arnot, in a pained tone; "but I did not think it would be to meet with insult."

"Insult! Quite the reverse. I should think that such as he ought to feel it an honor to be permitted a place among the second-class saints."

Mrs. Arnot's thoughts were very busy that afternoon. She was not by nature an innovator, and, indeed, was inclined to accept the established order of things without very close questioning. Her Christian life had been developed chiefly by circumstances purely personal, and she had unconsciously found walks of usefulness apart from the organized church work. But she was a devout worshipper and a careful listener to the truth. It had been her custom to ride to the morning service, and, as they resided some distance from the church, to remain at home in the evening, giving all in her employ a chance to go out.

Concerning the financial affairs of the church she was kept well informed, for she was a liberal contributor, and also to all other good causes presented. From earliest years her eye had always been accustomed to the phases presented by a fashionable church, and everything moved forward so quietly and with such sacred decorum that the thought of anything wrong did not occur to her.

But the truth that one who was endeavoring to lead a better life had been practically turned from the door of God's house seemed to her a monstrous thing. How much truth was there in her husband's sarcasm? How far did her church represent the accessible Jesus of Nazareth, to whom all were welcomed, or how far did it misrepresent him? Now that her attention was called to the fact, she remembered that the congregation was chiefly made up of the *élite* of the city, and that she rarely had seen any one present who did not clearly present the fullest evidence of respectability. Were those whom the Master most emphatically came to seek and save excluded? She determined to find out speedily.

Summoning her coachman, she told him that she wished to attend church that evening. She dressed herself very plainly, and entered the church closely veiled. Instead of going to her own pew, she asked the judicious and discriminating sexton for a seat. After a careless glance he pointed to one of the seats near the door, and turned his back upon her. A richly dressed lady and gentleman entered soon after, and he was all attention, marshalling them up the aisle into Mrs. Arnot's own pew, since it was known she did not occupy it in the evening. A few decent, plain-looking women, evidently sent thither by the wealthy families in whose employ they were, came in hesitatingly, and those who did not take seats near the entrance, as a matter of course, were motioned thither without ceremony. The audience room was but sparsely filled, large families being

represented by one or two members or not at all. But Mrs.
Arnot saw none of Haldane's class present—none who looked
as if they were in danger, and needed a kind, strong, rescuing hand—none who looked hungry and athirst for truth
because perishing for its lack. In that elegant and eminently respectable place, upholstered and decorated with
faultless taste, there was not a hint of publicans and sinners. One might suppose he was in the midst of the mil-
lennium, and that the classes to whom Christ preached had
all become so thoroughly converted that they did not even
need to attend church. There was not a suggestion of the
fact that but a few blocks away enough to fill the empty
pews were living worse than heathen lives.

The choir performed their part melodiously, and a master in music could have found no fault with the technical
rendering of the musical score. They were paid to sing,
and they gave to such of their employers as cared to be
present every note as it was written, in its full value. As
never before, it struck Mrs. Arnot as a performance. The
service she had attended hitherto was partly the creation of
her own earnest and devotional spirit. To-night she was
learning to know the service as it really existed.

The minister was evidently a conscientious man, for he
had prepared his evening discourse for his thin audience
as thoroughly as he had his morning sermon. Every word
was carefully written down, and the thought of the text was
exhaustively developed. But Mrs. Arnot was too far back
to hear well. The poor man seemed weary and discouraged
with the arid wastes of empty seats over which he must scat-
ter the seeds of truth to no purpose. He looked dim and
ghostly in the far-away pulpit, and in spite of herself his
sermon began to have the aspect of a paid performance,
the effect of which would scarcely be more appreciable than
the sighing of the wind without. The keenest theologian
could not detect the deviation of a hair from the received
orthodox views, and the majority present were evidently
satisfied that his views would be correct, for they did not

give very close attention. The few plain domestics near her dozed and nodded through the hour, and so gained some physical preparation for the toils of the week, but their spiritual natures were as clearly dormant as their lumpish bodies.

After the service Mrs. Arnot lingered, to see if any one would speak to her as a stranger and ask her to come again. Such was clearly not the habit of the congregation. She felt that her black veil, an evidence of sorrow, was a sort of signal of distress which ought to have lured some one to her side with a kind word or two, but beyond a few curious glances she was unnoticed. People spoke who were acquainted, who had been introduced to each other. As the worshippers (?) hastened out, glad to escape to regions where living questions and interests existed, the sexton, who had been dozing in a comfortable corner, bustled to the far end of the church, and commenced, with an assistant, turning out the lights on either side so rapidly that it seemed as if a wave of darkness was following those who had come thither ostensibly seeking light.

Mrs. Arnot hastened to her carriage, where it stood under the obscuring shadow of a tree, and was driven home sad and indignant—most indignant at herself that she had been so absorbed in her own thoughts and life that she had not discovered that the church to build and sustain which she had given so liberally was scarcely better than a costly refrigerator.

CHAPTER XXXIII

A DOUBTFUL BATTLE IN PROSPECT

THE painful impression made by the evening service that has been described acted as a rude disenchantment, and the beautiful church, to which Mrs. Arnot had returned every Sabbath morning with increasing pleasure, became as repulsive as it had been sacred and attractive. To her sincere and earnest spirit anything in the nature of a sham was peculiarly offensive; and what, she often asked herself, could be more un-Christlike than this service which had been held in his name?

The revelation so astonished and disheartened her that she was prone to believe that there was something exceptional in that miserable Sabbath evening's experience, and she determined to observe further and more closely before taking any action. She spoke frankly of her feelings and purposes to Haldane, and in so doing benefited the young man very much; for he was thus led to draw a sharp line between Christ and the Christlike and that phase of Christianity which is largely leavened with this world. No excuse was given him to jumble the true and the false together.

"You will do me a favor if you will quietly enter the church next Sunday morning and evening, and unobtrusively take one of the seats near the door," she said to him. "I wish to bring this matter to an issue as soon as possible. If you could manage to enter a little in advance of me, I would also be glad. I know how Christ received sinners, and I would like to see how we who profess to be representing him, receive those who come to his house."

Haldane did as she requested. In a quiet and perfectly unobtrusive manner he walked up the granite steps into the vestibule, and his coarse, gray suit, although scrupulously clean, was conspicuous in its contrast with the elegant attire of the other worshippers. He himself was conspicuous also; for many knew who he was, and whispered the information to others. A "jail-bird" was, indeed, a *rara avis* in that congregation, and there was a slight, but perfectly decorous, sensation. However greatly these elegant people might lack the spirit of Him who was "the friend of publicans and sinners," they would not for the world do anything that was overtly rude or ill-bred. Only the official sexton frowned visibly as the youth took a seat near the door. Others looked askance or glided past like polished icicles. Haldane's teeth almost chattered with the cold. He felt himself oppressed, and almost pushed out of the house, by the moral atmosphere created by the repellent thoughts of some who apparently felt the place defiled by his presence. Mrs. Arnot, with her keen intuition, felt this atmosphere also, and detected on the part of one or two of the officers of the Church an unchristian spirit. Although the sermon was an excellent one that morning, she did not hear it.

In the evening a lady draped in a black veil sat by Haldane. The service was but a dreary counterpart of the one of the previous Sabbath. The sky had been overcast and slightly threatening, and still fewer worshippers had ventured out.

Beyond furtive and curious glances no one noticed them save the sexton, who looked and acted as if Haldane's continued coming was a nuisance, which, in some way, he must manage to abate.

The young man waited for Mrs. Arnot at her carriage-door, and said as he handed her in:

"I have kept my word; but please do not ask me to come to this church again, or I shall turn infidel."

"I shall not come myself again," she replied, "unless there is a decided change."

The next morning she wrote notes to two of the leading officers of the church, asking them to call that evening; and her request was so urgent that they both came at the appointed hour.

Mrs. Arnot's quiet but clear and distinct statement of the evils of which she had become conscious greatly surprised and annoyed them. They, with their associates, had been given credit for organizing and "running" the most fashionable and prosperous church in town. An elegant structure had been built and paid for, and such a character given the congregation that if strangers visited or were about to take up their abode in the city they were made to feel that the door of this church led to social position and the most aristocratic circles. Of course, mistakes were made. People sometimes elbowed their way in who were evidently flaunting weeds among the patrician flowers, and occasionally plain, honest, but somewhat obtuse souls would come as to a Christian church. But people who were "not desirable"—the meaning of this phrase had become well understood in Hillaton—were generally frozen out by an atmosphere made so chilly, even in August, that they were glad to escape to other associations less benumbing. Indeed, it was now so generally recognized that only those of the best and most assured social position were "desirable," that few others ventured up the granite steps or sought admittance to this region of sacred respectability. And yet all this had been brought about so gradually, and so entirely within the laws of good breeding and ecclesiastical usage, and also under the most orthodox preaching, that no one could lay his finger on anything upon which to raise an issue.

The result was just what these officers had been working for, and it was vexatious indeed that, after years of successful manipulation, a lady of Mrs. Arnot's position should threaten to make trouble.

"My dear Mrs. Arnot," said one of these polished gentlemen, with a suavity that was designed to conciliate, but

which was nevertheless tinged with philosophical dogma-
tism, "there are certain things that will not mix, and the attempt to mingle them is wasting time on the impossible. It
is in accordance with the laws of nature that each class
should draw together according to their affinities and social
status. Our church is now entirely homogeneous, and
everything moves forward without any friction."

"It appears to me sadly machine-like," the lady remarked.

"Indeed, madam," with a trace of offended dignity, "is
not the Gospel ably preached?"

"Yes, but it is not obeyed. We have been made homogeneous solely on worldly principles, and not on those taught
in the Gospels."

They could not agree, as might have been supposed, and
Mrs. Arnot was thought to be unreasonable and full of impracticable theories.

"Very well, gentlemen," said Mrs. Arnot, with some
warmth, "if there can be no change in these respects, no
other course is left for me but to withdraw;" and the
religious politicians bowed themselves out, much relieved, feeling that this was the easiest solution of the
question.

Mrs. Arnot soon after wrote to the Rev. Dr. Barstow,
pastor of the church, for a letter of dismission. The good
man was much surprised by the contents of this missive.
Indeed, it so completely broke a chain of deep theological
speculation that he deserted his study for the street. Here
he met an officer of the church, a man somewhat advanced
in years, whom he had come to regard as rather reserved
and taciturn in disposition. But in his perplexity he ex-
hibited Mrs. Arnot's letter, and asked an explanation.

"Well," said the gentleman, uneasily, "I understand
that Mrs. Arnot is dissatisfied, and perhaps she has some
reason to be."

"Upon what grounds?" asked the clergyman hastily.

"Suppose we call upon her," was the reply. "I would

rather you should hear her reasons from herself; and, in fact, I would be glad to hear them also."

Half an hour later they sat in Mrs. Arnot's parlor.

"My dear madam," said Dr. Barstow, "are you willing to tell us frankly what has led to the request contained in this letter. I hope that I am in no way to blame."

"Perhaps we have all been somewhat to blame," replied Mrs. Arnot in a tone so gentle and quiet as to prove that she was under the influence of no unkindly feeling or resentment; "at least I feel that I have been much to blame for not seeing what is now but too plain. But habit and custom deaden our perceptions. The aspect of our church was that of good society—nothing to jar upon or offend the most critical taste. Your sermons were deeply thoughtful and profound, and I both enjoyed and was benefited by them. I came and went wrapped up in my own spiritual life and absorbed in my own plans and work, when, unexpectedly, an incident occurred which revealed to me what I fear is the *animus* and character of our church organization. I can best tell you what I mean by relating my experience and that of a young man whom I have every reason to believe wishes to lead a better life, yes, even a Christian life;" and she graphically portrayed all that had occurred, and the impressions made upon her by the atmosphere she had found prevalent, when she placed herself in the attitude of a humble stranger.

"And now," she said in conclusion, "do we represent Christ, or are we so leavened by the world that it may be doubted whether he would acknowledge us?"

The minister shaded his pained and troubled face with his hand.

"We represent the world," said the church officer emphatically; "I have had a miserable consciousness of whither we were drifting for a long time, but everything has come about so gradually and so properly, as it were, that I could find no one thing upon which I could lay my finger and say, This is wrong and I protest against it. Of course, if I had heard the sexton make such a remark to any one seeking to enter the house of God as was made to the young man you mention I should have interfered. And yet the question is one of great difficulty. Can such diverse classes meet on common ground?"

"My dear sir," said Mrs. Arnot earnestly, "I do not think we, as a church, are called upon to adjust these diverse classes, and to settle, on the Sabbath, nice social distinctions. The Head of the Church said, 'Whosoever will, let him come.' We, pretending to act in his name and by his authority, say, 'Whosoever is sufficiently respectable and well-dressed, let him come.' I feel that I cannot any longer be a party to this perversion.

"If we would preserve our right to be known as a Christian church we must say to all, to the poor, to the most sinful and debased, as well as to those who are now welcomed, 'Come'; and when they are within our walls they should be made to feel that the house does not belong to an aristocratic clique, but rather to him who was the friend of publicans and sinners. Christ adjusted himself to the diverse classes. Are we his superiors?"

"But, my dear madam, are there to be no social distinctions?"

"I am not speaking of social distinctions. Birth, culture, and wealth will always, and very properly, too, make great differences. In inviting people to our homes we may largely consult our own tastes and preferences, and neither good sense nor Christian duty requires that there should be intimacy between those unfitted for it by education and character. But a church is not our house, but God's house, and what right have we to stand in the door and turn away those whom he most cordially invites? Christ had his beloved disciple, and so we can have our beloved and congenial friends. But there were none too low or lowly for him to help by direct personal effort, by sympathetic contact, and I, for one, dare not ignore his example."

"Do you not think we can better accomplish this work by our mission chapel?"

"Where is your precedent? Christ washed the feet of fishermen in order to give us an example of humility, and to teach us that we should be willing to serve any one in his name. I heartily approve of mission chapels as outposts; but, as in earthly warfare, they should be posts of honor, posts for the brave, the sagacious, and the most worthy. If they are maintained in the character of second-class cars, they are to that extent unchristian. If those who are gathered there are to be kept there solely on account of their dress and humble circumstances, I would much prefer taking my chances of meeting my Master with them than in the church which practically excludes them.

"Christ said, 'I was a stranger, and ye took me in.' I came to our church as a stranger twice. I was permitted to walk in and walk out, but no one spoke to me, no one invited me to come again. It seems to me that I would starve rather than enter a private house where I was so coldly treated. I have no desire for startling innovations. I simply wish to unite myself with a church that is trying to imitate the example of the Master, and where all, whatever may be their garb or social and moral character, are cordially invited and sincerely welcomed."

Dr. Barstow now removed his hand from his face. It was pale, but its expression was resolute and noble.

"Mrs. Arnot, permit me to say that you are both right and wrong," he said. "Your views of what a church should be are right; you are wrong in wishing to withdraw before having patiently and prayerfully sought to inculcate a true Christian spirit among those to whom you owe and have promised Christian fidelity. You know that I have not very long been the pastor of this church, but I have already felt that something was amiss. I have been oppressed and benumbed with a certain coldness and formality in our church life. At the same time I admit, with contrition, that I have given way to my besetting sin. I am

naturally a student, and when once in my study I forget
the outside world. I am prone to become wholly occupied
with the thought of my text, and to forget those for whom
I am preparing my discourse. I, too, often think more of
the sermon than of the people, forgetting the end in the
means, and thus I fear I was becoming but a voice, a
religious philosophy, among them, instead of a living and
a personal power. You have been awakened to the truth,
Mrs. Arnot, and you have awakened me. I do not feel
equal to the task which I clearly foresee before me; I may
fail miserably, but I shall no longer darken counsel with
many words. You have given me much food for thought;
and while I cannot foretell the end, I think present duty
will be made clear. In times of perplexity it is our part to
do what seems right, asking God for guidance, and then
leave the consequences to him. One thing seems plain to
me, however, that it is your present duty to remain with
us, and give your prayers and the whole weight of your
influence on the side of reform."

"Dr. Barstow," said Mrs. Arnot, her face flushing
slightly, "you are right; you are right. I have been
hasty, and, while condemning others, was acting wrong
myself. You have shown the truer Christian spirit. I
will remain while there is any hope of a change for the
better."

"Well, Mrs. Arnot," said Mr. Blakeman, the elderly
church officer, "I have drawn you out partly to get your
views and partly to get some clearer views myself. I, too,
am with you, doctor, in this struggle; but I warn you both
that we shall have a hot time before we thaw the ice out of
our church."

"First pure, and then peaceable," said the minister
slowly and musingly; and then they separated, each feeling somewhat as soldiers who are about to engage in a severe
and doubtful battle.

CHAPTER XXXIV

A FOOTHOLD

THE skies did not brighten for Haldane, and he remained perplexed and despondent. When one wishes to reform, everything does not become lovely in this unfriendly world. The first steps are usually the most difficult, and the earliest experience the most disheartening. God never designed that reform should be easy. As it is, people are too ready to live the life which renders reform necessary. The ranks of the victims of evil would be doubled did not a wholesome fear of the consequences restrain.

Within a few short weeks the fortunes of the wealthy and self-confident youth had altered so greatly that now he questioned whether the world would give him bread, except on conditions that were painfully repugnant.

There was his mother's offer, it is true; but had Mrs. Haldane considered the nature of this offer, even she could scarcely have made it. Suppose he tried to follow out his mother's plan, and went to a city where he was unknown, could she expect an active young fellow to go to an obscure boarding-house, and merely eat and sleep? By an inevitable law the springing forces of his nature must find employment either in good or evil. If he sought employment of any kind the question would at once arise, "Who are you?" and sooner or later would come his history. In his long, troubled reveries he thought of all this, and the prospect of vegetating in dull obscurity at his mother's expense was as pleasant as that of being buried alive.

Moreover, he could not endure to leave Hillaton in utter

defeat. He was prostrate, and felt the foot of adverse fate upon his neck, but he would not acknowledge himself conquered. If he could regain his feet he would renew the struggle; and he hoped in some way to do so. As yet, however, the future was a wall of darkness.

Neither did he find any rest for his spiritual feet. For some reason he could not grasp the idea of a personal God who cared enough for him to give any practical help. In spite of all that Mrs. Arnot could say, his heart remained as cold and heavy as a stone within his breast.

But to some extent he could appreciate the picture she had presented. He saw one who, through weakness and folly, had fallen into the depths of degradation, patiently and bravely fighting his way up to a true manhood; and he had been made to feel that it was such a noble thing to do that he longed to accomplish it. Whether he could or no he was not sure, for his old confidence was all gone. But he daily grew more bent on making an honest trial, and in this effort a certain native persistency and unwillingness to yield would be of much help to him.

He was now willing, also, to receive any aid which self-respect permitted him to accept, and was grateful for the copying obtained for him by Mrs. Arnot. But she frankly told him that it would not last long. The question what he should do next pressed heavily upon him.

As he was reading the paper to Mr. Growther one evening, his eye caught an advertisement which stated that more hands were needed at a certain factory in the suburbs. He felt sure that if he presented himself in the morning with the others he would be refused, and he formed the bold purpose of going at once to the manufacturer. Having found the stately residence, he said to the servant who answered his summons:

"Will you say to Mr. Ivison that a person wishes to see him?"

The maid eyed him critically, and concluded, from his garb, to leave him standing in the hall.

Mr. Ivison left his guests in the parlor and came out, annoyed at the interruption.

"Well, what do you wish, sir?" he said, in a tone that was far from being encouraging, at the same time gaining an unfavorable impression from Haldane's dress.

"In the evening paper you advertised for more hands in your factory. I wish employment."

"Are you drunk, or crazy, that you thus apply at my residence?" was the harsh reply.

"Neither, sir; I—"

"You are very presuming, then."

"You would not employ me if I came in the morning."

"What do you mean? Who are you?"

"I am at least human. Can you give one or two moments to the consideration of my case?"

"One might afford that much," said the gentleman with a half-apologetic laugh; for the pale face and peculiar bearing of the stranger were beginning to interest him.

"I do not ask more of your time, and will come directly to the point. My name is Haldane, and, as far as I am concerned, you know nothing good concerning me."

"You are correct," said Mr. Ivison coldly. "I shall not need your services."

"Mr. Ivison," said Haldane in a tone that made the gentleman pause, "ought I to be a thief and a vagabond?"

"Certainly not."

"Then why do you, and all who, like you, have honest work to give, leave me no other alternative? I have acted wrongly and foolishly, but I wish to do better. I do not ask a place of trust, only work with others, under the eyes of others, where I could not rob you of a cent's worth if I wished. In the hurry and routine of your office you would not listen to me, so I come to-night and make this appeal. If you refuse it, and I go to the devil, you will have a hand in the result."

The prompt business-man, whose mind had learned to work with the rapidity of his machinery, looked at the troubled, half-desperate face a moment, and then said emphatically:

"By Jove, you are right! I'll give you work. Come to-morrow. Good-night, and good luck to your good intentions. But remember, no nonsense."

Here at last was a chance; here at last was regular employment. It was one step forward. Would he be able to hold it? This seemed doubtful on the morrow after he had realized the nature of his surroundings. He was set to work in a large room full of men, boys, and slatternly-dressed girls. He was both scolded and laughed at for the inevitable awkwardness of a new beginner, and soon his name and history began to be whispered about. During the noon recess a rude fellow flung the epithet of "jail-bird" at him, and, of course, it stuck like a burr. Never in all his life had he made such an effort at self-control as that which kept his hands off this burly tormentor.

He both puzzled and annoyed his companions. They knew that he did not belong to their class, and his bearing and manner made them unpleasantly conscious of his superiority; and yet all believed themselves so much more respectable than he, that they felt it was a wrong to them that he should be there at all. Thus he was predestined to dislike and ill-treatment. But that he could act as if he were deaf and blind to all that they could do or say was more than they could understand. With knit brows and firmly-closed lips he bent his whole mind to the mastery of the mechanical duties required of him, and when they were over he strode straight to his humble lodging-place.

Mr. Growther watched him curiously as he reacted into lassitude and despondency after the strain and tension of the day.

"It's harder to stand than 'tis to git along with me, isn't it?"

"Yes, much harder."

"O thunder! better give it up, then, and try something else."

"No, it's my only chance."

"There's plenty other things to do."

"Not for me. These vulgar wretches I am working with think it an outrage that a 'jail-bird,' as they call me, contaminates the foul air that they breathe. I may be driven out by them; but," setting his teeth, "I won't give up this foothold of my own accord."

"You might have been President if you had shown such grit before you got down."

"That's not pleasant to think of now."

"I might 'a known that; but it's my mean way of comfortin' people. A-a-h."

Haldane's new venture out into the world could scarcely have had a more painful and prosaic beginning; but, as he said, he had gained a "foothold."

There was one other encouraging fact, of which he did not know. Mr. Ivison sent for the foreman of the room in which Haldane had been set at work, and said:

"Give the young fellow a fair chance, and report to me from time to time how he behaves; but say nothing of this to him. If he gets at his old tricks, discharge him at once; but if he shows the right spirit, I wish to know it."

CHAPTER XXXV

"THAT SERMON WAS A BOMBSHELL"

THE following Sabbath morning smiled so brightly that one might be tempted to believe that there was no sin and misery in the world, and that such a church as Mrs. Arnot condemned was an eminently proper organization. As the congregation left their elegant homes, and in elegant toilets wended their way to their elegant church, they saw nothing in the blue sky and sunshine to remind them of the heavy shadows brooding over the earth. What more was needed than that they should give an hour to their æsthetic worship, as they had done in the past when the weather permitted, and then return to dinner and a nap and all the ordinary routine of life? There were no "beasts at Ephesus" to fight now. The times had changed, and to live in this age like an ancient Christian would be like going to Boston on foot when one might take a palace car. Hundreds of fully grown, perfectly sane people filed into the church, who complacently felt that in attending service once or twice a week, if so inclined, they were very good Christians. And yet, strange to say, there was a conspicuous cross on the spire, and they had named their church "St. Paul's."

St. Paul! Had they read his life? If so, how came they to satirize themselves so severely? A dwarf is the more to be pitied if named after a giant.

It was very queer that this church should name itself after the tent-maker, who became all things to all men, and who said, "I made myself servant unto all that I might gain the more."

It was very unfortunate for them to have chosen this saint, and yet the name, Saint Paul, had a very aristocratic sound in Hillaton, and thus far had seemed peculiarly fitted to the costly edifice on which it was carved.

And never had the church seemed more stately than on this brilliant Sabbath morning, never had its elegance and that of the worshippers seemed more in harmony.

But the stony repose and calm of their Gothic temple was not reflected in the faces of the people. There was a general air of perturbation and expectancy. The peculiar and complacent expression of those who are conscious of being especially well dressed and respectable was conspicuously absent. Annoyed, vexed, anxious faces passed into the vestibule. Knots of twos, threes, and half-dozens lingered and talked eagerly, with emphatic gestures and much shaking of heads. Many who disliked rough weather from any cause avoided their fellow-members, and glided hastily in, looking worried and uncomfortable. Between the managing officers, who had felicitated themselves on having secured a congregation containing the *crème de la crème* of the city, on one hand, and the disquieted Mr. Blakeman, who found the church growing uncomfortably cold, on the other, Mrs. Arnot's words and acts and the minister's implied pledge to bring the matter squarely to an issue, had become generally known, and a foreboding as of some great catastrophe oppressed the people. If the truth were known, there were very general misgivings; and, now that the people had been led to think, there were some uncomfortable aspects to the question. Even that august dignitary the sexton was in a painful dilemma as to whether it would be best to assume an air of offended dignity, or veer with these eddying and varying currents until sure from what quarter the wind would finally blow. He had learned that it was Mrs. Arnot whom he had twice carelessly motioned with his thumb into a back seat, and he could not help remarking to several of the more conservative members, that "it was very unjust and also unkind in Mrs. Arnot to palm herself off on him as an ordinary pusson, when for a long time it had been the plainly understood policy of the church not to encourage ordinary pussons."

But the rumor that something unusual was about to take place at St. Paul's brought thither on this particular Sabbath all kinds and descriptions of people; and the dignified functionary whose duty it was to seat them grew so hot and flustered with his unwonted tasks, and made such strange blunders, that both he and others felt that they were on the verge of chaos. But the most extraordinary appearing personage was no other than Mr. Jeremiah Growther; and, as with his gnarled cane he hobbled along at Haldane's side, he looked for all the world as if some grotesque and antique carving had come to life and was out for an airing. Not only the sexton, but many others, looked askance at the tall, broad-shouldered youth of such evil fame, and his weird-appearing companion, as they walked quite far up the aisle before they could find a seat.

Many rubbed their eyes to be sure it was not a dream. What had come over the decorous and elegant St. Paul's? When before had its dim, religious light revealed such scenes? Whence this irruption of strange, uncouth creatures—a jail-bird in a laborer's garb, and the profane old hermit, whom the boys had nicknamed "Jerry Growler," and who had not been seen in church for years.

Mrs. Arnot, followed by many eyes, passed quietly up to her pew, and bowed her head in prayer.

Prayer! Ah! in their perturbation some had forgotten that this was the place of prayer, and hastily bowed their heads also.

Mr. Arnot had been engaged in his business to the very steps, and much too absorbed during the week to hear or heed any rumors; but as he walked up the aisle he stared around in evident surprise, and gave several furtive glances over his shoulder after being seated. As his wife raised her head, he leaned toward her and whispered:

"What's the matter with Jeems? for, if I mistake not,

there are a good many second-class saints here to-day."
But not a muscle changed in Mrs. Arnot's pale face.
Indeed, she scarcely heard him. Her soul was and had
been for several days in the upper sanctuary, in the presence of God, pleading with him that he would return to this
• earthly temple which the spirit of the world had seemingly
usurped.

When Dr. Barstow arose to commence the service, a profound hush fell upon the people. Even his face and bearing impressed and awed them, and it was evident that he,
too, had climbed some spiritual mountain, and had been
face to face with God.

As he proceeded with the service in tones that were deep
and magnetic, the sense of unwonted solemnity increased.
Hymns had been selected which the choir could not perform, but must sing; and the relation between the sacred
words and the music was apparent. The Scripture lessons
were read as if they were a message for that particular congregation and for that special occasion, and, as the simple
and authoritative words fell on the ear the general misgiving
was increased. They seemed wholly on Mrs. Arnot's side;
or, rather, she was on theirs.

When, at last, Dr. Barstow rose, not as a sacred orator
and theologian who is about to *deliver* a sermon, but rather
as an earnest man, who had something of vital moment to
say, the silence became almost oppressive.

Instead of commencing by formally announcing his text,
as was his custom, he looked silently and steadily at his
people for a moment, thus heightening their expectancy.

"My friends," he began slowly and quietly, and there
was a suggestion of sorrow in his tone rather than of menace
or denunciation; "my friends, I wish to ask your calm and
unprejudiced attention to what I shall say this morning. I
ask you to interpret my words in the light of the word of
God and your own consciences; and if I am wrong in any
respect I will readily acknowledge it. Upon a certain occasion Christ said to his disciples, 'Ye know not what man-

ner of spirit ye are of'; and he at once proved how widely
his spirit differed from theirs. They accepted the lesson—
they still followed him, and through close companionship
eventually acquired his merciful, catholic spirit. But at
this time they did not understand him nor themselves.
Perhaps we can best understand the spirit *we* are of by
considering his, and by learning to know him better whom
we worship, by whose name we are called.

"During the past week I have been brought face to face
with the Christ of the Bible, rather than the Christ of theology and philosophy, who has hitherto dwelt in my study;
and I have learned with sorrow and shame that my spirit
differed widely from his. The Christ that came from heaven
thought of the people, and had compassion on the multitude.   I was engrossed with my sermons, my systems of
truth, and nice interpretations of passages that I may have
rendered more obscure. But I have made a vow in his
name and strength that henceforth I will no longer come
into this pulpit, or go into any other, to deliver sermons of
my own.   I shall no longer philosophize about Christ, but
endeavor to lead you directly to Christ; and thus you will
learn by comparison what manner of spirit you are of, and,
I trust, become imbued with his Spirit.   I shall speak the
truth in love, and yet without fear, and with no wordy disguise.   Henceforth I do not belong to you but to my Master, and I shall present the Christ who loved all, who died
for all, and who said to all, 'Whosoever will, let him come!'"

"You will find my text in the Gospel of St. John, the
nineteenth chapter and fifth verse:

"'Then came Jesus forth, wearing the crown of thorns
and the purple robe.   And Pilate saith unto them, Behold
the Man!'

"Let us behold him to-day, and learn to know him and
to know ourselves better.   If we discover any sad and fatal
mistake in our religious life, let us correct it before it is too
late."

It would be impossible to portray the effect of the ser-

mon that followed, coming, as it did, from a strong soul
stirred to its depths by the truth under consideration. The
people for the time being were swayed by it and carried
away. What was said was seen to be truth, felt to be
truth; and as the divine Man stood out before them luminous in his own loving and compassionate deeds, which
manifested his character and the principles of the faith he
founded, the old, exclusive, self-pleasing life of the church
shrivelled up as a farce and a sham.

"In conclusion," said Dr. Barstow, "what was the spirit
of this Man when he summoned publicans and fishermen to
be his followers? what was his spirit when he laid his hand
on the leper? what, when he said to the outcast, 'Neither
do I condemn thee; go and sin no more'? what, when to
the haughty Pharisees, the most respectable people of that
day, he threatened, 'Woe unto you!'

"He looked after the rich and almost perfect young man,
by whom he was nevertheless rejected, and loved him; he
also said to the penitent thief, 'To-day thou shalt be with
me in Paradise.' His heart was as large as humanity.
Such was his spirit."

After a moment's pause, in which there was a hush of
breathless expectancy, Dr. Barstow's deep tones were again
heard. "God grant that henceforth yonder doors may be
open to all whom Christ received, and with the same welcome that he gave. If this cannot be, the name of St.
Paul, the man who 'made himself the servant unto all that
he might gain the more,' can no longer remain upon this
church save in mockery. If this cannot be, whoever may
come to this temple, Christ will not enter it, nor dwell
within it."

The people looked at each other, and drew a long breath.
Even those who were most in love with the old system forgot Dr. Barstow, and felt for the moment that they had a
controversy with his Master.

The congregation broke up in a quiet and subdued manner. All were too deeply impressed by what they had heard

to be in a mood for talking as yet; and of the majority, it should be said in justice that, conscious of wrong, they were honestly desirous of a change for the better.

During the sermon Mr. Growther's quaint and wrinkled visage had worked most curiously, and there were times when he with difficulty refrained from a hearty though rather profane indorsement.

On his way home he said to Haldane, "I've lived like a heathen on Lord's day and all days; but, by the holy poker, I'll hear that parson hereafter every Sunday, rain or shine, if I have to fight my way into the church with a club."

A peculiar fire burned in the young man's eyes and his lips were very firm, but he made no reply. The Man whose portraiture he had beheld that day was a revelation, and he hoped that this divine yet human Friend might make a man of him.

"Well," remarked Mr. Arnot, sententiously, "that sermon was a perfect bombshell; and, mark my words, it will either blow the doctor out of his pulpit, or some of the first-class saints out of their pews."

But a serene and hopeful light shone from Mrs. Arnot's eyes, and she only said, in a low tone:

"The Lord is in his holy temple."

CHAPTER XXXVI

MR. GROWTHER FEEDS AN ANCIENT GRUDGE

THE problem in regard to the future of St. Paul's Church, which had so greatly burdened Dr. Barstow, was substantially solved. Christ had obtained control of the preacher's heart, and henceforth would not be a dogma, but a living presence, in his sermons. The Pharisees of old could not keep the multitudes from him, though their motives for following him were often very mixed. Although the philosophical Christ of theology, whom Dr. Barstow had ably preached, could not change the atmosphere of St. Paul's, the Christ of the Bible, the Man of Sorrows, the meek and lowly Nazarene, could, and the masses would be tempted to feel that they had a better right in a place sacred to his worship than those who resembled him in spirit as little as they did in the pomp of their life.

There would be friction at first, and some serious trouble. Mr. Arnot's judgment was correct, and some of the "first-class saints" (in their own estimation) would be "blown out of their pews." St. Paul's would eventually cease to be *the* fashionable Church *par excellence;* and this fact alone would be good and sufficient reason for a change on the part of some who intend to be select in their associations on earth, whatever relations with the "mixed multitude" they may have to endure in heaven. But the warmhearted and true-hearted would remain; and every church grows stronger as the Pharisees depart and the publicans and sinners enter.

The congregation that gathered at the evening service of

the memorable Sabbath described in the previous chapter was prophetic. Many of the wealthy and aristocratic members were absent, either from habit or disgust. Haldane, Mr. Growther, and many who in some respects resembled them, were present. "Jeems," the discriminating sexton, had sagaciously guessed that the wind was about to blow from another quarter, and was veering around also, as fast as he deemed it prudent. "Ordinary pussons" received more than ordinary attention, and were placed within earshot of the speaker.

But the problem of poor Haldane's future was not clear by any means. It is true a desire to live a noble life had been kindled in his heart, but as yet it was little more than a good impulse, an aspiration. In the fact that his eyes had been turned questioningly and hopefully toward the only One who has ever been able to cope with the mystery of evil, there was rich promise; but just what this divine Friend could do for him he understood as little as did the fishermen of Galilee. They looked for temporal change and glory; he was looking for some vague and marvellous change and exaltation.

But the Sabbath passed, and he remained his old self. Hoping, longing for the change did not produce it.

It was one of Mr. Growther's peculiarities to have a fire upon the hearth even when the evenings were so warm as not to require it. "Might as well kinder git ourselves used to heat," he would growl when Haldane remonstrated.

After the evening service they both lowered at the fire for some time in silence.

"Except ye be converted, and become as little children, ye shall not enter into the kingdom of heaven," had been Dr. Barstow's text; and, as is usually the case, the necessity of conversion had been made clearer than just what conversion is; and many more than the disquieted occupants of the quaint old kitchen had been sent home sorely perplexed how to set about the simple task of "believing." But it was a happy thing for all that they had been awakened to the fact that something must be done. After that sermon none could delude themselves with the hope that being decorous, well-dressed worshippers at St. Paul's would be all that was required.

But Mr. Growther needed no argument on this subject, and he had long believed that his only chance was, as he expressed it, "such an out-and-out shakin' to pieces, and makin' over agin that I wouldn't know myself." Then he would rub his rheumatic legs despondently and add, "But my speretual j'ints have got as stiff and dry as these old walkin' pins; and when I try to git up some good sort o' feelin' it's like pumpin' of a dry pump. I only feel real hearty when I'm a cussin'. A-a-h!"

But the day's experience and teaching had awakened anew in his breast, as truly as in Haldane's, the wish that he could be converted, whatever that blessed and mysterious change might be; and so, with his wrinkled face seamed with deeper and more complex lines than usual, the poor old soul stared at the fire, which was at once the chief source of his comfort and the emblem of that which he most dreaded. At last he snarled:

"I'm a blasted old fool for goin' to meetin' and gittin' all riled up so. Here, I haven't had a comfortable doze to-day, and I shall be kickin' around all night with nothin' runnin' in my head but 'Except ye be convarted, except ye be convarted'; I wish I had as good a chance of bein' convarted as I have of bein' struck by lightnin'."

"I wish I needed conversion as little as you," said Haldane despondently.

"Now look here," snapped the old man; "I'm in no mood for any nonsense to-night. I want you to know I never have been converted, and I can prove it to you plaguy quick if you stroke me agin the fur. You've got the advantage of me in this business, though you have been a hard cuss; for you are young and kind o' limber yet." Then, as he glanced at the discouraged youth, his manner changed, and in a tone that was meant to be kindly he ad.

ded, "There, there! Why don't you pluck up heart? If
I was as young as you be, I'd get converted if it took me
all summer."

Haldane shook his head, and after a moment slowly and
musingly said, as much to himself as to the giver of this
good advice:

"I'm in the Slough of Despond, and I don't know how
to get out. I can see the sunny uplands that I long to
reach, but everything is quaking and giving way under my
feet. After listening to Dr. Barstow's grand sermon this
morning, my spirit flamed up hopefully. Now he has
placed a duty directly in my path that I cannot perform
by myself. Mrs. Arnot has made it clear to me that the
manhood I need is Christian manhood. Dr. Barstow proves
out of the Bible that the first step toward this is conversion
—which seems to be a mysterious change which I but vaguely
understand. I must do my part myself, he says, yet I am
wholly dependent on the will and co-operation of another.
Just what am I to do? Just when and how will the help
come in? How can I know that it will come? or how can I
ever be sure that I have been converted?"

"O, stop splittin' hairs!" said Mr. Growther, testily.
"Hanged if I can tell you how it's all goin' to be brought
about—go ask the parson to clear up these p'ints for you
—but I can tell you this much: when you git converted
you'll know it. If you had a ragin' toothache, and it suddenly stopped and you felt comfortable all over, wouldn't
you know it? But that don't express it. You'd feel
more'n comfortable; you'd feel so good you couldn't hold
in. You'd be fur shoutin'; you wouldn't know yourself.
Why, doesn't the Bible say you'd be a new critter?
There'll be just such a change in your heart as there is
in this old kitchen when we come in on a cold, dark night
and light the candles, and kindle a fire. I tell you what
'tis, young man, if you once got converted your troubles
would be wellnigh over."

Though the picture of this possible future was drawn in

such homely lines, Haldane looked at it with wistful eyes.
He had become accustomed to his benefactor's odd ways
and words, and caught his sense beneath the grotesque imagery. As he was then situated, the future drawn by the
old man and interpreted by himself was peculiarly attractive. He was very miserable, and it is most natural, especially for the young, to wish to be happy. He had been
led to believe that conversion would lead to a happiness as
great as it was mysterious—a sort of miraculous ecstasy,
that would render him oblivious of the hard and prosaic
conditions of his lot. Through misfortune and his own
fault he possessed a very defective character. This character had been formed, it is true, by years of self-indulgence
and wrong, and Mrs. Arnot had asserted that reform would
require long, patient, and heroic effort. Indeed, she had
suggested that in fighting and subduing the evils of one's
own nature a man attained the noblest degree of knighthood. He had already learned how severe was the conflict
in which he had been led to engage.

But might not this mysterious conversion make things
infinitely easier? If a great and radical change were suddenly wrought in his moral nature, would not evil appetites
and propensities be uprooted like vile weeds? If a "new
heart" were given him, would not the thoughts and desires
flowing from it be like pure water from an unsullied spring?
After the "old things"—that is the evil—had passed away,
would not that which was noble and good spring up naturally, and almost spontaneously?

This was Mr. Growther's view; and he had long since
learned that the old man's opinions were sound on most
questions. This seemed, moreover, the teaching of the
Bible also, and of such sermons as he could recall. And
yet it caused him some misgivings that Mrs. Arnot had not
indicated more clearly this short-cut out of his difficulties.

But Mr. Growther's theology carried the day. As he
watched the young man's thoughtful face he thought the
occasion ripe for the "word in season."

"Now is the time," he said; "now while yer moral j'ints is limber. What's the use of climbin' the mountain on your hands and knees when you can go up in a chariot of fire, if you can only git in it?" and he talked and urged so earnestly that Haldane smiled and said:

"Mr. Growther, you have mistaken your vocation. You ought to have been a missionary to the heathen."

"That would be sendin' a thief to ketch a thief. But you know I've a grudge agin the devil, if I do belong to him; and if I could help git you out of his clutches it would do me a sight o' good."

"If I ever do get out I shall indeed have to thank you."

"I don't want no thanks, and don't desarve any. You're only giving me a chance to hit the adversary 'twixt the eyes," and the old man added his characteristic "A-a-h!" in an emphatic and vengeful manner, as if he would like to hit very hard.

Human nature was on the side of Mr. Growther's view of conversion. Nothing is more common than the delusive hope that health, shattered by years of wilful wrong, can be regained by the use of some highly extolled drug, or by a few deep draughts from some far-famed spring.

Haldane retired to rest fully bent upon securing this vague and mighty change as speedily as possible.

CHAPTER XXXVII

HOPING FOR A MIRACLE

M R. IVISON, Haldane's employer, was a worshipper at St. Paul's, and, like many others, had been deeply impressed by the sermon. Its influence had not wholly exhaled by Monday, and, as this gentleman was eminently practical, he felt that he ought to *do* something, as well as experience a little emotion. Thus he was led to address the following note to Haldane:

> Last week I gave you a chance; this week I am induced to give you a good word. While I warn you that I will tolerate no weak dallying with your old temptations, I also tell you that I would like to see you make a man of yourself, or, more correctly, perhaps, as Dr. Barstow would express it, be made a man of. If one wants to do right, I believe there is help for him (go and ask the Rev. Dr. Barstow about this); and if you will go right straight ahead till I see you can be depended upon, I will continue to speak good words to you and for you, and perhaps do more.   GEORGE IVISON.

This note greatly encouraged Haldane, and made his precarious foothold among the world's industries seem more firm and certain. The danger of being swept back into the deep water where those struggle who have no foothold, no work, no place in society would not come from the caprice or forgetfulness of his employer, but from his own peculiar temptations and weaknesses. If he could patiently do his duty in his present humble position, he justly believed that it would be the stepping-stone to something better. But, having learned to know himself, he was afraid of himself; and he had seen with an infinite dread what cold, dark depths yawn about one whom society shakes off as a vile and venomous thing, and who must eventually take evil and its consequences as his only portion. The hot, reeking apartment wherein he toiled was the first solid ground that he had felt beneath his feet for many days. If he could hold that footing, the water might shoal so that he could reach the land. It is true he could always look to his mother for food and clothing if he would comply with her conditions. But, greatly perverted as his nature had been, food and clothing, the maintenance of a merely animal life, could no longer satisfy him. He had thought too deeply, and had seen too much truth, to feed contentedly among the swine.

But the temptations which eventually lead to the swine —could he persistently resist these? Could he maintain a hard, monotonous routine of toil, with no excitements, no pleasures, with nothing that even approached happiness? He dared not give way; he doubted his strength to go forward alone with such a prospect. If conversion be a blessed miracle by which a debased nature is suddenly lifted up, and a harsh, lead-colored, prosaic world transfigured into the vestibule of heaven, he longed to witness it in his own experience.

It was while he was in this mood that his thoughts recurred to Dr. Marks, the good old clergyman who had been the subject of his rude, practical joke months before. He recalled the sincere, frank letter which led to their evening interview, and remembered with a thrill of hope the strong and mysterious emotion that had seized upon him as the venerable man took his hand in his warm grasp, and said in tones of pathos that shook his soul, "I wish I could lead you by loving force into the paths of pleasantness and peace." Wild and reckless fool as he then was, it had been only by a decided effort and abrupt departure that he had escaped the heavenly influences which seemed to brood in the quiet study where the good man prayed and spun the meshes of the nets which he daily cast for souls. If he could visit that study again with a receptive heart, might not the emotion that he had formerly resisted rise

like a flood, and sweep away his old miserable self, and he
become in truth a "new creature"?

The thought, having been once entertained, speedily
grew into a hope, and then became almost a certainty.
He felt that he would much rather see Dr. Marks than
Dr. Barstow, and that if he could feel that kind, warm
grasp again, an impulse might be given him which even
Mrs. Arnot's wise and gentle words could not inspire.

Before the week was over he felt that something must
be done either to soften his hard lot or to give him strength
to endure it.

The men, boys, and girls who worked at his side in the
mill were in their natures like their garb, coarse and soiled.
They resented the presence of Haldane for a twofold reason;
they regarded the intrusion of a "jail-bird" among them in
the light of an insult; they were still more annoyed, and
perplexed also, that this disreputable character made them
feel that he was their superior. Hence a system of petty
persecution grew up. Epithets were flung at him, and
practical jokes played upon him till his heart boiled with
anger or his nerves were irritated to the last degree of endurance. More than once his fist was clenched to strike;
but he remembered in time that the heavier the blow he
struck, the more disastrously it would react against himself.

After the exasperating experiences and noise of the day,
Mr. Growther's cottage was not the quiet refuge he needed.
Mr. Growther's growl was chronic, and it rasped on Haldane's overstrained nerves like the filing of a saw. Dr.
Barstow's sermons of the previous Sabbath had emphatically "riled" the old gentleman, and their only result, apparently, was to make him more out-of-sorts and vindictive
toward his poor, miserable little self than ever. He was so
irascible that even the comfortable cat and dog became
aware that something unusual was amiss, and, instead of
dozing securely, they learned to keep a wary and depreca-
tory eye on their master and the toes of his thick-soled
slippers.

"I've been goin' on like a darned old porkerpine," he said to Haldane one evening, "and if you don't git converted soon you'd better git out of my way. If you was as meek as Moses and twice as good you couldn't stand me much longer;" and the poor fellow felt that there was considerable truth in the remark.

The mill closed at an earlier hour on Saturday afternoon, and he determined to visit Dr. Marks if he could obtain permission from his employer to be absent a few hours on Monday morning. He wrote a note to Mr. Ivison, cordially thanking him for his encouraging words, but adding, frankly, that he could make no promises in regard to himself. "All that I can say, is," he wrote, "that I am trying to do right now, and that I am grateful to you for the chance you have given me. I wish to get the 'help' you suggest in your note to me, but, in memory of certain relations to my old pastor, Dr. Marks, I would rather see him than Dr. Barstow, and if you will permit me to be absent a part of next Monday forenoon I will esteem it a great favor, and will trespass on your kindness no further. I can go after mill-hours on Saturday, and will return by the first train on Monday."

Mr. Ivison readily granted the request, and even became somewhat curious as to the result.

When Mrs. Arnot had learned from Haldane the nature of his present employment, she had experienced both pleasure and misgivings. That he was willing to take and try to do such work rather than remain idle, or take what he felt would be charity, proved that there was more good metal in his composition than she had even hoped; but she naturally felt that the stinging annoyances of his position would soon become intolerable. She was not surprised, although she was somewhat perplexed, at the receipt of the following letter:

My dear Mrs. Arnot.—You have been such a true, kind friend to me, and have shown so much interest in my welfare, that I am led to give you a fuller insight into my present experiences and hopes. You know that I wish to be a Christian. You have made Christian manhood seem the most desirable thing that I can ever possess, but I make little or no progress toward it. Something must be done, and quickly too. Either there must be a great change in me, or else in my circumstances. As there is no immediate prospect of the latter, I have been led to hope that there can be such a change in me that I shall be lifted above and made superior to the exasperating annoyances of my condition. Yes, I am hoping even far more. If I could only experience the marvellous change which Dr. Barstow described so eloquently last Sunday evening, might I not do right easily and almost spontaneously? It is so desperately hard to do right now! If conversion will render my steep, thorny path infinitely easier, then surely I ought to seek this change by every means in my power. Indeed, there must be a change in me, or I shall lose even the foothold I have gained. I am subjected, all day long, to insult and annoyance. At times I am almost desperate and on the verge of recklessness. Every one of the coarse creatures that I am compelled to work with is a nettle that loses no chance to sting me; and there is one among them, a big, burly fellow, who is so offensive that I cannot keep my hands off him much longer if I remain my old self. You also know what a reception I must ever expect in the streets when I am recognized. The people act as if I were some sort of a reptile, which they must tolerate at large, but can, at least, shun with looks of aversion. And then, when I get to Mr. Growther's cottage I do not find much respite. It seems like ingratitude to write this, but the good old man's eccentric habit of berating himself and the world in general has grown wearisome, to say the least. I want to be lifted out of myself—far above these petty vexations and my own miserable weaknesses.

Once, before I left home, I played a rude joke on our good old pastor. Instead of resenting it he wrote me such a kind letter that I went to his study to apologize. While there his manner and words were such that I had to break away to escape a sudden and mysterious influence that inclined me toward all that is good. I have hoped that if I should visit him I might come under that influence again, and so be made a new and better man.

I have also another motive, which you will understand. Mother and I differ widely on many things, and always will; but I long to see her once more. I have been thinking of late of her many kindnesses—O that she had been less kind, less indulgent! But she cannot help the past any more than I can, and it may do us both good to meet once more. I do not think that she will refuse to see me or give me shelter for a few hours, even though her last letter seemed harsh.

I shall also be glad to escape for a few hours from my squalid and wretched surroundings. The grime of the sordid things with which I have so long been in contact seems eating into my very soul, and I long to sleep once more in my clean, airy room at home.

But I am inflicting myself too long upon you. That I have ventured to do so is due to your past kindness, which I can only wonder at, but cannot explain.
Gratefully yours,   E. HALDANE.

Mrs. Arnot was more than curious; she was deeply interested in the result of this visit, and she hoped and prayed earnestly that it might result in good. But she had detected an element in the young man's letter which caused her considerable uneasiness. His idea of conversion was a sudden and radical change in character that would be a sort of spiritual magic, contravening all the natural laws of growth and development. He was hoping to escape from his evil habits and weaknesses, which were of long growth, as the leper escaped from his disease, by a healing and momentary touch. He would surely be disappointed: might he not also be discouraged, and give up the patient and prayerful struggle which the sinful must ever wage against sin in this world? She trusted, however, that God had commenced a good work in his heart, and would finish it.

Even the sight of his native city, with its spires glistening in the setting sun, moved Haldane deeply, and when in the dusk he left the train, and walked once more through the familiar streets, his heart was crowded with pleasant and bitter memories, which naturally produced a softened and receptive mood.

He saw many well-remembered faces, and a few glanced at him as if he suggested one whom they had known. But he kept his hat drawn over his eyes, and, taking advantage of the obscurity of the night, escaped recognition.

"It is almost like coming back after one has died," he said to himself. "I once thought myself an important personage in this town, but it has got on better without me than it would have done with me. Truly, Mrs. Arnot is right—it's little the world cares for any one, and the absurdest of all blunders is to live for its favor."

It was with a quickly beating heart that he rang the bell at the parsonage, and requested to be shown up to Dr. Marks' study. Was this the supreme moment of his life, and he on the eve of that mysterious, spiritual change, of which he had heard so much, and the results of which would carry him along as by a steady, mighty impulse through earth's trials to heaven's glory? He fairly trembled at the thought.

The girl who had admitted him pointed to the open study door, and he silently crossed its threshold. The good old clergyman was bending over his sermon, to which he was giving his finishing touches, and the soft rays of the student's lamp made his white hair seem like a halo about his head.

The sacred quiet of the place was disturbed only by the quill of the writer, who was penning words as unworldly as himself. Another good old divine, with his Bible in his hand, looked down benignantly and encouragingly at the young man from his black-walnut frame. He was the sainted predecessor of Dr. Marks, and the sanctity of his life of prayer and holy toil also lingered in this study. Old volumes and heavy tomes gave to it the peculiar odor which we associate with the cloister, and suggested the prolonged spiritual musings of the past, which are so out of vogue in the hurried, practical world of to-day. This study was, indeed, a quiet nook—a little, slowly moving eddy left far behind by the dashing, foaming current of modern life; and Haldane felt impressed that he had found the hallowed place, the true Bethel, where his soul might be born anew.

CHAPTER XXXVIII

THE MIRACLE TAKES PLACE

"THE body of my sermon is finished; may the Lord breathe into it the breath of life!" ejaculated Dr. Marks, leaning back in his chair.

Haldane now secured his attention by knocking lightly on the open door. The old gentleman arose and came forward with the ordinary kindly manner with which he would greet a stranger.

"You do not remember me," said Haldane.

"I cannot say that I do. My eyesight is not as good as when I was at your age."

"I am also the last one you expect to see, but I trust I shall not be unwelcome when you know my motive for coming. I am Egbert Haldane, and I have hoped that your study would remain open, though nearly all respectable doors are closed against me."

"Egbert Haldane! Can I believe my eyes?" exclaimed the old clergyman, stepping eagerly forward.

"When last in this place," continued the youth, "I was led by your generous forgiveness of my rude behavior toward you to say, that if I ever wished to become a Christian I would come to you sooner than to any one else. I have come, for I wish to be a Christian."

"Now the Lord be praised! He has heard his servant's prayers," responded Dr. Marks fervently. "My study is open to you, my son, and my heart, too," he added, taking Haldane's hand in both of his with a grasp that emphasized his cordial words. "Sit down by me here, and tell me all that is on your mind."

This reception was so much kinder than he had even hoped, that Haldane was deeply moved. The strong, genuine sympathy unsealed his lips, and in honest and impetuous words he told the whole story of his life since their last interview. The good doctor was soon fumbling for his handkerchief, and as the story culminated, mopped his eyes, and ejaculated, "Poor fellow!" with increasing frequency.

"And now," concluded Haldane, "if I could only think that God would receive me as you have—if he would only change me from my miserable self to what I know I ought to be, and long to be—I feel that I could serve him with gratitude and gladness the rest of my life, even though I should remain in the humblest station; and I have come to ask you what I am to do?"

"He will receive you, my boy; he will receive you. No fears on that score," said the doctor, with a heartiness that carried conviction. "But don't ask me what to do. I'm not going to interfere in the Lord's work. He is leading you. If you wanted a text or a doctrine explained I'd venture to give you my views; but in this vital matter I shall leave you in God's hands, 'being confident of this very thing, that he which hath begun a good work in you will perform it until the day of Jesus Christ.' I once set about reforming you myself, and you know what a bungle I made of it. Now I believe the Lord has taken you in hand, and I shall not presume to meddle. Bow with me in prayer that he may speedily bring you into his marvellous light and knowledge." And the good man knelt and spread his hands toward heaven, and prayed with the simplicity and undoubting faith of an ancient patriarch.

Was his faith contagious? Did the pathos of his voice, his strongly manifested sympathy, combine with all that had gone before to melt the young man's heart? Or, in answer to the prayer, was there present One whose province it is to give life? Like the wind that mysteriously rises and comes toward one with its viewless, yet distinctly felt power,

Haldane was conscious of influences at work in his heart that were as potent as they were incomprehensible. Fear and doubt were passing away. Deep emotion thrilled his soul. Nothing was distinct save a rush of feeling which seemed to lift him up as on a mighty tide, and bear him heavenward.

This was what he had sought; this was what he had hoped; this strong, joyous feeling, welling up in his heart like a spring leaping into the sunlight, must be conversion.

When he arose from his knees his eyes were full of tears, but a glad radiance shone through them, and grasping the doctor's hand, he said brokenly:

"I believe your prayer has been answered. I never felt so strangely—so happy before."

"Come with me," cried the old man, impetuously, "come with me. Your mother must learn at once that her son, who 'was dead, is alive again';" and a few moments later Haldane was once more in the low carriage, on his way, with the enthusiastic doctor, to his old home.

"We won't permit ourselves to be announced," said the childlike old clergyman as they drove up the gravelled road. "We will descend upon your mother and sisters like an avalanche of happiness."

The curtains in the sitting-room were not drawn, and the family group was before them. The apartment was furnished with elegance and taste, but the very genius of dreariness seemed to brood over its occupants. The sombre colors of their mourning dresses seemed a part of the deep shadow that was resting upon them, and the depth and gloom of the shadow was intensified by their air of despondency and the pallor of their faces. The younger daughter was reading, but the elder and the mother held their hands listlessly in their laps, and their eyes were fixed on vacancy, after the manner of those whose thoughts are busy with painful themes.

Haldane could endure but a brief glance, and rushed in, exclaiming:

"Mother, forgive me!"

His presence was so unexpected and his onset so impetuous that the widow had no time to consider what kind of a reception she ought to give her wayward son, of whom she had washed her hands.

Her mother-love triumphed; her heart had long been sore with grief, and she returned his embrace with equal heartiness.

His sisters, however, had inherited more of their mother's conventionality than of her heart; and the fact that this young man was their brother did not by any means obliterate from their minds the other facts, that he had a very bad reputation and that he was abominably dressed. Their greeting, therefore, was rather grave and constrained, and suggested that there might have been a death in the family, and that their brother had come home to attend the funeral.

But the unworldly Dr. Marks was wholly absorbed in the blessed truth that the dead was alive and the lost found. He had followed Haldane into the apartment, rubbing his hands, and beaming general congratulation. Believing that the serene light of Heaven's favor rested on the youth, he had forgotten that it would be long before society relaxed its dark frown. It seemed to him that it was an occasion for great and unmixed rejoicing.

After some brief explanations had been given to the bewildered household, the doctor said:

"My dear madam, I could not deny myself the pleasure of coming with your son, that I might rejoice with you. The Lord has answered our prayers, you see, and you have reason to be the happiest woman living."

"I am glad, indeed," sighed the widow, "that some light is beginning to shine through this dark and mysterious providence, for it has been so utterly dark and full of mystery that my faith was beginning to waver."

"The Lord will not suffer you to be tempted above that you are able," said the clergyman, heartily. "When relief is essential it comes, and it always will come, rest assured.

Take comfort, madam; nay, let your heart overflow with joy without fear. The Lord means well by this young man. Take the unspeakable blessing he sends you with the gladness and gratitude of a child receiving gifts from a good Father's hands. Since he has begun the good work, he'll finish it."

"I hope so. I do, indeed, hope that Egbert will now come to his senses, and see things and duty in their true light, as other people do," ejaculated the widow, fervently. "If he had only taken the excellent advice you first gave him here how much better it would have been for us all! But now—" A dreary sigh closed the sentence.

"But now," responded the doctor, a little warmly, "the Lord has saved a soul from death, and that soul is your only son. It appears to me that this thought should swallow up every other; and it will, when you realize it," he concluded, heartily. "This world and the fashion of it passeth away. Since all promises well for the world to come, you have only cause for joy. As for my excellent advice, I was better pleased with it at the time than the Lord was. I now am thankful that he let it do no more harm than it did."

"We cannot help the past, mother," said Haldane, eagerly, "let us turn our eyes to the future, which is all aglow with hope. I feel that God has forgiven me, and the thought fills my heart with a tumult of joy. Your warm embrace assures me that you have also forgiven the wrong, the shame, and sorrow you have received at my hands. Henceforth it shall be my life-effort that you receive the reverse of all this. I at last feel within me the power to live as a true man ought."

"I trust your hopes may be realized, Egbert; I do, indeed; but you were so confident before—and then we all know what followed," concluded his mother, with a shudder.

"My present feeling, my present motives, in no respect resemble my condition when I started out before. I was then a conceited fool, ignorant of myself, the world, and the task I had attempted. But now I feel that all is different. Mother," he exclaimed with a rush of emotion, "I feel as if heaven had almost begun in my heart! why, then, do you cloud this bright hour with doubts and fears?"

"Well, my son, we will hope for the best," said his mother, endeavoring to throw off her despondency, and share in the spirit which animated her pastor. "But I have dwelt so long in sorrow and foreboding that it will require time before I can recover my old natural tone. These sudden and strong alternations of feeling and action on your part puzzle and disquiet me, and I cannot see why one brought up as you have been should not maintain a quiet, well-bred deportment, and do right as a matter of course, as your sisters do. And yet, if Dr. Marks truly thinks that you mean to do right from this time forward, I shall certainly take courage; though how we are going to meet what has already occurred I hardly see."

"I do, indeed, believe that your son intends to do right, and I also believe that the Lord intends to help him—which is of far greater consequence," said Dr. Marks. "I will now bid you good-night, as to-morrow is the Sabbath; and let me entreat you, my dear madam, in parting, to further by your prayer and sympathy the good work which the Lord has begun."

Haldane insisted on seeing the old gentleman safely back to his study. Their ride was a rather quiet one, each being busy with his own thoughts. The good man had found his enthusiasm strangely quenched in the atmosphere in which Mrs. Haldane dwelt, and found that, in spite of himself, he was sharing in her doubts and fears as to the future course of the erratic and impulsive youth at his side. He blamed himself for this, and tried to put doubt resolutely away. By a few earnest words he sought to show the young man that only as the grace of God was daily asked for and daily received could he hope to maintain the Christian life.

He now began to realize what a difficult problem was

before the youth. Society would be slow to give him credit
for changed motives and character, and as proof would take
only patient continuance in well-doing. The good doctor
now more than suspected that in his own home Haldane
would find much that was depressing and enervating.
Worse than all, he would have to contend with an excitable and ungoverned nature, already sadly warped and
biased wrongly. "What will be the final result?" sighed
the old gentleman to himself. But he soon fell back hopefully on his belief that the Lord had begun a good work and
would finish it.

Haldane listened attentively and gratefully to all that
his old friend had to say; and felt sure that he could and
would follow the advice given. Never before had right
living seemed so attractive, and the path of duty so luminous. But the thought that chiefly filled him with joy was
that henceforth he would not be compelled to plod forward
as a weary pilgrim. He felt that he had wings; some of the
divine strength had been given him. He believed himself
changed, renewed, transformed; he was confident that his
old self had perished and passed away, and that, as a new
creature, ennobling tendencies would control him completely. He felt that prayer would henceforth be as natural as breathing, and praise and worship, the strong and
abiding instincts of his heart.

CHAPTER XXXIX

VOTARIES OF THE WORLD

WHEN Haldane returned he found that his sisters had retired. He was not sorry, for he wished a long and unrestrained talk with his mother; but that lady pleaded that the events of the evening had so unnerved her, and that there was so much to be considered, that she must have quiet. In the morning they would try to realize their situation, and decide upon the best course to be pursued.

Even in his exaltation the last suggestion struck Haldane unpleasantly. Might not his mother mark out, and take as a test of his sincerity, some course that would accord with her ideas of right, but not with his? But the present hour was so full of mystical and inexplicable happiness that he gave himself up to it, believing that the divine hands, in which he believed himself to be, would provide for him as a helpless child is cared for.

The mill-people among whom he had worked the previous week would scarcely have recognized him as he came down to breakfast the following morning, dressed with taste and elegance. It was evident that his sisters could endure him with better grace than when clad in his coarse, working garb, redolent with the hitherto unimagined odors pertaining to well-oiled machinery. They, with his mother, greeted him, however, with the air of those who are in the midst of the greatest misfortunes, but who hope they see a coming ray of light

With their sincere but conventional ideas of life he was, in truth, a difficult problem. Nor can they be very greatly blamed. This youth, who might have been their natural protector against every scandalous and contemptuous word, and whose arm it would have been their pride to take before the world, had now such a reputation that only an affection all-absorbing and unselfish would be willing to brave the curious and scornful stare that follows one who had been so disgraced. Mrs. Haldane and her daughters were not without natural affection, but they were morbidly sensitive to public opinion. Like many who live somewhat secluded from the world, they imagined that vague and dreaded entity was giving them much more attention than it did. "What will people say?" was a terrible question to them.

Nothing could be further from their nature than an attempt to attract the world's attention by loud manners or flaunting dress; but it was essential to their peace that good society should regard them as eminently respectable, aristocratic, and high-toned—as a family far removed from vulgar and ordinary humanity. That their name, in the person of a son and brother, had been dragged through courts, criminal records, and jails, was an unparalleled disaster, that grew more overwhelming as they brooded over it. It seemed to them that the world's great eye was turned full upon them in scorn and wonder, and that only by maintaining their perfect seclusion, or by hiding among strangers, could they escape its cruel glare.

After all, their feelings were only morbid developments of the instincts of a refined womanly nature; but the trouble was, they had not the womanly largeness of heart and affection which would have made them equal to the emergency, however painful. Poor Mrs. Haldane was one of those unfortunate people who always fall below the occasion; indeed, she seldom realized it. Providence had now given her a chance to atone for much of her former weakness and ruinous indulgence, but her little mind was chiefly en-

grossed with the question, What can we do to smooth matters over, and regain something like our old standing in
society? As the result of a long consultation with her
daughters, it was concluded that their best course was to
go abroad. There they could venture out with him who
was the skeleton of the household, without having every
one turn and look after them with all kinds of comment
upon their lips. After several years in Europe they hoped
society would be inclined to forget and overlook the miserable record of the past few months.

That the young man himself would offer opposition to
the plan, and prefer to return to the scene of his disgrace,
and to his sordid toil, did not enter their minds.

In the enthusiasm of his new-born faith Haldane had
determined to face the public gaze, and hear Dr. Marks
preach. It is true, he had greatly dreaded the ordeal—
and for his mother and sisters, far more than for himself.
When he began to intimate something of this feeling his
mother promptly motioned to the waitress to withdraw
from the room. He then soon learned that they had not
attended church since Mrs. Haldane's return from her
memorable visit to Hillaton, and that they had no intention of going to-day.

"The very thought makes me turn faint and sick," said
the poor, weak gentlewoman.

"We should feel like sinking through the floor of the
aisle," chorused the pallid young ladies.

Haldane ceased partaking of his breakfast at once, and
leaned back in his chair.

"Do you mean to say," he asked gloomily, "that my
folly has turned this house into a tomb, and that you will
bury yourselves here indefinitely?"

"Well," sighed the mother, "if we live this wretched
life of seclusion, brooding over our troubles much longer,
smaller tombs will suffice us. You see that your sisters are
beginning to look like ghosts, and I'm sure I feel that I can
never lift up my head again. I know it is said that time

works wonders. Perhaps if we went abroad for a few years, and then resided in some other city, or in the seclusion of some quiet country place, we might escape this—'' and Mrs. Haldane finished with a sigh that was far worse than any words could have been. After a moment she concluded: ''But, of course, we cannot go out here, where all that has happened is so fresh, and uppermost in every one's mind. The more I think of it, the more decided I am that the best thing for us all is to go to some quiet watering-place in Europe, where there are but few, if any, Americans; and in time we may feel differently.''

Her son ate no more breakfast. He was beginning to realize, as he had not before, that he was in a certain sense a corpse, which this decorous and exquisitely refined family could not bury, but would hide as far as possible.

''You then expect me to go with you to Europe?'' he said.

''Certainly. We could not go without a gentleman.''

''That I scarcely am now, mother, in your estimation or in society's. I think you could get on better without me.''

''Now, Egbert, be sensible.''

''What am I to do in this secluded European watering-place, where there are no Americans, and at which we are to sojourn indefinitely?''

''I am sure I have not thought. Your sisters, at least, can venture out and get a breath of fresh air. It is time you thought of them rather than of yourself. You could amuse yourself with the natives, or by fishing and hunting.''

''Mother!'' he exclaimed, impetuously, ''I no longer desire to merely amuse myself. I wish to become a man, in the best sense of the word.''

Mrs. Haldane evidently experienced a disagreeable nervous shock at the sudden intensity of his manner, but she said, with rebuking quietness:

''I am sure I wish you to become such a man, thoroughly well bred, and thoroughly under self-control. It is my purpose to enable you to appear like a perfect gentleman from this time forward, and I expect that you will be one."

"What will I be but a well-dressed nonentity? what will I be but a coward, seeking to get away as far as possible from the place of my defeat, and to hide from its consequences?" he answered, with sharp, bitter emphasis.

"Egbert, your tendency to exaggeration and violent speech is more than I can bear in my weak, nervous condition. When you have thought this matter over calmly, and have realized how I and your sisters feel, you will see that we are right—that is, if Dr. Marks is correct, and you do really wish to atone for the past as far as it now can be done."

The young man paced restlessly up and down the room in an agitated manner, which greatly disquieted his mother and sisters.

"Can you not realize," he at last burst out, "that I, also, have a conscience? that I am no longer a child? and that I cannot see things as you do?"

"Egbert," exclaimed his elder sister, lifting her hand deprecatingly, "we are not deaf."

"If you will only follow your conscience," continued Mrs. Haldane, in her low monotone, "all will be well. It is your being carried away by gusts of impulse and violent passions that makes all the trouble. If you had followed your conscience you would at once have left Hillaton at my request, and hidden yourself in the seclusion that I indicated. If you had done so, you might have saved yourself and us from all that has since occurred."

"But I would have lost my self-respect. I should have done worse—"

"Self-respect!" interrupted his mother, with an expression akin to disgust flitting across her pale face. "How can you use that word after what has happened, and especially now that you are working among those vulgar factory people, and living with that profane old creature who goes by the name of 'Jerry Growler.' To think that you, who bear

your father's name, should have fallen so low! The daily
and hourly mortification of thinking of all this, here, where
for so many years there was not a speck upon our family
reputation, is more than flesh and blood can endure. Our
only course now is to go away where we are not known.
Our best hope is to make you appear like what your father
meant you should be, and try to forget that you have been
anything else; and if you have any sense of obligation to
us left you will do what you can to carry out our efforts.
Dr. Marks thinks you have met with 'a change of heart.'
I am sure you can prove it in no better way than by a
docile acquiescence in the wishes of one who has a natural
right to control you, and whose teachings," she added complacently, "had they been followed, would have enabled
you to hold up your head to-day among the proudest in
the land."

Haldane buried his face in his hands, and fairly groaned,
in his disappointment and sense of humiliation.

"Is it possible," asked one of his sisters "that you
thought that we could all go out to church to-day as
usual, and commence life to-morrow where he left off when
you first went away from home?"

"I expected nothing of the kind," said her brother, lifting up a face that was pale from suppressed feeling; "the
fact is, I have thought little about all this that is uppermost
in your minds. I have been all through the phase of shrinking from the world's word and touch, as if my whole being
were a diseased nerve. While in that condition I suffered
enough, God knows; but even in the police court I was not
made to feel more thoroughly that I was a disgraced criminal than I have been here, in my childhood's home. Perhaps you can't help your feeling; but the result is all the
same. Through the influence of a woman who belongs to
heaven rather than earth, I was led to forget the world and
all about it; I was led to wish to form a good character for
its own sake. I wanted to be rid of the debasing vices of
my nature which she had made me hate, and which would

separate me from such as she is. I wanted your forgiveness, mother. More than all, I wanted God's forgiveness, and that great change in my nature which he alone can bestow. I felt that Dr. Marks could help me, because I believed in him; and he did carry me, as it were, to the very gate of heaven. I expected, at least, a little sympathy from you all, and a God-speed as I went back to my work to-morrow. I even hoped that you might take me by the hand, and say to those who knew us here, 'My son was lost, but is found. He wishes to live a manly, Christian life, and all who are Christians should help him.' I find, on the contrary, that Christ and his words are forgotten; that I am regarded as a hideous and deformed creature, that must be disguised as far as possible, and spirited off to some remote corner of the earth, and there virtually buried alive. Thus different are the teachings of the Bible and the teachings of the world. I thought I could not endure my hard lot at Hillaton any longer, but I shall go back to it quite content."

As the youth uttered these words, with his usual impetuosity, his mother could only weep and tremble in her weak and nervous way; but his sisters exclaimed:

"Go back to your old mill-life at Hillaton!"

"Yes, by the first train, to-morrow."

"Well!" they chorused, with a long breath, but as all language seemed inadequate they added nothing to their exclamation.

Mrs. Haldane slowly wiped her eyes, and said, "Egbert is excited now, and does not realize how we feel. After he has thought it all over quietly he will see things in a different light, and will perceive that he should take counsel from his mother rather than from a stranger" (with peculiar emphasis on this word). "If he really wishes to do his duty as a Christian man, he will see that the first and most sacred obligations resting on him are to *us* and not to others, even though they may be more angelic than we are. You promised last evening that it would be your life-effort to make amends for the wrongs you have inflicted upon us; and. going back to your old, sordid life and vulgar associations would be a strange way of keeping this pledge. I suggest that we all retire to our rooms, and in the after part of the day we shall be calmer, and therefore more rational;" and the ladies quietly glided out, like black shadows. Indeed, they and their lives had become little more than attenuated shadows.

There is nothing which so thoroughly depletes and robs moral character of all substance—there is nothing which so effectually destroys all robust individuality—as the continuous asking of the question, "What will, people say?"

Poor Haldane went to his room, and paced it by the hour. He had learned thus early that the Christian life was not made up of sacred and beatific emotions, under the influence of which duty would become an easy, sun-illumined path.

He already was in sore perplexity as to what his duty was in this instance. Ought he not to devote himself to his mother and sisters, and hope that time would bring a healthful change in their morbid feeling? Surely what they asked would not seem hard in the world's estimation—a trip to Europe, and a life of luxurious ease and amusement—for society would agree with his mother, that he could be as good and Christian-like as he pleased in the meantime. The majority would say that if he could in part make amends by acquiescence in so reasonable a request, and one that promised so much of pleasure and advantage to himself, he ought certainly to yield.

But all that was good and manly in the young fellow's nature rose up against the plan. In the first place, he instinctively felt that his mother and sisters' views on nearly all subjects would be continually at variance with his own, since they were coming to look at life from such totally different standpoints. He also believed that he would be an ever-present burden and source of mortification to them. As a child and a boy he had been their idol. They had looked forward to the time when he, with irreproachable manners and reputation, would become their escort in the exclusive circles in which they were entitled to move. Now he was and would continue to be the insuperable bar to those circles; and by their sighs and manner he would be continually reminded of this fact. Fallen idols are a perpetual offence to their former worshippers, as they ever remind of the downfall of towering hopes.

With all his faults, Haldane had too much spirit to go through life as one who must be tolerated, endured, kept in the background, and concerning whom no questions must be asked.

He did think the matter over long and carefully, and concluded that even for his mother and sisters' sake it would be best that they should live apart. If he could thoroughly retrieve his character where he had lost it, they would be reconciled to him; if he could not, he would be less of a burden and a mortification absent than present.

When he considered his own feelings, the thought of skulking and hiding through life made his cheek tingle with shame and disgust. Conscience sided with his inclination to go back to his old, hard fight at Hillaton; and it also appeared to him that he could there better maintain a Christian life, in spite of all the odds against him, than by taking the enervating course marked out by his mother. He also remembered, with a faint thrill of hope, that whatever recognition he could get at Hillaton as a changed, a better man, it would be based on the rock of truth.

He therefore concluded to go back as he had intended, and with the decision came his former, happy, mystical feeling, welling up in his heart like the sweet refreshing waters of a spring, the consciousness of which filled his heart with courage and confidence as to the future.

"Surely," he exclaimed, "I am a changed, a converted man. These strange, sweet emotions, this unspeakable gladness of heart in the midst of so much that is painful and distracting, prove that I am. I have not taken this journey in vain."

Haldane met only his sisters at dinner, for the scene of the morning had prostrated his mother with a nervous headache. In spite of his efforts, it was a constrained and dismal affair, and all were glad when it was over.

In the evening they all met in Mrs. Haldane's room, and the young man told them his decision so firmly and quietly that, while they were both surprised and angry, they saw it was useless to remonstrate. He next drew such a dreary picture of the future as they had designed it, that they were half inclined to think he was right, and that his presence would be a greater source of pain than of comfort to them. He also convinced them that it would be less embarrassing for them to go to Europe alone than with his escort, and that the plan of going abroad need not be given up.

But Mrs. Haldane was strenuous on the point that he should leave Hillaton, accept of her old offer, and live a quiet, respectable life in some retired place where he was not known.

"I will not have it said," she persisted, "that my son is working as a common factory hand, nor will I have our name associated with that wretched old creature whose profanity and general outlandishness are the town-talk and the constant theme of newspaper squibs. You at least owe it to us to let this scandal die out as speedily as possible. If you will comply with these most reasonable requirements, I will see that you have an abundant support. If you will not, I have no evidence of a change in your character; nor can I see any better way than to leave you to suffer the consequences of your folly until you do come to your senses."

"Mother, do you think a young fellow of my years and energy could go to an out-of-the-way place, and just mope, eat, and sleep for the sake f being supported? I would rather starve first. I fear we shall never understand each other; and I have reached that point in life when I must follow my own conscience. I shall leave to-morrow morning before any of you are up; and in my old working clothes. Good-by;" and before they could realize it he had kissed them and left the room.

They weakly sighed as over the inevitable; but one of his sisters said, "He will be glad enough to come to your terms before winter."

CHAPTER XL

HUMAN NATURE

AT AN early hour Haldane, true to his purpose, departed from the home of his childhood in the guise of a laborer, as he had come.   His mother heard his step on the stairs, for she had passed a sleepless night, agitated by painful emotions.   She wished to call him back; she grieved over his course as a "dark and mysterious providence," as a misfortune which, like death, could not be escaped; but with the persistence of a little mind, capable of taking but a single and narrow view, she was absolutely sure she was right in her course, and that nothing but harsh and bitter experience would bring her wayward son to his senses.

Nor did it seem that the harsh experience would be wanting, for the morning was well advanced when he reached his place of work, and he received a severe reprimand from the foreman for being so late.   His explanation, that he had received permission to be absent, was incredulously received.   It also seemed that gibes, taunts, and sneers were flung at him with increasing venom by his ill-natured associates, who were vexed that they had not been able to drive him away by their persecutions.

But the object of their spite was dwelling in a world of which they knew nothing, and in which they had no part, and, almost oblivious of their existence, he performed his mechanical duty in almost undisturbed serenity.

Mr. Growther welcomed him back most heartily and with

an air of eager expectation, and when Haldane briefly but graphically narrated his experience, he hobbled up and down the room in a state of great excitement.

"You've got it! you've got it! and the genuine article, too, as sure as my name is Jeremiah Growther!" he exclaimed; "I'd give the whole airth, and anything else to boot, that was asked, if I could only git religion. But it's no use for me to think about it; I'm done, and cooled off, and would break inter ten thousand pieces if I tried to change myself. I couldn't feel what you feel any more than I could run and jump as you kin. My moral j'ints is as stiff as hedge-stakes. If I tried to git up a little of your feelin', it would be like tryin' to hurry along the spring by buildin' a fire on the frozen ground. It would only make one little spot soft and sloppy; the fire would soon go out: then it would freeze right up agin. Now, with you it's spring all over; you feel tender and meller-like, and everything good is ready to sprout. Well, well! if I do have to go to old Nick at last, I'm powerful glad he's had this set-back in your case."

Long and earnestly did Haldane try to reason his quaint friend out of his despairing views of himself. At last the old man said testily:

"Now, look here; you're too new-fledged a saint to instruct a seasoned and experienced old sinner like me. You don't know much about the Lord's ways yet, and I know all about the devil's ways. Because you've got out of his clutches (and I'm mighty glad you have) you needn't make light of him, and take liberties with him as if he was nobody, 'specially when Scripter calls him 'a roarin' lion.' If I was as young as you be, I'd make a dead set to git away from him; but after tryin' more times than you've lived years, I know it ain't no use. I tell you I can't feel as you feel, any more than you can squeeze water out of them old andirons. A-a-h!"

Haldane was silent, feeling that the old man's spiritual condition was too knotty a problem for him to solve.

After a few moments Mr. Growther added, in a voice that he meant to be very solemn and impressive:

"But I want you to enjoy your religious feelin's all the same. I will listen to all the Scripter readin' and prayin' you're willin' to do, without makin' any disturbance. Indeed, I think I will enjoy my wittles more, now that an honest grace can be said over 'em. An' when you read the Bible, you needn't read the cussin' parts, if yer don't want to. I'll read 'em to myself hereafter. I'll give you all the leeway that an old curmudgeon like myself kin; and I expect to take a sight o' comfort in seein' you goin' on your way rejoicin'."

And he did seem to take as much interest in the young man's progress and new spiritual experiences as if he alone were the one interested. His efforts to control his irritability and profanity were both odd and pathetic, and Haldane would sometimes hear him swearing softly to himself, with strange contortions of his wrinkled face, when in former times he would have vented his spite in the harshest tones.

Haldane wrote fully to Mrs. Arnot of his visit to his native city and its happy results, and enlarged upon his changed feelings as the proof that he was a changed man.

Her reply was prompt and was filled with the warmest congratulations and expressions of the sincerest sympathy. It also contained these words:

"I fear that you are dwelling too largely upon your feelings and experiences, and are giving to them a value they do not possess. Not that I would undervalue them—they are gracious tokens of God's favor; but they are not the grounds of your salvation and acceptance with God."

Haldane did not believe that they were—he had been too well taught for that—but he regarded them as the evidences that he was accepted, that he was a Christian; and he expected them to continue, and to bear him forward, and through and over the peculiar trials of his lot, as on a strong and shining tide.

Mrs. Arnot also stated that she was just on the eve of

leaving home for a time, and that on her return she would see him and explain more fully her meaning.

In conclusion, she wrote: "I think you did what was right and best in returning to Hillaton. At any rate, you have reached that age when you must obey your own conscience, and can no longer place the responsibility of your action upon others. But, remember, that you owe to your mother the most delicate forbearance and consideration. You should write to her regularly, and seek to prove that you are guided by principle rather than impulse. Your mother has much reason to feel as she does, and nothing can excuse you from the sacred duties you owe to her."

Haldane did write as Mrs. Arnot suggested. In a few days he received the following letter from his mother:

"We shall sail for Europe as soon as we can get ready for the journey. Our lawyer is making all the necessary arrangements for us. I will leave funds with him, and whenever you are ready in good faith to accept my offer, leave Hillaton, and live so that this scandal can die out, you can obtain from him the means of living decently and quietly. As it is, I live in daily terror lest you again do something which will bring our name into the Hillaton papers; and, of course, everything is copied by the press of this city. Will the time ever come when you will consider your mother's and sisters' feelings?"

For a time all went as well as could be expected in the trying circumstances of Haldane's life. His prayers for strength and patience were at first earnest, and their answers seemed assured—so assured, indeed, that in times of haste and weariness prayer eventually came to be hurried or neglected. Before he was aware of it, feeling began to ebb away. He at last became troubled, and then alarmed, and made great effort to regain his old, happy emotions and experiences; but, like an outgoing tide, they ebbed steadily away.

His face indicated his disquiet and anxiety, for he felt like one who was clinging to a rope that was slowly parting, strand by strand.

Keen-eyed Mr. Growther watched him closely, and was

satisfied that something was amiss. He was much concerned, and took not a little of the blame upon himself.

"How can a man be a Christian, or anything else that's
decent, when he keeps such cussed company as I be?" he
muttered. "I s'pose I kinder pisen and wither up his good
feelin's like a sulphuric acid fact'ry."

One evening he exclaimed to Haldane, "I say, young
man, you had better pull out o' here."

"What do you mean?"

"I'll give you a receipt in full and a good character, and
then you look for a healthier boardin'-place."

"Ah, I see! You wish to be rid of me?"

"No, you don't see, nuther. I wish you to be rid of
me."

"Of course, if you wish me to go, I'll go at once," said
Haldane, in a despondent tone.

"And go off at half-cock into the bargain? I ain't one
of the kind, you know, that talks around Robin Hood's
barn. I go straight in at the front door and out at the
back. It's my rough way of coming to the p'int at once.
I kin see that you're runnin' behind in speret'al matters,
and I believe that my cussedness is part to blame. You
don't feel good as you used to. It would never do to git
down at the heel in these matters, 'cause the poorest timber
in the market is yer old backsliders. I'd rather be what I
am than be a backslider. The right way is to take these
things in time, before you git agoin' down hill too fast. It
isn't that I want to git rid of you at all. I've kinder got
used to you, and like to have you 'round 'mazingly; but I
don't s'pose it's possible for you to feel right and live with
me, and so you had better cut stick in time, for you must
keep a-feelin' good and pi'us-like, my boy, or it's all up
with you."

"Then you don't want me to go for the sake of your
own comfort?"

"Not a bit of it. I only want you to git inter a place
that isn't so morally pisened as this, where I do so much

cussin'; for I will and must cuss as long as there's an atom left of me as big as a head of a pin. A-a-h!"

"Then I prefer to take my chances with you to going anywhere else."

"Think twice."

"I have thought more than twice."

"Then yer blood be on yer own head," said Mr. Growther with tragic solemnity, as if he were about to take Haldane's life. "My skirts is clear after this warnin'."

"Indeed they are. You haven't done me a bit of harm."

"Where does the trouble come from then? Who is a-harmin' you?"

"Well, Mr. Growther," said Haldane, wearily, "I hardly know what is the matter. I am losing zest and courage unaccountably. My old, happy and hopeful feelings are about all gone, and in their place all sorts of evil thoughts seem to be swarming into my mind. I have tried to keep all this to myself, but I have become so wretched that I must speak. Mrs. Arnot is away, or she might help me, as she ever does. I wish that I felt differently; I pray that I may, but in spite of all I seem drifting back to my old miserable self. Every day I fear that I shall have trouble at the mill. When I felt so strong and happy I did not mind what they said. One day I was asked by a workman, who is quite a decent fellow, how I stood it all? and I replied that I stood it as any well-meaning Christian man could. My implied assertion that I was a Christian was taken up as a great joke, and now they call me the 'pi'us jail-bird.' As long as I felt at heart that I was a Christian, I did not care; but now their words gall me to the quick. I do not know what to think. It seems to me that if any one ever met with a change I did. I'm sure I wish to feel now as I did then; but I grow worse every day. I am losing self-control and growing irritable. This evening, as I passed liquor saloons on my way home, my old appetite for drink seemed as strong as ever. What does it all mean?"

Mr. Growther's wrinkled visage worked curiously, and

at last he said in a tone and manner that betokened the deepest distress:

"I'm awfully afeerd you're a-backslidin'."

"I wish I had never been born," exclaimed the youth, passionately, "for I am a curse to myself and all connected with me. I know I shall have trouble with one man at the mill. I can see it coming, and then, of course, I shall be discharged. I seem destined to defeat in this my last attempt to be a man, and I shall never have the courage or hope to try again. If I do break down utterly, I feel as if I will become a very devil incarnate. O! how I wish that Mrs. Arnot was home."

"Now this beats me all out," said Mr. Growther, in great perplexity. "A while ago you felt like a saint and acted like one, now you talk and act as if Old Nick and all his imps had got a hold on ye. How do you explain all this, for it beats me?"

"I don't and can't explain. But here are the facts, and what are you going to do with them?"

"I ain't a-goin' to do nothin' with 'em except cuss 'em; and that's all I kin do in any case. You've got beyond my depth."

The sorely tempted youth could obtain but little aid and comfort, therefore, from his quaint old friend, and, equally perplexed and unable to understand himself, he sought to obtain such rest as his disquieted condition permitted.

As a result of wakefulness in the early part of the night, he slept late the following morning, and hastened to his work with scarcely a mouthful of breakfast. He was thus disqualified, physically as well as mentally, for the ordeal of the day.

He was a few minutes behind time, and a sharp reprimand from the foreman rasped his already jangling nerves. But he doggedly set his teeth and resolved to see and hear nothing save that which pertained to his work.

He might have kept his resolve had there been nothing more to contend with than the ordinary verbal persecution.

But late in the afternoon, when he had grown weary from the strain of the day, his special tormentor, a burly Irishman, took occasion, in passing, to push him rudely against a pert and slattern girl, who also was foremost in the tacit league of petty annoyance. She acted as if the contact of Haldane's person was a purposed insult, and resented it by a sharp slap of his face.

Her stinging stroke was like a spark to a magazine; but paying no heed to her, he sprang toward her laughing ally with fierce oaths upon his lips, and by a single blow sent him reeling to the floor. The machinery was stopped sharply, as far as possible, by the miscellaneous workpeople, to whom a fight was a boon above price, and with shrill and clamorous outcries they gathered round the young man where he stood, panting, like a wounded animal at bay.

His powerful antagonist was speedily upon his feet, and at once made a rush for the youth who had so unexpectedly turned upon him; and though he received another heavy blow, his onset was so strong that he was able to close with Haldane, and thus made the conflict a mere trial of brute force.

As Haldane afterward recalled the scene, he was conscious that at the time he felt only rage, and a mad desire to destroy his opponent.

In strength they were quite evenly matched, and after a moment's struggle both fell heavily, and Haldane was able to disengage himself. As the Irishman rose, and was about to renew the fight, he struck him so tremendous a blow on the temple that the man went to the floor as if pierced by a bullet, and lay there stunned and still.

When Haldane saw that his antagonist did not move, time was given him to think; he experienced a terrible revulsion. He remembered his profanity and brutal rage, he felt that he had broken down utterly. He was overwhelmed by his moral defeat, and covering his face with his hands, he groaned "Lost, lost!"

"By jocks," exclaimed a rude, half-grown fellow, "that clip would have felled an ox."

"Do you think he's dead?" asked the slattern girl, now thoroughly alarmed at the consequences of the blow she had given.

"Dead!" cried Haldane, catching the word, and, pushing all aside, he knelt over his prostrate foe.

"Water, bring water, for God's sake!" he said eagerly, lifting up the unconscious man.

It was brought and dashed in his face. A moment later, to Haldane's infinite relief he revived, and after a bewildered stare at the crowd around him, fixed his eyes on the youth who had dealt the blow, and then a consciousness of all that had occurred seemed to return. He showed his teeth in impotent rage for a moment, as some wild animal might have done, and then rose unsteadily to his feet.

"Go back to your work, all on ye," thundered the foreman, who, now that the sport was over, was bent on making a great show of his zeal; "as for you two bull-dogs, you shall pay dearly for this; and let me say to you, Mister Haldane, that the pious dodge won't answer any longer."

A moment later, with the exception of flushed faces and excited whisperings, the large and crowded apartment wore its ordinary aspect, and the machinery clanked on as monotonously as ever.

Almost as mechanically Haldane moved in the routine of his labor, but the bitterness of despair was in his heart.

He forgot that he would probably be discharged that day; he forgot that a dark and uncertain future was before him. He only remembered his rage and profanity, and they seemed to him damning proofs that all he had felt, hoped, and believed was delusion.

CHAPTER XLI

MRS. ARNOT'S CREED

WHEN Haldane entered the cottage that evening his eyes were bloodshot and his face so haggard that Mr. Growther started out of his chair, exclaiming: "Lord a' massy! what's the matter?"

"Matter enough," replied the youth, with a reckless oath. "The worst that I feared has happened."

"What's happened?" asked the old man excitedly.

"I've been fighting in the work-room like a bull-dog, and swearing like a pirate. That's the kind of a Christian I am, and always will be. What I was made for, I don't see," he added, as he threw himself into a chair.

"Well, well, well!" said Mr. Growther dejectedly, "I was in hopes she'd git here in time; but I'm afeered you've just clean backslid."

"No kind of doubt on that score," replied the young man, with a bitter laugh; "though I now think I never had very far to slide. And yet it all seems wrong and unjust. Why should my hopes be raised? why should such feelings be inspired, if this was to be the end? If I was foreordained to go to the devil, why must an aggravating glimpse of heaven be given me? I say it's all cruel and wrong. But what's the use! Come, let's have supper, one must eat as long as he's in the body."

It was a silent and dismal meal, and soon over. Then Haldane took his hat without a word.

"Where are you goin'?" asked Mr. Growther, anxiously.

"I neither know nor care."

"Don't go out to-night, I expect somebody."

"Who, in the name of wonder?"

"Mrs. Arnot."

"I could as easily face an angel of light now as Mrs. Arnot," he replied, pausing on the threshold; for even in his reckless mood the old man's wistful face had power to restrain.

"You are mistaken, Egbert," said a gentle voice behind him. "You can face me much more easily than an angel of light. I am human like yourself, and your friend."

She had approached the open door through the dusk of the mild autumn evening, and had heard his words. He trembled at her voice, but ventured no reply.

"I have come to see you, Egbert; you will not leave me."

"Mrs. Arnot," he said passionately, "I am not worth the trouble you take in my behalf, and I might as well tell you at once that it is in vain."

"I do not regard what I do for you as 'trouble,' and I know it is not in vain," she replied, with calm, clear emphasis.

Her manner quieted him somewhat; but after a moment he said:

"You do not know what has happened to-day, nor how I have been feeling for many days past."

"Your manner indicates how you feel; and you may tell me what has happened if you wish. If you prefer that we should be alone, come with me to my carriage, and in the quiet of my private parlor you can tell me all."

"No," said Haldane gloomily; "I am not fit to enter your house, and for other reasons would rather not do so. I have no better friend than Mr. Growther, and he already knows it all. I may as well tell you here; that is, if you are willing to stay."

"I came to stay," said Mrs. Arnot quietly; and sitting down, she turned a grave and expectant face toward him.

"I cannot find words in which to tell you my shame, and the utterness of my defeat."

"Yes, you can, Egbert. I believe that you have always told me the truth about yourself."

"I have, and I will again," he said desperately; "and yet it seems like profanation to describe such a scene to you." But he did describe it, briefly and graphically, nevertheless. As he spoke of his last fierce blow, which vanquished his opponent, Mr. Growther muttered:

"Sarved him right; can't help feelin' glad you hit 'im so hard; but then that's in keepin' with the cussedness of my natur'."

A glimmer of a smile hovered around Mrs. Arnot's flexible mouth, but she only asked quietly:

"Is that all?"

"I should think that was enough, after all that I had felt and professed."

"I fear I shall shock you, Egbert, but I am not very much surprised at your course. Indeed I think it was quite natural, in view of the circumstances. Perhaps my nature is akin to Mr. Growther's, for I am rather glad that fellow was punished; and I think it was very natural for you to punish him as you did. So far from despairing of you, I am the more hopeful of you."

"Mrs. Arnot!" exclaimed the youth in undisguised astonishment.

"Now do not jump to hasty and false conclusions from my words; I do not say that your action was right. In the abstract it was decidedly wrong, and for your language there is no other excuse save that an old, bad habit asserted itself at a time when you had lost self-control. I am dealing leniently with you, Egbert, because it is a trick of the adversary to tempt to despair as well as to over-confidence. At the same time I speak sincerely. You are and have been for some time in a morbid state of mind. Let my simple common-sense come to your aid in this emergency. The very conditions under which you have been working at the mill imposed a continuous strain upon your nervous power. You were steadily approaching a point where mere human endurance would give way. Mark, I do not say that you might not have been helped to endure longer, and to endure everything; but mere human nature could not have endured it much longer. It is often wiser to shun certain temptations, if we can, than to meet them. You could not do this; and if, taking into account all the circumstances, you could have tamely submitted to this insult, which was the culmination of long-continued and exasperating injury, I should have doubted whether you possessed the material to make a strong, forceful man. Of course, if you often give way to passion in this manner, you would be little better than a wild beast; but for weeks you had exercised very great forbearance and self-control—for one of your temperament, remarkable self-control—and I respect you for it. We are as truly bound to be just to ourselves as to others. Your action was certainly wrong, and I would be deeply grieved and disappointed if you continued to give way to such ebullitions of passion; but remembering your youth, and all that has happened since spring, and observing plainly that you are in an unhealthful condition of mind and body, I think your course was very natural indeed, and that you have no occasion for such despondency."

"Yes," put in Mr. Growther; "and he went away without his breakfast, and it was mighty little he took for lunch; all men are savages when they haven't eaten anything."

"Pardon me, Mrs. Arnot," said Haldane gloomily, "all this does not meet the case at all. I had been hoping that I was a Christian; what is more, it seems to me that I had had the feelings and experiences of a Christian."

"I have nothing to say against that," said the lady quietly; "I am very glad that you had."

"After what has occurred what right have I to think myself a Christian?"

"As good a right as multitudes of others."

"Now, Mrs. Arnot, that seems to me to be contrary to reason."

"It is not contrary to fact. Good people in the Bible, good people in history, and to my personal knowledge, too, have been left to do outrageously wrong things. To err is human; and we are all very human, Egbert."

"But I don't feel that I am a Christian any longer," he said sadly.

"Perhaps you are not, and never were. But this is a question that you can never settle by consulting your own feelings."

"Then how can I settle it?" was the eager response.

"By settling fully and finally in your mind what relation you will sustain to Jesus Christ. He offers to be your complete Saviour from sin. Will you accept of him as such? He offers to be your divine and unerring guide and example in your everyday life. Will you accept of him as such? Doing these two things in simple honesty and to the best of our ability is the only way to be a Christian that I know of."

"Is that all?" muttered Mr. Growther, rising for a moment from his chair in his deep interest in her words. She gave him an encouraging smile, and then turned to Haldane again.

"Mrs. Arnot," he said, "I know that you are far wiser in these matters than I, and yet I am bewildered. The Bible says we must be converted; that we must be born again. It seems to require some great, mysterious change that shall renew our whole nature. And it seemed to me that I experienced that change. It would be impossible for me to describe to you my emotions. They were sincere and profound. They stirred the very depths of my soul, and under their influence it was a joy to worship God and to do his will. Had I not a right to believe that the hour in which I first felt those glad thrills of faith and love was the hour of my conversion?"

"You had a right to hope it."

"But now, to-day, when every bad passion has been uppermost in my heart, what reason have I to hope?"

"None at all, looking to yourself and to your varying emotions."

"Mrs. Arnot, I am bewildered. I am all at sea. The Bible, as interpreted by Dr. Barstow and Dr. Marks, seems to require so much; and what you say is required is simplicity itself."

"If you will listen patiently, Egbert, I will give you my views, and I think they are correct, for I endeavor to take them wholly from the Bible. That which God requires is simplicity itself, and yet it is very much; it is infinite. In the first place, one must give up self-righteousness—not self-respect, mark you—but mere spiritual self-conceit, which is akin to the feeling of some vulgar people who think they are good enough to associate with those who are immeasurably beyond them, but whose superiority they are too small to comprehend. We must come to God in the spirit of a little child; and then, as if we were children, he will give to us a natural and healthful growth in the life that resembles his own. This is the simplest thing that can be done, and all can do it; but how many are trying to work out their salvation by some intricate method of human device, and, stranger still, are very complacent over the mechanical and abnormal results! All such futile efforts, of which many are so vain, must be cast aside. Listen to Christ's own words: 'Learn of me, for I am meek and lowly in heart.' He who would enter upon the Christian life, must come to Christ as the true scientist sits at the feet of nature—docile, teachable, eager to learn truth that existed long before he was born, and not disposed to thrust forward some miserable little system of his own. Nothing could be simpler, easier, or more pleasing to Christ himself than the action of Mary as she sat at his feet and listened to him; but many are like Martha, and are bustling about in his service in ways pleasing to themselves; and it is very hard for them to give up their own way. I've had to give up a great deal in my time, and perhaps you will.

"In addition to all trust in ourselves, in what we are and

what we have done, we must turn away from what we have felt; and here I think I touch your present difficulties. We are not saved by the emotions of our own hearts, however sacred and delightful they may seem. Nor do they always indicate just what we are and shall be. A few weeks since you thought your heart had become the abiding-place of all that was good; now, it seems to you to be possessed by evil. This is common experience; at one time the Psalmist sings in rapturous devotion; again, he is wailing in penitence over one of the blackest crimes in history. Peter is on the Mount of Transfiguration; again he is denying his master with oaths and curses. Even good men vary as widely as this; but Christ is 'the same, yesterday, to-day, and forever.' By good men I mean simply those who are sincerely wishing and trying to obtain mastery over the evil of their natures. If you still wish to do this, I have abundant hope for you—as much hope as ever I had.''

"Of what value, then, were all those strange, happy feelings which I regarded as the proofs of my conversion?'' Haldane asked, with the look of deep perplexity still upon his face.

"Of very great value, if you look upon them in their true light. They were evidences of God's love and favor. They showed how kindly disposed he is toward you. They can prove to you how abundantly able he is to reward all trust and service, giving foretastes of heavenly bliss even in the midst of earthly warfare. The trouble has been with you, as with so many others, that you have been consulting your variable emotions instead of looking simply to Christ, the author and finisher of our faith. Besides, the power is not given to us to maintain an equable flow of feeling for any considerable length of time. We react from exaltation into depression inevitably. Our feelings depend largely also upon earthly causes and our physical condition, and we can never be absolutely sure how far they are the result of the direct action of God's Spirit upon our minds. It is God's plan to work through simple, natural means, so that we may not be looking and waiting for the supernatural. And yet it would seem that many are so irrational that, when they find mere feeling passing away, they give up their hope and all relationship to Christ, acting as if the immutable love of God were changing with their flickering emotions."

"I have been just so irrational," said Haldane in a low, deep tone.

"Then settle it now and forever, my dear young friend, that Jesus Christ, who died to save you, wishes to save you every day and all the days of your life. He does not change a hair-breadth from the attitude indicated in the words, 'Come unto me; and whosoever cometh unto me I will in no wise cast out.'"

"Do you mean to say he feels that way toward me all the time, in spite of all my cantankerous moods?" asked Mr. Growther eagerly.

"Most certainly."

"I wouldn't a' thought it if I'd lived a thousand years."

"What, then, is conversion?" asked Haldane, feeling as if he were being led safely out of a labyrinth in which he had lost himself.

"In my view it is simply turning away from everything to Christ as the sole ground of our salvation and as our divine guide and example in Christian living."

"But how can we ever know that we are Christians?"

"Only by the honest, patient, continued effort to obey his brief command, 'Follow me.' We may follow near, or we may follow afar off; but we can soon learn whether we wish to get nearer to him, or to get away from him, or to just indifferently let him drop out of our thoughts. The Christian is one who holds and maintains certain simple relations to Christ. 'Ye are my friends,' he said, not if you feel thus and so, but, 'if ye do whatsoever I command you;' and I have found from many years' experience that 'his commandments are not grievous.' For every burden he imposes he gives help and comfort a hundred times.

The more closely and faithfully we follow him, the more surely do fear and doubt pass away. We learn to look up to him as a child looks in its mother's face, and 'his Spirit beareth witness with our spirit that we are his.' But the vital point is, are we following him? Feeling varies so widely and strangely in varied circumstances and with different temperaments that many a true saint of God would be left in cruel uncertainty if this were the test. My creed is a very simple one, Egbert; but I take a world of comfort in it. It contains only three words—Trust, follow Christ—that is all."

"It is so simple and plain that I am tempted to take it as my creed also," said Haldane, with a tinge of hope and enthusiasm in his manner.

"And yet remember," warned his friend earnestly, "there is infinite requirement in it. A child can make a rude sketch of a perfect statue that will bear some faint resemblance to it. If he persevere he can gradually learn to draw the statue with increasing accuracy. In taking this Divine Man as your example, you pledge yourself to imitate One whom you can ever approach but never reach. And yet there is no occasion for the weakest to falter before this infinite requirement, for God himself in spirit is present everywhere to aid all in regaining the lost image of himself. It is to no lonely unguided effort that I urge you, Egbert, but to a patient co-working with your Maker, that you may attain a character that will fit you to dwell at last in your kingly Father's house; and I tell you frankly, for your encouragement, that you are capable of forming such a character. I will now bid you good-night, and leave you to think over what I have said. But write to me or come to me whenever you wish."

"Good-night, Mr. Growther; hate yourself if you will, but remember that the Bible assures us that 'God is love'; you cannot hate him."

CHAPTER XLII

THE LEVER THAT MOVES THE WORLD

THE power of truth can scarcely be overestimated, and the mind that earnestly seeks it becomes noble in its noble quest. If this can be said of truth in the abstract, and in its humbler manifestations, how omnipotent truth becomes in its grandest culmination and embodied in a being capable of inspiring our profoundest fear and deepest love. One may accept of religious forms and philosophies, and be little changed thereby. One may be perfectly saturated with ecclesiasticism, and still continue a small-natured man. But the man that accepts of Jesus Christ as a personal and living teacher, as did the fishermen of Galilee, that man begins to grow large and noble, brave and patient.

Egbert Haldane has been sketched as an ordinary youth. There are thousands like him who have been warped and marred by early influences, but more seriously injured by a personal and wilful yielding to whatever form of evil proved attractive. The majority are not so unwary or so unfortunate as he was; but multitudes, for whom society has comparatively little criticism, are more vitiated at heart, more cold-blooded and deliberate in their evil. One may form a base character, but maintain an outward respectability; but let him not be very complacent over the decorous and conventional veneer which masks him from the world. If one imagines that he can corrupt his own soul and make it the abiding-place of foul thoughts, mean impulses, and shrivelling selfishness, and yet go forward very far in God's universe without meeting overwhelming disaster, he will find himself thoroughly mistaken.

The sin of another man finds him out in swift sequence upon its committal, and such had been Haldane's experience. He had been taught promptly the nature of the harvest which evil produces inevitably.

The terrible consequences of sin prevent and deter from it in many instances, but they have no very great reformatory power it would seem. Multitudes to-day are *in extremis* from destroying vices, and recognize the fact; but so far from reacting upward into virtue, even after vice (save in the intent of the heart) has ceased to be possible, there seems to be a moral inertia which nothing moves, or a reckless and increasing impetus downward.

It would appear that, in order to save the sinful, a strong, and yet gentle and loving, hand must be laid upon them. The stern grasp of justice, the grip of pain, law—human and divine—with its severe penalties, and conscience re-echoing its thunders, all lead too often to despondency, recklessness, and despair. It would be difficult to imagine a worse hell than vice often digs for its votaries, even in this world; and in spite of all human philosophies, and human wishes to the contrary, it remains a fact that the guilty soul trembles at a worse hereafter, and yet no sufferings, no fears, no fate can so appall as to turn the soul from its infatuation with that which is destroying it. More potent than commands, threats, and their dire fulfilment, is *love*, which wins and entreats back to virtue the man whom even Omnipotence could not drive back.

In the flood God overwhelmed the sinful world in sudden destruction, but the race continued sinning all the same. At last God came among men, and shared in their lot and nature. He taught them, he sympathized with them, he loved them, he died for them, and when the wondrous story is told as it should be, the most reckless pause to listen, the most callous are touched, and those who would otherwise despair in their guilt are led to believe that there is a heart large and tender enough to pity and save even such as the world is ready to spurn into a dishonored grave.

The love of God as manifested in Christ of Nazareth is doing more for humanity than all other influences combined. The best and noblest elements of our civilization can be traced either directly or indirectly to him, and shadows brood heavily over both the lands and hearts that neither know nor care for him.

It would seem, then, that not the wrath of God, but his love, is most effective in separating men from the evil which would otherwise destroy them. God could best manifest this love by becoming a man "made like unto his brethren"; for the love of God is ever best taught and best understood, not as a doctrine, but when embodied in some large-hearted and Christlike person.

Such a person most emphatically was Mrs. Arnot; and because of these divine characteristics her gentle, womanly hand became more potent to save young Haldane than were all the powers of evil and the downward impetus of a bad life to destroy.

How very many, like him, might be saved, were more women of tact and culture, large-hearted also and willing to give a part of their time to such noble uses!

By a personal and human ministry, the method that has ever been most effective in God's providence, Haldane was at last brought into close, intimate relations with the Divine Teacher himself. He was led to look away from his own fitful emotions and vague experiences to One who was his strong and unchanging friend. He was led to take as his daily guide and teacher the One who developed Peter the fisherman, Paul the bigot, Luther the ignorant monk, into what they eventually became, and it was not strange, therefore, that his crude, misshapen character should gradually assume the outlines of moral symmetry, and that strength should take the place of weakness. He commenced to learn by experience the truth which many never half believe, that God is as willing to lovingly fashion the spiritual life of some humble follower as he is to shape the destiny of those who are to be famous in the annals of the church and the world.

To Haldane's surprise he was not discharged from his humble position in Mr. Ivison's employ, and the explanation, which soon afterward appeared, gave him great encouragement. The man whom he had so severely punished in his outburst of passion, vented his spite by giving to the *Morning Courier* an exaggerated and distorted account of the affair, in which the youth was made to exchange places with himself, and appear as a coarse, quarrelsome bully.

When Haldane's attention was called to the paragraph his face flushed with indignation as he read it; but he threw the paper down and went to his work without a word of comment. He had already about despaired of anything like justice or friendly recognition from the public, and he turned from this additional wrong with a feeling not far removed from indifference. He was learning the value of Mrs. Arnot's suggestion, that a consciousness of one's own integrity can do more to sustain than the world's opinion, and her words on the previous evening had taught him how a companionship, and eventually a character, might be won that could compensate him for all that he had lost or might suffer.

His persecutor was, therefore, disappointed in seeing how little annoyance his spite occasioned, nor was his equanimity increased by a message from Mr. Ivison ordering his instant discharge.

The following morning the foreman of the room in which Haldane worked came to him with quite a show of friendliness, and said:

"It seems ye're in luck, for the boss takes an interest in ye. Read that; I wouldn't a' thought it."

Hope sprang up anew in the young man's breast as he read the following words:

EDITOR COURIER.—*Dear Sir:* You will doubtless give space for this correction in regard to the fracas which took place in my factory a day or two since. You, with all right-minded men, surely desire that no injustice should be done to any one in any circumstances. Very great injustice was done to young Haldane in your issue of to-day. I have taken pains to inform myself accurately, and have learned that he patiently submitted to a petty persecution for a long time, and at last gave way to natural anger under a provocation such as no man of spirit could endure. His tormentor, a coarse, ill-conditioned fellow, was justly punished, and I have discharged him from my employ. I have nothing to offer in extenuation of young Haldane's past faults, and, if I remember correctly, the press of the city has always been fully as severe upon him as the occasion demanded. If any further space is given to his fortunes, justice at least, not to say a little encouraging kindness, should be accorded to him, as well as severity. It should be stated that for weeks he has been trying to earn an honest livelihood, and in a situation peculiarly trying to him. I have been told that he sincerely wishes to reform and live a cleanly and decent life, and I have obtained evidence that satisfies me of the truth of this report. It appears to me that it is as mean a thing for newspapers to strike a man who is down, but who is endeavoring to rise again, as it is for an individual to do so, and I am sure that you will not consciously permit your journal to give any such sinister blow. Respectfully yours,   JOHN IVISON.

In editorial comment came the following brief remark:

We gladly give Mr. Ivison's communication a prominent place. It is not our intention to "strike" any one, but merely to record each day's events as they come to us. With the best intentions mistakes are sometimes made. We have no possible motive for not wishing young Haldane well—we do wish him success in achieving a better future than his past actions have led us to expect. The city would be much better off if all of his class were equally ready to go to work.

Here at least was some recognition. The fact that he was working, and willing to work, had been plainly stated, and this fact is an essential foundation-stone in the building up of a reputation which the world will respect.

Although the discharge of the leading persecutor, and Mr. Ivison's letter, did not add to Haldane's popularity at the mill, they led to his being severely let alone at first, and an increasingly frank and affable manner on the part of the young man, as he gained in patience and serenity, gradually disarmed those who were not vindictive and blind from prejudice.

· Poor Mrs. Haldane seemed destined to be her son's evil genius to the end. When people take a false view of life there seems a fatality in all their actions. The very fact that they are not in accord with what is right and true causes the most important steps of their lives to appear ill-timed, injudicious, and unnatural. That they are well-meaning and sincere does not help matters much, if both tact and sound principles are wanting. Mrs. Haldane belonged to the class that are sure that everything is right which seems right to them. True, it was a queer little jumble of religious prejudices and conventional notions that combined to produce her conclusions; but when once they were reached, no matter how absurd or defective they appeared to others, she had no more doubt of them than of the Copernican system.

Her motherly feelings had made her willing to take her son to some hiding-place in Europe; but since that could not be, and perhaps was not best, she had thoroughly settled it in her mind that he should accept of her offer and live at her expense the undemonstrative life of an oyster in the social and moral ooze of the obscurest mud-bank he could find. In this way the terrible world might be led to eventually leave off talking and thinking of the Haldane family—a consummation that appeared to her worth any sacrifice. When the morning paper brought another vile story (copied from the Hillaton "Courier") of her son's misdoings, her adverse view of his plans and character was confirmed beyond the shadow of a doubt. She felt that there was a fatality about the place and its associations for him, and her one hope was to get him away.

She cut the article from the paper and inclosed it to him with the accompanying note:

We go to New York this afternoon, and sail for Europe to-morrow. You send us in parting a characteristic souvenir, which I return to you. The scenes and associations indicated in this disgraceful paragraph seem more to your taste than those which your family have hitherto enjoyed as their right for many generations. While this remains true, you, of necessity, cut yourself off from your kindred, and we, who are most closely connected, must remain where our names cannot be associated with yours. I still cherish the hope, however, that you may find the way of the transgressor so hard that you will be brought by your bitter experience to accept of my offer and give the world a chance to forget your folly and wickedness. When you will do this in good faith (and my lawyer will see that it is done in good faith), you may draw on him for the means of a comfortable support. In bitter shame and sorrow, your mother,

EMILY HALDANE.

This letter was a severe blow to her son, for it contained the last words of the mother that he might not see for years. While he felt it to be cruelly unjust to him and his present aims, he was calm enough now to see that the distorted paragraph which led to it fitted in only too well with the past, and so had the coloring of truth. When inclined to blame his mother for not waiting for his versions of these miserable events and accepting of them alone, he was compelled to remember that she was in part awakened from her blind idolatry of him by the discovery of his efforts to deceive her in regard to his increasing dissipation. Even before he had entered Mr. Arnot's counting-room he had taught her to doubt his word, and now she had evidently lost confidence in him utterly. He foresaw that this confidence could be regained only by years of patient well-doing, and that she might incline to believe in him more slowly even than comparative strangers. But he was not disposed to be very angry and resentful, for he now had but little confidence in himself. He had been led, however, by his bitter experience and by Mrs. Arnot's faithful ministry to adopt that lady's brief but comprehensive creed. He was learning to trust in Christ as an all-powerful and personal friend; he was daily seeking to grasp the principles which Christ taught, but more clearly acted out, and which are essential to the formation of a noble character. He had thus complied with the best conditions of spiritual growth; and the crude elements of his character, which had been rendered more chaotic by evil, slowly began to shape themselves into the symmetry of a true man.

In regard to his mother's letter, all that he could do was to inclose to her, with the request that it be forwarded, Mr.

Ivison's defence of him, which appeared in the "Courier" of the following morning.

"You perceive," he wrote, "that a stranger has taken pains to inform himself correctly in regard to the facts of the case, and that he has for me some charity and hope. I do not excuse the wrong of my action on that occasion or on any other, but I do wish, and I am trying, to do better, and I hope to prove the same to you by years of patient effort. I may fail miserably, however, as you evidently believe. The fact that my folly and wickedness have driven you and my sisters into exile, is a very great sorrow to me, but compliance with your request that I should leave Hillaton and go into hiding would bring no remedy at all. I know that I should do worse anywhere else, and my self-respect and conscience both require that I should fight the battle of my life out here where I have suffered such disgraceful defeat."

CHAPTER XLIII

MR. GROWTHER "STUMPED"

ABOUT three weeks after the occasion upon which Haldane's human nature had manifested itself in such a disastrous manner as he had supposed, Mrs. Arnot, Dr. Barstow, and Mr. Ivison happened to find themselves together at an evening company.

"I have been wishing to thank you, Mr. Ivison," said the lady, "for your just and manly letter in regard to young Haldane. I think it encouraged him very much, and has given him more hopefulness in his work. How has he been doing of late? The only reply he makes to my questioning is, 'I am plodding on.'"

"Do you know," said Mr. Ivison, "I am beginning to take quite an interest in that young fellow. He has genuine pluck. You cannot understand, Mrs. Arnot, what an ordeal he has passed through. He is naturally as mettlesome as a young colt, and yet day after day he was subjected to words and actions that were to him like the cut of a whip."

"Mr. Ivison," said Mrs. Arnot, with a sudden moisture coming into her eyes, "I have long felt the deepest interest in this young man. In judging any one I try to consider not only what he does, but all the circumstances attending upon his action. Knowing Haldane's antecedents, and how peculiarly unfitted he was by early life and training for his present trials, I think his course since he was last released from prison has been very brave," and she gave a brief sketch of his life and mental states, as far as a delicate regard for his feelings permitted, from that date.

Dr. Barstow, in his turn, also became interested in the youth, not only for his own sake, but also in the workings of his mind and his spiritual experiences. It was the good doctor's tendency to analyze everything and place all psychological manifestations under their proper theological heads.

"I feel that I indirectly owe this youth a large debt of gratitude, since his coming to our church and his repulse, in the first instance, has led to decided changes for the better in us all, I trust. But his experience, as you have related it, raises some perplexing questions. Do you think he is a Christian?"

"I do not know. I think he is," replied Mrs. Arnot.

"When do you think he became a Christian?"

"Still less can I answer that question definitely."

"But would not one naturally think it was when he was conscious of that happy change in the study of good old Dr. Marks?"

"Poor Haldane has been conscious of many changes and experiences, but I do not despise or make light of any of them. It is certainly sensible to believe that every effect has a cause; and for one I believe that these strange, mystical, and often rich and rapturous experiences, are largely and perhaps wholly caused in many instances by the direct action of God's Spirit on the human spirit. Again, it would seem that men's religious natures are profoundly stirred by human and earthly causes, for the emotion ceases with the cause. It appears to me that if people would only learn to look at these experiences in a sensible way, they would be the better and wiser for them. We are thus taught what a grand instrument the soul is, and of what divine harmonies and profound emotions it is capable when played upon by any adequate power. To expect to maintain this exaltation with our present nature is like requiring of the athlete that he never relax his muscles, or of the prima donna that she never cease the exquisite trill which is but the momentary proof of what her present organization is capable. And yet it would appear that many; like poor Haldane, are tempted on one hand to entertain no Christian hope because they cannot produce these deep and happy emotions; or, on the other hand, to give up Christian hope because these emotions cease in the inevitable reaction that follows them. In my opinion it is when we accept of Christ as Saviour and Guide we become Christians, and a Christian life is the maintenance of this simple yet vital relationship. We thus continue branches of the 'true vine.' I think Haldane has formed this relationship."

"It would seem from your account that he had formed it, consciously, but a very brief time since," said Dr. Barstow, "and yet for weeks previous he had been putting forth what closely resembles Christian effort, exercising Christian forbearance, and for a time at least enjoying happy spiritual experiences. Can you believe that all this is possible to one who is yet dead in trespasses and sins?"

"My dear Dr. Barstow, I cannot apply your systematic theology to all of God's creatures any more than I could apply a rigid and carefully lined-out system of parental affection and government to your household. I know that you love all of your children, both when they are good and when they are bad, and that you are ever trying to help the naughty ones to be better. I am inclined to think that I could learn more sound theology on these points in your nursery and dining-room than in your study. I am sure, however, that God does not wait till his little bewildered children reach a certain theological mile-stone before reaching out his hand to guide and help them."

"You are both better theologians than I am," said Mr. Ivison, "and I shall not enter the lists with you on that ground; but I know what mill-life is to one of his caste and feeling, and his taking such work, and his sticking to it under the circumstances, is an exhibition of more pluck than most young men possess. And yet it was his only chance, for when people get down as low as he was they must take any honest work in order to obtain a foothold. Even now, burdened as he is by an evil name, it is difficult to see how he can rise any higher."

"Could you not give him a clerkship?" asked Mrs. Arnot.

"No, I could not introduce him among my other clerks. They would resent it as an insult."

"You could do this," said Mrs. Arnot with a slight flush, "but I do not urge it or even ask it. You are in a position to show great and generous kindness toward this young man. As he who was highest stooped to the lowliest, so those high in station and influence can often stoop to the humble and fallen with a better grace than those nearer to them in rank. If you believe this young man is now trustworthy, and that trusting him would make him still more so, you could give him a desk in your private office, and thus teach your clerks a larger charity. The influential and assured in position must often take the lead in these matters."

Mr. Ivison thought a moment, and then said: "Your proposition is unusual, Mrs. Arnot, but I'll think of it. I make no promises, however."

"Mr. Ivison," added Mrs. Arnot, in her smiling, happy way, "I hope you may make a great deal of money out of your business this year; but if, by means of it, you can also aid in making a good and true man, you will be still better off. Dr. Barstow here can tell you how sure such investments are."

"If I should follow your lead and that of Dr. Barstow, all my real estate would be in the 'Celestial City,'" laughed Mr. Ivison. "But I have a special admiration for the grace of clear grit, and this young fellow, in declining his mother's offer and trying to stand on his feet here in Hillaton, where every one is ready to tread him down, shows pluck, whatever else is wanting. I've had my eye on him for some time, and I'm about satisfied he's trying to do right. But it is difficult to know what to do for one with his ugly reputation.   I will see what can be done, however."

That same evening chilly autumn winds were blowing without, and Mr. Growther's passion for a wood fire upon the hearth was an indulgence to which Haldane no longer objected.   The frugal supper was over, and the two oddly diverse occupants of the quaint old kitchen glowered at the red coals in silence, each busy with his own thoughts.   At last Haldane gave a long deep sigh, which drew to him at once Mr. Growther's small twinkling eyes.

"Tough old world, isn't it, for sinners like us?" he remarked.

"Well, Mr. Growther, I've got rather tired of inveighing against the world; I'm coming to think that the trouble is largely with myself."

"Umph!" snarled the old man, "I've allers knowed the trouble was with me, for of all crabbed, cranky, cantankerous, old—"

"Hold on," cried Haldane, laughing, "don't you remember what Mrs. Arnot said about being unjust to one's self? The only person that I have ever known you to wrong is Jeremiah Growther, and it seems to me that you do treat him outrageously sometimes."

At the name of Mrs. Arnot the old man's face softened, and he rubbed his hands together as he chuckled, "How Satan must hate that woman!"

"I was in hopes that her words might lead you to be a little juster to yourself," continued Haldane, "and it has seemed to me that you, as well as I, have been in a better mood of late."

"I don't take no stock in myself at all," said Mr. Growther emphatically.   "I'm a crooked stick and allers will be —a reg'lar old gnarled knotty stick, with not 'nuff good timber in it to make a penny whistle.   That I haven't been in as cussin' a state as usual isn't because I think any better of myself, but your Mrs. Arnot has set me a-thinkin' on a new track.   She come to see me one day while you was at the mill, and we had a real speret'al tussel. I argufied my case in such a way that she couldn't git round it, and I proved to her that I was the driest and crookedest old stick that ever the devil twisted out o' shape when it was a-growin'. On a suddent she turned the argerment agin me in a way that has stumped me ever since. 'You are right, Mr. Growther,' she said, 'it was the devil and not the Lord that twisted you out of shape. Now who's the stronger,' she says, 'and who's goin' to have his own way in the end? Suppose you are very crooked, won't the Lord get all the more glory in making you straight, and won't his victory be all the greater over the evil one?' Says I, 'Mrs. Arnot, that's puttin' my case in a new light. If I should be straightened out, it would be the awfulest set-back Old Nick ever had; and if such a thing should happen he'd never feel sure of any one after that.' Then she turned on me kinder sharp, and says she, 'What right have you to say that God is allers lookin' round for easy work? What would you think of a doctor who would take only slight cases, and have nothing to do with people who were gittin' dangerous-like? Isn't Jesus Christ the great physician, and don't your common-sense tell you that he is jist as able to cure you as a little child?'

"I declare I was stumped. Like that ill-mannered cuss in the Scripter who thought his old clothes good enough for the weddin', I was speechless.

"But I got a worse knock down than that. Says she, 'Mr. Growther, I will not dispute all the hard things you have said of yourself (you see I had beat her on that line of argerment); I won't dispute all that you say (and I felt a little sot up agin, for I didn't know what she was a-drivin' at), but,' says she, 'I think you've got some natural feelin's. Suppose you had a little son, and while he was out in the street a wicked man should carry him off and treat him so cruelly that, instead of growin' to be strong and fine-lookin', he should become a puny, deformed little critter. Suppose at last you should hear where he was, and that he was longin' to escape from the cruel hands of his harsh master, who kept on a-treatin' of him worse and worse, would you, his father, go and coolly look at him and say, "If you was only a handsome boy, with a strong mind in a strong body, I'd deliver you out of this tyrant's clutches and take you back to be my son again; but since you are a poor, weak, deformed little critter, that can never do much, or be much, I'll leave you here to be abused and tormented as before"— is that what you would do, Mr. Growther?'

"Well, she spoke it all so earnest and real-like that I got off my guard, and I jist riz right up from my cheer, and I got hold of my heavy old cane there, and it seemed as if my hair stood right up on end, I was that mad at the old curmudgeon that had my boy, and I half shouts, 'No! that ain't what I'd do, I'd go for that cuss that stole my boy, and for every blow he'd given the little chap, I'd give him a hundred.'

"'But what would you do with the poor little boy?' she asks. At that I began to choke, my feelin's was so stirred up, and moppin' my eyes, I said, 'Poor little chap, all beaten and abused out o' shape! What would I do with him? Why, I couldn't do 'nuff for him in tryin' to make him forget all the hard times he'd had.' Then says she, 'You would twit the child with bein' weak, puny, and deformed, would you?' I was now hobblin' up and down the room in a great state of excitement, and says I, 'Mrs. Arnot, mean a man as I am, I wouldn't treat any human critter so, let alone my own flesh and blood, that had been so abused that it makes my heart ache to think on't.'

"'Don't you think you would love the boy a little even though he had a hump on his back and his features were thin and sharp and pale?' 'Mrs. Arnot,' says I, moppin' my eyes agin, 'if you say another word about the little chap I shall be struck all of a heap, fur my heart jist kinder— kinder pains like a toothache to do somethin' for him.' Then all of a suddent she turns on me sharp agin, and says she, 'I think you are a very inconsistent man, Mr.

Growther. You have been runnin' yourself down, and yet you claim to be better than your Maker. He calls himself our Heavenly Father, and yet you are sure that you have a kinder and more fatherly heart than he. You are one of his little, weak, deformed children, twisted all out of shape, as you have described, by his enemy and yours, and yet you the same as say that you would act a great deal more like a true father toward your child than he will toward his. You virtually say that you would rescue your child and be pitiful and tender toward him, but that your Heavenly Father will leave you in the clutches of the cruel enemy, or exact conditions that you cannot comply with before doing anything for you. Haven't you read in the Bible that "Like as a father pitieth his children, so the Lord pitieth them that fear him"? You think very meanly of yourself, but you appear to think more meanly of God. Where is your warrant for doing so?'

"The truth bust in on me like the sunlight into this old kitchen when we open the shutters of a summer mornin'. I saw that I was so completely floored in the argerment, and had made such a blasted old fool of myself all these years, that I just looked around for a knot-hole to crawl into. I didn't know which way to look, but at last I looked at her, and my withered old heart gave a great thump when I saw two tears a-standin' in her eyes. Then she jumps up and gives me that warm hand o' her'n and says: 'Mr. Growther, whenever you wish to know how God feels toward you, think how you felt toward that little chap that was abused and beaten all out o' shape,' and she was gone. Well, the upshot of it all is that I don't think a bit better of myself—not one bit—but that weakly little chap, with a peaked face and a hump on his back, that Mrs. Arnot made so real-like that I see him a-lookin' at me out of the cheer there half the time—he's a makin' me better acquainted with the Lord, for the Lord knows I've got a hump on my back and humps all over; but I keep a-sayin' to myself, 'Like as a father pitieth his children,' and I don't feel near

as much like cussin' as I used to. That little chap that
Mrs. Arnot described is doin' me a sight o' good, and if I
could find some poor little critter just like him, with no
one to look after him, I'd take him in and do for him in a
minit."

"Mr. Growther," said Haldane, huskily, "you have
found that poor misshapen, dwarfed creature that I fear
will never attain the proportions of a true man. Of course
you see through Mrs. Arnot's imagery. In befriending me
you are caring for one who is weak and puny indeed."

"Oh, you won't answer," said Mr. Growther with a
laugh. "I can see that your humps is growin' wisibly
less every day, and you're too big and broad-shouldered
for me to be a pettin' and a yearnin' over. I want jest
such a peaked little chap as Mrs. Arnot pictured out, and
that's doin' me such a sight o' good."

Again the two occupants of the old kitchen gazed at the
fire for a long time in silence, and again there came from
the young man the same long-drawn sigh that had attracted
Mr. Growther's attention before.

"That's the second time," he remarked.

"I was thinking," said Haldane, rising to retire, "whether
I shall ever have better work than this odious routine at the
mill."

Mr. Growther pondered over the question a few minutes,
and then said sententiously: "I'm inclined to think the Lord
gives us as good work as we're cap'ble of doin'. He'll pro-
mote you when you've growed a little more."

CHAPTER XLIV

GROWTH

THE next morning Haldane received a message directing him to report at Mr. Ivison's private office during the noon recess.

"Be seated," said that gentleman as the young man, wearing an anxious and somewhat surprised expression, entered hesitatingly and diffidently. "You need not look so troubled, I have not sent for you to find fault—quite the reverse. You have 'a friend at court,' as the saying goes. Not that you needed one particularly, for I have had my eye upon you myself, and for some days past have been inclined to give you a lift. But last evening Mrs. Arnot spoke in your behalf, and through her words I have been led to take the following step. For reasons that perhaps you can understand, it would be difficult for me to give you a desk among my other clerks. I am not so sensitive, now that I know your better aims, and it is my wish that you take that desk there, in this, my private office. Your duties will be very miscellaneous. Sometimes I shall employ you as my errand-boy, again I may intrust you with important and confidential business. I stipulate that you perform the humblest task as readily as any other."

Haldane's face flushed with pleasure, and he said warmly, "I am not in a position, sir, to consider any honest work beneath me, and after your kindness I shall regard any service I can render you as a privilege."

"A neat answer," laughed Mr. Ivison. "If you do your work as well I shall be satisfied. Pluck and good sense will make a man of you yet. I want you to understand distinctly that it has been your readiness and determination, not only to work, but to do any kind of work, that has won my good-will. Here's a check for a month's salary in advance. Be here to-morrow at nine, dressed suitably for your new position. Good-morning."

"Halloo! What's happened?" asked Mr. Growther as Haldane came in that evening with face aglow with gladness and excitement.

"According to your theory I've been promoted sure," laughed the youth, and he related the unexpected event of the day.

"That's jest like Mrs. Arnot," said Mr. Growther, rubbing his hands as he ever did when pleased; "she's allers givin' some poor critter a boost. T'other day 'twas me, now agin it's you, and they say she's helpin' lots more along. St. Peter will have to open the gate wide when she comes in with her crowd. 'Pears to me sometimes that I can fairly hear Satan a-gnashin' of his teeth over that woman. She's the wust enemy he has in town."

"I wish I might show her how grateful I am some day," said Haldane, with moistened eyes; "but I clearly foresee that I can never repay her."

"No matter if you can't," replied the old man. "She don't want any pay. It's her natur' to do these things."

Haldane gave his whole mind to the mastery of his new duties, and after a few natural blunders speedily acquired a facility in the diverse tasks allotted him. In a manner that was perfectly unobtrusive and respectful he watched his employer, studied his methods and habit of mind, and thus gained the power of anticipating his wishes. Mr. Ivison began to find his office and papers kept in just the order he liked, the temperature maintained at a pleasant medium, and to receive many little nameless attentions that added to his comfort and reduced the wear and tear of life to a hurried business-man; and when in emergencies Haldane was given tasks that required brains, he proved that he possessed a fair share of them.

After quite a lapse of time Mr. Ivison again happened to meet Mrs. Arnot, and he said to her:

"Haldane thinks you did him a great kindness in suggesting our present arrangement; but I am inclined to think you did me a greater, for you have no idea how useful the young fellow is making himself to me."

"Then you will have to find a new object of benevolence," answered the lady, "or you will have all your reward in this world."

"There it is again," said Mr. Ivison, with his hearty laugh, "you and Dr. Barstow give a man no peace. I'm going to take breath before I strike in again."

In his new employment, Haldane, from the first, had found considerable leisure on his hands, and after a little thought decided to review carefully the studies over which he had passed so superficially in his student days.

Mr. Growther persisted in occupying the kitchen, leaving what had been designed as the parlor or sitting-room of his cottage to dust and damp. With his permission the young man fitted this up as a study, and bought a few popular works on science, as the nucleus of a library. After supper he read the evening paper to Mr. Growther, who soon fell into a doze, and then Haldane would steal away to his own quarters and pursue with zest, until a late hour, some study that had once seemed to him utterly dry and unattractive.

Thus the months glided rapidly and serenely away, and he was positively happy in a mode of life that he once would have characterized as odiously humdrum. The terrible world, whose favor had formerly seemed essential, and its scorn unendurable, was almost forgotten; and as he continued at his duties so steadily and unobtrusively the hostile world began to unbend gradually its frowning aspect toward him. Those whom he daily met in business commenced with a nod of recognition, and eventually ended with a pleasant word. At church an increasing number began to speak to him, not merely as a Christian duty, but because the **young man's** sincere and earnest manner interested them and inspired respect.

The fact that he recognized that he was under a cloud and did not try to attract attention, worked in his favor. He never asked the alms of a kindly word or glance, by looking appealingly to one and another. It became his habit to walk with his eyes downcast, not speaking to nor looking toward any one unless first addressed. At the same time his bearing was manly and erect, and marked by a certain quiet dignity which inevitably characterizes all who are honestly trying to do right.

Because he asked so little of society it was the more disposed to give, and from a point of bare toleration it passed on to a willingness to patronize with a faint encouraging smile. And yet it was the general feeling that one whose name had been so sadly besmirched must be kept at more than arm's-length.

"He may get to heaven," said an old lady who was remarking upon his regular attendance at church, "but he can never hope to be received in good society again."

In the meantime the isolated youth was finding such an increasing charm in the companionship of the gifted minds who spoke to him from the printed pages of his little library that he felt the deprivation less and less.

But an hour with Mrs. Arnot was one of his chief pleasures, to which he looked forward with glad anticipation. For a long time he could not bring himself to go to her house or to take the risk of meeting any of her other guests, and in order to overcome his reluctance she occasionally set apart an evening for him alone and was "engaged" to all others. These were blessed hours to the lonely young fellow, and their memory made him stronger and more hopeful for days thereafter.

In his Christian experience he was gaining a quiet serenity and confidence. He had fully settled it in his mind, as Mrs. Arnot had suggested, that Jesus Christ was both willing and able to save him, and he simply trusted and tried to follow.

"Come," said that lady to him one evening, "it's time you found a nook in the vineyard and went to work."

He shook his head emphatically as he replied, "I do not feel myself either competent or worthy. Besides, who would listen to me?"

"Many might with profit. You can carry messages from Mr. Ivison, can you not take a message from your Divine Master? I have thought it all over, and can tell you where you will be listened to at least, and where you may do much good. I went, last Sunday, to the same prison in which I visited you, and I read to the inmates. It would be a moral triumph for you, Egbert, to go back there as a Christian man and with the honest purpose of doing good. It would be very pleasant for me to think of you at work there every Sabbath. Make the attempt, to please me, if for no better reason."

"That settles the question, Mrs. Arnot," said Haldane, with a troubled smile. "I would try to preach in Choctaw, if you requested it, and I fear all that I can say 'out o' my own head,' as Mr. Growther would put it, will be worse than Choctaw. But I can at least read to the prisoners; that is," he added, with downcast eyes and a flush of his old shame, "if they will listen to me, which I much doubt. You, with your large generous sympathies, can never understand how greatly I am despised, even by my own class."

"Please remember that I am of your class now, for you are of the household of faith. I know what you mean, Egbert. I am glad that you are so diffident and so little inclined to ask on the ground of your Christian profession that the past be overlooked. If there is one thing that disgusts me more than another it is the disposition to make one's religion a stepping-stone to earthly objects and the means of forcing upon others a familiarity or a relationship that is offensive to them. I cannot help doubting a profession of faith that is put to such low uses. I know that you have special reason for humility, but you must not let it develop into timidity. All I ask is that you read to such

poor creatures in the prison as will listen to you a chapter
in the Bible, and explain it as well as you can, and then
read something else that you think will interest them.''

Haldane made the attempt, and met, at first, as he feared,
with but indifferent success.   Even criminals looked at him
askance as he came in the guise of a religious teacher.   But
his manner was so unassuming, and the spirit ''I am better
than thou'' was so conspicuously absent, that a few were
disarmed, and partly out of curiosity, and partly to kill the
time that passed so slowly, they gathered at his invitation.
He sat down among them as if one of them, and in a voice
that trembled with diffidence read a chapter from the gospels.   Since he ''put on no airs,'' as they said, one and
another drew near until all the inmates of the jail were
grouped around him.   Having finished the chapter, Haldane
closed the Bible and said:

''I do not feel competent to explain this chapter.   Perhaps many of you understand it better than I do.   I did not
even feel that I was worthy to come here and read the chapter to you, but the Christian lady who visited you last Sunday asked me to come, and I would do anything for her.
She visited me when I was a prisoner like you, and through
her influence I am trying to be a better man.   I know, my
friends, from sad experience, that when we get down under
men's feet, and are sent to places like these, we lose heart
and hope; we feel that there is no chance for us to get up
again, we are tempted to be despairing and reckless; but
through the kindness and mercy of that good lady, Mrs.
Arnot, I learned of a kindness and mercy greater even than
hers.   The world may hate us, scorn us, and even trample us
down, and if we will be honest with ourselves we must admit
that we have given it some reason to do all this—at least I
feel that I have—but the world can't keep us down, and what
is far worse than the world, the evil in our own hearts can't
keep us down, if we ask Jesus Christ to help us up.   I am
finding this out by experience, and so know the truth of
what I am saying.   This Bible tells us about this strong,

merciful One, this Friend of publicans and sinners, and if you would like me to come here Sunday afternoons and read about him, I will do so very gladly, but I don't wish to force myself upon you if I'm not wanted."

"Come, my hearty, come every time," said an old sailor, with a resounding oath. "Tain't likely I'll ever ship with your captain, for sech as I've come to be couldn't pass muster. Howsumever, it's kind o' comfortin' to hear one talk as if there was plenty of sea-room, even when a chap knows he's drivin' straight on the rocks."

"Come, oh, come again," entreated the tremulous voice of one who was crouching a little back of his chair.

Haldane turned, and with a start recognized the fair young girl, whose blue eyes and Madonna-like face had, for a moment, even in the agony of his own shame, secured his attention while in the police court, more than a year before. She was terribly changed, and yet by that strange principle by which we keep our identity through all mutations, Haldane knew that she was the same, and felt that by a glance he could almost trace back her life through its awful descent to the time when she was a beautiful and innocent girl. As a swift dark tide might sweep a summer pinnace from its moorings, and dash it on the rocks until it became a crushed and shapeless thing, so passion or most untoward circumstances had suddenly drawn this poor young creature among coarse, destructive vices that had shattered the delicate, womanly nature in one short year into utter wreck.

"Come again," she whispered in response to Haldane's glance; "come soon, or else I shall be in my grave, and I've got the awful fear that it is the mouth of the bottomless pit. Otherwise I'd be glad to be in it."

"Poor child!" said Haldane, tears coming into his eyes.

"Ah!" she gasped, "will God pity me like that?"

"Yes, for the Bible says, 'The Lord is very pitiful and of tender mercy.' My own despairing thoughts have taught me to look for all of God's promises."

"You know nothing of the depths into which I have fallen," she said in a low tone; "I can see that in your face."

Again Haldane ejaculated, "Poor child!" with a heart-felt emphasis that did more good than the longest homily. Then finding the Bible story which commences, "And, behold, a woman in the city, which was a sinner," he turned a leaf down saying:

"I am neither wise enough nor good enough to guide you, but I know that Mrs. Arnot will come and see you. I shall leave my Bible with you, and, until she comes, read where I have marked."

Mrs. Arnot did come, and the pure, high-born woman shut the door of the narrow cell, and taking the head of her fallen sister into her lap, listened with responsive tears to the piteous story, as it was told with sighs, sobs, and strong writhings of anguish.

As the girl became calmer and her mind emerged from the chaos of her tempestuous and despairing sorrow, Mrs. Arnot led her, as it were, to the very feet of Jesus of Nazareth, and left her there with these words:

"He came to seek and save just such as you are—the lost. He is reaching down his rescuing hand of love to you, and when you grasp it in simple confiding trust you are saved."

Before the week closed, the poor creature forever turned her face away from the world in which she had so deeply sinned and suffered; but before she departed on the long journey, he who alone can grant to the human soul full absolution, had said to her, "Thy sins are forgiven; go in peace."

As Mrs. Arnot held her dying head she whispered, "Tell him that it was his tears of honest sympathy that first gave me hope."

That message had a vital influence over Haldane's subsequent life. Indeed these words of the poor dying waif were potent enough to shape all his future career. He was taught by them **the magnetic** power of sympathy, and **that he** who in the **depths of his heart** feels for his fellow-creatures, can **help them. He had** once hoped that **he** would dazzle men's eyes by **the** brilliancy of his career, but he had long since concluded **that he must plod along** the **lowly paths** of life. Until **his visit to the prison and** its results the thought had scarcely **occurred to him that** he could help others. He had felt that he had **been too sorely wounded himself ever to be more than an invalid in the** world's hospital; but he now began to learn that his very sin and suffering enabled him to approach nearer to those who were, as he was once, on the brink of despair or in the apathy of utter discouragement, and to aid them **more** effectively **because of his kindred experience.**

The truth that he, in the humblest possible way, could engage in **the noble work** for which he revered Mrs. Arnot, **came like a burst** of sunlight into his shadowed life, **and his visits to the prison** were looked forward to with increasing zest.

From reading the chapter merely he came to venture on a few comments. Then questions **were asked, and he tried** to answer some, and frankly **said he could** not **answer others.** But these questions stimulated his mind and led to thought and **wider** reading. **To his** own agreeable surprise, **as well** as that of his prison **class, he occasionally was** able **to bring,** on the following Sabbath, a very satisfactory answer to some of the questions; and this suggested the truth **that all** questions could be answered if only **time and wisdom** enough could be brought to bear **upon them.**

He gradually acquired a **facility in expressing his** thoughts, and, **better** still, **he had thoughts to express.** Some of the prisoners, who **were** in durance but **for a** brief time, asked **him to take a class in** the **Guy-Street Mission Chapel.**

"They will scarcely want me there as a teacher," he said with a slight flush.

But the superintendent **and pastor, after some hesitation** and inquiry, concluded they did want him there, and with some ex-prisoners as a nucleus, he unobtrusively formed a class near the door. The two marked characteristics of his Christian efforts—downright sincerity and sympathy—were like strong, far-reaching hands, and his class began to grow until it swamped the small neighboring classes with uncouth and unkempt-looking creatures that were drawn by the voice that asserted their manhood and womanhood in spite of their degradation. Finally, before another year ended, a large side-room was set apart for Haldane and his strange following, and he made every one that entered it, no matter how debased, believe that there were possibilities of good in them yet, and he was able to impart this encouraging truth because he so thoroughly believed it himself.

As he stood before that throng of publicans and sinners, gathered from the slums of the city, and, with his fine face lighted up with thought and sympathy, spoke to them the truth in such a way that they understood it and felt its power, one could scarcely have believed that but two years before he had been dragged from a drunken brawl to the common jail. The explanation is simple—he had followed closely that same divine Master who had taught the fishermen of Galilee.

CHAPTER XLV

LAURA ROMEYN

MRS. HALDANE and her daughters found European life so decidedly to their taste that it was doubtful whether they would return for several years. The son wrote regularly to his mother, for he had accepted of the truth of Mrs. Arnot's words that nothing could excuse him from the sacred duties which he owed to her. As his fortunes improved and time elapsed without the advent of more disgraceful stories, she also began to respond as frequently and sympathetically as could be expected of one taking her views of life. She was at last brought to acquiesce in his plan of remaining at Hillaton, if not to approve of it, and after receiving one or two letters from Mrs. Arnot, she was inclined to believe in the sincerity of his Christian profession. She began to share in the old lady's view already referred to, that he might reach heaven at last, but could never be received in good society again.

"Egbert is so different from us, my dears," she would sigh to her daughters, "that I suppose we should not judge him by our standards. I suppose he is doing as well as he ever will—as well indeed as his singularly unnatural disposition permits."

It did not occur to the lady that she was a trifle unnatural and unchristian herself in permitting jealousy to creep into her heart, because Mrs. Arnot had wielded a power for good over her son which she herself had failed to exert.

She instructed her lawyer, however, to pay to him an annuity that was far beyond his needs in his present frugal way of living.

This ample income enabled him at once to carry out a cherished purpose, which had been forming in his mind for several months, and which he now broached to Mrs. Arnot.

"For the last half year," he said, "I have thought a great deal over the possibilities that life offers to one situated as I am. I have tried to discover where I can make my life-work, maimed and defective as it ever must be, most effective, and it has seemed to me that I could accomplish more as a physician than in any other calling. In this character I could naturally gain access to those who are in distress of body and mind, but who are too poor to pay for ordinary attendance. There are hundreds in this city, especially little children, that, through vice, ignorance, or poverty, never receive proper attention in illness. My services would not be refused by this class, especially if they were gratuitous."

"You should charge for your visits, as a rule," said wise Mrs. Arnot. "Never give charity unless it is absolutely necessary."

"Well, I could charge so moderately that my attendance would not be a burden. I am very grateful to Mr. Ivison for the position he gave me, but I would like to do something more and better in life than I can accomplish as his clerk. A physician among the poor has so many chances to speak the truth to those who might otherwise never hear it. Now this income from my father's estate would enable me to set about the necessary studies at once, and the only question in my mind is, will they receive me at the university?"

"Egbert," said Mrs. Arnot, with one of those sudden illuminations of her face which he so loved to see, "do you remember what I said long ago, when you were a disheartened prisoner, about my ideal of knighthood? If you keep on you will fulfil it."

"I remember it well," he replied, "but you are mistaken. My best hope is to find, as you said upon another occasion, my own little nook in the vineyard, and quietly do my work there."

After considerable hesitation the faculty of the university received Haldane as a student, and Mr. Ivison parted with him very reluctantly. His studies for the past two years, and several weeks of careful review, enabled him to pass the examinations required in order to enter the Junior year of the college course.

As his name appeared among those who might graduate in two years, the world still further relaxed its rigid and forbidding aspect, and not a few took pains to manifest to him their respect for his resolute upward course.

But he maintained his old, distant, unobtrusive manner, and no one was obliged to recognize, much less to show, any special kindness to him, unless they chose to do so. He evidently shrank with a morbid sensitiveness from any social contact with those who, in remembrance of his past history, might shrink from him. But he had not been at the university very long before Mrs. Arnot overcame this diffidence so far as to induce him to meet with certain manly fellows of his class at her house.

In all the frank and friendly interchange of thought between Mrs. Arnot and the young man there was one to whom, by tacit consent, they did not refer, except in the most casual manner, and that was Laura Romeyn. Haldane had not seen her since the time she stumbled upon him in his character of wood-sawyer. He kept her image in a distant and doubly-locked chamber of his heart, and seldom permitted his thoughts to go thither. Thus the image had faded into a faint yet lovely outline which he had learned to look upon with a regret that was now scarcely deep enough to be regarded as pain. She had made one or two brief visits to her aunt, but he had taken care never to meet her. He had learned incidentally, however, that she had lost her father, and that her mother was far from well.

When calling upon Mrs. Arnot one blustering March evening, toward the close of his Junior year, that lady explained her anxious, clouded face by saying that her sister, Mrs. Romeyn, was very ill, and after a moment added, half in soliloquy, "What would she do without Laura?"

From this he gathered that the young girl was a loving daughter and a faithful nurse, and the image of a pale, yet lovely watcher rose before him with dangerous frequence and distinctness.

A day or two after he received a note from Mrs. Arnot, informing him that she was about to leave home for a visit to her invalid sister, and might be absent several weeks. Her surmise proved correct, and when she returned Laura came with her, and the deep mourning of the orphan's dress but faintly reflected the darker sorrow that shrouded her heart. When, a few sabbaths after her arrival, her veiled figure passed up the aisle of the church, he bowed his head in as sincere sympathy as one person can give for the grief of another.

For a long time he did not venture to call on Mrs. Arnot, and then came only at her request. To his great relief, he did not see Laura, for he felt that, conscious of her great loss and the memories of the past, he should be speechless in her presence. To Mrs. Arnot he said:

"Your sorrow has seemed to me such a sacred thing that I felt that any reference to it on my part would be like a profane touch; but I was sure you would not misinterpret my silence or my absence, and would know that you were never long absent from my thoughts."

He was rewarded by the characteristic lighting up of her face as she said:

"Hillaton would scarcely give you credit for such delicacy of feeling, Egbert, but you are fulfilling my faith in you. Neither have I forgotten you and your knightly conflict because I have not seen or written to you. You know well that my heart and hands have been full. And now a very much longer time must elapse before we can meet again. In her devotion to her mother my niece has overtaxed her strength, and her physical and mental depression is so great that our physician strongly recommends a year abroad. You can see how intensely occupied I have been in preparations for our hurried departure. We sail this week. I shall see your mother, no doubt, and I am glad I can tell her that which I should be proud to hear of a son of mine.''

The year that followed was a long one to Haldane. He managed to keep the even tenor of his way, but it was often as the soldier makes his weary march in the enemy's country, fighting for and holding, step by step, with difficulty. His intense application in his first year of study and the excitements of the previous years at last told upon him, and he often experienced days of extreme lassitude and weariness. At one time he was quite ill, and then he realized how lonely and isolated he was. He still kept his quarters at the hermitage, but Mr. Growther, with the kindest intentions, was too old and decrepit to prove much of a nurse.

In his hours of enforced idleness his imagination began to retouch the shadowy image of Laura Romeyn with an ideal beauty. In his pain and weakness her character of watcher—in which her self-sacrificing devotion had been so great as to impair her health—was peculiarly attractive. She became to him a pale and lovely saint, too remote and sacred for his human love, and yet sufficiently human to continually haunt his mind with a vague and regretful pain that he could never reach her side. He now learned from its loss how valuable Mrs. Arnot's society had been to him. Her letters, which were full and moderately frequent, could not take the place of her quiet yet inspiriting voice.

He was lonely, and he recognized the fact. While there were hundreds now in Hillaton who wished him well, and respected him for his brave struggle, he was too shadowed by disgraceful memories to be received socially into the homes that he would care to visit. Some of the church people invited him out of a sense of duty, but he recognized their motive, and shrank from such constrained courtesy with increasing sensitiveness.

But, though he showed human weakness and gave way

to long moods of despondency, at times inclining to murmur bitterly at his lot, he suffered no serious reverses. He patiently, even in the face of positive disinclination, maintanied his duties. He remembered how often the Divine Man, in his shadowed life, went apart for prayer, and honestly tried to imitate this example, so specially suited to one as maimed and imperfect as himself.

He found that his prayers were answered, that the strong Friend to whom he had allied his weakness did not fail him. He was sustained through the dark days, and his faith eventually brought him peace and serenity. He gained in patience and strength, and with better health came renewed hopefulness.

Although not a brilliant student, he was able to complete his university course and graduate with credit. He then took the first vacation that he had enjoyed for years, and, equipping himself with fishing-rod and a few favorite authors, he buried himself in the mountains of Maine.

His prison and mission classes missed him sadly. Mr. Growther found that he could no longer live a hermit's life, and began in good earnest to look for the "little, peaked-faced chap" that had grown to be more and more of a reality to him; but the rest of Hillaton almost forgot that Haldane had ever existed.

In the autumn he returned, brown and vigorous, and entered upon his studies at the medical school connected with the university with decided zest. To his joy he found a letter from Mrs. Arnot, informing him that the health of her niece was fully restored, and that they were about to return. And yet it was with misgivings that he remembered that Laura would henceforth be an inmate of Mrs. Arnot's home. As a memory, however beautiful, she was too shadowy to disturb his peace. Would this be true if she had fulfilled all the rich promises of her girlhood, and he saw her often?

· With a foreboding of future trouble he both dreaded and longed to see once more the maiden who had once so deeply stirred his heart, and who in the depths of his disgrace had

not scorned him when accidentally meeting him in the guise
and at the tasks of a common laborer.

It was with a quickened pulse that he read in the "Spy,"
one Monday evening, that Mrs. Arnot and niece had arrived
in town. It was with a quicker pulse that he received a note
from her a few days later asking him to call that evening,
and adding that two or three other young men whom he
knew to be her especial favorites would be present.

Because our story has confined itself chiefly to the relations existing between Haldane and Mrs. Arnot, it must not
be forgotten that her active sympathies were enlisted in behalf of many others, some of whom were almost equally at-
tached to her and she to them.

After a little thought Haldane concluded that he would
much prefer that his first interview with Laura should be in
the presence of others, for he could then keep in the background without exciting remark.

He sincerely hoped that when he saw her he might find
that her old power over him was a broken spell, and that
the lovely face which had haunted him all these years,
growing more beautiful with time, was but the creation of
his own fancy. He was sure she would still be pretty, but
if that were all he could go on his way without a regretful
thought. But if the shy maiden, whose half-entreating,
compassionate tones had interrupted the harsh rasping of
his saw years ago, were the type of the woman whom he
should meet that evening, might not the bitterest punishment of his folly be still before him?

He waited till sure that the other guests had arrived,
and then entered to meet, as he believed, either a hopeless
thraldom or complete disenchantment.

As he crossed the threshold of the parlor the pleasure of
seeing Mrs. Arnot again, and of receiving her cordial greeting, obliterated all other thoughts from his mind.

He had, however, but a moment's respite, for the lady
said:

"Laura, my friend Mr. Haldane."

He turned and saw, by actual vision, the face that in fancy he had so often looked upon. It was not the face that he expected to see at all. The shy, blue-eyed maiden, who might have reminded one of a violet half hidden among the grass, had indeed vanished, but an ordinary pretty woman had not taken her place.

He felt this before he had time to consciously observe it, and bowed rather low to hide his burning face; but she frankly held out her hand and said, though with somewhat heightened color also:

"Mr. Haldane, I am glad to meet you again."

Then, either to give him time to recover himself, or else, since the interruption was over, she was glad to resume the conversation that had been suspended, she turned to her former companions. Mrs. Arnot also left him to himself a few moments, and by a determined effort he sought to calm the tumultuous riot of his blood. He was not phlegmatic on any occasion; but even Mrs. Arnot could not understand why he should be so deeply moved by this meeting. She ascribed it to the painful and humiliating memories of the past, and then dismissed his manner from her mind. He speedily gained self-control, and, as is usual with strong natures, became unusually quiet and undemonstrative. Only in the depths of his dark eyes could one have caught a glimpse of the troubled spirit within, for it was troubled with a growing consciousness of an infinite loss.

CHAPTER XLVI

MISJUDGED

THE young men who were Mrs. Arnot's guests were naturally attracted to Laura's side, and she speedily proved that she possessed the rare power of entertaining several gentlemen at the same time, and with such grace and tact as to make each one feel that his presence was both welcome and needed in the circle.

Mrs. Arnot devoted herself to Haldane, and showed how genuine was her interest in him by taking up his life where his last letter left it, and asking about all that had since occurred. Indeed, with almost a mother's sympathy, she led him to speak of the experiences of the entire year.

"It seems to me," he said, "that I have scarcely more than held my ground."

"To hold one's ground, at times requires more courage, more heroic patience and fortitude, than any other effort we can make. I have been told that soldiers can charge against any odds better than they can simply and coolly stand their ground. But I can see that you have been making progress. You have graduated with honor. You are surely winning esteem and confidence. You have kept your faith in God, and maintained your peculiar usefulness to a class that so few can reach: perhaps you are doing more good than any of us, by proving that it is a fact and not a theory that the fallen can rise."

"You are in the world, but not of it," he said; and then, as if anxious to change the subject, asked. "Did you see my mother?"

Although Mrs. Arnot did not intend it, there was a slight constraint in her voice and manner as she replied: "Yes, I took especial pains to see her before I returned, and went out of my way to do so. I wished to assure her how well you were doing, and how certain you were to retrieve the past, all of which, of course, she was very glad to hear."

"Did she send me no message?" he asked, instinctively feeling that something was wrong.

"She said that she wrote to you regularly, and so, of course, felt that there was no need of sending any verbal messages."

"Was she not cordial to you?" asked the young man, with a dark frown.

"She was very polite, Egbert. I think she misunderstands me a little."

His face flushed with indignation, and after a moment's thought he said bitterly, and with something like contempt, "Poor mother! she is to be pitied."

Mrs. Arnot's face became very grave, and almost severe, and she replied, with an emphasis which he never forgot:

"She is to be loved; she is to be cherished with the most delicate consideration and forbearance, and honored—yes, honored—because she is your mother. You, as her son, should never say, nor permit any one to say a word against her. Nothing can absolve you from this sacred duty. Remember this as you hope to be a true man."

This was Mrs. Arnot's return for the small jealousy of her girlhood's friend.

He bowed his head, and after a moment replied: "Mrs. Arnot, I feel, I know, you are right. I thank you."

"Now you are my knight again," she said, her face suddenly lighting up. "But come; let us join the others, for they seem to have hit upon a very mirthful and animated discussion."

Laura's eye and sympathies took them in at once as they approached, and enveloped them in the genial and magnetic influences which she seemed to have the power of exerting.

Although naturally and deeply interested in his interview with Mrs. Arnot, Haldane's eyes and thoughts had been drawn frequently and irresistibly to the object of his old-time passion. She was, indeed, very different from what he had expected. The diffident maiden, so slight in form and shy in manner, had not developed into a drooping lily of a woman, suggesting that she must always have a manly support of some kind near at hand. Still less had she become a typical belle, and the aggressive society girl who captures and amuses herself with her male admirers with the grace and sang froid of a sportive kitten that carefully keeps a hapless mouse within reach of her velvet paw. The pale and saint-like image which he had so long enshrined within his heart, and which had been created by her devotion to her mother, also faded utterly away in the presence of the reality before him. She was a veritable flesh-and-blood woman, with the hue of health upon her cheek, and the charm of artistic beauty in her rounded form and graceful manner. She was a revelation to him, transcending not only all that he had seen, but all that he had imagined.

Thus far he had not attained a moral and intellectual culture which enabled him even to idealize so beautiful and perfect a creature. She was not a saint in the mystical or imaginative sense of the word, but, as a queen reigning by the divine right of her surpassing loveliness and grace in even Hillaton's exclusive society, she was practically as far removed from him as if she were an ideal saint existing only in a painter's haunted imagination.

Nature had dowered Laura Romeyn very richly in the graces of both person and mind; but many others are equally favored. Her indescribable charm arose from the fact that she was very receptive in her disposition. She had been wax to receive, but marble to retain. Therefore, since she had always lived and breathed in an atmosphere of culture, refinement, and Christian faith, her character had the exquisite beauty and fragrance which belongs to a rare flower to which all the conditions of perfect development have been supplied. Although the light of her eye was serene, and her laugh as clear and natural as the fall of water, there was a nameless something which indicated that her happy, healthful nature rested against a dark background of sorrow and trial, and was made the richer and more perfect thereby.

Her self-forgetfulness was contagious. The beautiful girl did not look from one to another of the admiring circle for the sake of picking up a small revenue of flattery. From a native generosity she wished to give pleasure to her guests; from a holy principle instilled into her nature so long ago that she was no longer conscious of it, she wished to do them good by suggesting only such thoughts as men associate with pure, good women; and from an earnest, yet sprightly mind, she took a genuine interest herself in the subjects on which they were conversing.

By her tact, and with Mrs. Arnot's efficient aid, she drew all into the current of their talk. The three other young men who were Mrs. Arnot's guests that evening were manly fellows, and had come to treat Haldane with cordial respect. Thus for a time he was made to forget all that had occurred to cloud his life. He found that the presence of Laura kindled his intellect with a fire of which he had never been conscious before. His eyes flashed sympathy with every word she said, and before he was aware he, too, was speaking his mind with freedom, for he saw no chilling repugnance toward him in the kindly light of her deep blue eyes. She led him to forget himself and his past so completely that he, in the excitement of argument, inadvertently pronounced his own doom. In answer to the remark of another, he said:

"Society is right in being conservative and exclusive, and its favor should be the highest earthly reward of a stainless life. The coarse and the vulgar should be taught that they cannot purchase it nor elbow their way into it, and those who have it should be made to feel that losing it is like losing life, for it can never be regained. Thus

society not only protects itself, but prevents weak souls
from dallying with temptation.''

So well-bred was Laura that, while her color deepened
at his words, she betrayed no other consciousness that they
surprised her. But he suddenly remembered all, and the
blood **rushed** tumultuously to his **face, then left it very
pale.**

"What I have said is true, **nevertheless,''** he added
quietly and decisively, as if in answer to these thoughts;
''and losing one's place in society may be worse than losing
life.''

He felt that this was true, as he looked at the beautiful
girl before him, so kind and gentle, and yet so unapproach-
able by him; and, what is more, he saw in her face pitying
acquiescence to **his words. As her aunt's protégé, as a young
man trying to reform, he felt that he would have her good
wishes and courteous** treatment, but never anything more.

"Egbert, I take issue with you,'' began Mrs. Arnot
warmly; but further remark was interrupted by the entrance of a gentleman, who was announced as

''Mr. Beaumont.''

There was a nice distinction between the greeting given
by Mrs. Arnot to this gentleman and that which she had
bestowed upon Haldane and her other guests. His reception was simply the perfection of quiet courtesy, **and no one**
could have been sure that the lady was glad to see him.
She merely welcomed him as a social equal to her parlors,
and then turned again to her friends.

But Laura **had a** kindlier greeting for the new-comer.
While her manner **was** equally undemonstrative, her eyes
lighted up with **pleasure** and the color deepened in her
cheeks. It was evident that they were old acquaintances,
and that he had found previous occasions for making himself **very** agreeable.

Mr. Beaumont did not care **to** form one of a circle. He
was in the world's estimation, possibly in his own, a complete circle in himself, rounded out and perfect on every

side. He was the only son in one of the oldest and most aristocratic families in the city; he was the heir of very large wealth; his careful education had been supplemented by years of foreign travel; hs was acknowledged to be the best connoisseur of art in Hillaton; and to his irreproachable manners was added an irreproachable character. "He is a perfect gentleman," was the verdict of the best society wherever he appeared.

Something to this effect Haldane learned from one of the young men with whom he had been spending the evening, as they bent their steps homeward—for soon after Mr. Beaumont's arrival all took their departure.

That gentleman seemed to bring in with him a different atmosphere from that which had prevailed hitherto. Although his bow was distant to Haldane when introduced, his manner had been the perfection of politeness to the others. For some reason, however, there had been a sudden restraint and chill. Possibly they had but unconsciously obeyed the strong will of Mr. Beaumont, who wished their departure. He was almost as resolute in having his own way as Mr. Arnot himself. Not that he was ever rude to any one in any circumstances, but he could politely freeze objectionable persons out of a room as effectually as if he took them by the shoulders and walked them out. There was so much in his surroundings and antecedents to sustain his quiet assumption, that the world was learning to say, "By your leave," on all occasions.

Haldane was not long in reaching a conclusion as he sat over a dying fire in his humble quarters at the hermitage. If he saw much of Laura Romeyn he would love her of necessity by every law of his being. Assuring himself of the hopelessness of his affection would make no difference to one of his temperament. He was not one who could coolly say to his ardent and impetuous nature, "Thus far, and no farther." There was something in her every tone, word, and movement which touched chords within his heart that vibrated pleasurably or painfully.

This power cannot be explained. It was not passion. Were Laura far more beautiful, something in her manner or character might speedily have broken the spell by which she unconsciously held her captive. His emotion in no respect resembled the strong yet restful affection that he entertained for Mrs. Arnot. Was it love? Why should he love one who would not love in return, and who, both. in the world's and his own estimation, was infinitely beyond his reach? However much his reason might condemn his feelings, however much he might regret the fact, his heart trembled at her presence, and, by some instinct of its own, acknowledged its mistress. He was compelled to admit to himself that he loved her already, and that his boyhood's passion had only changed as he had changed, and had become the strong and abiding sentiment of the man. She only could have broken the power by becoming commonplace, by losing the peculiar charm which she had for him from the first. But now he could not choose; he had met his fate.

One thing, however, he could do, and that he resolved upon before he closed his eyes in sleep in the faint dawning of the following day. He would not flutter as a poor moth where he could not be received as an accepted lover.

This resolution he kept. He did not cease calling upon Mrs. Arnot, nor did the quiet warmth of his manner toward her change; but his visits became less frequent, he pleading the engrossing character of his studies, and the increasing preparation required to maintain his hold on his mission-class; but the lady's delicate intuition was not long in divining the true cause. One of his unconscious glances at Laura revealed his heart to her woman's eye as plainly as could any spoken words. But by no word or hint did Mrs. Arnot reveal to him her knowledge. Her tones might have been gentler and her eyes kinder; that was all. In her heart, however, she almost revered the man who had the strength and patience to take up this heavy and hopeless burden, and go on in the path of duty without a word.

How different was his present course from his former passionate clamor for what was then equally beyond his reach! She was almost provoked at her niece that she did not appreciate Haldane more.   But would she wish her peerless ward to marry this darkly shadowed man, to whom no parlor in Hillaton was open save her own?   Even Mrs. Arnot would shrink from this question.

Laura, too, had perceived that which Haldane meant to hide from all the world.   When has a beautiful woman failed to recognize her worshippers?   But there was nothing in Laura's nature which permitted her to exult over such a discovery.   She could not resent as presumption a love that was so unobtrusive, for it became more and more evident as time passed that the man who was mastered by it would never voluntarily give to her the slightest hint of its existence.   She was pleased that he was so sensible as to recognize the impassable gulf between them, and that he did not go moaning along the brink, thus making a spectacle of himself, and becoming an annoyance to her.   Indeed, she sincerely respected him for his reticence and self-control, but she also misjudged him; for he was so patient and strong, and went forward with his duties so quietly and steadily, that she was inclined to believe that his feelings toward her were not very deep, or else that he was so constituted that affairs of the heart did not give him very much trouble.

CHAPTER XLVII

LAURA CHOOSES HER KNIGHT

"WHY, Laura, how your cheeks burn!" exclaimed Mrs. Arnot as she entered her niece's room one afternoon.

"Now, don't laugh at me for being so foolish, but I have become absurdly excited over this story. Scott was well called the 'Wizard of the North.' What a spell he weaves over his pages! When reading some of his descriptions of men and manners in those old chivalric times, I feel that I have been born some centuries too late—in our time everything is so matter-of-fact, and the men are so prosaic. The world moves on with a steady business jog, or, to change the figure, with the monotonous clank of uncle's machinery. My castle in the air would be the counterpart of those which Scott describes."

"Romantic as ever," laughed her aunt; "and that reminds me, by the way, of the saying that romantic girls always marry matter-of-fact men, which, I suppose, will be your fate. I confess I much prefer our own age. Your stony castles make me shiver with a sense of discomfort; and as for the men, I imagine they are much the same now as then, for human nature does not change much."

"O, auntie, what a prosaic speech! Uncle might have made it himself. The idea of men being much the same now! Why, in that day there were the widest and most picturesque differences between men of the same rank. There were horrible villains, and then to vanquish these and undo the mischief they were ever causing, there were

knights *sans peur et sans reproche.*   But now a gentleman is
a gentleman, and all made up very much in the same style,
like their dress coats.   I would like to have seen at least
one genuine knight—a man good enough and brave enough
to do and to dare anything to which he could be impelled
by a most chivalric sense of duty.   About the most heroic
thing a man ever did for me was to pick up my fan.''

Mrs. Arnot thought of one man whose heart was almost
breaking for her, and yet who maintained such a quiet,
masterful self-control that the object of his passion, which
had become like a torturing flame, was not subjected to even
the slightest annoyance; and she said, ''You are satirical to-
day.   In my opinion there are as true knights now as your
favorite author ever described.''

''Not in Hillaton,'' laughed Laura, ''or else their disguise is perfect.''

''Yes, in Hillaton,'' replied Mrs. Arnot, with some
warmth, ''and among the visitors at this house.   I know
of one who bids fair to fulfil my highest ideal of knighthood, and I think you will do me the justice to believe that
my standard is not a low one.''

''Auntie, you fairly take away my breath!'' said Laura,
in the same half-jesting spirit.   ''Where have my eyes been?
Pray, who is this paragon, who must, indeed, be nearly
perfect, to satisfy your standard?''

''You must discover him for yourself; as you say, he
appears to be but a gentleman, and would be the last one
in the world to think of himself as a knight, or to fill your
ideal of one.   You must remember the character of our age.
If one of your favorite knights should step, armed *cap-à-pie*,
out of Scott's pages, all the dogs in town would be at his
heels, and he would probably bring up at the station-house.
My knight promises to become the flower of his own age.
Now I think of it, I do not like the conventional word
'flower,' as used in this connection, for my knight is steadily growing strong like a young oak.   I hope I may live to
see the man he will eventually become.''

"You know well, auntie," said Laura, "that I have not meant half I have said. The men of our day are certainly equal to the women, and I shall not have to look far to find my superior in all respects. I must admit, however, that your words have piqued my curiosity, and I am rather glad you have not named this 'heart of oak,' for the effort to discover him will form a pleasant little excitement."

"Were I that way inclined," said Mrs. Arnot, smiling, "I would be willing to wager a good deal that you will hit upon the wrong man."

Laura became for a time quite a close student of human nature, observing narrowly the physiognomy and weighing the words and manner, of her many gentleman acquaintances; but while she found much to respect, and even to admire, in some, she was not sure that any one of them answered to her aunt's description. Nor could she obtain any further light by inquiring somewhat into their antecedents. As for Mrs. Arnot, she was considerably amused, but continued perfectly non-committal.

After Laura had quite looked through her acquaintances Haldane made one of his infrequent calls, but as Mr. Beaumont was also present she gave to her quondam lover scarcely more than a kindly word of greeting, and then forgot his existence. It did not occur to her, any more than it would to Haldane himself, that he was the knight.

Mr. Arnot, partly out of a grim humor peculiarly his own, and partly to extenuate his severity toward the youth, had sent to his niece all the city papers containing unfavorable references to Haldane, and to her mind the associations created by those disgraceful scenes were still inseparable from him. She honestly respected him for his resolute effort to reform, as she would express it, and as a sincere Christian girl she wished him the very best of success, but this seemed as far as her regard for him could ever go. She treated him kindly where most others in her station would not recognize him at all, but such was the delicacy and refinement of her nature that she shrank from one who had been capable of acts like his. The youth who had annoyed her with his passion, whom she had seen fall upon the floor in gross intoxication, who had been dragged through the streets as a criminal, and who twice had been in jail, was still a vivid memory. She knew comparatively little about, and did not understand, the man of to-day. Beyond the general facts that he was doing well and doing good, it was evident that, by reason of old and disagreeable associations, she did not wish to hear much about him, and Mrs. Arnot had the wisdom to see that time and the young man's own actions would do more to remove prejudice from the mind of her niece, as well as from the memory of society in general, than could any words of hers.

Of course, such a girl as Laura had many admirers, and among them Mr. Beaumont was evidently winning the first place in her esteem. Whether he were the knight that her aunt had in mind or no, she was not sure, but he realized her ideal more completely than any man whom she had ever met. He did, indeed, seem the "perfect flower of his age," although she was not so sure of the oak-like qualities. She often asked herself wherein she could find fault with him or with all that related to him, and even her delicate discrimination could scarcely find a vulnerable point. He was fine-looking, his heavy side-whiskers redeeming his face from effeminacy; he was tall and elegant in his proportions; his taste in his dress was quiet and faultless; he possessed the most refined and highly cultured mind of any man whom she had known; his family was exceedingly proud and aristocratic, but as far as there can be reason for these characteristics, this old and wealthy family had such reason. Laura certainly could not find fault with these traits, for from the first Mr. Beaumont's parents had sought to pay her especial attention. It was quite evident that they thought that the orphaned girl who was so richly dowered with wealth and beauty might make as good a wife for their matchless son as could be found, and such an opinion on their part was, indeed, a high compliment to Laura's birth and breeding.

No one else in Hillaton would have been thought of with any equanimity.

The son was inclined to take the same view as that entertained by his parents, but, as the party most nearly interested, he felt it incumbent upon him to scrutinize very closely and deliberately the woman who might become his wife, and surely this was a sensible thing to do.

There was nothing mercenary or coarse in his delicate analysis and close observation. Far from it. Mr. Beaumont was the last man in the world to look a lady over as he would a bale of merchandise. More than all things else, Mr. Beaumont was a *connoisseur*, and he sought Mrs. Arnot's parlors with increasing frequency because he believed that he would there find the woman best fitted to become the chief ornament of the stately family mansion.

Laura had soon become conscious of this close tentative scrutiny, and at first she had been inclined to resent its cool deliberateness. But, remembering that a man certainly has a right to learn well the character of the woman whom he may ask to be his wife, she felt that there was nothing in his action of which she could complain; and it soon became a matter of pride with her, as much as anything else, to satisfy those fastidious eyes that hitherto had critically looked the world over, and in vain, for a pearl with a lustre sufficiently clear. She began to study his taste, to dress for him, to sing for him, to read his favorite authors; and so perfect was his taste that she found herself aided and enriched by it. He was her superior in these matters, for he had made them his life-study. The first hour that she spent with him in a picture-gallery was long remembered, for never before had those fine and artistic marks which make a painting great been so clearly pointed out to her. She was brought to believe that this man could lead her to the highest point of culture to which she could attain, and satisfy every refined taste that she possessed. It seemed as if he could make life one long gallery of beautiful objects, through which she might stroll in elegant leisure, ever conscious that he who stood by to minister and explain was looking away from all things else in admiration of herself.

The prospect was too alluring. Laura was not an advanced female, with a mission; she was simply a young and lovely woman, capable of the noblest action and feeling should the occasion demand them, but naturally luxurious and beauty-loving in her tastes, and inclined to shun the prosaic side of life.

She made Beaumont feel that she also was critical and exacting. She had lived too long under Mrs. Arnot's influence to be satisfied with a man who merely lived for the pleasure he could get out of each successive day. He saw that she demanded that he should have a purpose and aim in life, and he skilfully met this requirement by frequently descanting on æsthetic culture as the great lever which could move the world, and by suggesting that the great question of his future was how he could best bring this culture to the people. As a Christian, she took issue with him as to its being *the* great lever, but was enthusiastic over it as a most powerful means of elevating the masses, and she often found herself dreaming over how much a man gifted with Mr. Beaumont's exquisite taste and large wealth could do by placing within the reach of the multitude objects of elevating art and beauty.

By a fine instinct she felt, rather than saw, that Mrs. Arnot did not specially like the seemingly faultless man, and was led to believe that her aunt's ideal knight was to be found among some of the heartier young men who were bent on doing good in the old-fashioned ways; and, with a tendency not unnatural in one so young and romantic, she thought of her aunt as being a bit old-fashioned and prosaic herself. In her youthful and ardent imagination Beaumont came to fill more and more definitely her ideal of the modern knight—a man who summed up within himself the perfect culture of his age, and who was proposing to diffuse that culture as widely as possible.

"You do not admire Mr. Beaumont," said Laura a little abruptly to her aunt one day.

"You are mistaken, Laura; I do admire him very much."

"Well, you do not like him, then, to speak more correctly; he takes no hold upon your sympathies."

"There is some truth in your last remark, I must admit. For some reason he does not. Perhaps it is my fault, and I have sometimes asked myself, Is Mr. Beaumont capable of strong affection or self-sacrificing action? has he much heart?"

"I think you do him injustice in these respects," said Laura warmly.

"Quite probably," replied Mrs. Arnot, adding with a mischievous smile, which brought the rich color to her niece's cheeks, "Perhaps you are in a better position to judge of his possession of these qualities than I am. Thus far he has given me only the opportunity of echoing society's verdict—He is a perfect gentleman. I wish he were a better Christian," she concluded gravely.

"I think he is a Christian, auntie."

"Yes, dear, in a certain æsthetic sense. But far be it from me to judge him. Like the rest of the world, I respect him as an honorable gentleman."

A few days after this conversation Mr. Beaumont drove a pair of coal-black horses to Mrs. Arnot's door, and invited Laura to take a drive. When, in the twilight, she returned, she went straight to her aunt's private parlor, and, curling down at her knees, as was her custom when a child, said:

"Give me your blessing, auntie; your congratulations, also—I hope, although I am not so sure of these. I have found my knight, though probably not yours. See!" and she held up her finger, with a great flashing diamond upon it.

Mrs. Arnot took the girl in her arms and said, "I do bless you, my child, and I think I can congratulate you also. On every principle of worldly prudence and worldly foresight I am sure I can. It will be very hard ever to give you up to another; and yet I am growing old, and I am glad that you, who are such a sacred charge to me, have chosen one who stands so high in the estimation of all, and who is so abundantly able to gratify your tastes."

"Yes, auntie, I think I am fortunate," said Laura, with complacent emphasis. "I have found a man not only able to gratify all my tastes—and you know that many of them are rather expensive—but he himself satisfies my most critical taste, and even fills out the ideal of my fancy."

Mrs. Arnot gave a sudden sigh.

"Now, auntie, what, in the name of wonder, can that foreboding sigh mean?"

"You have not said that he satisfied your heart."

"O, I think he does fully," said Laura, hastily, though with a faint misgiving. "These tender feelings will come in their own good time. We have not got far enough along for them yet. Besides, I never could have endured a passionate lover. I was cured of any such tastes long ago, you remember," she added, with a faint laugh.

"Poor Egbert!" ejaculated Mrs. Arnot, with such sad emphasis that Laura looked up into her face inquiringly as she asked:

"You don't think he will care much, do you?"

"Yes, Laura; you know he will care, perhaps more deeply than I do; but I believe that he will wish you happiness as truly and honestly as myself."

"O, auntie! how can it be that he will care as much as yourself?"

"Is it possible, Laura, that you have failed to detect his regard for you in all these months? I detected it at a glance, and felt sure that you had also."

"So I did, auntie, long since, but I supposed it was, as you say, a mere regard that did not trouble him much. I should be sorry to think that it was otherwise."

"At all events, it has not troubled you much, whatever it may have cost him. You hardly do Haldane justice. Your allusion to his former passion should remind you that he still possesses the same ardent and impetuous nature, but it is under control. You cannot return his deep, yet unobtrusive, love, and, as the world is constituted, it is probably well for you that this is true; but I cannot bear that it should have no better reward than your last rather contemptuous allusion.''

"Forgive me, auntie; I did not imagine that he felt as you seem to think. Indeed, in my happiness and preoccupation, I have scarcely thought of him at all. His love has, in truth, been unobtrusive. So scrupulously has he kept it from my notice that I had thought and hoped that it had but little place in his mind. But if you are right, I am very, very sorry. Why is the waste of these precious heart-treasures permitted?'' and gathering tears attested her sincerity.

"That is an old, old question, which the world has never answered. The scientists tell us that by a law of nature no force is ever lost. If this be true in the physical world, it certainly should be in the spiritual. I also believe that an honest, unselfish love can enrich the heart that gives it, even though it receives no other reward. But you have no occasion to blame yourself, Laura. It is one of those things which never could have been helped. Besides, Haldane is serving a Master who is pledged to shape seeming evils for his good. I had no thought of speaking of him at all, only your remark seemed so like injustice that I could not be silent. In the future, moreover, you may do something for him. Society is too unrelenting, and does not sufficiently recognize the struggle he has made, and is yet making; and he is so morbidly sensitive that he will not take anything that even looks like social alms. You will be in a position to help him toward the recognition which he deserves, for I should be sorry to see him become a lonely and isolated man. Of course, you will have to do this very carefully, but your own graceful tact will best guide you in this matter. I only wish you to appreciate the brave fight he is making and the character he is forming, and not to think of him merely as a commonplace, well-meaning man, who

is at last trying to do right, and who will be fairly content
with life if he can secure his bread and butter."

"I will remember what you say, and do my very best,"
said Laura earnestly, "for I do sincerely respect Mr. Haldane for his efforts to retrieve the past, and I should despise
myself did I not appreciate the delicate consideration he has
shown for me if he has such feelings as you suppose.
Auntie!" she exclaimed after a moment, a sudden light
breaking in upon her, "Mr. Haldane is your knight."

"And a very plain, prosaic knight, no doubt, he seems
to you."

"I confess that he does, and yet when I think of it I
admit that he has fought his way up against tremendous
odds. Indeed, his present position in contrast with what
he was involves so much hard fighting that I can only
think of him as one of those plain, rugged men who have
risen from the ranks."

"Look for the plain and rugged characteristics when he
next calls," said Mrs. Arnot quietly. "One would have
supposed that such a rugged nature would have interposed
some of his angles in your way."

"Forgive me, auntie; I am inclined to think that I know
very little about your knight; but it is natural that I should
much prefer my own. Your knight is like one of those remorseful men of the olden time who, partly from faith and
partly in penance for past misdeeds, dons a suit of plain
heavy iron armor, and goes away to parts unknown to fight
the infidel. My knight is clad in shining steel; nor is the
steel less true because overlaid with a filagree of gold; and
he will make the world better not by striking rude and ponderous blows, but by teaching it something of his own fair
courtesy and his own rich culture."

"Your description of Haldane is very fanciful and a little
far-fetched," said Mrs. Arnot, laughing; "should I reply in
like vein I would only add that I believe that he will henceforth keep the 'white cross' on his knightly mantle un-
stained. Already he seems to have won a place in that

ancient and honorable order established so many centuries ago, the members of which were entitled to inscribe upon their shields the legend, 'He that ruleth his own spirit is better than he that taketh a city.' But we are carrying this fanciful imagery too far, and had better drop it altogether. I know that you will do for Haldane all that womanly delicacy permits, and that is all I wish. Mr. Beaumont's course toward you commands my entire respect. He long since asked both your uncle's consent and mine to pay you his addresses, and while we, of course, gave our approval, we have left you wholly free to follow the promptings of your own heart. In the world's estimation, Laura, it will be a brilliant alliance for each party; but my prayer shall be that it may be a happy and sympathetic union, and that you may find an unfailing and increasing content in each other's society. Nothing can compensate for the absence of a warm, kind heart, and the nature that is without it is like a home without a hearth-stone and a fire; the larger and more stately it is, the colder and more cheerless it seems.''

Laura understood her aunt's allusion to her own bitter disappointment, and she almost shivered at the possibility of meeting a like experience.

CHAPTER XLVIII

MRS. ARNOT'S KNIGHT

IT will not be supposed that Haldane was either blind or indifferent during the long months in which Beaumont, like a skilful engineer, was making his regular approaches to the fair lady whom he would win. He early foresaw what appeared to him would be the inevitable result, and yet, in spite of all his fortitude, and the frequency with which he assured himself that it was natural, that it was best, that it was right, that this peerless woman should wed a man of Beaumont's position and culture, still that gentleman's assured deliberate advance was like the slow and torturing contraction of the walls of that terrible chamber in the Inquisition which, by an imperceptible movement, closed in upon and crushed the prisoner. For a time he felt that he could not endure the pain, and he grew haggard under it.

"What's the matter, my boy?" said Mr. Growther abruptly to him one evening. "You look as if something was a-gnawin' and a-eatin' your very heart out."

He satisfied his old friend by saying that he did not feel well, and surely one sick at heart as he was might justly say this.

Mr. Growther immediately suggested as remedies all the drugs he had ever heard of, and even volunteered to go after them; but Haldane said with a smile,

"I would not survive if I took a tenth part of the medicines you have named, and not one of them would do me any good. I think I'll take a walk instead."

Mr. Growther thought a few moments, and muttered to himself, "What a cussed old fool I've been to think that rhubob and jallup could touch his case! He's got something on his mind,' and with a commendable delicacy he forbore to question and pry.

Gradually, however, Haldane obtained patience and then strength to meet what seemed inevitable, and to go forward with the strong, measured tread of a resolute soldier.

While passing through his lonely and bitter conflict he learned the value and significance of that ancient prophecy, "He is despised and rejected of men; a man of sorrows and acquainted with grief; and we hid, as it were, our faces from him." How long, long ago God planned and purposed to win the sympathy and confidence of the suffering by coming so close to them in like experience that they could feel sure—yes, know—that he felt with them and for them.

Never before had the young man so fully realized how vital a privilege it was to be a disciple of Christ—to be near to him—and enjoy what resembled a companionship akin to that possessed by those who followed him up and down the rugged paths of Judea and Galilee.

When, at last, Laura's engagement became a recognized fact, he received the intelligence as quietly as the soldier who is ordered to take and hold a position that will long try his fortitude and courage to the utmost.

As for Laura, the weeks that followed her engagement were like a beautiful dream, but one that was created largely by the springing hopes and buoyancy of youth, and the witchery of her own vivid imagination. The springtime had come again, and the beauty and promise of her own future seemed reflected in nature. Every day she took long drives into the country with her lover, or made expeditions to picture galleries in New York; again, they would visit public parks or beautiful private grounds in which the landscape gardener had lavished his art. She lived and fairly revelled in a world of beauty, and for the time it intoxicated her with delight.

There was also such a chorus of congratulation that she could not help feeling complacent. Society indorsed her choice so emphatically and universally that she was sure she had made no mistake. She was caused to feel that she had carried off the richest prize ever known in Hillaton, and she was sufficiently human to be elated over the fact.

Nor was the congratulation all on one side. Society was quite as positive that Beaumont had been equally fortunate, and there were some that insisted that he had gained the richer prize. It was known that Laura had considerable property in her own name, and it was the general belief that she would eventually become heiress of a large part of the colossal fortune supposed to be in the possession of Mr. and Mrs. Arnot. In respect to character, beauty, accomplishments—in brief, the minor considerations in the world's estimation—it was admitted by all that Laura had few superiors. Mr. Beaumont's parents were lavish in the manifestations of their pleasure and approval. And thus it would seem that these two lives were fitly joined by the affinity of kindred tastes, by the congenial habits of equal rank, and by universal acclamation.

Gradually, however, the glamour thrown around her new relationship by its very novelty, by unnumbered congratulations, and the excitement attendant on so momentous a step in a young lady's life, began to pass away. Every fine drive in the country surrounding the city had been taken again and again; all the fine galleries had been visited, and the finer pictures admired and dwelt upon in Mr. Beaumont's refined and quiet tones, until there was little more to be said. Laura had come to know exactly why her favorite paintings were beautiful, and precisely the marks which gave them value. The pictures remained just as beautiful, but she became rather tired of hearing Mr. Beaumont analyze them. Not that she could find any fault with what he said, but it was the same thing over and over again. She became, slowly and unpleasantly, impressed with the thought that, while Mr. Beaumont would probably take the most correct view of every object that met his eye, he would always take the same view, and, having once heard him give an opinion, she could anticipate on all future occasions just what he would say. We all know, by disagreeable experience, that no man is so wearisome as he who repeats himself over and over again without variation, no matter how approved his first utterance may have been. Beaumont was remarkably gifted with the power of forming a correct judgment of the technical work of others in all departments of art and literature, and to the perfecting of this accurate æsthetic taste he had given the energies of his maturer years. He had carefully scrutinized in every land all that the best judges considered pre-eminently great and beautiful, but his critical powers were those of an expert, a connoisseur, only. His mind had no freshness or originality. He had very little imagination. Laura's spirit would kindle before a beautiful painting until her eyes suffused with tears. He would observe coolly, with an eye that measured and compared everything with the received canons of art, and if the drawing and coloring were correct he was simply—satisfied.

Again, he had a habit of forgetting that he had given his artistic views upon a subject but a brief time before, and would repeat them almost word for word, and often his polished sentences and quiet monotone were as wearisome as a thrice-told tale.

As time wore on the disagreeable thought began to suggest itself to Laura that the man himself had culminated; that he was perfected to the limit of his nature, and finished off. She foresaw with dread that she might reach a point before very long when she would know all that he knew, or, at least, all that he kept in his mind, and that thereafter everything would be endless repetition to the end of life. He dressed very much the same every day; his habits were very uniform and methodical. In the world's estimation he was, indeed, a bright luminary, and he certainly resembled the heavenly bodies in the following respects. Laura was learning that she could calculate his orbit to a nicety, and know beforehand what he would do and say in given conditions. When she came to know him better she might be able to trace the unwelcome resemblance still further, in the fact that he did not seem to be progressing toward anything, but was going round and round in a habitual circle of thought and action, with himself as the centre of his universe.

Laura resisted the first and infrequent coming of these thoughts, as if they were suggestions of the evil one; but, in spite of all effort, all self-reproach, they would return. Sometimes as little a thing as an elegant pose—so perfect, indeed, as to suggest that it had been studied and learned by heart years ago—would occasion them, and the happy girl began to sigh over a faint foreboding of trouble.

By no word or thought did she ever show him what was passing in her mind, and she would have to show such thoughts plainly before he would even dream of their existence, for no man ever more thoroughly believed in himself than did Auguste Beaumont. He was satisfied he had learned the best and most approved way of doing everything, and as his action was always the same, it was, therefore, always right. Moreover, Laura eventually divined, while calling with him on his parents, that the greatest heresy and most aggravated offence that any one could be guilty of in the Beaumont mansion would be to find fault with Auguste. It would be a crime for which neither reason nor palliation could be found.

Thus the prismatic hues which had surrounded this man began to fade, and Laura, who had hoped to escape the prose of life, was reluctantly compelled to admit to herself at times that she found her lover tiresomely prosy and "splendidly null."

In the meantime Haldane had finished the studies of his second year at the medical college, and had won the respect of his instructors by his careful attention to the lectures, and by a certain conscientious, painstaking manner, rather than by the display of any striking or brilliant qualities.

One July evening, before taking his summer vacation, he called on Mrs. Arnot. The sky in the west was so threatening, and the storm came on so rapidly, that Mr. Beaumont did not venture down to the city, and Laura, partly to fill a vacant hour, and partly to discover wherein the man of to-day, of whom her aunt could speak in such high terms, differed from the youth that she, even as an immature girl, despised, determined to give Haldane a little close observation. When he entered she was at the piano, practicing a very difficult and intricate piece of music that Beaumont had recently brought to her, and he said:

"Please do not cease playing. Music, which is a part of your daily fare, is to me a rarely tasted luxury, for you know that in Hillaton there are but few public concerts even in winter."

She gave him a glance of genuine sympathy, as she remembered that only at a public concert where he could pay his way to an unobtrusive seat could he find opportunity to enjoy that which was a part of her daily life. In no parlor save her aunt's could he enjoy such refining pleasures, and for a reason that she knew well he had rarely availed himself of the privilege. Then another thought followed swiftly: "Surely a man so isolated and cut off from these æsthetic influences which Mr. Beaumont regards as absolutely essential, must have become uncouth and angular in his development." The wish to discover how far this was true gave to her observation an increasing zest. She generously resolved, however, to give him as rich a musical banquet as it was in her power to furnish, if his eye and manner asked for it.

"Please continue what you were playing," he added, "it piques my curiosity."

As the musical intricacy which gave the rich but tangled fancies of a master-mind proceeded, his brow knit in perplexity, and at its close he shook his head and remarked:

"That is beyond me. Now and then I seemed to catch glimpses of meaning, and then all was obscure again."

"It is beyond me, too," said Mrs. Arnot with a laugh. "Come, Laura, give us something simple. I have heard severely classical and intricate music so long that I am ready to welcome even 'Auld lang syne.'"

"I also will enjoy a change to something old and simple," said Laura, and her fingers glided into a selection which Haldane instantly recognized as Steibelt's Storm Rondo.

As Laura glanced at him she saw his deepening color, and then it suddenly flashed upon her when she had first played that music for him, and her own face flushed with annoyance at her forgetfulness. After playing it partly through she turned to her music-stand in search of something else, but Haldane said:

"Please finish the rondo, Miss Romeyn;" adding, with a frank laugh, "You have, no doubt, forgotten it; but you once, by means of this music, gave me one of the most deserved and wholesome lessons I ever received."

"Your generous acknowledgment of a fancied mistake at that time should have kept me from blunders this evening," she replied in a pained tone.

With a steady glance that held her eyes he said very quietly, and almost gently:

"You have made no blunder, Miss Romeyn. I do not ignore the past, nor do I wish it to be ignored with painstaking care. I am simply trying to face it and overcome it as I might an enemy. I may be wrong, for you know I have had little chance to become versed in the ways of good society; but it appears to me that it would be better even for those who are to spend but a social hour together that they should be free from the constraint which must exist when there is a constant effort to shun delicate or dangerous ground. Please finish the rondo; and also please remember that the ice is not thin here and there," he added with a smile.

Laura caught her aunt's glance, and the significant lighting up of her face, and, with an answering smile, she said:

"If you will permit me to change the figure, I will suggest that you have broken the ice so completely that I shall take you at your word, and play and sing just what you wish;" and, bent upon giving the young man all the pleasure she could, she exerted her powers to the utmost in widely varied selections; and while she saw that his technical knowledge was limited, it was clearly evident that he possessed a nature singularly responsive to musical thoughts and effects; indeed, she found a peculiar pleasure and incentive in glancing at his face from time to time, for she saw reflected there the varied characteristics of the melody. But once, as she looked up to see how he liked an old English ballad, she caught that which instantly brought the hot blood into her face.

Haldane had forgotten himself, forgotten that she belonged to another, and, under the spell of the old love song, had dropped his mask. She saw his heart in his gaze of deep, intense affection more plainly than spoken words could have revealed it.

He started slightly as he saw her conscious blush, turned pale instead of becoming red and embarrassed, and, save a slight compression of his lips, made no other movement. She sang the concluding verse of the ballad in a rather unsympathetic manner, and, after a light instrumental piece devoid of sentiment, rose from the piano.

Haldane thanked her with frank heartiness, and then added in a playful manner that, although the concert was over, he was weather-bound on account of the shower, and would therefore try to compensate them for giving him shelter by relating a curious story which was not only founded on fact, but all fact; and he soon had both of his auditors deeply interested in one of those strange and varied experiences which occasionally occur in real life, and which he had learned through his mission class. The tale was so full of lights and shadows that now it provoked to laughter, and again almost moved the listeners to tears. While the narrator made as little reference to himself as possible, he unconsciously and of necessity revealed how practically and vitally useful he was to the class among whom he was working. Partly to draw him out, and partly to learn more about certain characters in whom she had become interested, Mrs. Arnot asked after one and another of Haldane's "difficult cases." As his replies suggested inevitably something of their dark and revolting history, Laura again forgot herself so far as to exclaim:

"How can you work among such people?"

After the words were spoken she was already to wish that she had bitten her tongue out.

"Christ worked among them," replied he gravely, and then he added, with a look of grateful affection toward Mrs. Arnot, "Besides, your aunt has taught me by a happy experience that there are some possibilities of a change for the better in 'such people.' "

"Mr. Haldane," said Laura impetuously, and with a burning flush, "I sincerely beg your pardon. As you were speaking you seemed so like my aunt in refinement and character that you banished every other association from my mind."

His face lighted up with a strong expression of pleasure, and he said:

"I am glad that those words are so heartily uttered, and that there is no premeditation in them; for if in the faintest and furthest degree I can even resemble Mrs. Arnot, I shall feel that I am indeed making progress."

"I shall say what is in my mind without any constraint whatever," said Mrs. Arnot. "Years ago, Egbert, when once visiting you in prison, to which you had been sent very justly, I said in effect, that in rising above yourself and your circumstances, you would realize my ideal of knighthood. You cannot know with what deep pleasure I tell you to-night that you are realizing this ideal even beyond my hopes."

"Mrs. Arnot," replied Haldane, in a tone that trembled slightly, "I was justly sent to that prison, and to-night, no doubt, I should have been in some other prison-house of human justice—quite possibly," he added, in a low, shuddering tone, "in the prison-house of God's justice—if you had not come like an angel of mercy—if you had not borne with me, taught me, restrained me, helped me with a patience closely akin to Heaven's own. It is the hope and prayer of my life that I may some day prove how I appreciate all that you have done for me. But, see; the storm is over, as all storms will be in time. Good-night, and good-by," and he lifted her hand to his lips in a manner that was at once so full of homage and gratitude, and also the grace of natural and unstudied action, that there came a rush of tears into the lady's eyes.

Laura held out her hand and said: "Mr. Haldane, you cannot respect me more than you have taught me to respect you."

He shook his head at these words, involuntarily intimating that she did not know, and never could, but departed without trusting himself to reply.

The ladies sat quite a long time in silence. At length Laura remarked with a sigh:

"Mr. Haldane is mistaken. The ice is thin here and there, but I had no idea that there were such depths beneath it."

Mrs. Arnot did not reply at once, and when she did perhaps she had in mind other experiences than those of her young friend, for she only said in a low musing tone:

"Yes, he is right. All storms will be over in time."

CHAPTER XLIX

A KNIGHTLY DEED

THE year previous Haldane had buried himself among the mountains of Maine, but he resolved to spend much of the present summer in the city of New York, studying such works of art as were within his reach, haunting the cool, quiet libraries, and visiting the hospitals, giving to the last, as a medical student, the most of his time. He found himself more lonely and isolated among the numberless strange faces than he had been in the northern forests. He also went to his native city for the purpose of visiting Dr. Marks, and as the family mansion was closed, took a room at the hotel. His old acquaintances stood far aloof at first, but when Dr. Marks carried him off with friendly violence to the parsonage, and kept him there as a welcome guest, those who had known him or his family concluded that they could shake hands with him, and many took pains to do so, and to congratulate him on the course he was taking. Dr. Marks' parsonage was emphatically the Interpreter's house to him, and after a brief visit he returned to New York more encouraged with the hope that he would eventually retrieve the past than ever he had been before.

But events now occurred which promised to speedily blot out all possibility of an earthly future. In answer to his letter describing his visit to Dr. Marks, he received from Mrs. Arnot a brief note, saying that the warm weather had affected her very unfavorably, and that she was quite ill and had been losing strength for some weeks. On this ground he must pardon her brief reply. Her closing words were, "Persevere, Egbert. In a few years more the best homes in the land will be open to you, and you can choose your society from those who are honorable here and will be honored hereafter."

There were marks of feebleness in the handwriting, and Haldane's anxiety was so strongly aroused in behalf of his friend that he returned to Hillaton at once, hoping, however, that since the heats of August were nearly over, the bracing breath of autumn would bring renewed strength.

After being announced he was shown directly up to Mrs. Arnot's private parlor, and he found himself where, years before, he had first met his friend. The memory of the bright, vivacious lady who had then entertained him with a delicate little lunch, while she suggested how he might make his earliest venture out into the world successful, flashed into his mind, with thronging thoughts of all that had since occurred; but now he was pained to see that his friend reclined feebly on her lounge, and held out her hand without rising.

"I am glad you have come," she said with quiet emphasis, "for your sympathy will be welcome, although, like others, you can do nothing for us in our trouble."

"Mrs. Arnot," he exclaimed in a tone of deep distress, "you are not seriously ill?"

"No," she replied, "that is not it. I'm better, or will be soon, I think. Laura, dear, light the gas, please, and Egbert can read the telegrams for himself. You once met my sister, Mrs. Poland, who resides in the South, I think."

"Yes, I remember her very well. There was something about her face that haunted me for months afterward."

"Amy was once very beautiful, but ill-health has greatly changed her."

In the dusk of the evening Haldane had not seen Laura and Mr. Beaumont, as he entered, and he now greeted them with a quiet bow; but Laura came and gave him her hand, saying:

"We did not expect you to return so soon, Mr. Haldane."

"After hearing that Mrs. Arnot was ill I could not rest till I had seen her, and I received her note only this morning."

He now saw that both Laura's eyes and Mrs. Arnot's were red with weeping.

The latter, in answer to his questioning, troubled face, said: "The yellow fever has broken out in the city where my sister resides. Her husband, Mr. Poland, has very important business interests there, which he could not drop instantly. She would not leave him, and Amy, her daughter, would not leave her mother. Indeed, before they were aware of their danger the disease had become epidemic, and Mr. Poland was stricken down. The first telegram is from my sister, and states this fact; the second there is from my niece, and it breaks my heart to read it," and she handed it to him and he read as follows:

"The worst has happened. Father very low. Doctor gives little hope. I almost fear for mother's mind. The city in panic—our help leaving—medical attendance uncertain. It looks as if I should be left alone, and I helpless. What shall I do?"

"Was there ever a more pathetic cry of distress?" said Mrs. Arnot, with another burst of grief. "Oh that I were strong and well, and I would fly to them at once."

"Do you think I could do any good by going?" asked Laura, stepping forward eagerly, but very pale.

"No," interposed Mr. Beaumont, with sharp emphasis; "you would only become an additional burden, and add to the horrors of the situation."

"Mr. Beaumont is right; but you are a noble woman even to think of such a thing," said Haldane, and he gave her a look of such strong feeling and admiration that a little color came into her white cheeks.

"She does not realize what she is saying," added Mr. Beaumont. "It would be certain death for an unacclimated Northener to go down there now."

Laura grew very pale again. She had realized what she

was saying, and was capable of the sacrifice; but the man who had recognized and appreciated her heroism was not the one who held her plighted troth.

Paying no heed to Beaumont's last remark, Haldane snatched up the daily paper that lay upon the table, and turned hastily to a certain place for a moment, then, looking at his watch, exclaimed eagerly:

"I can do it if not a moment is wasted. The express train for the South leaves in an hour, and it connects with all the through lines. Miss Romeyn, please write for me, on your card, an introduction to your cousin, Miss Poland, and I will present it, with the offer of my assistance, at the earliest possible moment."

"Egbert, no!" said Mrs. Arnot, with strong emphasis, and rising from her couch, though so ill and feeble. "I will not permit you to sacrifice your life for comparative strangers."

He turned and took her hand in both of his, and said:

"Mrs. Arnot, there is no time for remonstrance, and it is useless. *I am going*, and no one shall prevent me." Then he added, in tones and with a look of affection which she never forgot, "Deeply as I regret this sad emergency, I would not, for ten times the value of my life, lose the opportunity it gives me. I can now show you a small part of my gratitude by serving those you love. Besides, as you say, that telegram is such a pathetic cry of distress that, were you all strangers, I would obey its unconscious command. But haste, the card!"

"Egbert, you are excited; you do not realize what you are saying!" cried the agitated lady.

He looked at her steadily for a moment, and then said, in a tone so quiet and firm that it ended all remonstrance, "I realize fully what I am doing, and it is my right to decide upon my own action. To you, at least, I never broke my word, and I assure you that I will go. Miss Romeyn, will you oblige me by instantly writing that card? Your aunt is not able to write it."

His manner was so authoritative that Laura wrote with a trembling hand:

The bearer is a very dear friend of aunt's.   How brave and noble a man he is you can learn from the fact that he comes to your aid now.   In deepest sympathy and love,   LAURA.

"Good-by, my dear, kind friend," said Haldane cheerily to Mrs. Arnot while Laura was writing; "you overrate the danger.   I feel that I shall return again, and if I do not, there are many worse evils than dying."

"Your mother," said Mrs. Arnot, with a low sob.

"I shall write to her a long letter on the way and explain everything."

"She will feel that it never can be explained."

"I cannot help it," replied the young man resolutely; "I know that I am doing right, or my conscience is of no use to me whatever."

Mrs. Arnot put her arms around his neck as if she were his mother, and said in low, broken tones:

"God bless you, and go with you, my true knight; nay, let me call you my own dear son this once.   I will thank you in heaven for all this, if not here," and then she kissed him again and again.

"You have now repaid me a thousand-fold," he faltered, and then broke away.

"Mr. Haldane," said Laura tearfully, as he turned to her, "Cousin Amy and I have been the closest friends from childhood, and I cannot tell you how deeply I appreciate your going to her aid.   I could not expect a brother to take such a risk."

Haldane felt that his present chance to look into Laura's face might be his last, and again, before he was aware, he let his eyes reveal all his heart.   She saw as if written in them, "A brother might not be willing to take the risk, but I am."

"Do I then render you a special service?" he asked, in a low tone.

"You could not render me a greater one."

"Why, this is better than I thought," he said. "How fortunate I was in coming this evening! There, please do not look so distressed. A soldier takes such risks as these every day, and never thinks of them. You have before you a happy life, Miss Laura, and I am very, very glad. Good courage, and good-by," and his manner now was frank, cheerful, and brotherly.

She partly obeyed an impulse to speak, but checked it, and tremblingly bent her head; but the pressure she gave his hand meant more than he or even she herself understood at the time.

"Good-by, Mr. Beaumont," he said, hurriedly. "I need not wish you happiness, since you already possess it;" and he hastened from the room and the house without once looking back.

A moment later they heard his rapid resolute tread echoing from the stony pavement, but it speedily died away.

Laura listened breathlessly at the window until the faintest sound ceased. She had had her wish. She had seen a man who was good enough and brave enough to face any danger to which he felt impelled by a chivalric sense of duty. She had seen a man depart upon as knightly an expedition as any of which she had ever read, but it was not her knight.

"This young Haldane is a brave fellow, and I had no idea that there was so much of him," remarked Mr. Beaumont in his quiet and refined tones. "Really, take it all together, this has been a scene worthy of the brush of a great painter."

"Oh, Auguste!" exclaimed Laura; "how can you look only on the æsthetic side of such a scene?" And she threw herself into a low chair and sobbed as if her heart would break.

Mr. Beaumont was much perplexed, for he found that all of his elegant platitudes were powerless either to comfort or to soothe her.

"Leave her with me," said Mrs. Arnot. "The excitements of the day have been too much for her. She will be better to-morrow."

Mr. Beaumont was glad to obey. He had been accustomed from childhood to leave all disagreeable duties to others, and he thought that Laura had become a trifle hysterical. "A little lavender and sleep is all that she requires," he remarked to himself as he walked home in the starlight. "But, by Jove! she is more lovely in tears than in smiles."

That he, Auguste Beaumont, should risk the loss of her and all his other possessions by exposing his precious person to a loathsome disease did not enter his mind.

"Oh, auntie, auntie, I would rather have gone myself and died, than feel as I do to-night," sobbed Laura.

" 'Courage' was Egbert's last word to you, Laura," said Mrs. Arnot, "and courage and faith must be our watchwords now. We must act, too, and at once. Please tell your uncle I wish a draft for five hundred dollars immediately, and explain why. Then inclose it in a note to Egbert, and see that Michael puts it in his hands at the depot. Write to Egbert not to spare money where it may be of any use, or can secure any comfort. We cannot tell how your aunt Amy is situated, and money is always useful. We must telegraph to your Cousin Amy that a friend is coming. Let us realize what courage, prayer, and faith can accomplish. Action will do you good, Laura."

The girl sprang to her feet and carried out her aunt's wishes with precision. That was the kind of "lavender" which her nature required.

After writing all that her aunt dictated, she added on her own part:

If the knowledge that I honor you above other men can sustain you, rest assured that this is true; if my sympathy and constant remembrance can lighten your burdens, know that you and those you serve will rarely be absent from my thoughts. You make light of your heroic act. To me it is a revelation. I did not know that men could be so strong and noble in our day. Whether such

words are right or conventional, I have not even thought. My heart is full
and I must speak them. That God may bless you, aid you in serving those I
love so dearly, and return you in safety, will be my constant prayer.

Auntie falters out one more message, "Tell Egbert that sister Amy's household have not our faith; suggest it, teach it if you can." Farewell, truest of
friends. LAURA ROMEYN.

Mr. Growther was asleep in his chair when Haldane entered, and he stole by him and made preparations for departure with silent celerity. Then, valise in hand, he
touched his old friend, who started up, and exclaimed:

"Lord a' massy, where did you come from, and where
yer goin'? You look kinder sperit like. I say, am I
awake? I was dreamin' you was startin' off to kill somebody."

"Dreams go by contraries. It may be a long time before
we meet again. But we shall have many a good talk over
old times, if not here, why, in the better home, for your
'peaked-faced little chap' will surely lead you there," and
he explained all in a few brief sentences. "And now, my
kind, true friend, good-by. I thank you from my heart for
the shelter you have given me, and for your stanch friendship when friends were so few. You have done all that you
could to make a man of me, and now that you won't have
time to quarrel with me about it, I tell you to your face
that you are not a mean man. There are few larger-
hearted, larger-souled men in this city," and before the
bewildered old gentleman could reply, he was gone.

"Lord a' massy, Lord a' massy," groaned Mr. Growther,
"the bottom is jest fallin' out o' everything. If he dies
with the yellow-jack I'll git to cussin' as bad as ever."

Haldane found Mrs. Arnot's coachman at the depot
with the letter Laura had written. As he read it his face
flushed with the deepest pleasure. Having a few moments
to spare, he pencilled hastily:

"MISS ROMEYN—I have received from Michael the letter with the draft.
Say to Mrs. Arnot I shall obey both the letter and spirit of her instructions.
Let me add for myself that my best hopes are more than fulfilled. That you,

who know all my past, could write such words seems like a heavenly dream. But I assure you that you overestimate both the character of my action and the danger. It is all plain, simple duty, which hundreds of men would perform as a matter of course. I ask but one favor, please look after Mr. Growther. He is growing old and feeble; I owe him so much—Mrs. Arnot will tell you. Yours—"

"He couldn't write a word more, Miss, the train was a movin' when he jumped on," said Michael when he delivered the note.

But that final word had for Laura no conventional meaning. She had long known that Haldane was, in truth, hers, and she had deeply regretted the fact, and would at any time have willingly broken the chain that bound him, had it been in her power. Would she break it to-night? Yes, unhesitatingly; but it would now cost her a pain to do so, which, at first, she would not understand. On that stormy July evening when she gave Haldane a little private concert she had obtained a glimpse of a manhood unknown to her before, and it was full of pleasing suggestion. To-night that same manhood which is at once so strong, and yet so unselfish and gentle, had stood out before her distinct and luminous in the light of a knightly deed, and she saw with the absoluteness of irresistible conviction that such a manhood was above and beyond all surface polish, all mere æsthetic culture, all earthly rank—that it was something that belonged to God, and partook of the eternity of his greatness and permanence.

By the kindred and noble possibilities of her own womanly nature, she was of necessity deeply interested in such a man, having once recognized him; and now for weeks she must think of him as consciously serving her in the most knightly way and at the hourly risk of his life, and yet hoping for no greater reward than her esteem and respect. While she knew that he would have gone eagerly for her aunt's sake, and might have gone from a mere sense of duty, she had been clearly shown that the thought of serving her had turned his dangerous task into a privilege and a joy. Could she follow such a man daily and hourly with her thoughts, could she in vivid imagination watch his self-sacrificing efforts to minister to, and save those she loved, with only the cool, decorous interest that Mr. Beaumont would deem proper in the woman betrothed to himself? The future must answer this question.

When Haldane had asked for a ticket to the southern city to which he was destined, the agent stared at him a moment and said:

"Don't you know yellow fever is epidemic there?"

"Yes," replied Haldane with such cold reserve of manner that no further questions were asked; but the fact that he, a medical student, had bought a ticket for the plague-stricken city was stated in the "Courier" the following morning. His old friend Mr. Ivison soon informed himself of the whole affair, and in a glowing letter of eulogy made it impossible for any one to charge that Mrs. Arnot had asked the young man to go to the aid of her relatives at such tremendous personal risk. Indeed it was clearly stated, with the unimpeachable Mr. Beaumont as authority, that she had entreated him not to go, and had not the slightest expectation of his going until he surprised her by his unalterable decision.

After reading and talking over this letter, sustained as it had been by years of straightforward duty, even good society concluded that it could socially recognize and receive this man; and yet, as the old lady had remarked, there was still an excellent prospect that he would enter heaven before he found a welcome to the exclusive circles of Hillaton.

CHAPTER L

"O DREADED DEATH!"

HALDANE found time in the enforced pauses of his journey to write a long and affectionate letter to his mother, explaining all, and asking her forgiveness again, as he often had before. He also wrote to Mrs. Arnot a cheerful note, in which he tried to put his course in the most ordinary and matter-of-fact light possible, saying that as a medical student it was the most natural thing in the world for him to do.

As he approached the infected city he had the train chiefly to himself, and he saw that the outgoing trains were full, and when at last he walked its streets it reminded him of a household of which some member is very ill, or dead, and the few who were moving about walked as if under a sad constraint and gloom. On most faces were seen evidences of anxiety and trouble, while a few were reckless.

Having obtained a carriage, he was driven to Mr. Poland's residence in a suburb. He dismissed the carriage at the gate, preferring to quietly announce himself. The sultry day was drawing to a close as he walked up the gravelled drive that led to the house. Not even the faintest zephyr stirred the luxuriant tropical foliage that here and there shadowed his path, and yet the stillness and quiet of nature did not suggest peace and repose so much as it did death. The motionless air, heavily laden with a certain dead sweetness of flowers from the neighboring garden, might well bring to mind the breathless silence and the heavy atmosphere of the chamber in which the lifeless form and the fading funeral wreath are perishing together.

So oppressed was Haldane he found himself walking softly and mounting the steps of the piazza with a silent tread, as if he were in truth approaching the majesty of death. Before he could ring the bell there came from the parlor a low, sad prelude, played on a small reed organ that had been built in the room, and then a contralto voice of peculiar sweetness sang the following words with such depth of feeling that one felt that they revealed the innermost emotion of the heart:

> O priceless life! warm, throbbing life,
> With thought and love and passion rife,
>   I cling to thee.
> Thou art an isle in the ocean wide;
> Thou art a barque above the tide;
> How vague and void is all beside!
>   I cling to thee.
>
> O dreaded death! cold, pallid death,
> Despair is in thy icy breath;
>   I shrink from thee.
> What victims wilt thou next enroll?
> Thou hast a terror for my soul
> Which will nor reason can control;
>   I shrink from thee.

Then followed a sound that was like a low sob. This surely was Amy, Laura's cousin-friend, and already she had won the whole sympathy of his heart.

After ringing the bell he heard her step, and then she paused, as he rightly surmised, to wipe away the thickly falling tears. He was almost startled when she appeared before him, for the maiden had inherited the peculiar and striking beauty of her mother. Sorrow and watching had brought unusual pallor to her cheeks; but her eyes were so large, so dark and intense, that they suggested spirit rather than flesh and blood.

"I think that this is Miss Poland," commenced Haldane in a manner that was marked by both sympathy and respect, and he was about to hand her his card of introduction, when she stepped eagerly forward and took his hand, saying: "You are Mr. Haldane. I know it at a glance."

"Yes, and wholly at your service."

Still retaining his hand, she looked for a second into his face, as if she would read his soul and gauge the compass of his nature; so intent and penetrating was her gaze, that Haldane felt that if there had been any wavering or weakness on his part she would have known it as truly as himself.

Her face suddenly lighted up with gratitude and friendliness, and she said, earnestly:

"I *do* thank you for coming. I had purposed asking you not to take so great a risk for us, but to return; for, to be frank with you, our physician has told me that your risk is terribly great; but I see that you are one that would not turn back."

"You are right, Miss Poland." Then he added, with a frank smile, "There is nothing terrible to me in the risk you speak of. I honestly feel it a privilege to come to your aid, and I have but one request to make: that you will let me serve you in any way and every way possible. By any hesitancy and undue delicacy in this respect you will greatly pain me."

"Oh!" she exclaimed in a low and almost passionate tone, "I am so glad you have come, for I was almost desperate."

"Your father?" asked Haldane very gravely.

"He is more quiet, and I try to think he is better, but doctor won't say that he is. Ah, there he is coming now."

A carriage drove rapidly to the door, and the physician sprang up the steps as if the hours were short for the increasing pressure of his work.

"Miss Amy, why are you here yet? I hoped that you and your little sister were on your way to the mountains," he said, taking her hand.

"Please do not speak of it again," she replied. "I cannot leave father and mother, and Bertha, you know, is too young and nervous a child to be forced to go away alone. We must all remain together, and hope the best from your skill."

"God knows I'm doing all in my power to save my dear old friend Poland," said the physician huskily, and then he shook his head as if he had little hope. "How is he now?"

"Better, I think. Dr. Orton, this is the friend of whom I spoke, Mr. Haldane."

"You have always lived at the North?" asked the physician, looking the young man over with a quick glance.

"Yes, sir."

"Do you realize the probable consequences of this exposure to one not acclimated?"

"Dr. Orton, I am a medical student, and I have come to do my duty, which here will be to carry out strictly your directions. I have only one deep cause for anxiety, and that is that I may be taken with the disease before I can be of much use. So please give me work at once."

"Give me your hand, old fellow. You do our profession credit, if not fully fledged. You are right, we must all do what we can while we can, for the Lord only knows how many hours are left to any of us. But, Amy, my dear, it makes me feel like praying and swearing in the same breath to find you still in this infernal city. A friend promised to call this morning and take you and your sister away."

"We cannot go."

"Well, well, as long as the old doctor is above ground he will try to take care of you; and this young gentleman can be invaluable if he can hold on for a while before following too general a fashion. Come, sir, I will install you as nurse at once."

"Doctor, Doctor Orton, what have you brought for me?" cried a childish voice, and a little girl, fair and blue-eyed, came fluttering down the stairs, intercepting them on the way to Mr. Poland's room.

"Ah! there's my good little fairy," said the kind-hearted man, taking her in his arms and kissing her. "Look in my pockets, little one, and see what you can find."

With delightful unconsciousness of the shadows around her the child fumbled in his pockets and soon pulled out a picture-book.

"No candy yet?" she exclaimed in disappointment.

"No candy at all, Bertha, nothing but good plain food till next winter. You make sure of this, I suppose," he said significantly to the elder sister.

"Yes, as far as possible. I will wait for you here."

They ascended to a large airy room on the second floor. Even to Haldane, Mr. Poland appeared far down in the dark valley; but he was in that quiet and conscious state which follows the first stage of the fever, which in his case, owing to his vigorous frame, had been unusually prolonged.

Without a word the doctor felt the sick man's pulse, who bent upon him his questioning eyes. From the further side of the bed, Mrs. Poland, sitting feebly in her chair, also fixed upon the physician the same intense searching gaze that Haldane had sustained from the daughter. Dr. Orton looked for a moment into her pale, thin face, which might have been taken as a model for agonized anxiety, and then looked away again, for he could not endure its expression.

"Orton, tell me the truth; no wincing now," said Mr. Poland in low, thick utterance.

"My dear old friend, it cuts me to the heart to say it, but if you have anything special that you would like to say to your family I think you had better say it now."

"Then I am going to die," said the man and both his tone and face were full of awe; while poor Mrs. Poland looked as if *in extremis* herself.

"This return and rapid rise of fever at this late day looks very bad," said the physician, gloomily, "and you insisted on knowing the truth."

"You ever were an honest friend, Orton; I know you have done your best for me, and, although worked to death, have come to see me often. I leave my family in your charge. God grant I may be the only one to suffer. May I see the children?"

"Yes, a few moments; but I do not wish them to be in this room long."

"Don't go just yet, Orton. I—to tell you the truth, I feel that dying is rather serious business, and you and I have always taken life somewhat as a good joke. Call the girls."

They came and stood by their mother. Amy was beyond tears, but little Bertha could not understand it, and with difficulty could be kept from clambering upon the bed to her father.

"Amy's naughty, she keeps me away from you, papa. I've been wanting to see you all day, and Amy won't let me."

The doctor and Haldane retired to the hallway.

There was an unutterable look in the dying man's eyes as he fixed them on the little group.

"How can I leave you? how can I leave you?" he groaned.

At this the child began to cry, and again struggled to reach her father. She was evidently his idol, and he prayed, "Wherever I go—whatever becomes of me, God grant I may see that child again."

"Mother," he said (he always called his wife by that endearing name), "I'm sure you are mistaken. I want to see you all again with such intense longing that I feel I shall. This life can't be all. My hearts·revolts at it. It's fiendish cruelty to tear asunder forever those who love as we do. As I told you before, I'm going to take my chances with the publican. Oh! that some one could make a prayer! Orton!" he called feebly.

The doctor entered, leaving the door open.

"Couldn't you offer a short prayer? You may think it

unmanly in me, but I am in sore straits, and I want to see these loved ones again."

"Haldane," cried Dr. Orton, "here, offer a prayer, for God's sake, if you can. I feel as if I were choking."

Without any hesitancy or mannerism the Christian man knelt at Mr. Poland's bedside and offered as simple and natural a prayer as he would have spoken to the Divine Man in person had he gone to him in Judea, centuries ago, in behalf of a friend. His faith was so absolute that he that was petitioned became a living presence to those who listened.

"God bless you, whoever you are," said the sick man. "Oh, that does me good! It's less dark. It seems to me that I've got hold of a hand that can sustain me."

"Bress de Lord!" ejaculated an old negress who sat in a distant corner.

"I install this young man as your nurse to-night," said Dr. Orton, huskily; "I'll be here in the morning. Come, little girls, go now."

"We shall meet again, Amy; we shall meet again, Bertie, darling; remember papa said it and believed it."

Haldane saw a strange blending of love and terror in Amy's eyes as she led her little and bewildered sister from the room.

Dr. Orton took him one side and rapidly gave his directions. "His pulse," he said, "indicates that he may be violent during the night; if so, induce Mrs. Poland to retire, if possible. I doubt if he lives till morning." He then told Haldane of such precautions as he should take for his own safety, and departed.

The horrors of that night cannot be portrayed. As the fever rose higher and higher, all evidence of the kind, loving husband and father perished, and there remained only a disease-tortured body. The awful black vomit soon set in. The strong physical nature in its dying throes taxed Haldane's powerful strength to the utmost, and only by constant effort and main force could he keep the sufferer

in his bed. Mrs. Poland and the old colored woman who
assisted her would have been totally unequal to the occasion. Indeed, the wife was simply appalled and overwhelmed with grief and horror, for the poor man, unconscious of all save pain, and in accordance with a common
phase of the disease, filled the night with unearthly cries
and shrieks. But before the morning dawned, instead of
tossing and delirium there was the calm serenity of death.

As Haldane composed the form for its last sleep he
said:

"My dear Mrs. Poland, your faithful watch is ended,
your husband suffers no more; now, surely you will yield
to my entreaty and go to your room. I will see that everything is properly attended to."

The poor woman was bending over her husband's ashes,
almost as motionless as they, and her answer was a low cry
as she fell across his body in a swoon.

Haldane lifted her gently up, and carried her from the
room.

Crouching at the door of the death-chamber, her eyes
dilated with horror, he found poor Amy.

"Is mother dead also?" she gasped.

"No, Miss Amy. She only needs your care to revive
speedily. Please lead the way to your mother's apartment."

"I think there is a God, and that he sent you," she
whispered.

"You are right," he replied, in the natural hearty tone
which is so potent in reassuring the terror-stricken. "Courage, Miss Amy; all will be well at last. Now let me help
you like a brother, and when your mother revives, I will
give her something to make her sleep; I then wish you to
sleep also."

The poor lady revived after a time, and tried to rise that
she might return to her husband's room, but fell back in
utter weakness.

"Mrs. Poland," said Haldane gently, "you can do no
good there. You must live for your children now."

She soon was sleeping under the influence of an opiate.

"Will you rest, too, Miss Amy?" asked Haldane.

"I will try," she faltered; but her large, dark eyes looked as if they never would close again.

Returning to the room over which so deep a hush had fallen, Haldane gave a few directions to the old negress whom he left in charge, and then sought the rest he so greatly needed himself.

CHAPTER LI

"O PRICELESS LIFE!"

WHEN Haldane came down the following morning he found Bertha playing on the piazza as unconscious of the loss of her father as the birds singing among the trees of their master. Amy soon joined them, and Haldane saw that her eyes had the same appealing and indescribable expression, both of sadness and terror, reminding one of some timid and beautiful animal that had been brought to bay by an enemy that was feared inexpressibly, but from which there seemed no escape.

He took her hand with a strong and reassuring pressure.

"Oh," she exclaimed with a slight shudder, "how can the sun shine? The birds, too, are singing as if there were no death and sorrow in the world."

"Only a perfect faith, Miss Amy, can enable us, who do know there is death and sorrow, to follow their example."

"It's all a black mystery to me," she replied, turning away.

"So it was to me once."

An old colored man, the husband of the negress who had assisted Haldane in his watch, now appeared and announced breakfast.

It was a comparatively silent meal, little Bertha doing most of the talking. Amy would not have touched a mouthful had it not been for Haldane's persuasion.

As soon as Bertha had finished, she said to Haldane:

"Amy told me that you did papa ever so much good last evening: now I want to see him right away."

"Does she not know?" asked Haldane in a low tone.

Amy shook her head. "It's too awful. What can I tell her?" she faltered.

"It is indeed inexpressibly sad, but I think I can tell the child without its seeming awful to her, and yet tell her the truth," he replied. "Shall I try to explain?"

"Yes, and let me listen, too, if you can rob the event of any of its unutterable horror."

"Will Bertie come and listen to me if I will tell her about papa?"

The child climbed into his lap at once, and turned her large blue eyes up to his in perfect faith.

"Don't you remember that papa spoke last night of leaving you; but said you would surely meet again?"

At this the child's lip began to quiver, and she said: "But papa always comes and kisses me good-by before he goes away."

"Perhaps he did, Bertie, when you were asleep in your crib last night."

"Oh yes, now I'm sure he did if he's gone away, 'cause I 'member he once woke me up kissing me good-by."

"I think he kissed you very softly, and so you didn't wake. Our dear Saviour, Jesus, came last night, and papa went away with him. But he loves you just as much as ever, and he isn't sick any more, and you will surely see him again."

"Do you think he will bring me something nice when he comes?"

"When you see him again he will have for you, Bertie, more beautiful things than you ever saw before in all your life, but it may be a long time before you see him."

The child slipped down from his knees quite satisfied and full of pleasant anticipation, and went back to her play on the piazza.

"Do you believe all that?" asked Amy, looking as if Bertha had been told a fairy tale.

"I do, indeed. I have told the child what I regard as

the highest form of the truth, though expressed in simple language. Miss Amy, I know that your father was ever kind to you. Did he ever turn coldly away from any earnest appeal of yours?"

"Never, never," cried the girl, with a rush of tears.

"And can you believe that his Heavenly Father turned from his touching appeal last night? Christ said to those who were trusting in him, 'I will come again and receive you unto myself; that where I am there ye may be also.' As long as your father was conscious, he was clinging to that divine hand that has never failed one true believer in all these centuries. Surely, Miss Amy, your own reason tells you that the poor helpless form that we must bury to-day is not your father. The genial spirit, the mind that was a power out in the world, the soul with its noble and intense affections and aspirations—these made the man that was your father. Therefore I say with truth that the man, the imperishable part, has gone away with him who loved humanity, and who has prepared a better place for us than this earth can ever be under the most favoring circumstances. You can understand that the body is but the changing, perishing shadow.

"When you compare the poor, disease-shattered house in yonder room, with the regal spirit that dwelt within it, when you compare that prostrate form—which, like a fallen tree in the forest, is yielding to the universal law of change—with the strong, active, intelligent man that was your father, do not your very senses assure you that your father has gone away, and, as I told Bertha, you will surely see him again? It may seem to you that what I said about the good-by kiss was but a fiction to soothe the child, but in my belief it was not. Though we know with certainty so little of the detail of the life beyond, we have two good grounds on which to base reasonable conjecture. We know of God's love; we know your father's love; now what would be natural in view of these two facts? I think we can manage to keep Bertha from seeing that which is no longer her father, and thus every memory of him will be pleasant. We will leave intact the impression which he himself made when he acted consciously, for this which now remains is not himself at all."

Further conversation was interrupted by the arrival of Dr. Orton; but Haldane saw that Amy had grasped at his words as one might try to catch a rope that was being lowered to him in some otherwise hopeless abyss.

"I feared that such might be the end," said the doctor, gloomily, on learning from Haldane the events of the night; "it frequently is in constitutions like his." Then he went up and saw Mrs. Poland.

The lady's condition gave him much anxiety, but he kept it to himself until they were alone. After leaving quieting medicines for her with Amy, and breaking utterly down in trying to say a few words of comfort to the fatherless girl, he motioned to Haldane to follow him.

"Come with me to the city," he said, "and we will arrange for such disposal of the remains as is best."

Having informed Amy of the nature of his errand, and promising to telegraph Mrs. Arnot, Haldane accompanied the physician to the business part of town.

"You have been a godsend to them," said the kind-hearted old doctor, blowing his nose furiously. "This case comes a little nearer home than any that has yet occurred; but then the bottom is just falling out of everything, and it looks as if we would all go before we have a frost. It seems to me, though, that I can stand anything rather than see Amy go. She is engaged to a nephew of mine—as fine a fellow as there is in town, if I do say it, and I love the girl as if she were my own child. My nephew is travelling in Europe now, and I doubt if he knows the danger hanging over the girl. If anything happens to her it will about kill him, for he idolizes her, and well he may. I'm dreadfully anxious about them all. I fear most for Mrs. Poland's mind. She's a New England lady, as I suppose you know—wonderfully gifted woman, too much brain power for that fragile body of hers. Well, perhaps you did not understand all that was said last night; but Mrs. Poland has always been a great reader, and she has been carried away by the materialistic philosophy that's in fashion nowadays. Queer, isn't it? and she two-thirds spirit herself. Her husband and my best friend was as genial and whole-souled a man as ever lived, fond of a good dinner, fond of a joke, and fond of his family to idolatry. His wife had unbounded influence over him, or otherwise he might have been a little fast; but he always laughed at what he called her 'Yankee notions,' and said he would not accept her philosophy until she became a little more material herself. Poland was a square, successful business man, but I fear he did not lay up much. He was too open-hearted and free-handed—a typical Southerner I suppose you would say at the North, that is, those of you who don't think of us as all slave-drivers and slave-traders. I expect the North and South will have to have a good, square, stand-up fight before they understand each other."

"God forbid!" ejaculated Haldane.

"Well, I don't think you and I will ever quarrel. You may call us what you please if you will take care of Poland's family."

"I have already learned to have a very thorough respect both for your head and heart, Doctor Orton."

"I'm considerably worse than they average down here. But as I was telling you, Mrs. Poland was a New England woman, and to humor her her husband employed such white servants as could be got in the city, and poor trash they were most of the time. When the fever appeared they left instantly. Poland bought the old colored people who are there with the place, and gave them their freedom, and only they have stood by them. What they would have done last night if you had not come, God only knows. Poor Amy, poor Amy!" sighed the old doctor tempestuously; "she's the prettiest and pluckiest little girl in the city. She's half frightened out of her wits, I can see that, and yet nothing but force could get her away. For my nephew's sake and her own I tried hard to induce her to go, but she stands her ground like a soldier. What is best now I hardly know. Mrs. Poland is so utterly prostrated that it might cost her life to move her. Besides, they have all been so terribly exposed to the disease that they might be taken with it on the journey, and to have them go wandering off the Lord knows where at this chaotic time looks to me about as bad as staying where they are, and I can look after them. But we'll see, we'll see." And in like manner the sorely troubled old gentleman talked rapidly on, till they reached the undertaker's, seemingly finding a relief in thus unburdening his heart to one of whose sympathy he felt sure, and who might thus be led to feel a deeper interest in the objects of his charge.

Even at that time of general disaster Haldane's abundant funds enabled him to secure prompt attention. It was decided that Mr. Poland's remains should be placed in a receiving vault until such time as they could be removed to the family burying-ground in another city, and before the day closed everything had been attended to in the manner which refined Christian feeling would dictate.

Before parting with Haldane, Doctor Orton had given him careful directions what to do in case he recognized symptoms of the fever in any of the family or himself. "Keep Amy and Bertha with their mother all you can," he said; "anything to rouse the poor woman from that stony despair into which she seems to have fallen."

The long day at length came to an end. Haldane of necessity had been much away, and he welcomed the cool and quiet evening; and yet he knew that with the shadow of night, though so grateful after the glare and heat to which he had been subjected, the fatal pestilence approached the nearer, as if to strike a deadlier blow. As the pioneer forefathers of the city had shut their doors and windows at nightfall, lest their savage and lurking foes should send a fatal arrow from some dusky covert, so now again, with the close of the day, all doors and windows must be shut against a more subtle and remorseless enemy, whose viewless shafts sped with a surer aim in darkness.

Amy had spent much of the day in unburdening her heart in a long letter to her cousin Laura, in which in her own vivid way she portrayed the part Haldane had acted toward them. She had also written to her distant and unconscious lover, and feeling that it might be the last time, she had poured out to him a passion that was as intense and yet as pure as the transparent flame that we sometimes see issuing from the heart of the hard-wood maple, as we sit brooding over our winter fire.

"Come and sit with us, and as one of us," she had said to Haldane, and so they had all gathered at the bedside of the widow, who had scarcely strength to do more than fix her dark, wistful eyes on one and another of the group. She was so bewildered and overwhelmed with her loss that her mind had partially suspended its action. She saw and heard everything; she remembered it all afterward; but now the very weight of the blow had so stunned her that she was mercifully saved from the agony of full consciousness.

Little Bertha climbed upon Haldane's lap and pleaded for a story.

"Yes, Bertie," he said, "and I think I know a story that you would like. You remember I told you that your papa had gone away with Jesus; would you not like to hear a story about this good friend of your papa's?"

"Yes, yes, I would. Do you know much about him?"

"Quite a good deal, for he's my friend too. I know one true story about him that I often like to think of. Listen, and I will tell it to you. Jesus is the God who made us, and he lives 'way up above the sky. But he not only made us, Bertie, but he also loves us, and in order to show us how he loves us he is always coming to this world to do us good; and once he came and lived here just like a man, so that we might all be sure that he cared for us and wanted to make us good and happy. Well, at that time when he lived here in this world as a man he had some true friends who loved him and believed in him. At a certain time they were all staying on the shore of a sea, and one evening Jesus told his friends to take a little boat and go over to the other side of the sea, and he would meet them there. Then Jesus, who wanted to be alone, went up the side of the mountain that rose from the water's edge. Then night came and it began to grow darker and darker, and at last it was so dark that the friends of Jesus that were in the boat could only see a very little way. Then a moaning, sighing wind began to rise, and the poor men in the boat saw that a storm was coming, and they pulled hard with their oars in hopes of getting over on the other side before the storm became very bad; but by the time they reached the very middle of the sea, the wind began to blow furiously, just as you have seen it blow when the trees bent 'way over toward the ground, and some perhaps were broken down. A strong wind at sea makes the water rise up in waves, and these waves began to beat against the boat, and before very long some of the highest ones would dash into it. The men pulled with their oars with all their might, but it was of no use; the wind was right against them, and though they did their best hour after hour, they still could get no nearer the shore. How sad and full of danger was their condition! the dark, dark night was above and around them, the dark, angry waves dashing by and over them, the cold, black depths of water beneath them, and no sound in their ears but the wild, rushing storm. What do you think became of them?"

"I'm afraid they were drowned," said Bertha, looking up with eyes that were full of fear and trouble.

"Have you forgotten Jesus?"

"But he's 'way off on the side of the mountain."

"He is never so far from his friends but that he can see them and know all about them. He saw these friends in the boat, for Jesus can see in the darkness as well as in the light; and when the night grew darkest, and the waves were highest, and his friends most weary and discouraged, he came to them so that they might know that he could save them, when they felt they could not save themselves. And he came as no other help could have come—walking over the very waves that threatened to swallow up his friends; and when he was near to them he called out, 'Be of good cheer, it is I; be not afraid.' Then he went right up to the boat and stepped into it among his friends. Oh! what a happy change his coming made, for the winds ceased, the waves went down, and in a very little while the boat reached the sea-shore. The bright sun rose up, the darkness fled away, and the friends of Jesus were safe. They have been safe ever since. Nothing can harm Jesus' friends. He takes care of them from day to day, from year to year, and from age to age. Whenever they are in trouble or pain or danger he comes to them as he did to his friends in the boat, and he brings them safely through it all. Don't you think he is a good friend to have?"

"Isn't I too little to be his friend?"

"No, indeed; no one ever loved little children as he does. He used to take them in his arms and bless them, and he said, 'Suffer them to come to me'; and where he lives he has everything beautiful to make little children happy."

"And you say papa is with him?"

"Yes, papa is with him."

"Why can't we all go to him now?"

"As soon as he is ready for us he will come for us."

"I wish he was ready for mamma, Amy, and me now, and then we could all be together. It's so lonely without papa. Oh! I'm so tired," she added after a few moments, and a little later her head dropped against Haldane's breast, and she was asleep.

"Mr. Haldane," said Amy in a low, agitated voice, "have you embodied your faith in that story to Bertha?"

"Yes, Miss Amy."

"Why do you think"—and she hesitated. "How do you know," she began again, "that any such Being as Jesus exists and comes to any one's help?"

"Granting that the story I have told you is true, how did his disciples know that he came to their help? Did not the hushed winds prove it? Did not the quieted waters prove it? Did not his presence with them assure them of it? By equal proof I know that he can and will come to the aid of those who look to him for aid. I have passed through darker nights and wilder storms than ever lowered over the Sea of Galilee, and I know by simple, practical, happy experience that Jesus Christ, through his all-pervading Spirit, has come to me in my utter extremity again and again, and that I have the same as felt his rescuing hand. Not that my trials and temptations have been greater than those of many others, but I have been weaker than others, and I have often been conscious of his sustaining power when otherwise 1 would have sunk beneath my burden. This is not a theory, Miss Amy, nor the infatuation of a few ignorant people. It is the downright experience of multitudes in every walk of life, and, on merely scientific grounds, is worth as much as any other experience. This story of Jesus gains the sympathy of little Bertha; it also commands the reverent belief of the most gifted and cultivated minds in the world."

"Oh, that I could believe all this; but there is so much mystery, so much that is dark." Then she glanced at her mother, who had turned away her face and seemed to be sleeping, and she asked: "If Christ is so strong to help and save, why is he not strong to prevent evil? Why is there a cry of agony going up from this stricken city? Why must father die who was everything to us? Why must mother suffer so? Why am I so shadowed by an awful fear? Life means so much to me. I love it," she continued in low yet passionate tones. "I love the song of birds, the breath of flowers, the sunlight, and every beautiful thing. I love sensation. I am not one who finds a tame and tranquil pleasure in the things I like or in the friends I love. My joys thrill every nerve and fibre of my being. I cling to them, I cannot give them up. A few days ago life was as full of rich promise to me as our tropical spring. It is still, though I will never cease to feel the pain of this great sorrow, and yet this horrible pit of death, corruption, and nothingness yawns at my very feet. Mr. Haldane," she said in a still lower and more shuddering tone, "I have a terrible presentiment that I shall perish with this loathsome disease. I may seem to you, who are so quiet and brave, very weak and cowardly; but I shrink from death with a dread which you cannot understand and which no language can express. It is repugnant to every instinct of my being, and I can think of it only with unutterable loathing. If I were old and feeble, if I had tasted all the joys of life, I might submit, but not now, not now. I feel with father that it is fiendish cruelty to give one such an intense love of life and then wrench it away; and, passionately as I love life, there is one far more dear. There is that in your nature which has so won my confidence that I can reveal to you my whole heart. Mr. Haldane, I love one who is like you, manly and noble, and dearly as I prize life, I think I could give it away in slow torture for his sake, if required. How often my heart has thrilled to see his eyes kindle with his foolish admiration, the infatuation of love which makes its object beautiful at least to the lover. And now to think that he does not know what I suffer and fear, to think that I may never see him again, to think that when he returns I may be a hideous mass of corruption that he cannot even approach. Out upon the phrases 'beneficent nature,' and 'natural law.' Laws which permit such things are must unnatural, and to endow one with such a love of life, such boundless capabilities of enjoying life, and then at the supreme moment when the loss will be most bitterly felt to snatch it away, looks to me more like the work of devilish ingenuity than of a 'beneficent nature.' I feel with father, it is fiendish cruelty."

Haldane bowed his head among Bertha's curls to hide the tears that would come at this desperate cry of distress; but Amy's eyes were hard and dry, and had the agonized look which might have been their expression had she been enduring physical torture.

"Miss Amy," he said brokenly after a moment, "you forget that your father said, 'If this life is all, it is fiendishly cruel to tear us from that which we have learned to love so dearly,' and I agree with him.   But this life is not all; the belief that human life ends at death is revolting to reason, conscience, and every sense of justice.   If this were true the basest villain could escape all the consequences of his evil in a moment, and you who are so innocent, so exquisite in your spiritual organization, so brave and noble that you can face this awful fear in your devotion to those you love—you by ceasing to breathe merely would sink to precisely the same level and be no different from the lifeless clay of the villain.   Such monstrous injustice is impossible; it outrages every instinct of justice, every particle of reason that I have.

"Miss Amy, don't you see that you are like the disciples in the boat out in the midst of the sea?   The night is dark above you, the storm is wild around you, the waves are dashing over you, the little boat is frail, and there are such cold, dark depths beneath it.   But we can't help these things.   We can't explain the awful mystery of evil and suffering; sooner or later every human life becomes enveloped in darkness, storm, and danger.   That wave-tossed boat in the midst of the sea is an emblem of the commonest human experience.   On the wide sea of life, numberless little barks are at this moment at the point of foundering. Few are so richly freighted as yours, but the same unknown depths are beneath each.   But, Miss Amy, I pray you remember the whole of this suggestive Bible story.   Those imperilled disciples were watched by a loving, powerful friend.   He came to their aid, making the very waves that threatened to engulf the pathway of his rescuing love.   He saved those old-time friends. They are living to-day, they will live forever. I can't explain the dark and terrible things of which this world is full, I cannot explain the awful mystery of evil in any of its forms. I know the pestilence is all around us; I know it seems to threaten your precious, beautiful life. I recognize the fact, as I also remember the fact of the darkness and storm around the little boat. But I also know with absolute certainty that there is one who can come to your rescue, whose province it is to give life, deathless life, life more rich and full of thrilling happiness than you have ever dreamed of, even with your vivid imagination."

"How, how can you know this? What *proof* can you give me?" she asked; and no poor creature, whose life was indeed at stake, ever bent forward more eagerly to catch the sentence of life or death, than did Amy Poland the coming answer.

"I know it," he replied more calmly, "on the strongest possible grounds of evidence—my own experience, the experience of Mrs. Arnot, who is sincerity itself, and the experience of multitudes of others. Believers in Jesus Christ have been verifying his promises in every age, and in every possible emergency and condition of life, and if their testimony is refused, human consciousness is no longer a basis of knowledge. No one ever had a better friend than Mrs. Arnot has been to me; she has been the means of saving me from disgrace, shame, and everything that was base, and I love her with a gratitude that is beyond words, and yet I am not so conscious of her practical help and friendship as that of the Divine Man who has been my patient unwavering friend in my long, hard struggle."

Under his words, the hard, dry despair of Amy had given way to gentler feelings, which found expression in low, piteous sobbing.

"Oh, when will he come to me?" she asked, "for I cannot doubt after such words."

"When you most need him, Miss Amy. It is your privilege to ask his comforting and sustaining presence now; but he will come when he sees that you most need him."

"If ever poor creatures needed such a friend as you have described, we need him now," faltered Mrs. Poland, turning her face toward them and then they knew that she had heard all.

Amy sprang to her embrace, exclaiming, "Mother, is it possible that we can find such a friend in our extremity?"

"Amy, I am bewildered, I am overwhelmed."

Haldane carried little Bertha to her crib and covered her with an afghan. Then coming to the lady's side he took her hand and said gently, and yet with that quiet firmness which does much to produce conviction: "Mrs. Poland, before leaving your husband to his quiet sleep we read words which Jesus Christ once spoke to a despairing, grief-stricken woman. Take them now as if spoken to you. 'Jesus said unto her, I am the resurrection and the life: he that believeth in me, though he were dead, yet shall he live; and whosoever liveth and believeth in me shall never die.' As your husband said to you, you will all surely meet again."

Then he lifted her hand to his lips in a caress that was full of sympathy and respect, and silently left the room.

CHAPTER LII

A MAN VERSUS A CONNOISSEUR

AMY'S sad presentiment was almost verified. She was very ill, and for hours of painful uncertainty Haldane watched over her and administered the remedies which Dr. Orton left; and indeed the doctor himself was never absent very long, for his heart was bound up in the girl. At last, after a wavering poise, the scale turned in favor of life, and she began to slowly revive.

Poor Mrs. Poland was so weak that she could not raise her head or hand, but, with her wistful, pathetic eyes, followed every motion, for she insisted on having Amy in the same room with herself. Aunt Saba, the old negress, to whom Mr. Poland had given her freedom, continued a faithful assistant. Bound to her mistress by the stronger chain of gratitude and affection, she served with fidelity in every way possible to her; and she and her husband were so old and humble that death seemingly had forgotten them.

Before Amy was stricken down with the fever the look of unutterable dread and anxiety that was so painful to witness passed away, and gave place to an expression of quiet serenity.

"I need no further argument," she had said to Haldane; "Christ has come across the waves of my trouble. I am as sure of it as I am sure that you came to my aid. I do not know whether mother or Bertha or I will survive, but I believe that God's love is as great as his power, and that in some way and at some time all will come out for the best. I have written to my friend abroad and to Auntie

Arnot all about it, and now I am simply waiting. O, Mr. Haldane, I am so happy to tell you," she had added, "that I think mother is accepting the same faith, slowly and in accordance with her nature, but surely nevertheless. I am like father, quick and intense in my feelings. I feel that which is false or that which is true, rather than reason it out as mother does."

Aunt Saba and her husband managed to take care of Bertha and keep her mind occupied; but before Amy's convalescence had proceeded very far the little girl was suddenly prostrated by a most violent attack of the disease, and she withered before the hot fever like a fragile flower in a simoom. Haldane went hastily for Dr. Orton, but he gave scarcely a hope from the first.

During the night following the day on which she had been stricken down a strange event occurred.[1] The sultry heat had been followed by a tropical thunder-storm, which had gathered in the darkness, and often gave to the midnight a momentary and brighter glare than that of the previous noon. The child would start as the flashes grew more intense, for they seemed to distress her very much.

As Haldane was lifting her to give her a drink he said: "Perhaps Bertie will see papa very soon."

Hearing the word "papa," the child forgot her pain for a moment and smiled. At that instant there was a blinding flash of lightning, and the appalling thunder-peal followed without any interval.

Both Mrs. Poland and Amy gave a faint and involuntary cry of alarm, but Haldane's eyes were fixed on the little smiling face that he held so near to his own. The smile did not fade. The old, perplexed expression of pain did not come back, and after a moment he said quietly and very gently:

---

[1] It is stated on high medical authority that "all patients suffer more during thunder-showers," and an instance is given of a physician who was suffering from this fever, and who was killed as instantly, by a vivid flash and loud report, as if he had been struck by the lightning.

"Bertie is with her father;" and he lifted her up and carried her to her mother, and then to Amy, that they might see the beautiful and smiling expression of the child's face.

But their eyes were so blinded by tears that they could scarcely see the face from which all trace of suffering had been banished almost as truly as from the innocent spirit.

Having laid her back in the crib, and arranged the little form as if sleeping, he carried the crib, with Aunt Saba's help, to the room where Mr. Poland had died. Then he told the old negress to return and remain with her mistress, and that he would watch over the body till morning.

That quiet watch by the pure little child, with a trace of heaven's own beauty on her face, was to Haldane like the watch of the shepherds on the hillside near Bethlehem. At times, in the deep hush that followed the storm, he was almost sure that he heard, faint and far away, angelic minstrelsy and song.

Haldane's unusually healthful and vigorous constitution had thus far resisted the infection, but after returning from the sad duty of laying little Bertha's remains by those of her father, he felt the peculiar languor which is so often the precursor of the chill and subsequent fever. Although he had scarcely hoped to escape an attack, he had never before realized how disastrous it would be to the very ones he had come to serve. Who was there to take care of him? Mrs. Poland was almost helpless from nervous prostration. Amy required absolute quiet to prevent the more fatal relapse, which is almost certain to follow exertion made too early in convalescence. He knew that if he were in the house she would make the attempt to do something for him, and he also knew it would be at the risk of her life. Old Aunt Saba was worn out in her attendance on Bertha, Amy, and Mrs. Poland. Her husband, and a stranger who had been at last secured to assist him, were required in the household duties.

He took his decision promptly, for he felt that he had

but brief time in which to act. Going to Mrs. Poland's room, he said to her and Amy:

"I am glad to find you both so brave and doing as well as you are on this sad, sad day. I do not think you will take the disease, Mrs. Poland; and you, Miss Amy, only need perfect quiet in order to get well Please remember, as a great favor to me, how vitally important is the tranquillity of mind and body that I am ever preaching to you, and don't do that which fatigues you in the slightest degree, till conscious of your old strength. And now I am going away for a little while. This is a time when every man should be at his post of duty. I am needed elsewhere, for I know of a case that requires immediate attention. Please do not remonstrate," he said, as they began to urge that he should take some rest; "my mission here has ended for the present and my duty is elsewhere. We won't say good-by, for I shall not be far away;" and although he was almost faint from weakness, his bearing was so decided and strong, and he appeared so bent on departure, that they felt that it would hardly be in good taste to say anything more.

"We are almost beginning to feel that Mr. Haldane belongs to us," said Amy to her mother afterward, "and forget that he may be prompted by as strong a sense of duty to others."

As Haldane was leaving the house Dr. Orton drove to the door. Before he could alight the young man climbed into his buggy with almost desperate haste.

"Drive toward the city," he said so decisively that the doctor obeyed.

"What's the matter, Haldane? Speak, man; you look sick."

"Take me to the city hospital. I am sick."

"I shall take you right back to Mrs. Poland's," said the doctor, pulling up.

Haldane laid his hands on the reins, and then explained his fears and the motive for his action.

"God bless you, old fellow; but you are right. Any

effort now would cost Amy her life, and she would make it if you were there. But you are not going to the hospital."

Dr. Orton's intimate acquaintance with the city enabled him to place Haldane in a comfortable room near his own house, where he could give constant supervision to his case. He also procured a good nurse, whose sole duty was to take care of the young man. To the anxious questioning of Mrs. Poland and Amy from time to time, the doctor maintained the fiction, saying that Haldane was watching a very important case under his care; "and you know his way," added the old gentleman, rubbing his hands, as if he were enjoying something internally, "he won't leave a case till I say it's safe, even to visit you, of whom he speaks every chance he gets;" and thus the two ladies in their feeble state were saved all anxiety.

They at length learned of the merciful ruse that had been played upon them by the appearance of their friend at their door in Dr. Orton's buggy. As the old physician helped his patient, who was still rather weak, up the steps, he said with his hearty laugh:

"Haldane has watched over that case, that he and I told you of, long enough. We now turn the case over to you, Miss Amy. But all he requires is good living, and I'll trust to you for that. He's a trump, if he is a Yankee. But drat him, I thought he'd spoil the joke by dying, at one time."

The sentiments that people like Mrs. Poland and her daughter, Mrs. Arnot, and Laura, would naturally entertain toward one who had served them as Haldane had done, and at such risk to himself, can be better imagined than portrayed. They looked and felt infinitely more than they were ever permitted to say, for any expression of obligation was evidently painful to him.

He speedily gained his old vigor, and before the autumn frosts put an end to the epidemic, was able to render Dr. Orton much valuable assistance.

Amy became more truly his sister than ever his own had been to him. Her quick intuition soon discovered his secret

—even the changing expression of his eyes at the mention of Laura's name would have revealed it to her—but he would not let her speak on the subject. "She belongs to another," he said, "and although to me she is the most beautiful and attractive woman in the world, it must be my lifelong effort not to think of her."

His parting from Mrs. Poland and Amy tested his self-control severely. In accordance with her impulsive nature, Amy put her arms about his neck as she said brokenly:

"You were indeed God's messenger to us, and you brought us life. As father said, we shall all meet again."

On his return, Mrs. Arnot's greeting was that of a mother; but there were traces of constraint in Laura's manner. When she first met him she took his hand in a strong, warm pressure, and said, with tears in her eyes:

"Mr. Haldane, I thank you for your kindness to Amy and auntie as sincerely as if it had all been rendered to me alone."

But after this first expression of natural feeling, Haldane was almost tempted to believe that she shunned meeting his eyes, avoided speaking to him, and even tried to escape from his society, by taking Mr. Beaumont's arm and strolling off to some other apartment, when he was calling on Mrs. Arnot. And yet if this were true, he was also made to feel that it resulted from no lack of friendliness or esteem on her part.

"She fears that my old-time passion may revive, and she would teach me to put a watch at the entrance of its sepulchre," he at length concluded; "she little thinks that my love, so far from being dead, is a chained giant that costs me hourly vigilance to hold in lifelong imprisonment."

But Laura understood him much better than he did her. Her manner was the result of a straightforward effort to be honest. Of her own free will, and without even the slightest effort on the part of her uncle and aunt to incline her toward the wealthy and distinguished Mr. Beaumont, she had accepted all his attentions, and had accepted the man himself. In the world's estimation she would not have the slightest ground to find fault with him, for, from the first, both in conduct and manner, he had been irreproachable.

When the telegram which announced Mr. Poland's death was received, he tried to comfort her by words that were so peculiarly elegant and sombre, that, in spite of Laura's wishes to think otherwise, they struck her like an elegiac address that had been carefully prearranged and studied; and when the tidings of poor little Bertha's death came, it would occur to Laura that Mr. Beaumont had thought his first little address so perfect that he could do no better than to repeat it, as one might use an appropriate burial service on all occasions. He meant to be kind and considerate. He was "ready to do anything in his power," as he often said. But what was in his power? As telegrams and letters came, telling of death, of desperate illness, and uncertain life, of death again, of manly help, of woman-like self-sacrifice in the same man, her heart began to beat in quick, short, passionate throbs. But it would seem that nothing could ever disturb the even rhythm of Beaumont's pulse. He tried to show his sympathy by turning his mind to all that was mournful and sombre in art and literature. One day he brought to her from New York what he declared to be the finest arrangement of dirge music for the piano extant, and she quite surprised him by declaring with sudden passion that she could not and would not play a note of it.

In her deep sorrow and deeper anxiety, in her strange and miserable unrest, which had its hidden root in a cause not yet understood, she turned to him again and again for sympathy, and he gave her abundant opportunity to seek it, for Laura was the most beautiful object he had ever seen; and therefore, to feast his eye and gratify his ear, he spent much of his time with her; so much, indeed, that she often grew drearily weary of him. But no matter when or how often she would look into his face for quick, heartfelt appreciation, she saw with instinctive certainty that, more than lover, more than friend, and eventually, more than husband, he was, and ever would be, a connoisseur. When she smiled he was admiring her, when she wept he was also admiring her. Whatever she did or said was constantly being looked at and studied from an æsthetic standpoint by this man, whose fastidious taste she had thus far satisfied. More than once she had found herself asking: "Suppose I should lose my beauty, what would he do?" and the instinctive answer of her heart was: "He would honorably try to keep all his pledges, but would look the other way."

Before she was aware of it, she had begun to compare her affianced with Haldane, and she found that the one was like a goblet of sweet, rich wine, that was already nearly exhausted and cloying to her taste; the other was like a mountain spring, whose waters are pure, ever new, unfailing, prodigally abundant, inspiring yet slaking thirst.

But she soon saw whither such comparisons were leading her, and recognized her danger and her duty. She had plighted her faith to another, and he had given her no good reason to break that faith. Laura had a conscience, and she as resolutely set to work to shut out Haldane from her heart, as he, poor man, had tried to exclude her image, and from very much the same cause. But the heart is a wayward organ and is often at sword's-point with both will and conscience, and frequently, in spite of all that she could do, it would array Haldane on the one side and Beaumont on the other, and so it would eventually come to be, the man who loved her, *versus* the connoisseur who admired her, but whose absorbing passion for himself left no place for any other strong feeling.

CHAPTER LIII

EXIT OF LAURA'S FIRST KNIGHT

HALDANE was given but little time for quiet study, for, before the year closed, tidings came from his mother, who was then in Italy, that she was ill and wished to see him. Poor Mrs. Haldane had at last begun to understand her son's character better, and to realize that he would retrieve the past. She also reproached herself that she had not been more sympathetic and helpful to him, and was not a little jealous that he should have found better and more appreciative friends than herself. And, at last, when she was taken ill, she longed to see him, and he lost not a moment in reaching her side.

Her illness, however, did not prove very serious, and she improved rapidly after a young gentleman appeared who was so refined in his manners, so considerate and deferential in his bearing toward her that she could scarcely believe that he was the same with the wild, wretched youth who had been in jail, and, what was almost as bad, who had worked in a mill.

Haldane made the most of his opportunities in seeing what was beautiful in nature and art while in the old world, but his thoughts turned with increasing frequency to his own land—not only because it contained the friends he loved so well, but also because events were now rapidly culminating for that great struggle between the two jarring sections that will eventually form a better and closer union on the basis of a mutual respect, and a better and truer knowledge of each other.

When Mrs. Haldane saw that her son was determined to take part in the conflict, he began to seem to her more like his old unreasonable self. She feebly remonstrated as a matter of course, and proved to her own satisfaction that it was utter folly for a young man who had the enjoyment of such large wealth as her son to risk the loss of everything in the hardships and dangers of war. He was as kind and considerate as possible, but she saw from the old and well-remembered expression of his eyes that he would carry out his own will nevertheless, and therefore she and his sisters reluctantly returned with him.

Having safely installed them in their old home, and proved by the aid of Dr. Marks and some other leading citizens of his native city that they had no further occasion to seclude themselves from the world, he returned to Hillaton to aid in organizing a regiment that was being recruited there, and in which Mr. Ivison had assured him of a commission. By means of the acquaintances he had made through his old mission class, he was able to secure enlistments rapidly, and although much of the material that he brought in was unpromising in its first appearance, he seemed to have the faculty of transforming the slouching dilapidated fellows into soldiers, and it passed into general remark that "Haldane's company was the roughest to start with and the best disciplined and most soldierly of them all when ordered to the seat of war."

The colonelcy of the regiment was given to Mr. Beaumont, not only on account of his position, but also because of his large liberality in fitting it out. He took a vast interest in the æsthetic features of its equipment, style of uniform, and like matters, and he did most excellent service in insisting on neatness, good care of weapons, and a soldierlike bearing from the first.

While active in this work he rose again in Laura's esteem, for he seemed more manly and energetic than he had shown himself to be before; and what was still more in his favor, he had less time for the indulgence of his taste as a connoisseur with her fair but often weary face as the object of contemplation.

She, with many others, visited the drill-ground almost daily, and when she saw the tall and graceful form of Mr. Beaumont issuing from the colonel's tent, when she saw him mount his superb white horse, which he managed with perfect skill, when she saw the sun glinting on his elegant sword and gold epaulets, and heard his sonorous orders to the men, she almost felt that all Hillaton was right, and that she had reason to be proud of him, and to be as happy as the envious belles of the city deemed her to be. But in spite of herself, her eyes would wander from the central figure to plain Captain Haldane, who, ignoring the admiring throng, was giving his whole attention to his duty.

Before she was aware, the thought began to creep into her mind, however, that to one man these scenes were military pageants, and to the other they meant stern and uncompromising war.

This impression had speedy confirmation, for one evening when both Mr. Beaumont and Haldane happened to be present, Mrs. Arnot remarked in effect that her heart misgive her when she looked into the future, and that the prospect of a bloody war between people of one race and faith was simply horrible.

"It will not be very bloody," remarked Mr. Beaumont, lightly. "After things have gone about so far the politicians on both sides will step in and patch up a compromise. Our policy at the North is to make an imposing demonstration. This will have the effect of bringing the fire-eaters to their senses, and if this won't answer we must get enough men together to walk right over the South, and end the nonsense at once. I have travelled through the South, and know that it can be done."

"Pardon me, colonel," said Haldane, "but since we are not on the drill-ground I have a right to differ with you. I anticipate a very bloody, and, perhaps, a long war. I have not seen so much of the South, but I have seen something of its people. The greatest heroism I ever saw manifested in my life was by a young Southern girl, and if such are their women we shall find the men foemen abundantly worthy of our steel. We shall indeed have to literally walk over them, that is, such of us as are left and able to walk. I agree with Mrs. Arnot, and I tremble for the future of my country."

Mr. Beaumont forgot himself for once so far as to say, "Oh, if you find such cause for trembling—" but Laura's indignant face checked further utterance.

"I propose to do my duty," said Haldane, with a quiet smile, though a quick flush showed that he felt the slur, "and it will be your duty, Colonel, to see that I do."

"You have taught us that the word duty means a great deal to you, Egbert," said Mrs. Arnot, and then the matter dropped. But the animus of each man had been quite clearly revealed, and the question would rise in Laura's mind, "Does not the one belittle the occasion because little himself?" Although she dreaded the coming war inexpressibly, she took Haldane's view of it. His tribute to her cousin Amy also touched a very tender chord.

On the ground of having secured so many recruits Mr. Ivison urged that Haldane should have the rank of major, but at that time those things were controlled largely by political influence and favoritism, and there were still not a few in Hillaton who both thought and spoke of the young man's past record as a good reason why he should not have any rank at all. He quietly took what was given him and asked for nothing more.

All now know that Mr. Beaumont's view was not correct, and as the conflict thickened and deepened that elegant gentleman became more and more disgusted. Not that he lacked personal courage, but, as he often remarked, it was the "horrid style of living" that he could not endure. He could not find an æsthetic element in the blinding dust or unfathomable mud of Virginia.

As was usually the case, there was in the regiment a soldier gifted with the power and taste for letter-writing, and he kept the local papers quite well posted concerning affairs

in the regiment. One item concerning Beaumont will indicate the condition of his mind. After describing the "awful" nature of the roads and weather, the writer added,
"The Colonel looks as if in a chronic state of disgust."

Suddenly the regiment was ordered to the far Southwest.
This was more than Beaumont could endure, for in his view
life in that region would be a burden under any circumstances. He coolly thought the matter over, and concluded
that he would rather go home, marry Laura, and take a tour
in Europe, and promptly executed the first part of his plan
by resigning on account of ill-health. He had a bad cold,
it is true, which had chiefly gone to his head and made him
very uncomfortable, and so inflamed his nose that the ex-
amining physician misjudged the exemplary gentleman, rec-
ommending that his resignation be accepted, more from the
fear that his habits were bad than from any other cause.
But by the time he reached Hillaton his nose was itself
again, and he as elegant as ever. The political major had
long since disappeared, and so Haldane started for his distant field of duty as lieutenant-colonel.

The regimental letter-writer chronicled this promotion in
the Hillaton "Courier" with evident satisfaction.

"Lieut.-Col. Haldane," he wrote, "is respected by all and liked by the majority. He keeps us rigidly to our duty, but is kind and considerate nevertheless. He is the most useful officer I ever heard of. Now he is chaplain and
again he is surgeon. He coaxes the money away from the men and sends it
home to their families, otherwise much of it would be lost in gambling. Many
a mother and wife in Hillaton hears from the absent oftener because the Colonel urges the boys to write, and writes for those who are unable. To give
you a sample of the man I will tell you what I saw not long ago. The roads
were horrible as usual, and some of the men were getting played out on the
march. The first thing I knew a sick man was on the Major's horse (he was
Major then), and he was trudging along in the mud with the rest of us, and
carrying the muskets of three other men who were badly used up.[1] We want

---

[1] I cannot refrain here from paying a tribute to my old schoolmate and
friend, Major James Cromwell, of the 124th New York Volunteers, whom I
have seen plodding along in the mud in a November storm, a sick soldier rid-
ing his horse, while he carried the accoutrements of other men who were giving out from exhaustion. Major Cromwell was killed while leading a charge
at the battle of Gettysburg.

the people of Hillaton to understand, that if any of us get back we won't hear anything more against Haldane. Nice, pretty fellows, who don't like to get their boots muddy, as our ex-Colonel, for instance, may be more to their taste, but they ain't to ours."

Laura read this letter with cheeks that reddened with shame and then grew very pale.

"Auntie," she said, showing it to Mrs. Arnot, "I cannot marry that man. I would rather die first."

"I do not wonder that you feel so," replied Mrs. Arnot emphatically. "With all his wealth and culture I neither would nor could marry him, and would tell him so. I have felt sure that you would come to this conclusion, but I wished your own heart and conscience to decide the matter."

But before Laura could say to Mr. Beaumont that which she felt she must, and yet which she dreaded, for his sake, to speak, a social earthquake took place in Hillaton.

Mr. Arnot was arrested! But for the promptness of his friends to give bail for his appearance, he would have been taken from his private office to prison as poor Haldane had been years before.

It would be wearisome to tell the long story of his financial distress, which he characteristically kept concealed from his wife. Experiences like his are only too common. With his passion for business he had extended it to the utmost limit of his capital. Then came a time of great depression and contraction. Prompted by a will that had never been thwarted, and a passion for routine which could endure no change, he made Herculean effort to keep everything moving on with mechanical regularity. His strong business foresight detected the coming change for the better in the business world, and with him it was only a question of bridging over the intervening gulf. He sank his own property in his effort to do this; then the property of his wife and Laura, which he held in trust. Then came the great temptation of his life. He was joint trustee of another very large property, and the co-executor was in Europe, and would be absent for years. In order to use some of the funds of this property it was necessary to have the signature of this gentleman. With the infatuation of those who dally with this kind of temptation, Mr. Arnot felt sure that he could soon make good all that he should use in his present emergency, and, therefore, forged the name of the co-trustee. The gentleman returned from Europe unexpectedly, and the crime was discovered and speedily proved.

It was now that Mrs. Arnot proved what a noble and womanly nature she possessed. Without palliating his fault, she ignored the whole scoffing, chattering world, and stood by her husband with as wifely devotion as if his crime had been misfortune, and he himself had been the affectionate considerate friend that she had believed he would be, when as a blushing maiden she had accepted the hand that had grown so hard, and cold, and heavy.

Mr. Beaumont was stunned and bewildered. At first he scarcely knew what to do, although his sagacious father and mother told him very plainly to break the engagement at once. But the trouble with Mr. Beaumont upon this occasion was that he was a man of honor, and for once he almost regretted the fact. But since he was, he believed that there was but one course open for him. Although Laura was now penniless, and the same almost as the daughter of a man who would soon be in State prison, he had promised to marry her. She must become the mistress of the ancient and aristocratic Beaumont mansion.

He braced himself, as had been his custom when a battle was in prospect, and went down to the beautiful villa which would be Laura's home but a few days longer.

As he entered, she saw that he was about to perform the one heroic act of his life, but she was cruel enough to prevent even that one, and so reduced his whole career to one consistently elegant and polished surface.

He had taken her hand, and was about to address her in the most appropriate language, and with all the dignity of self-sacrifice, when she interrupted him by saying briefly:

"Mr. Beaumont, please listen to me first. Before the

most unexpected event occurred.which has made so great a change in my fortunes, and I may add, in so many of my friends, I had decided to say to you in all sincerity and kindness that I could not marry you. I could not give you that love which a wife ought to give to a husband. I now repeat my decision still more emphatically.''

Mr. Beaumont was again stunned and bewildered. A woman declining to marry him!

"Can nothing change your decision?" he faltered, fearing that something might.

"Nothing," she coldly replied, and with an involuntary expression of contempt hovering around her flexible mouth.

"But what will you do?" he asked, prompted by not a little curiosity.

"Support myself by honest work," was her quiet but very decisive answer.

Mr. Beaumont now felt that there was nothing more to be done but to make a little elegant farewell address, and depart, and he would make it in spite of all that she could do.

The next thing she heard of him was that he had started on a tour of Europe, and, no doubt, in his old character of a connoisseur, whose judgment few dared to dispute.

CHAPTER LIV

ANOTHER KNIGHT APPEARS

THE processes of law were at length complete, and Mr. Arnot found himself in a prison cell, with the prospect that years must elapse before he would receive a freedom that now was dreaded almost more than his forced seclusion. After his conviction he had been taken from Hillaton to a large prison of the State, in a distant city.

"I shall follow you, Thomas, as soon as I can complete such arrangements as are essential," Mrs. Arnot had said, "and will remain as near to you as I can. Indeed, it will be easier for Laura and me to commence our new life there than here."

The man had at last begun to realize the whole truth. True to his nature, he thought of himself first, and saw that his crime, like a great black hand, had dragged him down from his proud eminence of power and universal respect, away from his beloved business, and had shut him up in this narrow, stony sepulchre, for what better was his prison cell than a tomb to a man with his tireless mind? The same mind which like a giant had carried its huge burden every day, was still his; but now there was nothing for it to do. And yet it would act, for constant mental action had become a necessity from a lifetime of habit. Heretofore his vast business taxed every faculty to the utmost. He had to keep his eye on all the great markets of the world; he had to follow politicians, diplomats, and monarchs into their secret councils, and guess at their policy in order to shape his own business policy. His interests were so large and far-reaching that it had been necessary for him to take a glance over the world before he could properly direct his affairs from his private office. For years he had been commanding a small army of men, and with consummate skill and constant thought he had arrayed the industry of his army against the labors of like armies under the leadership of other men in competition with himself. His mind had learned to flash with increasing speed and accuracy to one and another of all these varied interests. But now the great fabric of business and wealth, which he had built by a lifetime of labor, had vanished like a dream, and nothing remained but the mind that had constructed it.

"Ah!" he groaned again and again, "why could not mind and memory perish also?"

But they remained, and were the only possessions left of his great wealth.

Then he began to think of his wife and Laura. He had beggared them, and, what was far worse, he had darkened their lives with the shadow of his own disgrace. Wholly innocent as they were, they must suffer untold wretchedness through his act. In his view he was the cause of the broken engagement between his niece and the wealthy Mr. Beaumont, and now he saw that there was nothing before the girl but a dreary effort to gain a livelihood by her own labor, and this effort rendered almost hopeless by the reflected shame of his crime.

His wife also was growing old and feeble. At last he realized he had a wife such as is given to but few men—a woman who was great enough to be tender and sympathetic through all the awful weeks that had elapsed since the discovery of his crime—a woman who could face what she saw before her and utter no words of repining or reproach.

He now saw how cold and hard and unappreciative he had been toward her in the days of his prosperity, and he cursed himself and his unutterable folly.

Thus his great powerful mind turned in vindictive rage against itself. Memory began to show him with mocking finger and bitter jibes where he might have acted more wisely in his business, more wisely in his social relations, and especially more wisely and humanely, to say the least, in his own home. It seemed to take a fiendish delight in telling him how everything might have been different, and how he, instead of brooding in a prison cell, might have been the most honored, useful, wealthy, and happy man in Hillaton.

Thus he was tortured until physical exhaustion brought him a brief respite of sleep. But the next day it was the same wretched round of bitter memories and vain but torturing activity of mind. Day after day passed and he grew haggard under his increasing mental distress. His mind was like a great driving wheel, upon which all the tremendous motive power is turned without cessation, but for which there is nothing to drive save the man himself, and seemingly it would drive him mad.

At last he said to himself, "I cannot endure this. For my own sake, for the sake of my wife and Laura, it were better that an utter blank should take the place of Thomas Arnot. I am, and ever shall be, only a burden to them. I am coming to be an intolerable burden to myself."

The thought of suicide, once entertained, grew rapidly in favor, and at last it became only a question how he could carry out his dark purpose. With this definite plan before him he grew calmer. At last he had something to *do* in the future, and terrible memory must suspend for a time its scorpion lash while he thought how best to carry out his plan.

The suicide about to take the risk of endless suffering is usually desirous that the intervening moments of his "taking off" should be as painless as possible, and Mr. Arnot began to think how he could make his exit momentary. But his more tranquil mood, the result of having some definite action before him, led to sleep, and the long night passed in unconsciousness, the weary body clogging the wheels of conscious thought.

The sun was shining when he awoke; but with returning consciousness came memory and pain, and the old cowardly desire to escape all the consequences of his sin by death. He vowed he would not live to see another day, and once more he commenced brooding over the one question, how he would die. As he took up this question where he had dropped it the previous night, the thought occurred to him what a long respite he had had from pain. Then like a flash of lightning came another thought:

"Suppose by my self-destroying act I pass into a condition of life in which there is no sleep, and memory can torture without cessation, without respite? True, I have tried to believe there is no future life, but am I sure of it? Here I can obtain a little rest. For hours I have been unconscious, through the weight of the body upon my spirit. How can I be sure that the spirit cannot exist separately and suffer just the same? I am not suffering now through my body, and have not been through all these terrible days. My body is here in this cell, inert and motionless, painless, while in my mind I am enduring the torments of the damned. The respite from suffering that I have had has come through the weariness of my body, and here I am planning to cast down the one barrier that perhaps saves me from an eternity of torturing thought and memory."

He was appalled at the bare possibility of such a future; reason told him that such a future was probable, and conscience told him that it was before him in veritable truth. He felt that wherever he carried memory and his present character he would be most miserable, whether it were in Dante's Inferno, Milton's Paradise, or the heaven or hell of the Bible.

There was no more thought of suicide. Indeed, he shrank from death with inexpressible dread.

Slowly his thoughts turned to his wife, the woman who had been so true to him, the one human being of all the

world who now stood by him. She might help him in his
desperate strait. She seemed to have a principle within
her soul which sustained her, and which might sustain
him. At any rate, he longed to see her once more, and
ask her forgiveness in deep contrition for his base and life-
long failure to "love, honor, and cherish her," as he had
promised at God's altar and before many witnesses.

The devoted wife came and patiently entered on her
ministry of love and Christian faith, and out of the chaos
of the fallen man of iron and stone there gradually emerged
a new man, who first became in Christ's expressive words
"a little child" in spiritual things, that he might grow naturally and in the symmetry of the enduring manhood which
God designs to perfect in the coming ages.

Mrs. Arnot's sturdy integrity led her to give up everything to her husband's creditors, and she came to the city
of her new abode wherein the prison was located almost
penniless. But she brought letters from Dr. Barstow, Mr.
Ivison, and other Christian people of Hillaton. These were
presented at a church of the denomination to which she belonged, and all she asked was some employment by which
she and Laura could support themselves. These letters secured confidence at once. There was no mystery—nothing
concealed—and, although so shadowed by the disgrace of
another, the bearing of the ladies inspired respect and won
sympathy. A gentleman connected with the church gave
Laura the position of saleswoman in his bookstore, and to
Mrs. Arnot's little suburban cottage of only three rooms
kind and interested ladies brought sewing and fancy-work.
Thus they were provided for, as God's people ever are in
some way.

Mrs. Arnot had written a long letter to Haldane before
leaving Hillaton, giving a full account of their troubles,
with one exception. At Laura's request she had not mentioned the broken engagement with Beaumont.

"If possible, I wish to see him myself before he knows,"
she had said. "At least, before any correspondence takes

place between us, I wish to look into his eyes, and if I see the faintest trace of shrinking from me there, as I saw it in Mr. Beaumont's eyes, I will never marry him, truly as I love him."

Mrs. Arnot's face had lighted up with its old-time expression, as she said:

"Laura, don't you know Egbert Haldane better than that?"

"I can't help it," she had replied with a troubled brow; "the manner of nearly every one has changed so greatly that I must see him first."

Haldane did not receive Mrs. Arnot's first letter. He was at sea with his regiment, on his way to the far South-west, when the events in which he would have been so deeply interested began to occur. After reaching his new scene of duty, there were constant alternations of march and battle. In the terrible campaign that followed, the men of the army he was acting with were decimated, and officers dropped out fast. In consequence, Haldane, who received but two slight wounds, that did not disable him, was promoted rapidly. The colonel of the regiment was killed soon after their arrival, and from the command of the regiment he rose, before the campaign was over, to command a brigade, and then a division; and he performed his duties so faithfully and ably that he was confirmed in this position.

Mrs. Arnot's first letter had followed him around for a time, and then was lost, like so many others in that time of dire confusion. Her second letter after long delay reached him, but it was very brief and hurried, and referred to troubles that he did not understand. From members of his old regiment, however, rumors reached him of some disaster to Mr. Arnot, and wrong-doing on his part, which had led to imprisonment.

Haldane was greatly shocked at the bare possibility of such events, and wrote a most sympathetic letter to Mrs. Arnot, which never reached her. She had received some of his previous letters, but not this one.

By the time the campaign was over one of Haldane's
wounds began to trouble him very much, and his health
seemed generally broken down from exposure and over-
exertion. As a leave of absence was offered him, he availed
himself of it and took passage to New York.

Three or four letters from his mother had reached him,
but that lady's causeless jealousy of Mrs. Arnot had grown
to such proportions that she never mentioned her old
friend's name.

The long days of the homeward voyage were passed by
Haldane in vain conjecture. Of one thing he felt sure, and
that was that Laura was by this time, or soon would be,
Mrs. Beaumont; and now that the excitement of military
service was over, the thought rested on him with a weight
that was almost crushing.

One evening Mr. Growther was dozing as usual between
his cat and dog, when some one lifted the latch and walked
in without the ceremony of knocking.

"Look here, stranger, where's yer manners?" snarled
the old gentleman. Then catching a glimpse of the well-
remembered face, though now obscured by a tremendous
beard, he started up, exclaiming,

"Lord a' massy! 'taint you, is it? And you compared
yourself with that little, peaked-faced chap that's around
just the same—you with shoulders as broad as them are,
and two stars on 'em too!"

The old man nearly went beside himself with joy. He
gave the cat and dog each a vigorous kick, and told them
to "wake up and see if they could believe their eyes."

It was some time before Haldane could get him quieted
down so as to answer all the questions that he was longing
to put; but at last he drew out the story in full of Mr.
Arnot's forgery and its consequences.

"Has Mr. Beaumont married Miss Romeyn?" at last he
faltered.

"No; I reckon not," said Mr. Growther dryly.

"What do you mean?" asked Haldane sharply.

"Well, all I know is that he didn't marry her, and she ain't the kind of a girl to marry him, whether he would or no, and so they ain't married."

"The infernal scoundrel!" thundered Haldane, springing to his feet. "The—"

"Hold on!" cried Mr. Growther. "O Lord a' massy! I half believe he's got to swearin' down in the war. If he's backslid agin, nothin' but my little, peaked-faced chap will ever bring him around a nuther time."

Haldane was stalking up and down the room in strong excitement and quite oblivious of Mr. Growther's perplexity.

"The unutterable fool!" he exclaimed, "to part from such a woman as Laura Romeyn for any cause save death."

"Well, hang it all! if he's a fool that's his business. What on 'arth is the matter with you? I ain't used to havin' bombshells go off right under my nose as you be, and the way you are explodin' round kinder takes away my breath."

"Forgive me, my old friend; but I never had a shot strike quite as close as this. Poor girl! poor girl! What a prospect she had a few months since. True enough, Beaumont was never a man to my taste; but a woman sees no faults in the man she loves; and he could have given her everything that her cultivated taste could wish for. Poor girl, she must be broken-hearted with all this trouble and disappointment."

"If I was you, I'd go and see if she was," said Mr. Growther, with a shrewd twinkle in his eyes. "I've heerd tell of hearts bein' mended in my day."

Haldane looked at him a moment, and, as he caught his old friend's meaning, he brought his hand down on the table with a force that made everything in the old kitchen ring again.

"O Lord a' massy!" ejaculated Mr. Growther, hopping half out of his chair.

"Mr. Growther," said Haldane, starting up, "I came to

have a very profound respect for your sagacity and wisdom
years ago, but to-night you have surpassed Solomon himself. I shall take your most excellent advice at once and
go and see."

"Not to-night—"

"Yes, I can yet catch the owl train to-night. Good-by
for a short time."

"No wonder he took the rebs' works, if he went for 'em
like that," chuckled Mr. Growther, as he composed himself
after the excitement of the unexpected visit. "Now I know
what made him look so long as if something was a-gnawin'
at his heart; so I'm a-thinkin' there'll be two hearts
mended."

Haldane reached the city in which Mrs. Arnot resided
early in the morning, and as he had no clew to her residence, he felt that his best chance of hearing of her would
be at the prison itself, for he knew well that she would seek
either to see or learn of her husband's welfare almost daily.
In answer to his inquiries, he was told that she would be
sure to come to the prison at such an hour in the evening
since that was her custom.

He must get through the day the best he could, and so
strolled off to the business part of the city, where was
located the leading hotel, and was followed by curious eyes
and surmises. Major-generals were not in the habit of inquiring at the prison after convicts' wives.

As he passed a bookstore, it occurred to him that an exciting story would help kill time, and he sauntered in and
commenced looking over the latest publications that were
seductively arranged near the door.

"I'll go to breakfast now, Miss," said the junior clerk
who swept the store.

"Thank you. Oh, go quickly," murmured Laura Romeyn to herself, as with breathless interest she watched the
unconscious officer, waiting till he should look up and recognize her standing behind a counter. She was destined to
have her wish in very truth, for when he saw her he would

be so surely off his guard from surprise that she could see into the very depths of his heart.

Would he never look up ? She put her hand to her side, for anticipation was so intense as to become a pain. She almost panted from excitement. This was the supreme moment of her life, but the very fact of his coming to this city promised well for the hope which fed her life.

"Ah, he is reading. The thought of some stranger holds him, while my intense thoughts and feelings no more affect him than if I were a thousand miles away. How strong and manly he looks! How well that uniform becomes him, though evidently worn and battle-stained! Ah! two stars upon his shoulder! Can it be that he has won such high rank? What will he think of poor me, selling books for bread? Egbert Haldane, beware! If you shrink from me now, even in the expression of your eye, I stand aloof from you forever."

The man thus standing on the brink of fate, read leisurely on, smiling at some quaint fancy of the author, who had gained his attention for a moment.

"Heigh ho!" he said at last, "this stealing diversion from a book unbought is scarcely honest, so I will—"

The book dropped from his hands, and he passed his hands across his eyes as if to brush away a film. Then his face lighted up with all the noble and sympathetic feeling that Laura had ever wished or hoped to see, and he sprang impetuously toward her.

"Miss Romeyn," he exclaimed. "Oh, this is better than I hoped."

"Did you hope to find me earning my bread in this humble way?" she faltered, deliciously conscious that he was almost crushing her hand in a grasp that was all too friendly.

"I was hoping to find *you*—and Mrs. Arnot," he added with a sudden deepening of color. "I thought a long day must elapse before I could learn of your residence."

"Do you know all?" she asked, very gravely.

"Yes, Miss Romeyn," he replied with moistening eyes, "I know all. Perhaps my past experience enables me to sympathize with you more than others can. But be that as it may, I do give you the whole sympathy of my heart; and for this brave effort to win your own bread I respect and honor you more, if possible, than I did when you were in your beautiful home at Hillaton."

Laura's tears were now falling fast, but she was smiling nevertheless, and she said, hesitatingly:

"I do not consider myself such a deplorable object of sympathy; I have good health, a kind employer, enough to live upon, and a tolerably clear conscience. Of course I do feel deeply for auntie and uncle, and yet I think auntie is happier than she has been for many years. If all had remained as it was at Hillaton, the ice around uncle's heart would have grown harder and thicker to the end; now it is melting away, and auntie's thoughts reach so far beyond time and earth, that she is forgetting the painful present in thoughts of the future."

"I have often asked myself," exclaimed Haldane, "could God have made a nobler woman? Ah! Miss Laura, you do not know how much I owe to her."

"You have taught us that God can make noble men also."

"I have merely done my duty," he said, with a careless gesture. "When can I see Mrs. Arnot?"

"I can't go home till noon, but I think I can direct you to the house."

"Can I not stay and help you sell books? Then I can go home with you."

"A major-general behind the counter selling books would make a sensation in town, truly."

"If the people were of my way of thinking, Miss Laura Romeyn selling books would make a far greater sensation."

"Very few are of your way of thinking, Mr. Haldane."

"I am heartily glad of it," he ejaculated.

"Indeed!"

"Pardon me, Miss Romeyn" he said with a deep flush, "you do not understand what I mean." Then he burst out impetuously, "Miss Laura, I cannot school myself into patience. I have been in despair so many years that since I now dare to imagine that there is a bare chance for me, I cannot wait decorously for some fitting occasion. But if you can give me even the faintest hope I will be patience and devotion itself."

"Hope of what?" said Laura faintly, turning away her face.

"Oh, Miss Laura, I ask too much," he answered sadly.

"You have not asked anything very definitely, Mr. Haldane," she faltered.

"I ask for the privilege of trying to win you as my wife."

"Ah, Egbert," she cried, joyously, "you have stood the test; for if you had shrunk, even in your thoughts, from poor, penniless Laura Romeyn, with her uncle in yonder prison, you might have tried in vain to win me."

"God knows I did not shrink," he said eagerly, and reaching out his hand across the counter.

"I know it too," she said shyly.

"Laura, all that I am, or ever can be, goes with that hand."

She put her hand in his, and looking into his face with an expression which he had never seen before, she said:

"Egbert, I have loved you ever since you went, as a true knight, to the aid of cousin Amy."

And thus they plighted their faith to each other across the counter, and then he came around on her side.

We shall not attempt to portray the meeting between Mrs. Arnot and one whom she had learned to look upon as a son, and who loved her with an affection that had its basis in the deepest gratitude.

Our story is substantially ended. It only remains to be said that Haldane, by every means in his power, showed gentle and forbearing consideration for his mother's feelings, and thus she was eventually led to be reconciled to his choice, if not to approve of it.

"After all, it is just like Egbert," she said to her daughters, "and we will have to make the best of it."

Haldane's leave of absence passed all too quickly, and in parting he said to Laura:

"You think I have faced some rather difficult duties before, but there was never one that could compare with leaving you for the uncertainties of a soldier's life."

But he went nevertheless, and remained till the end of the war.

Not long after going to the front he was taken prisoner in a disastrous battle, but he found means of informing his old friend Dr. Orton of the fact. Although the doctor was a rebel to the backbone, he swore he would "break up the Confederacy" if Haldane was not released, and through his influence the young man was soon brought to his friend's hospitable home, where he found Amy installed as housekeeper. She was now Mrs. Orton, for her lover returned as soon as it was safe for him to do so after the end of the epidemic. He was now away in the army, and thus Haldane did not meet him at that time; but later in the conflict Colonel Orton in turn became a prisoner of war, and Haldane was able to return the kindness which he received on this occasion. Mrs. Poland resided with Amy, and they both were most happy to learn that they would eventually have a relative as well as friend in their captive, for never was a prisoner of war made more of than Haldane up to the time of his exchange.

Years have passed. The agony of the war has long been over. Not only peace but prosperity is once more prevailing throughout the land.

Mr. and Mrs. Arnot reside in their old home, but Mrs. Egbert Haldane is its mistress. Much effort was made to induce Mr. Growther to take up his abode there also, but he would not leave the quaint old kitchen, where he said "the little peaked-faced chap was sittin' beside him all the time."

At last he failed and was about to die.   Looking up into Mrs. Arnot's face, he said:

"I don't think a bit better of myself.   I'm twisted all out o' shape.   But the little chap has taught me how the Good Father will receive me."

The wealthiest people of Hillaton are glad to obtain the services of Dr. Haldane, and to pay for them; they are glad to welcome him to their homes when his busy life permits him to come; but the proudest citizen must wait when Christ, in the person of the poorest and lowliest, sends word to this knightly man, "I am sick or in prison"; "I am naked or hungry."

THE END